POSITIVE & LIFE-CHANGIN

CHECK THEM OUT!

Time Traveler

Book 1

Book 2

Book 3

Book 4

Katrina Kahler

Table of Contents

Book 1
The Discovery

Prologue

The Trial

At first, it was a gentle rumble, like thunder in the distance. It vibrated beneath my feet and shook the walls. Then the subtle shaking turned to tremors, shooting so hard through the wooden floorboards that they began to pull up out of the floor. Earthquake, it had to be an earthquake! There was no shaking the last time we did this, so what had changed? Panic set in and I wanted to tell my brother I'd changed my mind. But it was too late. The shaking suddenly became violent, sending me to my knees, with Kate, my best friend alongside me.

Oliver, on the other hand, whooped in excitement. Typical of my brother to think this was something to be jumping for joy about instead of being worried! But he was the genius. And he should be the one realizing something was wrong. Terribly wrong!

We pulled ourselves up using the furniture and clung tightly to whatever we could in order to stay on our feet. Kate's face was pale, and her mouth was open in both shock and excitement. I'm sure my expression was no different.

Without warning, trinkets from around the room and a pile of books that had been stacked neatly next to the workbench lifted into the air, hovering all on their own as if gravity no longer affected them.

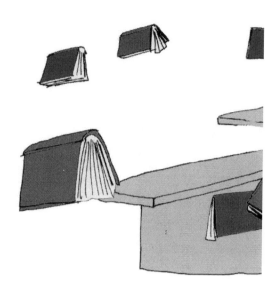

The shaking that had paused for a moment picked up again violently; I waited for the house to collapse on top of us, burying us alive. Bad idea, this was a very bad idea! Cracks appeared on the walls, and I clung to Kate's hand. Oliver backed his way towards us and to my surprise, grabbed my other hand, gulping.

"I think we made a mistake," I swore I heard him say, but the crackling sound filling the room stole his words away. I took a breath to try and ask him to repeat what he'd said, and then a gust of wind snatched my voice away from me.

Then, for a split second, time stood still. A heavy silence enveloped the room. I wasn't sure what was more frightening, the silence, or the shaking of the objects as they hovered before our eyes. It was the same and yet so different. What had we done wrong?

Then, it was as if time abruptly sped up. Everything blurred into a faded haze around us, and the woozy sensation in my stomach rose to my throat in a nauseating rush. I squeezed Kate and Oliver's hands tighter. Unable to maintain my grip, I felt them being dragged away from me.

My gut twisted as I was lifted off my feet, my scream dying in my throat.

What seemed like a few seconds later, I landed sharply on my butt and heard grunts from Kate and Oliver as well. I opened my eyes, blinking as I tried to take in my surroundings.

Very different surroundings.

I had a sinking feeling our experiment had worked. But instead of being overjoyed and excited, I was terrified. Totally and utterly terrified.

Chapter 1

Three Weeks Earlier

"This project is going to be the worst," I muttered as I set my books in my locker, wishing I could delay it a few more days. I'd already put it off a week and now only had the weekend to complete my entire project so that it was ready to present to the class on Monday.

Sometimes I hated school.

"Oh, come on. It won't be that bad." Kate Roberts, my best friend since kindergarten, smiled in an effort to cheer me up. But I wasn't in a mood to be happy. She wouldn't give up, however, and tried one more comment. "Your face will freeze like that, Holly."

"Now you sound like my mom." I shook my head at her with a frustrated sigh.

Kate grinned and shut her locker door. "Well, what's so bad about a family tree project? It's easy. I sat down with my grandmother, and once she got talking, I had enough material for five projects, at least."

I pulled out the textbooks I'd need for this weekend's batch of homework and shoved them hard into my messenger bag. "I don't exactly have a chatty grandmother, and my grandpa died before me, or my brother was born. So it's not that simple for me. I only have my brother and my mom. And Mom doesn't like me digging into our family history at all. At least not Dad's side. She's never told us anything about him."

I fidgeted with my necklace. Most days, I never gave my dad any thought, but with our latest project in history class revolving around who we came from and who our ancestors were, it was all I'd thought of for the past few weeks. Too bad I had no idea about my father's side of the family. No idea at all.

I didn't even know what my dad looked like.

"Maybe now your mom will fill you in on all the details, especially if you tell her it's for a grade," Kate turned to me hopefully as we walked from our lockers towards the front of the school.

All around us, kids bustled, racing to get to the buses. We didn't take a bus. We got to walk since we only lived two streets over from the middle school. One of the benefits of a small town was what Mom always said, and I agreed with her. I loved being able to walk to and from school, or to the center of town. It made everything so easy and gave me more time with my best friend.

As we walked, I wanted to believe Kate's words. Mom refused to say anything about the man who was my father, but perhaps this could be my one chance to figure out who he really was. If I said I needed to know for a school project, surely she'd be obligated to give me answers, right? My grade depended on it.

"Oh my gosh," Kate whispered and grabbed my arm hard to pull me to a sudden stop. "There he is...the boy of your dreams."

I rolled my eyes, but at the same time, I shyly tucked a loose strand of hair behind my ear as I stared across the front lawn of the school. Zac Fredericks. Cutest boy in the seventh grade and the coolest. I'd had a crush on him for years, along with half the girl population. He had short dark hair, blue eyes that always seemed to be smiling, and he was tall. A good head taller than me. I smiled wider when he glanced in my direction. My hands grew sweaty, and I clutched at Kate, unsure of what to do. Panic set in and all I heard was my pulse pounding in my ears.

"Is he looking at me?" I whispered, shocked.

"I think so. Wave or something," Kate replied, shaking my arm.

I lifted my hand to do just that when another girl

breezed past me, her brown ponytail swinging from side to side as she moved quickly in Zac's direction.

She waved and called out, "Hey Zac! Wait for me!"

Immediately I dropped my hand, my face burning hot as I watched Jade Nielsen run to catch up with Zac and his friends. They weren't together, but Jade liked to make it look like they were, hanging on his arm and laughing at everything he said. You'd think they were in high school or something by the way she acted sometimes. She was one of those girls who strutted around as though she were better than everyone else. It made Mom click her tongue in disapproval and tell me how grateful she was that I didn't act that way.

"She is so annoying," I groused as I turned away, Kate following behind me. Mom might be right, but Zac seemed to drift towards Jade and her friends. I sniffed hard with frustration and walked faster to get away from them.

"She's so fake. Jake will see through her one of these days."

"You sure about that? She's got him wound around her finger, and she knows it, too." I frowned at Kate, still trying to get over my embarrassment at waving at Zac. I just hoped that he didn't realize.

Clutching at the strap of my bag, I tried to tune out Jade's obnoxiously loud laughter as we walked towards the sidewalk, leaving the school behind. At least with the weekend ahead, I wouldn't have to see her until Monday, not that it was any consolation. Our projects were due on Monday, and of course Jade was in our class. She'd spent the last three days telling the class all about her family history and how incredible it was. According to her, her great, great, great whatever grandfather was in the Civil War and had earned himself a medal of honor. She teased everyone with artifacts she was going to have her mom bring to school so she could show them off. Genuine artifacts that her grandfather actually used.

And me? I had half a family tree because I had no idea who my father even was.

"You're grinding your teeth again," Kate said, nudging my arm.

"Why does she have to be so rude? Like why?"

"Because that's how she is, you know that. All eyes on her or no eyes," Kate said, laughing. "Your presentation will be fine, Holly. The only person you have to impress is the teacher, remember?"

I scoffed. "Mrs. Clarke, who's already made it pretty clear Jade is her favorite student? She doesn't care that I have the highest marks in the class, without even trying to get on her good side, the way Jade does. She's one of those teachers, you know. Easily pulled into the popular kids' world. Hate it, hate all of it."

I couldn't wait to get through one more year of middle school and be in high school. I kept going back and forth on whether it would be better or not, but at least I'd have a wider selection of classes, classes that hopefully Jade

Nielsen would not be taking.

We reached my house first, and Kate waved me off as I hurried to get inside and finish up my project. The only thing I'd done so far was written down all the names on Mom's side but hadn't done any actual research yet. Tests in other classes had kept me busy studying all week; I was also still getting up the nerve to ask Mom about my dad again.

"Mom, you home?" I called out as I opened the front door and stepped inside.

"In the office, honey!" she replied.

Mom worked from home most of the week and only had to go into the head office in town on Mondays. I dropped my bag at the bottom of the stairs then wringing my hands as I held my breath, I went to find her in her office. Papers were scattered everywhere, and there were images of items hung on the wall, tacked up until there was hardly any space left. Mom worked in marketing. Her job kept her busy the majority of the time, but me and Oliver, my older brother, never complained. She took good care of us, and we tried not to make her life stressful.

Until right now of course.

"Hey, kiddo, how was school?" she asked, looking up with a smile.

"Good, I guess," I mumbled. Taking a breath, I continued, "Mom? Remember I told you I had this huge project in history class?"

"Hmm," she mused, jotting something down on a post-it note. "What was it again?"

"We're supposed to research our ancestors," I explained, pacing around her office. "You know…who they were, where they came from or if they did anything interesting. We're supposed to write up our family tree, too, you know like…add as much information as we can. But…but I was hoping I could go to school on Monday with both sides of the family tree filled out…and not just you know, your side?"

Mom stopped scribbling and leaned back in her chair. Her eyes narrowed as she tossed her pen on the desk. "We've talked about this before, Holly."

"I know, but it's for a project," I pleaded. "Why can't I just know my dad's name? Who he was?"

"I'm not going through this again," she said, using that Mom voice that most kids respected and stopped pushing. But not me.

"Why can't I know? I'm twelve now. I can handle the truth!"

"You don't need details about his side. My side is interesting enough," Mom insisted. "If you had done your research, you'd know your family migrated from England and that your grandfather was a well-known scientist. He studied physics and the manipulation of time. He was a very important man who received several awards for his work."

I groaned with frustration, wanting to pull my hair out. "Yeah, that's awesome, but what about Dad's side? What if there's someone buried in his family tree that's even greater?"

"A scientist isn't enough for you?" she asked, and I heard the warning in her voice to stop pushing for answers I wasn't going to get.

What can I say? I got my stubbornness from Mom. Neither her words nor her tone of voice was going to stop me. "It is," I replied, "but I just want to know…and this is my chance! What's so wrong with knowing?"

Mom stood and turned her back to me, crossing her arms. "Holly, you don't understand. Your dad left us, alright? He walked out one day and never came back. He left us! You were only a baby, and your brother wasn't even two!" She whipped around, and angry tears shone in her eyes. "He doesn't deserve to have his children know who he is."

"But—"

"No! No buts! He's gone from our lives, and as far as

13

I'm concerned he doesn't exist."

Her harsh words had me taking a step back, but I didn't ask again. The last thing I wanted to do was make Mom relive the pain of that day. And here I was doing just that.

"Mom, I'm sorry," I whispered, hating myself for not thinking of what it would do to her. She loved our father and then he just up and left her. He broke her heart and even after all these years, it still hurt her.

I still wanted to know about him, but I'd have to find out on my own.

Mom came over and hugged me, kissing the top of my head. "I understand how you feel, and I get it, but I'm not ready to go down that road. Not yet. Now," she said sniffing hard and clearing her throat, "why don't you go downstairs and see if you can find some fun stuff about your grandpa? I'm sure there are a few trinkets of his you can use."

I nodded and left her office. With no other alternative, I went back to my school bag and grabbed my history book along with my project notes for class. Mom said Grandpa was a scientist, but I doubted we had any cool looking invention or gizmo I could use. That didn't mean I wouldn't find one in the basement, though.

My brother, Oliver was a super smart techno genius. He had skipped eighth grade and was already in high school. The basement was where he messed around with computers and whatever gadgets he could find and take apart that Mom wouldn't miss, or ones that he'd dug out of dumpsters.

When I headed down to the basement, I breathed a sigh of relief to find that he was nowhere in sight. At least he wouldn't be in my way.

He was family, and I loved Oliver, but he tended to go into these long-winded explanations of whatever new high-tech device he was working on in the hopes of taking it to the tech fair over the summer. None of that interested me, and I usually wound up making up an excuse to leave him alone with his tinkering.

Setting my history book down, I sifted through the items on his workbench, but there was nothing that looked old enough to convince my teacher or the class. None of it looked finished either. Gears and levers were piled in various places along with nuts and bolts and things that I had no idea about.

"Darn it," I whispered, tapping my fingers on the table trying to think.

Mom said there might be boxes down here, but I didn't see any. Maybe I'd find something in the attic? I only had a few days to find some physical objects I could use in my presentation, preferably something cool to outdo the antique items Jade would bring to class next week. With desperation driving me on, I sprinted out of the basement, up to the top floor, and stared up at the string dangling overhead. Technically we were not supposed to go into the attic. The ladder was old and rickety, and Mom said it was too dangerous for us to be using it. But I needed something for my project. Anything! I couldn't stand to see Jade showing off and getting all the praise from our teacher. Again.

Desperate times called for desperate measures.

"Holly! I'm going to the grocery store," Mom called out, interrupting my thoughts. "Let your brother know where I've gone. If he ever comes out of his room, that is!"

Beaming at my stroke of luck, I called out, "Will do! Bye, Mom!"

"You don't have to sound so excited that I'm leaving," she yelled back with a laugh. "I'll be back in an hour or so!"

I waited, bouncing on my feet for her to leave. The car started outside, and I heard the squeaking of the brakes as she reversed down the long drive. I counted to twenty in my head, then jumped up and grabbed the string for the ladder. It unfolded loudly and nearly smacked me in the head as dust fell around me. Once it was down, I tested my weight on it, holding my breath. When it didn't collapse, I grinned. Then, taking it one step at a time, I climbed up into the attic.

Chapter 2

I sneezed for the fourth time in a row as the dusty air tickled my senses and second-guessed my genius idea of going up to the attic in the first place. With my hand over my mouth, I looked around for the light and found a long string that was attached to a bulb overhead, hanging down in the center of the attic. The hair on the back of my neck stood on end, but that was silly. There was nothing up there except boxes and spiders.

But still…I glanced back to make sure the ladder was still there in case I needed a quick getaway. I tugged the string and the single lightbulb popped on.

"Alright," I said, looking around. "If I was a box of Grandpa's stuff, where would I be?"

I started to my right, picking up boxes and opening them just enough to see what was inside. Most of them were filled with old clothes or toys that used to belong to Oliver or me. Other than that, all I found was some stuff that looked like it belonged to Mom and was from years ago.

After about thirty minutes, I'd found nothing except dead bugs, spider webs that kept getting caught in my hair, and one horrible encounter with a mirror that made me scream and jump about three feet in the air.

With my heart still racing from that experience, I planted my hands on my hips and tapped my toe, annoyed. Mom said she had stuff of Grandpa's, but where was it? Surely I'd be able to find something interesting, but I didn't have much more time before she arrived home. I was about to give up when I turned and spotted a box shoved all the way towards the back against the wall.

"What's in that box?" I asked myself curiously as I hurried towards it.

It was a large cardboard box in near perfect condition, except for a layer of dust that had collected on top. Using a t-shirt from one of the other boxes, I wiped it clean and carefully opened the flaps.

"Jackpot." I grinned as I eagerly pulled back the other flaps. Dragging the box in the direction of the light so that it shone inside the dark depths, I peered inside. Sitting on top was a manila envelope. I picked that up first and sat back on my heels as I opened it. "Photos?"

I dumped them out on the floor and carefully moved them around. Mom was in most of the images, along with younger versions of Oliver and me and a few pictures of our grandparents. All of a sudden, my hand froze in place, hovering over another photograph with two faces smiling back at me. The woman was Mom when she was younger, but the guy beside her, I didn't know his face. At the same time though, I was certain that I did.

"Dad?" I breathed out the word, and with a shaky hand, picked up the picture.

They looked so happy, holding hands and smiling at whoever had taken the photo. Mom had her head rested on his shoulder, and her eyes seemed to sparkle. The photographer had captured her expression beautifully. My pulse raced. I couldn't help but smile as I gently ran my fingers over the image.

Tears started to burn in my eyes. What happened? Why had he left her? Quickly brushing the tears away, I looked down and stared at the other photos. There was one of the same man standing on his own, and I took in every detail of the photo in my hand. I knew beyond any doubt that he was my father.

Every other photo was of him with Mom. Or photos of him and…him and Oliver.

And me.

I couldn't bear to pick up the photo of the man holding a tiny bundle wrapped tightly in a pink blanket. Me. He was holding me. And the pride on his face instantly filled me with warmth. He loved us. In every picture, I saw his love, felt it pouring out of the photos and across time.

The last one I found was of the four of us together. I knew I looked like Mom, but Oliver was the spitting image of our dad. They had the same brown hair and blue eyes and the same complexion. I stared at the image, excited to find a sign that my dad existed. Then intense anger took hold.

Throwing the pictures down, I jumped to my feet and paced around the attic, glaring down at the photos as I fought back the tears.

"Why did you leave us?" I snapped. "Why? You're so happy in those pictures and you just…you just left us!"

My chest heaved from ranting, but as quick as the anger came over me, it began to fade away, until I was at a loss for what I should feel. Mom said he went out one day and never came home. What if something happened to him and they just never found out what it was? Maybe he wasn't still out there. Maybe…maybe he was…

But no, I wasn't going to think about that. He was alive, and I wouldn't let myself think the worst.

I went up there expecting to find things that had belonged to Grandpa and instead, found pictures of a man, a man who was my father, a man who I might never even meet. I couldn't stay there forever, though and I definitely couldn't leave the pictures lying around in case Mom made a trip up here. I gathered them up and stuffed them back in the envelope. I couldn't decide if I was going to pack them back into the box where I'd found them, or take them with me. Setting them aside for the moment, I dug around inside the box, hoping to find more about my dad.

I pulled out a few bulky sweaters that looked like a man's…a pair of old boots, pocket knives, and a few other random items. I came across awards of Grandpa's in frames, along with notebooks with his name on the front and filled with his old scribbles. At least, if nothing else, I had something of his to use for my presentation. Down at the very bottom of the box, my fingers brushed across something hard and metallic feeling. Frowning, I reached in and had to use both hands to pull it out.

"What are you?" I asked myself, looking for a way to open the box.

A thin, metal handle rested on top, but when I tugged it, the lid remained firmly closed. I spun the box around and puffed my cheeks out in aggravation when I spotted a keyhole on the front.

"Locked. Typical!"

I dug around in the box, searching for a key, but after emptying it and turning it upside down just to be sure, there was no key to be found.

"That's not helpful at all." I drummed my fingers on the top of the metal box wondering how I could get it open.

All the tools were in the basement. Maybe a screwdriver would work? It was the best I could come up with, and just in time. A car door slammed outside, and I jumped. Mom was back! I threw everything back into the box, but when it came to the envelope with pictures, I hesitated. Not willing to leave all the photos behind, I pushed through them and found the image of the four of us, shoved it in my back pocket, picked up the box, and hurried down the ladder of the attic. I got the ladder folded up at the same time the door opened downstairs.

I heard Mom talking to herself and the crinkling of paper bags. Any second now, she was going to call upstairs for us to help, but I had to get this box to the basement first. I peeked around the hall and down the stairs, but her steps trailed away and back outside.

Holding the metal box tightly in my arms, I raced downstairs, slipping and sliding on the hardwood floor as I hurried onwards to the basement. I just made it, closing the door behind me when Mom stomped back inside. I rushed to the workbench and set the metal box down as I heard Mom's voice calling out for Oliver and me to come and help her. After throwing an old sweater over the box so it would be out of sight, I tried to calm my breathing as well as my racing heart and trudged back upstairs to help.

"Oh, there you are," Mom said, appearing in the basement doorway and making me jump.

"Gah! Oh, my gosh, Mom!"

She laughed. "Sorry. Find anything useful for your project down there?"

Placing my hand behind my back so she couldn't see my crossed fingers I nodded. "Yeah, I found a ton of stuff to use. I think my presentation is going to be great."

"Good, I was hoping I hadn't lost the few things I'd managed to save." She pushed the bags across the counter and sighed. "Hey, I'm sorry about earlier. I know I lost my temper a bit."

"No, I get it, it's fine," I assured her and closed the basement door behind me. "Groceries?"

She smiled. "Yep! And go and get your brother, would you? I think he's got his headphones on and can't hear me calling."

I knew he definitely couldn't hear anything since I'd screamed a few times while I was up in the attic and yelled even more than that. Hoping that Mom wouldn't somehow magically know I'd been searching in the attic and found the photos she'd kept hidden, I darted upstairs to grab Oliver.

"Hey!" I yelled when I opened his door.

He was hunched over his desk with his headphones on, head bobbing to the rock music blasting out of them. I grabbed his arm when he didn't respond, and he leaped off his chair with a yell. "Seriously, Holly?"

I laughed at his wide-eyed gaze. "Sorry. Mom's back from the store. She needs help with the groceries."

"I'll be down in a second."

"Oliver? Could you uh, help me with something later tonight?"

His brow crinkled as he set his headphones aside. "What is it?"

"Something I found in the attic."

"The attic?" He repeated confused. "Why were you in the attic? We're not supposed to be up there. Does Mom know?"

"No, and she's not going to know."

"Unless I tell her."

"Well, if you tell her, you're going to get yourself into trouble, too," I pointed out. "I did it while you were here with me alone so you should've known I was up there."

He crossed his arms and sighed. "Really? You want to play that game?"

"I just need your help opening this metal box I found. It's locked, and I couldn't find a key."

"No way, if you found a box up there that's locked, then it's meant to be locked and left alone," he moved past me towards the door.

Stepping around him to block his path, I pulled the photo from my back pocket and held it out for him to see. He stared agape at the image as he processed what he was looking at. "Where did you get this?"

I let him take it. "In the attic. It was in the same box I found the metal container in."

"That's...that's Dad," he whispered. "Isn't it?"

"I think so. There's a ton of pictures up there with all of us, and he's in most of them," I explained. "There are some clothes and other things that I think were his, but I can't get the box open. There's no key."

He ran his hand through his hair and grinned. "I had

23

no idea I looked so much like him."

I smiled and stared at the photo. "Yeah, you do. Bet you act just like him, too."

"This metal box," he said and reluctantly handed the picture back to me, "you think it's got more of Dad's stuff in it?"

"You two coming or what?" Mom yelled up the stairs.

"On our way!" I called back and shrugged at Oliver. "Maybe. Help me later? It's already on your workbench down there."

"And Mom, what are we going to tell her?"

"Are you crazy!" I hissed. "She doesn't want us to know anything about our father! We keep this between us, deal? At least for now." He didn't appear convinced. "Oliver, please, you know how much this stresses Mom out. Let's keep it between us. Please? I won't ask you for anything for six months!"

He tapped his chin, and the mischievous grin that spread across his face had me rolling my eyes. "What else will you do for me?"

"Really?" I sighed.

"Yeah, really. How about you have to do all my inside chores for three months." He stared back at me, and I could see he was serious.

"Two," I argued. "And I won't tell Mom about you almost burning down the house two weeks ago with your experiments in the basement." I held out my hand knowing I'd won the argument. He took my hand and shook it, hard.

"Ouch!" I moaned.

He winked. "We'll head down after dinner and see about this box of yours."

Did we have to wait until after dinner? My feet itched to take him down there straight away, but Mom couldn't know what we were up to. I'd just have to keep myself busy with something else until we could sneak down there later. All the while though, I wondered what secrets the box had hidden inside.

Dinner was spent with Oliver and me exchanging glances across the table and anxiously waiting for it to be over. Oliver finished eating first and asked if he could be excused to work on something downstairs. I helped Mom clean up, and once she was settled in the living room watching TV, I backed towards the basement.

"I have to go do some more work on my project," I told her.

"You sure you have enough information on your grandpa? I could always tell you a ton of stories about him and his crazy experimenting from when I was a kid." She laughed. "I swear sometimes Oliver acts just like him."

"I think I have enough. My project will be just fine." I turned and tried not to sprint too excitedly down the stairs.

Oliver was already bent over the box with a screwdriver in his hand, but I could tell he was frustrated. He chewed on his bottom lip so hard I was surprised it wasn't bleeding.

"You can't get it open?"

He set the screwdriver down as he shook his head, wiping sweat from his forehead. "No luck yet. I'm not sure I can pick the lock."

"You think we could smash it open?"

"And if there's something breakable inside, we'll wreck it," he pointed out.

I cringed. "You're right. Do you have anything else to get it open with?" I tugged on the handle again and took the screwdriver from him to give it a try myself, but after a few minutes of struggling, I tossed the tool aside with a grunt of annoyance.

Oliver took it back to stare at the lock. "I have some better tools upstairs. I might be able to break the hinges and open it that way, but it's going to take time."

"Guess I won't have anything cool to show for my project," I mumbled. "So much for showing up stupid Jade

Nielson."

"That girl? She still giving you trouble?" he asked.

"Just normal trouble. She was telling everyone all week how cool her great something grandpa was in the Civil War. And me, I don't even know who my dad is," I said, pulling out the photograph again and plopping onto a stool.

Oliver sat beside me and looked at the photo. "Maybe you don't know your dad, but you do have a grandpa who did some pretty neat things with science," Oliver said. "He was a pioneer of his time, a real genius."

"Yeah I know; I guess I just hoped this would be the time we'd finally get some answers about our father. Now I'm going to have to give my presentation and announce to the entire class that I don't know who my dad is."

Oliver gave me a sympathetic look. We had our typical sibling moments when we didn't get along, but I knew my brother was always there for me. And when it came to our dad, we both wanted to solve that mystery.

"No, but look what you found today. Those pictures? It's more than we've ever had before. Maybe those photos and the other stuff in the attic will give us some answers. And whatever's in this," he said, resting his hand on the metal box, "it won't be a mystery forever."

"I hope not."

"Don't let that girl, Jade get to you," he said, nudging my arm. "She's not very smart."

"I know that," I sighed. "But everyone still likes her. She's the most popular girl in the grade."

"You think everyone likes her, but they just put on an act."

I blinked. "How would you know? You're the most socially awkward person I've ever met."

He laughed loudly as he hopped off his stool and safely tucked the box away. "I might be that, but I pay attention. Now go on, leave me alone in my dungeon of solitude," he teased. "Don't you have homework to do on our family?"

I grudgingly slid off the stool and held out the picture to him. "You want to keep this?"

He looked at it long and hard but handed it back to me. "No, you found it. You hold onto it."

Carefully, I tucked it away again and picked up my papers to head back to my room. I thought about what Oliver had said about Jade. And I spent the rest of the night convincing myself my project would be just as great as hers, even without the artifacts and the medal of honor story that she was planning to present.

But by Sunday night, I'd forgotten all about what Oliver had said to me and was back to feeling sorry for myself.

Chapter 3

For the first three classes of the day, I worried about history and my oral presentation. Kate tried to cheer me up, but nothing worked. I'd caught a glimpse of her project earlier that morning, and seeing both sides of her family tree filled out only reminded me that only half my tree was finished. I had no information about my dad, not even his name. I considered digging out a picture of his face from the box in the attic, at least, but it felt weird to have that on there and not his name. Jade would accuse me of cutting it out of a magazine or something, and I wasn't going to give her any more reason to make fun of me.

I tried to think of any excuse not to give my presentation, thinking of the smirk on Jade's face when she saw the blank space for my father. She'd laugh, I knew she'd laugh. Perhaps I could fake being sick. Mrs. Clarke wasn't that bright when it came to students finding ways to get out of her class.

There was one kid who was maybe there one day a week. Every other day, he found an excuse to leave the room or simply spent the time in the bathroom. Mrs. Clarke didn't pay attention to the students she didn't like. She wasn't that great a teacher. Faking sick, yeah, I could get away with that.

"Holly? We're going to be late," Kate said, and I blinked, realizing I'd been staring intently at my locker. "It'll be fine, you'll see," she nudged me reassuringly.

"Or I could be sick," I said and coughed harshly until my eyes watered. Kate stared at me with a bland look. I sighed. "Yeah, yeah alright, let's go."

We made it to history class right as the bell rang, and hurried to take our seats. I pulled out the chart and the report that I'd spent the weekend working on.

I also had the framed picture of my grandpa posing proudly for the camera.

As well, I had the award he'd received for his amazing work in the field of physics.

Over the weekend, when my mom was out of the house, I'd managed to sneak back up to the attic and grab Grandpa's things from the box hidden against the wall. My mom assumed I'd found them in the basement. I guessed she'd packed them away so long ago that she had no idea where she'd stored them.

But at least I didn't have to admit I'd been in the attic and discovered the box she had obviously wanted to keep hidden.

As far as my grandpa was concerned though, the experiments he did, as well as his in-depth study of time, were pretty cool. And over the weekend, I learned a lot about him. Oliver and I spent ages reading through the notebooks I'd found, and Oliver helped me work on my slides for my presentation. Without him explaining Grandpa's notes to me, I'd have no idea what I was telling my classmates. But even though Oliver and I found it interesting, I was still worried that no one in my class would care about it. Especially not compared to Jade's presentation about her war hero ancestor.

"Alright class, settle down," Mrs. Clarke said, clapping her hands as she walked inside. "Now then, I hope you all have your presentations ready. We'll get through as many as we can today."

She picked up the dreaded hat, and the class groaned in unison. I swear she did it on purpose. She could just go alphabetically through the class names. But oh no, she had to dump all our names in a hat and draw them out randomly. I crossed my fingers under my desk as she reached in for the first name. Thankfully, the name she called out wasn't mine.

"Jade. It looks like you're up first," Mrs. Clarke announced, already beaming at her.

I would never understand what people saw in that girl. She was exactly as her name said, jaded and annoying. She was also not very bright at all, but she still spent her days making fun of all the smart people.

"Awesome!" she said excitedly. "Do you have all the things my mom dropped off?"

"I do, right here. Now, remember, these artifacts are antiques and very valuable. So, you can't pass them around, ok? Everyone will have to come up and look at them closer after your presentation."

"Sure thing, Mrs. C."

I mimed gagging, and Kate stifled a laugh behind her hand while Jade set up her slideshow on the computer. She had numerous photos of an old man that looked nothing like her. Mrs. Clarke helped lay out several items in small, shadowboxes and the class muttered excitedly at the sight of the old civil war era pistol, or part of it at least, as well as a medal, a knife, and an old uniform shirt. I slumped in my chair and wished I could disappear.

Jade flipped off the lights and started in on her presentation. It wasn't hard to miss that she was staring at Zac nearly the entire time and he was staring right back. He even winked at her. Winked! I slumped even lower and glanced at the photograph of my grandpa. Mom swore she had more things of his lying around, but I tore our house apart over the weekend and found nothing cool to show, aside from the few things in the box in the attic. Jade talked on and on, flipping through slides and the class oohed and ahhed in all the right places. By the end, most kids were nearly out of their seats for their chance to look at the artifacts up close.

"Zac, how about your row comes up first?" Jade suggested happily and took her place beside the items so she could show them off.

"OMG!" I heard Kate whisper, and I smirked in agreement.

Could Jade make herself any more obvious? Why weren't she and Zac a thing yet? She batted her eyelashes as he asked her about the pistol, leaning closer to him as if she was going to kiss him right there in class! When my row was called up, I followed the others, ready to take a quick glimpse and dart back to my seat. I didn't want to stand there and stare at Jade and the casual but cool way she styled her hair, or her cute pink top and blue skinny jeans. I tugged at the hem of the oversized sweater I'd thrown on that morning because I was cold. Then I smoothed down my frizzy hair, self-conscious of how uncool I probably looked.

"Are you ready to do yours?" Jade whispered to me in an undertone as I joined the group who had been asked to view all the items on display.

"Why wouldn't I be?" I replied sharply.

She shrugged casually. "Just wondering how you fill out a tree with only half the tree."

I glared at her, opening my mouth to tell her off for being so mean. Of course, she had to know my business, didn't she? But what right did she have to comment on that? As tempted as I was to say something back, Mrs. Clarke was right there, and I wasn't going to spend the rest of class in the principal's office. Gritting my teeth and imagining myself lunging across the table and tackling Jade to the floor, I returned to my seat and sank back into my chair with my head in my hands. I was not going to let her get to me. I rubbed my sleeve over my eyes and glared at her.

"Hey Holly, you ok?"

I froze, then slowly turned. "Zac?"

"Yeah," he said, smiling. "You look upset. Just wanted to make sure you were alright?"

Was this really happening? I subtly pinched my arm and smiled through the sharp pain. Yep, this was real. "Yeah, I'm good, just had something in my eye." My crush was speaking to me. The cutest guy in the class was asking me if I was alright. I smiled and tried not to act like an idiot. "Who did you do your project on?" I asked quietly.

"Er, no one interesting. Just my great-uncle. He did something with astronomy I think."

"Oh wow! That's pretty cool," I said, thankful my voice sounded normal, and I wasn't gushing. I caught Kate's wide-eyed look behind him as she returned to her spot.

"You think so? I wasn't sure," Zac said. It was the first time I'd ever heard him sound self-conscious.

"Trust me; it's neat. My grandpa worked in physics and did something with time."

I glanced up towards the front to see Jade packing up her things and handing them to Mrs. Clarke. All the while though, her narrowed gaze was focused on me and filled with the promise of getting me back for talking to Zac. All I did was smile at her, loving how red her face had turned.

"With time? That sounds *really* cool!" Zac asked, his smile widening with what seemed like genuine interest.

I opened my mouth to answer, but Mrs. Clarke picked up the hat and called us back to attention. "Let's see who goes next," she said and drew out another slip of paper. "Holly, you're up."

Jade took her seat as I stood and said to Zac, "Wish me luck!"

He smiled back, giving me the confidence I needed. I moved to the front and uploaded my presentation on the computer. I then set up the photograph of my grandpa along with his award, and dove right in. I told everyone about my grandpa and his work in the labs. I started to get into the experiments he did, but as I looked out over the class, I saw half of them with their eyes closed. Kate, a true friend, did her best to look intrigued. A few people started laughing at the back of the class.

"Settle down," Mrs. Clarke scolded, also sounding bored.

Inwardly, I groaned and tried to push through the rest of my speech. I looked over the class once more, ready to stare at the back wall, so I didn't have to see all the bored faces. That was when I spotted Zac. The interest on his face was genuine, and it bolstered my confidence. My crush was interested in my presentation! I continued, nearly at the end, and was ready to finish strong when a chair scraping across the floor caught my attention.

Jade. The mean look on her face told me she saw just how interested Zac was. Clearly, I had drawn her attention to it, and now she was trying to distract him. I choked on my next few words and had to stop and clear my throat. A few snickers echoed around the room, and I quickly ended my speech. There was a polite smattering of applause, but no compliments from Mrs. Clarke as she had done for Jade's project. I avoided Jade as I sat back down, but I felt her glare from across the room all the same.

"Good job," Kate said to me, but it was Zac who tapped me on the shoulder.

"He was a pretty cool dude, your grandpa," he whispered as Mrs. Clarke called out the next name. "Nice presentation."

"Thanks," I mumbled.

"Yeah, Holly," Jade added in a whisper loud enough for everyone to hear. "That was such a great presentation. I'm so glad we spent the time hearing all about your stuffy old grandpa in a lab." She laughed at her joke and I half-hoped Zac would say something to make her shut up. But he was silent.

So much for my crush caring about me. I spent the rest of class doodling in my notebook and wishing Zac hadn't said anything in the first place. Him being nice to me gave me hope that I had a chance with him, but now…now I knew that would never happen. Not with Jade hanging around. I rested my cheek on my palm and wondered how bad it would be if I didn't talk for the rest of the year. It was March. I could make it work.

Why did I even like Zac? He was cute and funny, but once he was around his friends or Jade, he acted completely different. I would never change myself to fit in. Last year when we started middle school, Kate and I had promised ourselves that.

And I wasn't about to break that promise now for some boy, no matter how much I wished I could be like Jade, even if only for a day to see what it would be like. I liked my oversized sweaters and not always perfect hair. I didn't wear makeup, and I liked painting my nails outrageous colors instead of getting a manicure all the time.

I was me, and I wasn't going to apologize for it. Not one bit.

I picked at my usual sandwich for lunch; I wasn't interested in eating right then.

Instead, I pulled out bits of salad and dropped them on my plate. The great speech I'd given myself barely an hour ago, about being myself and not worrying about girls like Jade, did nothing to lift my spirits now.

"You're really going to let it bug you?" Kate asked as she nibbled on her sandwich.

"Huh?"

"Jade and her presentation."

I tossed down the food in my hands. "It's not just that. Zac was talking to me, you heard him, and the second she opened her mouth, he forgot I existed. Why do people react like that around her? Why?"

I shoved my tray aside and wished I could fake being sick enough to go home early. Though I might be able to convince the school nurse, Mom would see right through me, like always. I was terrible at lying to her. I'm still not sure how I got through the whole weekend without telling her about the metal box I'd found along with the photos.

I had the family photo I'd found with me at school. I hadn't been able to leave it at home; not now that I had something of Dad. I wanted to take it out and look at it, but I hadn't told Kate about my weekend yet. I loved her to death, but she liked to ask non-stop questions. I knew I'd get emotional over my father, and having that happen at school was not part of the plan. I was still reeling from Jade's glaring and her snide comments about me not knowing who my dad was.

"There's Zac now," Kate said, interrupting my thoughts as she nodded her head towards the cafeteria doors. "Why don't you go over and say hi?"

"Are you insane?" I whispered and ducked lower. "I can't do that!"

"Why not? What's the worst that can happen? He was trying to talk to you in class."

I stared at her like she'd lost her mind. "Gee, I don't know. He laughs at me, doesn't want to talk to me, and the entire school sees it! My presentation was bad enough. I don't need to make my life any worse."

She shook her head as I attempted to calm my racing

heart. At the same time, Zac and his friends went to sit at their usual table, joking and laughing loudly about who knows what.

"You said it yourself, though," she said quietly, "he was interested in your presentation, and I doubt he said what he did for a laugh."

"And?"

"And maybe it's worth taking a risk now and then. Come on, Holly. You always dream of being adventurous, well now's your chance. Go do something a little crazy for once."

I groaned. But deep down inside, I knew Kate was right. Was I this much of a coward that I couldn't even talk to one boy? I took a deep breath and pushed back from the table. Kate smiled encouragingly. I was about to head over and talk to him about my grandpa's experiments when Jade's loud squeal cut through the cafeteria. She and her gaggle of friends ran to Zac's table and sat down without even asking, taking over any empty seats. She leaned in close and placed her hand on his arm, whispering something to him that had him laughing hysterically a few seconds later.

Promptly, I sat back down and continued tearing apart my sandwich. This time, I imagined it was Jade I was tearing apart.

"Oh Holly, I'm sorry," Kate sighed. "She won't be around forever you know."

"Yeah, in a year we'll be at high school with more boys for her to throw herself at," I muttered angrily. "Whatever…it's fine."

Kate looked like she wanted to say more, but stopped talking and finished eating her lunch instead. Every few seconds, I glanced across the cafeteria at the other table and froze. Jade was looking pointedly at me. She winked and leaned against Zac's side.

"I'll see you later," I muttered to Kate as I stood. I

dumped my food in the trash, set down my tray, and disappeared into a bathroom stall for the last few minutes of lunch telling myself to get it together. I would just have to stop crushing on Zac so hard. There were plenty of boys in this school, not like I *had* to have a boyfriend. I just thought it would be nice.

If I was honest with myself though, the real reason I wanted one was so I could rub it in Jade's face.

The bell rang, and I stepped out of the stall to splash water on my face and get ready for the rest of the day. I took out the family photo for a few seconds, smiling down at the happy people caught in that moment forever.

"I'm going to figure out what happened to you, Dad," I whispered. "One way or another."

I tucked it safely away again and headed off to my next class, vowing to put Zac and Jade, and any other useless nonsense behind me. For a few hours at least.

Chapter 4

During the days after the incident in the cafeteria, I tried to act like my old happy self, but couldn't seem to manage it. Jade continued to shoot me obnoxious looks and Zac was back to pretty much ignoring me. By the time Friday rolled around, I was ready for the weekend to start so I could have a few days not stressing about the drama in my life. At dinner that night, I felt Mom's eyes on me. I tried to eat but was too upset about Jade and Zac to get much food down. When I pushed my plate away, she sighed.

"Is this about your presentation in class this week?" she asked.

"What? No, no that went fine," I promised. "And that was like four days ago."

"Then what's got you all upset? This isn't like you."

I didn't want to tell her it had to do with a boy at school, but I couldn't think of a good enough lie; not one that she would believe. "I thought someone liked me. Now I'm not so sure, that' all. It's not a big deal, Mom, promise."

"Alright," she said, but I knew I hadn't convinced her.

Thankfully she turned to Oliver next, and I was off the hook for the moment at least. My brother talked and talked about his project and all the tech that went into it. I nodded right along with Mom, but I'm pretty sure neither of us understood what he was going on about. He kept on with his explanation anyway. I think he just needed to talk some nights. My brother wasn't the best at making friends and was always the quiet kid at school. At home, he could be himself. We loved him no matter how nerdy he sounded.

When we were cleaning up after dinner, he pulled me aside and whispered, "Meet me in the basement. I have something to show you."

The metal box! I'd been so wrapped up in Zac and Jade I'd forgotten all about it. "You got the box open?" I asked, but stopped when I saw Mom appear behind him.

"What's going on with you two?" she asked.

"Nothing," we replied in unison.

"Right, sure. Keep your secrets. But I know when you're getting along too well," she warned, winking as she said it. "Go on about your mischief. I'll finish the dishes."

"Thanks, Mom!" We bolted out of the kitchen to the sound of her laughter. I headed straight for the basement while Oliver raced up to his room to grab the box. Pacing back and forth impatiently, I tugged at my sweater sleeves until I finally heard his feet pounding down the stairs. "Finally!"

"Sorry, your highness," he teased and set the heavy box down on the workbench.

"Did you already look?" I asked, hoping he had, and also that he hadn't at the same time. It was torture waiting to see what was in that box and if it held any answers to who our Dad was...is.

"No, I was being nice and waiting for you. It took me the last two nights to pry into the thing," Oliver muttered as he pulled off the blanket he'd used to cover it up. His hands rested on the top, and he looked at me. "Ready?"

I nodded, too excited to say anything. Holding my breath, I watched as he lifted the lid and we both eagerly peered inside. But there was nothing immediately awesome in view, except for some brownish paper. "What is that?"

"An envelope of some kind."

I reached in and pulled it out. "Maybe it's got more photos?" But this one looked older, much older. The envelope was heavily faded and worn at the corners as if someone had used it quite frequently. Peeking inside, I shook my head. "Nope, no photos."

I started to pull out the contents to see what they were but stopped when Oliver tugged on my sleeve. His jaw had dropped open, and his eyes were scrunched in confusion. "What?"

"What is this?" he indicated the box in front of us.

I stared at the box but had no idea what I was looking at or what the contents could be. "Looks like one of your crazy inventions."

"Well, it's not. So, what is it?"

"You're the genius, remember? You tell me."

But my brother who knew everything looked more lost than I did. Inside the box was a device, kind of a battery looking thing with colored wires sticking out of it. At one end it was attached to another weird device...thing. It was topped with a heap of strange dials and knobs of varying sizes all marked with numbers, but not in any order that made sense to me.

There was also a fine layer of dust that Oliver began to gently brush away with a rag from his workbench while I dumped out everything from the envelope. No pictures this time, but lots of loose papers and scraps of notes. Hopefully, something in there could tell us what we'd just found. The papers were mostly handwritten, the scribble so small I could barely read it, and the cursive was atrocious. It looked a lot like Oliver's mad writing when he started a new project. I spread out the papers and waited for Oliver to make sense of them all.

"Any ideas?" I asked after a few minutes of him reading through the notes and watching his brow wrinkle more than I thought possible. "It's all gibberish to me."

"These were Grandpa's notes," he whispered in awe and glanced back at the box. He held up one of the nicer looking note pages and showed me the signature at the bottom. It was nearly impossible to read, but I could make out the last name: Peterson. Mom signed it the same way. She had kept her original name after Dad disappeared and it was all we ever knew.

"Really?" Too bad we didn't open this box earlier. I could've taken it to school and shown it off, whatever it is. "Does it say what it is?"

"I think so," he said slowly, running his fingers through his thick brown hair that looked so much like Dad's.

"I guess we know you take after Grandpa then," I mused, fiddling with the knobs. But Oliver reached out and stopped me. "What?" I frowned at him. "I'm sure I'm not going to break it."

"No," he said shaking with excitement. "No, just hang on a minute."

"Hang on for what?"

He flipped through the pages of notes then set them in a specific order on the table, pushing me to the side. He mumbled under his breath, words that made no sense to me, numbers and whatnot. I sighed, frustrated we hadn't found anything related to Dad and even more upset I couldn't have used this to show up Jade and her old weapons. A crazy invention was definitely more exciting than old civil war stuff that you could find anywhere, any day of the week. Too bad I missed my chance and here I was back to wallowing in misery over her and Zac and my inability to understand why he didn't like me as much as he did her.

I turned for the stairs, not sure what I was going to do in my room when Oliver grabbed my sweater and dragged me back. "Where do you think you're going?"

"Out of the way of you and whatever mad science this is."

"No, no trust me," he said, tapping his finger on one of the note pages. "You're going to want to see this. Just hang on one second."

I hopped up on a stool and watched as he ran his finger over some chart sketched out on the paper in front of him. He bit his tongue between his front teeth. It was the same thing I did when I was concentrating. He then and fiddled with the knobs and dials, turning each one carefully as if afraid it would break off in his hands. There was something almost comforting about watching him working on our grandpa's invention. It was as if we were meant to find it so that Oliver could…I don't know…finish what Grandpa had started? Maybe tinker with it more and see what he could make of it? Part of me almost felt like I was watching Grandpa at work instead of Oliver. We never got to meet our grandpa. He died five years before Oliver was born, and Mom only talked about him every now and again.

Oliver's hand stretched to the far side of the device to a switch I hadn't noticed earlier. He sucked in a deep breath, closed his eyes and flipped it across.

Sparks shot out of it from all sides, and I leaped back with a yelp of alarm. It sputtered then stopped, tried to start one more time, and stopped again.

"What are you two doing down there?" Mom called from the top of the stairs after the door creaked open.

I opened my mouth to tell her Oliver was about to set the house on fire, but he clapped his hand over my lips and replied, "Nothing! We're hust tinkering like always. We're fine."

"Is something burning?"

"No, nothing. Just some old wires I was messing with. Don't worry; I have the fire extinguisher!"

"Alright, but if you set this house on fire, you're grounded for a year, at least!"

Mom's steps retreated, and the door closed again. I shoved Oliver's hand aside, and we both stared at the gadget in the box. The sparks had stopped flying, but I was wary of getting any closer to it. "What did you just do?"

He ignored my question and pushed on the wires; I guess making sure they were all connected. He wiggled a few more pieces of it, ran his fingers down the notes, then went to flip the switch again. I backed away, ready to bolt upstairs if the thing decided to blow up. But this time when it whirred to life, it only sparked once then hummed as it stayed on.

"I started it up again," he said, nodding with pride at his achievement.

Too bad I didn't share the sentiment. "Yeah, I see that, but what is it?"

"It's a relocation device," he whispered, running his fingers over it carefully as it continued to whir with power. A blue sort of glow came off it, almost pulsing like some weird heartbeat, and I took another step back, just in case. Oliver might be willing to risk his fingers, but I wasn't.

"Speak English, oh great inventor."

He remained focused on the gadget as he attempted to explain, "I'm pretty sure it's a time machine. I could be wrong. Some of these codes are hard to make out. I'll need more time with the notes to study them and see if I'm right or not in my assumptions, but as of this moment—"

"Wait," I interrupted, once my mind caught up with his words. "Did you say time machine?"

"Yeah, something that relocates objects to the past or

the future. You know, like in the movies...except for this one...this one's real!"

I looked from him to the machine and burst out laughing. "You're kidding, right? That stuff isn't real! That's why it's in the movies. There's no way our grandpa invented a time machine and then stuffed it into this box to sit up in our attic for years and years and years!"

My face ached from laughing so hard. Oliver looked hurt, but I couldn't help my reaction. "I'm sorry, bro, but maybe Grandpa was just messing around with wiring and stuff. I don't think it actually works."

These past few days had been weird, and I was suddenly impatient to leave the basement and go upstairs to my bedroom. Kate would be messaging me soon for our usual Friday night chat about the past week at school.

I patted Oliver on the back sympathetically. "Sorry, I'm not laughing at you, I promise. But you have to admit...a time machine? Come on."

"What if I could prove it works?" he said.

"How? You're going to take us back in time?" I joked.

"No, not without testing it. Moving us through time would be stupid," he replied in a serious tone. "We should start with something small, something that's not alive, just in case things get hairy." He glanced around, muttering about what he could use.

"Oliver, you can't be serious," I said, my laughter gone. Now I was a bit worried about my brother's sanity. "Oliver, did you hear me? It won't work!"

"I bet you it will. Ah, here we go." He pointed to a book that had caught his eye.

It was my history book, the one I'd misplaced earlier in the week. Oliver picked it up and set it beside the box. Then, he unhinged the side panel of the box near where the device sat and lined it up with the book.

"What are you doing with my history book?"

"Just hold on a second." He twisted the knobs and dials, checking his watch, as I stepped closer to see what he was doing. "We'll set it for ten minutes earlier, that should be enough."

"You're not making any sense." I tried to grab my book, but he blocked my way. "Seriously?" I scoffed at him. "I need that!"

If Mrs. Clarke were to ask where my book was again on Monday and I had to tell her my brother sent it back in time, I'd be in more trouble than ever.

"You don't need it now; it's Friday," he muttered, nudging me away.

He made a few more adjustments and flipped the switch. Then he took my hand and dragged me away from the table. I wanted to grab my book back, but the blue glow that had been dull just seconds before burned brighter as the whirring grew louder and louder. Sparks flew from the gadget, and I jumped. The lights around us flickered on and off as the device shook in its box. The tools on the workbench shook and vibrated with the force of the device's movements. My heart began to pound in my chest as I stared intently at my book. Then, without warning, a beam of light shot out and engulfed it. All around my book, loose items suddenly lifted into the air, hovering as if held by some invisible force.

"Oliver," I said alarmed, but he was grinning like a madman.

"Just wait!"

The items floating in the air shook. The light from the box burned so brightly, we had to cover our faces with our hands. I still wanted to see what was going on though, and I peeked through my fingers, squinting against the light. My book lifted off the table, just a few inches, and then with a loud popping noise, it disappeared. The light faded and the device stopped glowing as the whirring slowed to where it had been before. My book was gone; completely and utterly gone.

"What…what just happened?" I whispered, on the border of confused and panicked. "Oliver, what just happened!"

"Your book is now ten minutes in the past." He bowed, flourishing his hand as he added, "You're welcome, and I believe you owe me an apology."

"You…you sent it back?"

"Yes, to 7:50 pm precisely. Pretty neat, huh?"

I picked up his arm and stared at his watch. It was eight o'clock. "Oliver, I need my book. Bring it back! Now!"

"It's not coming back, ever."

I frowned, shaking my head. "No, no it has to come back."

"It can't. It's gone from this timeline forever, well at least I'm pretty sure it has. I'll have to read through the notes more thoroughly, so I fully understand what Grandpa intended with this machine. But for the moment, your book will not return to this timeline, at least not easily."

I stared at him blankly. Nothing coming out of his mouth made sense anymore, and I wanted to pull at his hair until he made my book reappear. That stupid machine. Of course, he just had to start it up and see what it would do. Now I had no textbook! Mrs. Clarke would use that as an excuse to give me lunch detention for a month. And Jade…she would go on and on if she caught wind that my crazy brother was messing around with a time machine. She'd spread rumors so fast; everyone would start calling me loony Holly before the week was over!

Oliver was still rambling on and on about how he had sent the book back in time. According to him, this meant if we wanted to get it back, someone from the past would have to send it to the future. But even that wouldn't work because of some condition or other about a time loop. My head ached so much I stopped listening and waited for him to stop talking.

He finally had to take a breath, and I grabbed his shoulders. "Oliver, I need my textbook!"

"Will you forget about the book!" he exclaimed. "Do you have any idea what our grandpa discovered? All those years where he concentrated on theories and ideas, and they all paid off! He invented a real-life working time machine!"

"I think I hate you right now," I muttered with a grunt of annoyance. "I really think I do."

"Whatever. Forget about your stupid book and try to understand what we just did. We sent something back in time! That's incredible!" Wildly, he looked around as he whispered, "Now we should try something else."

"Yeah, how about we send *you* back in time."

The look he gave me was so serious, I flinched. "That's not funny, Holly. You can't just send someone back like that. Do you have any idea what could happen?"

I opened my mouth to say something, but then Mom began to call down to us again.

"What are you two doing down there? I thought I

47

heard some weird noises and then the lights flickered. Oliver, if you blow fuses out again, there will have to be a limit to the amount of tinkering you're allowed to do!"

"Sorry, Mom, it was nothing. Just a little power surge. Won't happen again," Oliver yelled back before I could say anything.

We held our breaths, waiting to see if she'd come downstairs to check on us, but the door closed again, and we relaxed. I stared at my brother as he started messing with the knobs once more, twisting this one then that one and tugging on the wires.

"You aren't going to use it again tonight, are you?" I asked.

"No, I want to read through more of these notes. Want to help?"

"Sure, why not," I said sarcastically and hopped back up on my stool. "Let's read about Grandpa's time machine."

He scoffed as he slid some of the pages towards me. "I can't understand why you don't think it's real. You saw your book disappear. How else would you explain it?"

I wished I had a better explanation, but logically there wasn't one. My textbook was gone. Sighing with frustration, I picked up the notes and tried to read through them, but Grandpa's handwriting was horrible and after a while, my eyes started to hurt from squinting in the dim light of the single light bulb.

"I don't even understand what I'm reading," I said through a yawn a little while later. "But it does sound like some of the same stuff from my presentation."

"It should. Those theories were our grandfather's basis for making this," Oliver said as he flipped over another page. "It sounds like he only had a chance to test it a few times before he had to lock it away." He frowned and shook his head as he sat back. "Seems like Grandpa might have been worried about someone taking it away from him."

I took the page that he passed to me. It was dated

March 18th, 1990. "Huh, who would've tried to take it? Didn't Mom say he worked for a university?"

"Yeah, but it doesn't sound like it was his employer. Sounded like he had a partner. He keeps referring to someone with only the initial T. It's weird." Oliver rubbed his eyes and looked ready to keep digging through the notes for more answers, but the door creaked open again, and he rushed to cover the machine.

"Ok, you two, I know it's a Friday night, but enough tinkering for now. Head on up to bed, alright? It's nearly ten o'clock already."

I picked up Oliver's wrist to check the time. I was very late for messaging Kate, but at least I had a good reason.

"We'll be up in a few minutes, Mom," I called out to her before returning my attention to the machine.

"Swear you won't say anything to Mom," Oliver whispered as he powered down the device and closed up the box. "Holly, please. Mom won't understand what this is. She'll take it away; she'll probably even throw it out. She won't understand, and I'll be in so much trouble for mucking around with it."

I crossed my arms, tapping my socked foot on the floor. I knew we should tell our mother. My conscious told me it was the right thing to do, especially after what I just saw. It was obvious how dangerous this thing could be. But if I did tell her about it, then I'd have to admit I was in the attic. Oliver and I would both wind up in trouble, and I didn't want to spend my first few weeks of summer grounded over this. And getting Oliver in trouble would only make my life miserable somewhere along the way. As well, this new mystery surrounding Grandpa and the machine was the most fascinating thing we'd ever discovered in our entire lives.

I wanted to know more about it and figure out this T person Grandpa knew. A partner maybe? And who was responsible for trying to take away Grandpa's work?

"I won't tell her," I finally said. My curiosity was too strong to let Mom know what we were up to. "But you can't mess with it unless I'm around. Deal?"

He took my hand. "Deal. And you can't mess with it either, alright? That's all I need is to have you send yourself back in time, and me being grounded for life over it."

I had no intention of messing around with that machine, especially since I didn't even understand what it all meant. As I trudged upstairs and brushed my teeth before heading into my room for the night, I wondered about my textbook and where it had gone. Oliver said it would never come back because it was no longer in this timeline. So then what timeline was it in? I tried to make sense of it all, but it only made my headache worse than it already was. On the bright side, I now had something to occupy my thoughts all weekend instead of thinking about Zac and Jade.

I stood in front of my bedroom mirror for a few minutes, tugging at my long hair and wondering what I could do differently to make myself stand out. But that was stupid. I liked how I looked. I had my own unique style. I puffed out my cheeks, annoyed, and fell into bed.

After I pulled my laptop open to check if Kate was still on messenger, I saw the five messages she'd left asking why I'd missed our usual Friday night chat time. She was still online, and I replied that I'd been busy with some crazy thing my brother was working on. As I typed, the events of the last couple of hours played over in my mind, and I realized my brother was right. This find was incredible.

He had sent my textbook back in time.

I found myself giggling with disbelief. Oliver had done something totally amazing, and it had happened right before my eyes.

I guess I'd previously denied it, but now that I'd accepted it, I couldn't stop thinking about it and wondering what we were going to do next with this incredible machine.

I messaged Kate and told her she had to come over the following morning as early as she could.

My brother has discovered the most insane thing! You have to see it for yourself!

She asked me what it was, but I couldn't even begin to explain it through messenger, and just begged her to come over instead. For once, Oliver had done something cool, and I hadn't even given him credit for figuring it all out. Realizing he was online right then as well, I sent him a quick smiley face. I was annoyed about my textbook, but he had made it time-travel. I would never be capable of that!

He sent me back a thumbs up and said that while Mom was out with her friends the following day, we'd see what else we could get it to do.

When I got off the computer to read for a bit before going to sleep, all I could think about was sending Jade back in time, laughing as she got stuck in the Middle Ages. Or worse, the sixties. She had ranted one whole month about hippies and their lack of fashion sense. Yeah, I'd send her back there and make her suffer in super wide bell-bottom flared pants and horrible tie-dyed prints.

Then I'd have Zac all to myself. The thought kept me smiling until I finally drifted off to sleep.

Chapter 5

Saturday morning rolled around, and instead of sleeping in like I usually did, I bolted downstairs the second I heard Mom leave. It was her day to go shopping, hang out with some of her friends, and essentially have a thinking day as she called it. As soon as Oliver and I were old enough, she'd started having these days and left us at home all alone. We didn't mind. Mom worked her butt off during the week, sometimes well into the evening. As well as that, she took care of my brother and I. If she wanted a day all to herself, that was just fine by us.

And for the day ahead, it suited us perfectly.

Oliver was already in the kitchen when I reached it, scoffing down a bowl of cereal. I made myself the same, wanting to eat before Kate showed up. He eyed me funnily but didn't say anything until the doorbell rang.

"Are you expecting someone today, Holly?" he asked, an annoyed expression on his face.

"It's just Kate," I told him and ran through the house to get the door. "I had to let her know!"

"You said it was our secret," he argued as he followed me and stopped me from opening the door. "We can't let anyone in on this!"

"We said we wouldn't tell Mom," I corrected. "And Kate won't tell anyone else."

"How do you know?"

I rolled my eyes. "Because it's Kate and we've been friends for like our entire lives." I tried shoving him out of the way, but he leaned on the door harder. "Come on, Oliver. Please? Trust your baby sister."

"I trust you; I don't exactly trust your friend who likes to do a lot of talking."

"She won't tell a soul. I promise."

He didn't look convinced but stepped aside so I could open the door anyway. I grinned to see Kate bouncing on the front porch. "Hey!" I smiled at her. "Sorry. We were having a discussion."

"About me?" She glanced from me to Oliver. "Did I do something wrong?"

"No," I said, the same time my brother said, "Not yet."

Kate frowned. "Should I go?"

"No, he's just paranoid. Stay, please, we have a lot to tell you."

"I still don't think this is a good idea," Oliver murmured. "She could tell someone, and then it'll all be ruined. Do you want that to happen?"

I looked at Kate and raised my eyebrows, making a face to indicate what she needed to do. She stepped up to Oliver and cleared her throat as she held up her hand. "I swear that I will not tell a soul about whatever you two are going to tell me or show me, or whatever this is. Holly wasn't very specific last night," she added, grinning at Oliver and giving him a quick wink.

Oliver's cheeks flushed, and I stifled a laugh. My brother's behavior around girls was always fun to watch. He shoved his hands shyly into his pockets and looked like he was ready to bolt, just to get away from Kate's wide smile and shining eyes.

"Please? I'm good at keeping secrets, honest. Ask Holly. I haven't told anyone about her crush on Zac," Kate said in a rush.

"Kate!" I gasped in alarm as she clapped a hand over her mouth.

"Well, that's reassuring," Oliver said dryly.

"Oh, come on, this is bigger than my crush," I said and gave him the best puppy dog stare I could, while Kate did the same.

"I'll never ask you for anything ever again. Just let her see it, please? Pretty, pretty please?"

He shoved his hands into his pockets as he tried to decide, hesitating for a moment before nodding.

"But if she says anything and gets us in trouble, I'm blaming you," he said, pointing a warning finger in my direction.

"I won't! Thanks, Oliver!" Kate said, and he mumbled something under his breath as he headed in the direction of the basement.

"Alright, spill!" Kate demanded. "What are you two up to?"

"I might not have been completely honest with you about my family tree project," I confessed, pausing in my spot. I had something a bit more important to share with Kate before I mentioned the time machine.

I called out to Oliver and told him we'd be down in the basement shortly then turned back to the kitchen to finish eating my breakfast. Starting from the beginning, I told Kate about my adventure in the attic when I was searching for something of my grandpa's. I'd always told her that our dad wasn't part of our lives. But she never asked any questions about him, and I never gave her any specific details. Now things had changed, and I decided I was going to tell her everything.

"When Oliver was two," I began, "Mom said that our dad left the house to run some errands and he just never came back."

"What? I didn't realize that's what happened all those years ago. All I knew was that she wouldn't tell you about him," Kate said soothingly. "I'm really sorry, Holly."

"It's ok. Mom doesn't talk about him ever, and we still don't know what happened to him. When we were given the family tree project about our families and all, I hoped she would tell me more, but she refused. So, I went hunting for answers." I pulled out the photograph that I'd kept in my back pocket all week and showed it to her. "That's him, that's my dad."

Kate smiled at our family photo. "Your parents look so happy. And now I can see where Oliver gets his looks. He looks nothing like you or your mom."

I had to agree. "I found the photo in the attic, tucked away in a box with a bunch of other things that I think were his, my dad's I mean. There's so many pictures of him smiling with Mom and us. They're all hidden away in that box. I just don't understand why he would walk out on us like that."

Tears burned in my eyes and I hastily wiped them away before I started crying and couldn't stop. It always hurt, knowing he had left us, but it hurt even more now that I knew how perfect our family appeared to have been. Were we not enough for him? Was it me? Or Oliver? Mom only ever told me once that our dad had loved us. She mentioned it one single time. After that, she refused to talk about him up, ever.

"Anyway," I said when I could talk again without

worrying about breaking down, "when I found these pictures, I found something else, too."

"Clues about your dad?"

"No, there was nothing except the pictures and some old clothes. But, I did find something that belonged to our grandpa."

"The scientist?"

I nodded as I carefully tucked the photograph in my pocket again. "There was this metal box buried with all the other stuff. It was locked, and at first, I hoped there might be something about Dad in it. I asked Oliver to help me break into it, but Kate...oh man, you won't believe what we found in that box!"

"Well, where is it?"

"Downstairs." I quickly took Kate's hand, and we hurried towards the basement door. When we reached the bottom of the steps, we saw Oliver maneuvering the metal box into position. But he hadn't opened it up yet.

I turned to Kate, "I'm not exactly sure I can tell you what it is."

Kate huffed. "You're killing me here."

"I know, I know, but trust me, it's worth every second you have to wait."

I nodded to Oliver and with one more worried frown at Kate, he opened the box and slid the side panel away. Kate moved closer and bit her lip as she looked at the wires and the device inside.

Oliver flipped it on. At least this time it didn't spark, but it glowed blue again, and the whirring filled the basement. The pulsing seemed stronger this time around, too. Whatever Oliver had done to it, seemed to have made it run more smoothly or something.

"Uh, what is it? Some weird vacuum cleaner in a box?" she teased.

"Watch carefully," Oliver said, reaching for an empty plastic container that had been sitting on a nearby shelf. He positioned it exactly where my textbook had been before the book was zapped into the past forever.

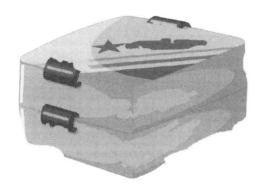

I pulled Kate back a safe distance, practically dancing in place with excitement to see if the device would do the same thing with the plastic container. Part of me said that my brother and I were both crazy and nothing had actually happened the night before; that somehow we dreamed about it, and my textbook was still in the house somewhere.

But the machine had to work again. I wasn't ready to see the most awesome find of our lives fail after only one chance to try it out. Oliver adjusted the dials and knobs once more, and I wondered where he was sending the plastic container. I figured he would tell us before the show started. Kate opened her mouth, probably to start asking a billion questions. But I held up my hand.

"Patience, you'll see," I promised.

"I think you're both nuts," she whispered.

I laughed. "You know...we just might be."

"Alright girls, get ready to watch this old container disappear from our timeline and go back in time an hour," Oliver said and flipped the second switch.

"Wait, what did he just say?" Kate asked as Oliver forced us back a bit further. "Holly, what did he say?"

"Watch, or you'll miss it!" I urged her with a nudge of my elbow.

Just as it had previously, the blue glow from the machine increased tenfold, and all of the small objects around it suddenly lifted into the air, vibrating the same as before. Kate gasped and grabbed my arm hard, tugging on it as if I couldn't already see what was happening. I felt her pulse racing just as fast as mine was, as the beam of light shot out of the end of the device and surrounded the plastic container. Kate's mouth dropped open in awe. I'm sure mine was doing the same even though I'd witnessed this event once before. Now that I knew what was happening, I was even more amazed to watch it all take place.

The whirring intensified with each passing second and the light burned so brightly, we all had to cover our eyes. The air around the container vibrated with the force of the device, and this time, I felt the tremor through the ground at my feet.

Then, just when I didn't think the light could get any brighter, there was a loud pop.

"Holly! What's happening?" Kate yelled, panicking. I pointed at the place the container had been as the light dimmed and the whirring engine of the device slowed down.

Oliver whooped and leaped into the air. "Oh man! Did you see that? Definitely not a fluke!"

I high-fived him. I was just as thrilled as he was to see it had worked again. We'd done it, or rather…he had done it. Kate took a few steps towards the table and lifted her hand to point. I knew exactly how she felt, but this time, for some reason, a weird nagging started in my gut. A shiver raced down my spine, and I crinkled my nose at it, confused.

I should be excited.

So why was I suddenly a little bit afraid of what we'd discovered?

"The container," Kate finally managed to gasp. "The container is gone!"

Chapter 6

Kate rushed over to where the plastic container had been just moments before. She moved her hand over the spot, then smiled as if she finally understood everything. She bent down, looking around underneath the table, then walked behind it, searching.

"Uh, Kate, what are you doing?" Oliver asked.

"It's a magic trick, right?" she said, her voice muffled as she bent down even lower, swiping her arm under the workbench as if the missing item would be down there somewhere.

I frowned. "Kate, it wasn't a trick."

"Sure it wasn't. You two actually sent something back in time an hour." She laughed and rolled her eyes as though she'd caught us out trying to trick her.

Oliver and I exchanged a look. "We really did. Seriously!" He gave her a convincing stare, but Kate was back by our sides shaking her head.

"I don't do magic tricks," Oliver added. "I deal with facts and science, and the fact is the blue plastic container that was sitting on this bench a few moments ago, is gone. Poof, back in time one hour. We're never going to see it again."

She laughed like we were playing a prank on her and I wasn't sure how to convince her that this was real. Then again, if I saw what she'd just seen, I wouldn't think it was real either. She continued to laugh, and Oliver's cheeks reddened in annoyance. But she wouldn't stop, so I took her by the arm and dragged her upstairs.

"We're going to go hang out in my room," I told my brother.

"She has to believe it's real!" he replied angrily.

"This is the discovery of the century. Not some stupid joke!"

"We'll talk about it later," I insisted, and with Kate still shaking with the giggles, we bounded up the two flights of stairs to my bedroom and shut the door. "You could've just played along to make him feel better," I scolded her and frowned.

"I'm sorry," she said, wiping a tear from her eye as she plopped onto my bed. "But time travel? Come on, that's movie stuff."

"Maybe, or maybe he's onto something. That metal box with the weird device inside, I found it mixed in with all my grandpa's other things, and Dad's. It's weird that Mom would have an invention like that just lying around and not realize it."

"A time machine," Kate repeated blandly. "Holly, have you guys been watching too many science fiction movies? Are you sure you and your brother didn't dream this all up somehow?"

I sat down in my desk chair and propped my feet on the bed. "Yes, I'm sure!"

"Well, I guess strange things happen around here when Oliver is involved," she teased.

I giggled at her comment. "Yeah, like a time machine existing and working."

We laughed together for a few minutes; then I began to wonder if Oliver had discovered anything else.

"We found all my grandpa's old notes," I explained in a more serious tone. "He wrote down something about having to lock the machine away because someone was trying to take it from him. And he had a partner, someone who he referred to as T."

"You sound like you fell into some science mystery novel," Kate mused. "At least you can't say you had a boring weekend."

Absently I nodded, my mind racing back over what Oliver and I had learned and I debated on going back downstairs to keep an eye on him. I hoped he wasn't going to do something stupid like fiddle around with that machine by himself. What if it blew up on him? Or worse? What if, despite what Kate said about it all being a trick, what if he accidentally sent himself somewhere he shouldn't go?

A horrible thought started in my mind, and no matter what I did, I couldn't shake the image from my head.

Kate frowned at me. "Holly?"

"Uh, what?"

"Your face is going to get stuck like that if you're not careful!" She tossed one of my pillows at me. "What are you thinking about so hard?"

Should I tell her? Since finding the pictures of Dad, the few details I knew surrounding the day he'd disappeared kept replaying over and over in my head, like Jade's obnoxious squeal of laughter.

But should I confide in Kate? I loved her. She was my best friend, and I was beginning to worry she'd think I was weird. The ideas running around in my mind didn't make sense and made me sound crazy. I was already a ten on the nerd scale. I wasn't sure I wanted to start making headway on the insane person scale, as well.

"Spill. What's on your mind?" Kate urged again.

"It's just really strange, I guess," I started slowly. "My dad disappeared so suddenly, and then years later I find this thing in the attic. I can't help wondering if what happened to him had something to do with that metal box."

Kate pursed her lips, and I was sure she was about to tell me I was going too far.

"Think about it logically," she said, raising her eyebrows as if to prove a point. "If your dad disappeared because of that time-machine, and I'm not saying that it really is a time machine, but if it is, how would it have taken him away?

You said it yourself; your grandpa died before your brother was born and your dad didn't vanish until after you were born. Your grandpa was no longer around then, so how could he have used his machine to make your dad disappear?"

I opened my mouth to tell her how it could still be possible, then closed it.

"It's impossible, Holly." She shook her head at me. "I think you can let go of the theory that your dad was thrown back in time by that box in your basement."

I sighed. "It was a bit out there, huh?"

She held up her thumb and forefinger a couple of inches apart as if I was only slightly off. But she meant that I was way off.

We grinned at each other. "Do you have to stay at home all day?" she asked, abruptly changing the subject.

Yes, was what I wanted to say. I was convinced that Oliver and I were onto something. I felt an urgent need to go back downstairs and keep going through Grandpa's notes, maybe even get that large cardboard box out of the attic and see if there were any other helpful notes in there that might give us some clues. But Kate still thought all this was a neat trick, and I could tell she was anxious to do something fun.

Rather than making her suffer and hang around the house while Oliver and I continued searching for clues, I gave in. "I could call Mom. What do you want to do?"

"I think you and your brother need to get out of this house," she suggested. "Let's go get some ice cream from the shop. It'll be fun!"

We didn't live that far from our small town center, and Mom usually allowed me to go there with Kate, as long as Oliver went with us. I doubted he'd agree to that today, but it was worth a shot. I told Kate I'd call Mom and hurried downstairs to call her from the phone in the kitchen.

She answered on the first ring. "Everything ok at home?" she asked.

"Yeah, we're fine, Mom. Kate came over, and we wondered if we could go get ice cream in town."

"Did you ask your brother if he would go with you?"

I bit my lip and sighed. "I don't think Oliver wants to, but it's such a nice day, and we won't be gone long. Please, Mom?"

I heard her mumble something, probably to her girlfriends, and then came back on the line. "You're to take your cell phone with you, and you're only allowed to go to the ice cream store and come straight back. I want you to text me when you get there and text me when you're walking home. OK?"

"Really?" I asked, not believing she was saying yes.

"Really. But I don't want you gone all day, only an hour or so, alright? And make sure your brother knows where you're going."

"Love you, Mom!"

"Love you too, honey. Remember. Text me when you get there."

I promised I would then put down the phone and hurried back upstairs to tell Kate we were free to go. "I just have to tell Oliver. Wait for me by the front door."

She bounded excitedly down the stairs behind me, and I hurried down one more flight to the basement. I heard tools tapping and Oliver grumbling as he sat hunched over the workbench. I jumped when I saw a bright blue flash of light.

"Oliver!"

"What do you want?" he asked, moving even closer to the machine.

"Look, just because Kate thinks it's a trick, it doesn't mean I do," I said sincerely.

"I know it works, but she's more skeptical, you know. And I do want to find out how Grandpa made this machine and I also want to know about his partner. It's all very cool. You know that. Don't worry about Kate."

He rubbed a hand over his face and offered me an apologetic smile. "Yeah, ok."

"Well, Mom said Kate, and I could go into town to get ice cream. Want to come with us?"

He tapped his fingers loudly on the table, and I waited for him to say no, but to my surprise, he nodded. "Why not? I could use a break. All of Grandpa's notes are giving me a headache. His handwriting is tiny; I can barely read it."

"Perfect, let's go then."

He set aside his tools and carefully turned off the machine then covered the metal box before pushing it towards the back of the workbench. He followed me upstairs and went to grab his jacket. When Kate realized he was coming too, she smiled wider. I didn't want to ask, but I had a feeling she might think my brother was cute. And that would start a whole other conversation I wasn't sure I wanted to have. I slipped into my jacket, and with my cell phone and keys in my hands, we left the house behind and headed into town.

The March air was chilly, and the sun hadn't popped out from behind the clouds yet to warm up the day. I shoved my hands deeper into my pockets and debated getting hot chocolate instead of ice cream once we reached the store. We talked about school, well mostly Kate and I talked about school and the people in our classes. At the same time, Oliver rolled his eyes and made some aggravated sound about how much we worried about the popular kids.

"You know, when you get older, you're not going to want to waste your time on all that stuff," he said as we turned down another street and the ice creamery sign appeared.

"Yeah, but we still have one more year before high school," Kate argued.

"And we have to deal with these people for that year," I added, kicking a pebble on the sidewalk. "Stupid Jade."

Oliver nudged me with his elbow. "What did I say about not caring about that girl?"

"She can't help it," Kate said, even though I was shaking my head, trying to get her to stop. "They're crushing on the same boy."

"That Zac guy?" Oliver looked at me, and I knew he was going to tell me what he told me every time he found out I had a crush on someone. "You do know you're only twelve, right?"

Kate interrupted him. "But he's the best looking boy in our class, and I think on some level, he's crushing on Holly, too."

Oliver raised his eyebrows at that. "Really?" I saw the big brother protective glint in his eyes and wished Kate hadn't said anything.

"He's very smart," I said defensively. "He was also very interested in Grandpa's work until Jade made fun of me about it."

"People who aren't smart will always make fun of people who are," Oliver said, as we reached the ice cream store. "It makes them feel better about themselves. And if Zac has a crush on you, then he'll eventually stop hanging out with girls like Jade."

Oliver held open the door, and I followed Kate inside, while at the same time typing a quick message to Mom to let her know we'd arrived. But then, an unexpected gasp from Kate caused me to freeze in my spot. Whipping around, I looked to see what had caught her attention.

I heard the sound of her dreaded laughter, before catching sight of the person I never wanted to see outside of school. But there she was, Jade Nielsen, sitting in the corner booth with two of her friends, plus a couple of boys from our class.

And Zac.

All I could do was stare as he watched her eat her ice cream. She giggled loudly, covering her mouth with a hand, her nails painted bright pink and her outfit as pretty as always. I wanted to hide, to disappear. I'd grabbed my old fleece jacket before heading out the door of our house because it was warm and comfy, not because it looked good on me. I also hadn't bothered to spend much time fixing my hair. I'd raced out of bed and got dressed quickly, too excited to see the time machine work again to worry about how I looked. I wanted to turn around and walk right out the door again, but Kate grabbed my arm and pulled me towards the counter. Oliver moved to block the group from my view, directing us forwards to get our ice cream.

When it was our turn to order, I wasn't even sure what I wanted anymore. Oliver ended up choosing for me and decided on a large waffle cone with scoops of chocolate chip and milk chocolate. I thanked him as he handed over the money to pay.

"Don't let it bother you so much," he whispered. "Jade's not worth it. And Zac's not either if he wants to hang out with girls like her."

I nodded, but I wasn't convinced. I wanted it to be me with Zac in the booth, eating ice cream together and laughing. I wondered what they even talked about. Zac was a top student in our science and math classes and Jade, well, she was on the student council and was in charge of all the decorating for functions. I didn't want to say she was stupid because she was manipulatively smart. But she wasn't book-smart.

We sat at a table by the front of the shop near the windows to wait for our orders to be ready. I tried not to focus on the sound of Jade's laughter sounding loudly from the other side of the store. Kate and Oliver talked about random things, and I attempted to join in, but every time Jade laughed, I wanted to throw something at her.

Finally, our order came up, and Kate jumped up to grab it.

"See? Now you've got ice cream, and we can eat it on our way home," Oliver said.

"So much for a fun outing," I mumbled, as Kate came back with our ice orders and handed me mine. Usually, my mouth would be watering at the sight of the huge waffle cone. But right then, it was the last thing I felt like eating.

I took it from her and thanked her as I stood up to follow Oliver out the door.

"Holly, hey."

I paused, wishing I hadn't heard Zac's voice behind me. Slowly, I turned around, hoping my hair didn't look as messy as I'd previously thought. Running a hand quickly over the top of my head, to smooth back any frizzy, loose strands, I smiled shyly. "Oh, hey. I didn't know you were in here," I lied.

"Yeah, just hanging out with some friends. What are you guys up to?"

I felt Oliver's glare from behind me. "Just grabbing some ice cream. Kate and I have been working on a project with my brother, and we needed a break." I looked past Zac to see Jade shooting me daggers with her eyes. I smiled for real this time and turned back to see Zac grinning.

"You know, I was hoping to talk to you about all that stuff your grandpa studied," he said.

"You seemed pretty interested," I replied, excited to have a chance to talk to him. But before I could ask if he wanted to join us for a walk back to my place, or to the park close by, Jade got up from their table and moved towards us.

"Oh! Holly, I didn't realize you were here!" she said brightly. "I would've asked you to join us, but looks like you're busy hanging out with your brother." She said it in that mocking tone as if I should be embarrassed to be seen in public with my older brother.

"Yeah, so?" I snapped. "Some people get along with their siblings."

"Yeah," Zac said with a grin, surprising us both. "I go into town with my little sister all the time."

Inwardly, I laughed with delight, watching Jade try to recover from her horrible joke, but she failed to find words. Zac gave me his attention again, and I thought my ice cream would melt in my hands because I was blushing so badly all over.

"So ah, maybe if you're not busy later this weekend, we can hang out or something?" he asked.

"Yeah, that would be cool," I agreed. "I think we follow each other on Instagram. You can message me there if you want?"

I heard Kate giggle beside and I nudged her discreetly with my elbow. My heart pounded loudly, and I was surprised no one else in the shop heard it.

Zac pulled out his cell and asked for my phone number. I recited it to him, and he texted me right away. "There, now you've got my number," he said with a grin. "Text me tomorrow. Promise?"

I bobbed my head. "I will."

He said hi to Kate and even introduced himself to my brother briefly before he and his friends left the shop leaving a slack-jawed Jade looking like she wanted to strangle me. I took a big bite of my ice cream and ate it, turned my back on her, and the three of us left her and her gaggle of friends behind.

Kate thankfully waited until we were far enough away from any other pedestrians before she let out a whoop of excitement and jumped up and down like a maniac. While at the same time, Oliver texted Mom for us to tell her we were on our way back to the house.

"Oh man! You should've seen yourself! See? I told you! I so told you!" Kate blurted.

"Yeah, I get it," I said through my laughter.

"Are you happy now?" Oliver asked. I caught the way he looked at Kate like she was borderline for the nut house.

My cheeks warmed impossibly more, and I ate my ice cream, unable to stop grinning. "Yeah, I think I am."

"Good, because there's something else I want to show you guys today."

"With the time machine thingy?" Kate asked warily. "You know, seeing the same trick twice isn't always exciting."

"What if it isn't the same trick?"

I stopped walking and looked my brother dead in the eye. I didn't like that look on his face or the way he was beginning to walk faster to get ahead of me. "Oliver, what are you planning to do?" I asked, rushing to catch up. "Oliver?"

"I have an idea, and I want to test it out. We still have a few hours until Mom gets home."

"What are you going to do?" Kate's tone was still teasing.

She really thought Oliver was practicing some sort of magician's trick and not actually tampering with things I was pretty sure he didn't fully understand. He was smart, but those notes came from our grandpa who was pretty much a genius. I hadn't worried too much when my brother was using the machine to make an old plastic container disappear, but the way he was avoiding me had my gut sinking to the ground.

"Oliver, you're not going to do what I think you're going to do, are you?" I whispered.

He shrugged. "Why not? We won't know how well it works until we test all theories."

"No, you're not going to do this!"

"What's he going to do?" Kate asked, hurrying after him. "Oliver?"

He refused to answer and tossed his empty ice cream cup in a nearby trash can before continuing quickly towards our house. I couldn't eat the rest of mine because my stomach had begun to churn so badly. Even my obsession with Zac had been pushed aside with the worry of what my brother was planning to do.

"Oliver, you can't do this. What if something goes wrong? What if you get hurt...or worse?" I added, thinking of what had happened to Dad. Regardless of what Kate had said about it being impossible, part of me still felt my father's disappearance was tied to the machine we'd found.

"Nothing bad is going to happen to me, at least I don't think it will."

"Oliver, that's not encouraging!" I shook my head, but it was to no avail.

Racing along behind him, I followed him down the pavement that led to our front door. He pulled his key from his pocket, unlocked the door and darted inside, quickly disappearing out of sight. I could hear his feet thumping down the basement stairs as I turned and beckoned for Kate to hurry.

When she finally reached the front door, she trailed behind me, down the steps to the basement. "What's going on? Why are you guys in such a rush?"

"He's going to use that machine on himself!"

Kate stopped dead in her tracks, looking more confused than ever. "So he's going to do the trick again and this time, make himself disappear? He'll come right back though, won't he?"

"It's real," I told her, needing her to understand. "Oliver didn't just make that plastic container disappear. He sent it back in time. We'll never see it again." I approached Oliver, my pulse racing as I watched him hastily pull the machine into view. "And if you do this to yourself, Oliver, you might not come back!"

He arranged the box on the table, so it faced outwards

71

this time, messing with the dials and knobs as if he hadn't even heard me.

"Oliver!" I gasped, trying to stop him. "I'll tell Mom!"

He turned around with a pleading look in his eyes. "No, don't, please."

"Then why are you doing this?"

He turned back to the box, messed with the knobs some more and shrugged. "Because. I want to be something great, just like Grandpa was. All I do is sit down here all day long messing around with things. But can you imagine what people would think of me if I could get this time-machine working? A time machine started by our grandpa and finished by his grandson!"

When he faced me, I saw the emotion in his eyes. I'd never realized how hard it must have been for my brother to grow up without a dad; maybe even harder than it had been for me.

"Dad was gone before I ever had a chance to show him what I could do," Oliver said, his voice insistent. "And Grandpa died before I was born. If I can get the machine to work though …maybe he'll know that his grandson did something great."

I should have still said no. I should have grabbed my cell from my pocket and called Mom. But I didn't do either. Instead, I nodded, and taking Kate's hand, I dragged her back towards the bottom of the stairs and out of the line of the machine's rays.

"Holly?" Kate glanced at me with wide eyes, and then looked towards my brother. "What's going on?"

"Hopefully we're going to watch my brother perform another trick," I told her. "But this time, this time you'll believe us."

Chapter 7

Rather than leaving the machine on the table, Oliver picked it up in his hands and faced us. I wanted to close my eyes when he reached for the switch that he'd maneuvered the last two times.

"Here I go," he mumbled as he flipped the switch and the machine hummed to life once more.

The lights flickered, and objects around the basement hovered in the air. Kate and I grabbed hold of the railing, trying to keep our feet on the ground. The vibration was stronger this time, much stronger. Blue light crackled from the machine and surrounded Oliver. I thought I heard him yell in pain or panic; I wasn't sure which, but I could barely make him out because of the blinding light.

"Oliver!" I called, but there was no reply.

Time seemed to stand still in front of me as a strong wind whipped up around the room, lifting even more objects into the air. It was a struggle to remain on my feet, and I gripped tighter to the railing. The room blurred. Everything was out of focus, and all I could see of Oliver was a hazy figure within the chaos that rushed around him.

"Oliver!" I screamed once more. "Oliver, answer me!"

But my words were whipped away, and I stared at Kate, taking in the horror and fear that filled her features. I clenched my teeth as I grabbed a firmer hold of the railing. Then with no warning whatsoever, an audible pop sounded.

It was a noise that was becoming increasingly familiar, but this time, along with that popping sound, it wasn't my history book or a useless plastic container that disappeared before us. This time, it was my brother.

Oliver and the machine had vanished into thin air. The objects that were just a second earlier, hovering around us, fell to the floor. Kate and I stumbled over each other, rushing to the spot where Oliver had stood just a moment ago.

"Where did he go?" Kate spun in a circle then paced frantically around the room. "Holly? Answer me!"

My hand lifted to my mouth; then I felt my lips drop open as I realized what had happened. "He did it. He really did it. Oh my gosh!"

I paused for a moment to take it all in. "Oh my gosh! Oh my gosh! Oh my gosh!" Stunned and in shock, I repeated the words over and over and over.

"What did he do? Where's he gone?" Kate was back in front of me, holding my shoulders and giving me a hard shake. "Holly!"

"We tried to tell you," I said and giggled, feeling close to hysterics. This had to be a dream, it really did, but the proof was right in front of me...or not I guess. I was filled with fear, but at the same time, I could not help the excitement bubbling inside. "That was a time machine, and Oliver just sent himself somewhere else to prove it was real." I wondered if he went far enough back to see our dad, but that would be crazy.

We had no idea exactly what this machine would do, and I prayed he wouldn't have taken such a big risk so soon, at least not without me.

"No, no that's not real," Kate mumbled and stepped away from me. "This isn't possible."

"But it is," I told her, trying to get her to understand. "Kate, my grandpa was a genius, and something tells me he left all this behind so one day, Oliver would find his work. Maybe even set about finishing what he...started."

I frowned as a gust of wind rushed past us both, ruffling our hair and stirring the papers on the workbench.

"Did you feel that?" I asked, worried that maybe I was going a little crazy after all.

But my friend nodded, trembling with excitement or fear, I couldn't tell which.

The gust came again, and we yelped in alarm as it nearly knocked us off our feet. Papers and small items whirled around us as if a cyclone had sprung up in the room and threatened to take us away with it. We struggled to pull ourselves out of the bursts of air, grabbing hold of the stair railing once more as the lights flickered and a crackling sound filled the basement. The hairs on my arms stood on end, and though part of me knew I should shield my eyes, I couldn't help but stare at the spot Oliver had disappeared from only moments before.

The crackling noise turned deafening, and my eyes widened in alarm to see blue light appearing out of nothing in the center of the storm. It sparked out in all directions and just when I expected it to catch something alight and burn our house to the ground, the same pop happened again.

All of a sudden, Oliver stood before us, his hair a total mess but he was grinning madly from ear to ear. He still held the whirring machine in his hands. It continued to hum, but the sound was gradually decreasing along with the fading glow of the blue light.

"Oliver!" I rushed off the steps and threw my arms around him, ruffling his hair at the same time. "You idiot! Don't scare me like that! Where did you go?"

"Don't you mean when?" he asked, laughing at his own joke.

"It's not funny," I scolded even though I was grinning right along with him.

"I went back and found something you might want." He reached under his arm and removed the history book he'd sent back in time the previous night. I stared at it, not ready to believe it actually still existed.

I was also struggling to comprehend the fact that he'd gone back in time and retrieved it.

"Pretty neat, huh?" the grin on his face could not have grown wider if he tried.

Kate crept towards us and looked from me to Oliver and back again. "You...you went back in time?"

"Yep, just to last night so I could get this book back."

Kate gulped, and I couldn't blame her for being out of sorts. It was the third time I'd seen the machine work, and I was still at a loss for how or why it worked. My friend ran her hands through her hair, but a slow smile lifted her lips. "Wow...have I ever told you how happy I am that we're best friends?"

I hugged her with one arm, studying my history book. "Same."

"So, you two want to try it out or not?"

We exchanged a glance then fell into hysterical laughter. "No way," Kate burst out. "No, way!" she repeated once more. Then after a moment's hesitation, she added, "I mean, is it safe? It seemed to work for you. But would it work for all of us? How do we even do it and when would we go back to?"

Her questions continued, and I was thrilled at her enthusiasm. She had turned from a total skeptic to someone who finally believed that the time machine was real. She was now as excited as Oliver.

But when I saw the pair of them smiling at one another and I realized they were serious, I stopped to process what they were saying. A voice in my head immediately screamed... *This is a terrible idea!*

Oliver had somehow managed to get the machine to work for himself. But what if it was a fluke and the next time, it took us too far back? Or it took us forward instead? What if the machine got stuck somewhere and we weren't able to get back to our real timeline? The worries mounted the more I let my imagination run wild with what could happen and just how dangerous it all was. Oliver said it himself; once something was sent back from this timeline, there was no getting it back. Unless the machine came with us and everything worked out perfectly, the way it had when he retrieved my textbook. But what were the chances of that happening again?

"I know that look," Kate said, and I shook my head to see them both watching me.

"What look? I don't have a look," I mumbled, setting my textbook down.

"Yeah, you do. Your face gets all scrunchy, and you look like you're ready to burp or let one rip," Kate said through her giggling. Oliver spurted with laughter behind her, and I rolled my eyes.

"What?" Kate giggled again. "I'm just saying."

"Even if I have that look, it doesn't mean anything," I said, crossing my arms.

"Yeah it does," Oliver argued. "It means you're going to say no and ruin our fun."

Kate's head bobbed in agreement. "It's true. That's the...Holly's no fun face."

"Five minutes ago, you still thought all this was a trick," I pointed out, "and now you're ready to just what...hop into that crackling blue light and disappear?"

Kate shrugged. "Guess so. Come on, Holly! This is an adventure! You're always talking about wanting to do something cool and different! Think of the stories we could tell from this," she urged when I paced away from her and Oliver. "You'd get to do something that Jade would never dream of doing."

I stopped mid-step. That was true. Jade didn't have a genius brother who could discover a time machine and tinker with it enough to get it to work. For once, I would have something that only I could do. And though I might never be able to tell her, I was pretty sure that made me cooler than her and her perfect nails, and her civil war artifacts.

"If we're going to do this, we have to do it soon,"

Oliver said. "Mom will be back home in a few hours, and I don't want to be reappearing when she's here."

I grunted, shifting from one foot to the other as my conscious warred with itself inside my head. Kate clasped her hands together and stuck out her lower lip. Pouting! My best friend had resorted to pouting to try and convince me to go along with this crazy plan.

"Does it hurt?" I asked Oliver.

"Nope, feels kind of weird, but it doesn't hurt," he promised. "Worst scenario is that you're going to have a very bad hair day when we land where we're going."

"Where are we going to go?" Kate was shaking. She was bursting with excitement. "Can we go to the future?"

He shook his head as he set the machine on the workbench. "I think it's in the notes somewhere, but I'd have to study the device to figure out how to get us safely into the future and back. The future can be tricky, but the past…well…it's complicated, too, but those were the first notes I found, so that's what I've figured out so far. I don't want to test future travel just yet."

I couldn't believe I had agreed to this, but I finally nodded. Kate jumped up and down then hugged me so hard I swore I felt my ribs crack. "Can't…breathe!"

"Sorry!" She set me on my feet and danced around on the spot. "Oh man, this is going to be insane! Where are we going, or sorry," she said when Oliver's brow arched, "when are we going?"

"Well, I went back a day," he said. "We could try a bit farther back."

"Where did you land when you traveled?" I asked, joining him and Kate at the workbench.

"The same place where I left from. Maybe we could go back about a month?"

We nodded in agreement and watched curiously as he mumbled under his breath, checked his watch, and jotted down notes on scrap pieces of paper. I was always

78

fascinated by my brother and how smart he was. I might not always tell him like I should I guess, but he was the smartest person I knew. I wondered if Dad was the same way. Once again my mind told me his disappearance had something to do with the machine we'd found and were now tampering with. What if Mom came home today and found her kids gone, just like Dad? What would she think?

What if Dad was the T person Grandpa referred to in his notes? Mom still hadn't told us Dad's name, so I had no idea if that could be the case or not.

"I think I've got it," Oliver announced suddenly, and I put my thoughts about our dad away for another day. Oliver fiddled with the dials and knobs again as Kate, and I huddled close by, waiting for what would come next. "A month ago on Saturday, Mom was gone. We were here on our own, and then we went into town," he said. "Remember that day, Holly?"

"Think so, but are you sure we'll be in the house when no one else is."

"If my calculations are correct then, yes," he stated. "It's the perfect date for us all to go back to because no one else was here on that day. So that will work...I think."

"Oliver, why do you not sound so certain?"

"There's always a chance for error," he said.

"Why don't we go to a time when there were people around?" Kate asked. "You know...so we know that we really are in the past?"

Oliver frowned. "Not sure that's a good idea. If we see our other selves, I'm not sure exactly what that could do. It's safer to try and appear when no one else is here. It has to be a day when we were all out of the house. See that clock on the workbench? It shows the date, so we'll know we've gone back in time."

Kate and I nodded. I did not want to cause some unknown problem if we were seen when we went back. So, I figured what Oliver was suggesting, made sense.

79

"Right, I think we're set to go," he said as he picked up the machine and gripped hold of it firmly. "Hang on tight. It's going to be a bumpy ride."

Kate held onto his right arm, and I held his left. He flipped the switch, and the machine loudly whirred to life. The pulsing blue light matched the unsteady beating of my heart. It was racing wildly in my chest as I held my breath. My whole body vibrated, and soon, the three of us watched as items in the room lifted and hovered in the air. I dug my fingers harder into Oliver's arm, hoping he'd forgive me for probably leaving bruises. The crackling blue light shot out from the machine in his arms and crackled around us. My hair stood on end, and a weird, giddy sensation filled me. I laughed.

I realized that when Oliver had trialed the device on himself earlier, and I thought I'd heard him gasp in pain, he'd been laughing, which was what we were all doing now. We couldn't help it. Then the light-headedness set it. We were spinning; spinning around so fast I thought I was going to be sick. My eyes were clenched tightly closed. I didn't dare to open them. Not that I'd be able to as they seemed glued shut and pulled tightly into their sockets.

A pop made me jump, and when my feet hit the ground, I knew without a doubt that we were not in the present anymore.

I glanced up from where Oliver, Kate, and I had landed in a heap on the basement floor. Trying to orient myself, I glanced at the clock on the workbench in an attempt to read the date and time. But I was still so shaken, it appeared blurry, and I was struggling to read it properly.

"Oh my gosh," I heard Kate whisper in disbelief. "We're back in your basement!"

Chapter 8

"Did we come back to the right time, Oliver? A month back…like you said?" I whispered the words, afraid someone might overhear us and know we were down here.

Oliver pushed to his feet, leaving the machine on the floor. "Yeah, think so."

"What do you mean you think so?"

I watched his face pale, and he gulped. "Uh, well, I might have miscalculated by a little bit."

"How much is a little bit?"

Footsteps stomped overhead, and the three of us hunkered down as if whoever was upstairs would know we were in the basement and rush down to see what was going on. I smacked Oliver on the arm, and he winced, shooting me a glare. After taking a closer look at the clock, I'd realized we were definitely farther than a month in the past.

It was January 5th which meant we were still on winter break.

"Oliver! Are you downstairs?" a woman's voice called.

"It's Mom!" I hissed in a panicked whisper. "Mom's here!"

"I know," he replied quietly, as he picked up the machine and motioned for us to back into the shadows of the basement. "Come on; we have to stay out of sight."

Kate and I moved with him beneath the stairs and behind stacks of boxes. "What do we do?" Kate asked as the footsteps moved closer to the top of the stairs.

"Oliver?" Mom's voice was clearer than ever.

Oliver was focused intently on the time machine, hurriedly turning the dials and checking his watch. "I need a few seconds…just have to make a couple of adjustments."

I watched him closely, while at the same time, my pulse throbbed at the base of my throat. Silently, I urged him to hurry, before Mom decided to come down the stairs looking for him.

"There. It's ready." Oliver glanced towards us and told us to grab hold. I knew he wanted us to get back to our time zone before anything bad took place. And I definitely wanted the same thing. But when he flipped the switch, nothing happened. No whirring, no bright blue light. Nothing. He shook the gadget, rattling it in its box angrily.

"No! Come on!" he muttered.

"Are we stuck here?" Kate asked, her eyes wide with fear.

I waited for him to reply. We couldn't be stuck. That would be bad. We had to get back! I didn't even know what would happen if we were stuck in the past with ourselves. "Oliver. On a scale of one to ten, how bad is this, and be honest with me!"

He shook his head, mumbling under his breath…words and calculations and things I didn't understand. He rambled on and on as Mom yelled again, but when no answer came from the basement, she moved away, and I breathed a sigh of relief. But Oliver was losing it. I grabbed his shoulders firmly and gave him a hard shake.

"Oliver! Look at me!"

His head snapped up, and he chewed on his bottom lip. "What?"

"Can we get back or not?" I repeated. "English, please."

He fumbled with the machine in his hands, and I worried he was going to say no. But he gave me a different answer entirely, "Maybe…I don't know. Something malfunctioned. I need to fix it."

"Well, your tools are mostly down here, right?" I nodded to the workbench. "Get what you need. We'll keep an eye out for you."

I could see that Kate looked as freaked out as I felt, but she stood up with me, her eyes darting toward the staircase.

"Oliver," I said in a firm voice, "you have to get us back home. We can't stay here."

"Yes I know," he replied as he jumped to his feet. "I just need a few minutes."

He hurried to the workbench while Kate and I stood at the bottom of the stairs, out of sight of anyone who might open the door, but close enough we could see and hear what was happening in the house above. I wracked my brain, trying to remember what we'd all been doing back on the 5th of January. But that was nearly three months ago. It had been so cold outside during winter break, and we'd had so much snow that we mostly stayed indoors…but if it was the week that I thought it was…at some point we did head outside.

"I'm ready!"

I jumped at the sound of my voice yelling through the house upstairs. Clapping my hand quickly over my mouth, I tried to keep myself from yelling in alarm. Kate twisted her hands anxiously together as she watched Oliver. She then looked back to the basement door, her eyes never stopping.

"Di you find your brother yet?" Mom asked, from the top of the stairs.

I saw the handle turn and made ready to grab Oliver, but then I heard my brother's voice booming through the house.

"Who's ready to lose?" he yelled in a mocking tone.

"Whatever! I'm going to beat you both," Mom said through her laughter. Their footsteps moved to the front of the house, the door opened, then closed again, and finally, we were alone. There was no one else inside except us, huddled in the basement.

I remembered we had gone outside for most of the afternoon. We had played games out in the snow. But meanwhile, Oliver was still mumbling under his breath beside me as he continued to mess around with the machine. I didn't want to make him any more nervous. So I kept my urges for him to hurry up, to myself, dancing from one foot to the other.

"No...no it's not down here!" Oliver exclaimed anxiously.

"What isn't?" I asked, rushing to the table.

"My calibrator. It's gotta be upstairs in my room."

"Where?"

"On my desk, looks like a compass, but it's digital — where are you going?"

Ignoring his question, I was already halfway up the stairs before he could try to stop me. At the top, I paused and listened, but I heard our laughter outside and sprinted from the basement door, up the next flight of stairs and into Oliver's room. Thankfully, his room was pretty well organized. I moved towards his desk, searching for the calibrator thing that he needed. We had to get back to our proper time zone. I was not going to remain stuck in the past.

As for Oliver, I wasn't even sure he knew what would happen if we were stuck here.

After a few moments of frantic searching on top of the desk, I yanked open drawer after drawer then let out a quiet woot of celebration when I found what I was looking for. I poked my head out of his room again, making sure the coast was clear then darted down the first set of stairs.

"Holly, hurry up," Oliver hissed, and I saw his and Kate's faces in the basement doorway.

I held up the calibrator, and he nodded to indicate that I'd grabbed the right thing. I made ready to sprint back towards them when the front door abruptly swung open.

84

I froze, caught between the front entry and the basement door, holding my breath. Oliver whispered my name to move, but I couldn't. It was like my feet were suddenly glued to the floor. Slowly, I glanced over my shoulder and immediately noticed the familiar pink knit scarf and the green jacket that was being worn by a familiar figure…myself…Holly, in the past. She was humming under her breath as she kicked the snow from her boots. She hadn't seen me yet.

Finally, I got my feet to move in a quiet attempt to sneak back to the basement door. I only had a few feet to go. My past-self was still busy, muttering under her breath about having to pee in the middle of a snowball fight.

So close…I was so close…

"Hey!"

I cursed and heard Oliver and Kate gasp.

"Who are you?" my past-self asked in surprise. "I'm calling the cops!"

Even as Oliver whispered a harsh no, I started to turn around. The second I made eye contact with myself, everything changed. The jaw of my past-self dropped, and she rubbed her eyes as if she were dreaming. Then the room began to spin. I became that dizzy, I almost couldn't see straight.

"What is this?" my past-self asked, confused and freaked out. "What's going on?"

"I'm you," I replied, trying to stay upright. "Just…just act like you never saw me."

Why did I feel so funny? My limbs were light; so light. I felt like I could float away if I weren't careful. Horrified at what was happening to me, I was startled to hear my other-self scream in alarm. I looked up to see her holding her hands before her face, but they weren't solid anymore.

They were translucent. And the translucent effect was spreading.

"No," she whispered. "What's going on! Help me!"

I tried to reach out as if to help myself but stopped short. My own hands were fading right before my eyes. I staggered backward, not ready to believe what I was seeing.

I was disappearing and soon…soon I would be nothing.

Frozen in fear, I lifted my gaze and locked eyes with my past-self. "I think I made a terrible mistake."

Book 2
The Impact

Chapter 1

I stared at my hand, disappearing before my eyes. My past-self had her mouth open in silent horror. I was ready to join her when a hand closed around my shoulder and dragged me towards the open basement door, taking the calibrator from my hand as we went.

"What are you doing?" I asked Oliver as he and Kate guided me to the basement.

I was still fading away, and Kate bounced on her feet as she panicked. Oliver frantically tinkered with the device, not answering my question.

"Oliver!"

His hands shook as he fiddled with the device and the calibrator. "You're not supposed to see yourself! We have to get out of here. NOW!" He mumbled under his breath, and his fingers moved faster, trying to get the machine going again.

Another finger vanished before my eyes. "Oliver, what happens if we can't go back?" I asked, my voice shaking with fear. "Oliver!"

"You disappear," he yelped. I froze at his words. "You disappear forever."

I gulped as my pinkie vanished next. "Please hurry," I begged.

He turned his attention back to the box, and a few seconds later it hummed to life, the familiar blue light emanating from it. He twisted the dials and turned the knobs, calling for me and Kate to hurry over to him.

Upstairs, I heard my own scream and the front door open. The other me was screaming for Mom and Oliver. I could hear the sounds clearly.

But at the same time, the basement had begun vibrating and shaking as it had before when we vanished into the past. The light crackled up Oliver's arms, and the same giddy feeling hit me again. This time though, I could not bring myself to laugh. Not when my entire hand that I tried to place on Oliver's arm was gone. I held Kate's hand tightly with my other hand, which so far was still intact. All around us, random items and objects of different shapes and sizes floated and hovered in the air.

We spun around and around until I waited to be sick for sure this time, then with a loud pop everything suddenly stopped and we were standing in the exact same place in the basement. Oliver clutched the machine as its humming slowed and the blue light receded into it.

"Did we do it?" I asked, afraid to check and see if I was whole again. "Oliver? Kate? Can someone at least tell me if my hand is back?"

"Yeah, your hand's back," Kate exclaimed and grabbed hold of it to confirm.

I glanced at it clasped in hers and sank to the floor in relief. Oliver set the machine back on his workbench and checked the clock in the basement then picked up his phone and checked that too. "Oh my gosh, we made it back."

"I vote we don't do that again," I mumbled from the floor, staring up at the ceiling. "Like ever."

Kate plopped down beside me, nodding in agreement, but Oliver remained quiet. I sat up enough to see him slouched on the stool and to my surprise, grinning like a madman.

"Oliver?"

Slowly, he turned to stare at us, and a laugh escaped him. "Do you have any idea what we just did?" he asked through his laughter. "Do you know what this means?"

"Yeah, it means your sister almost disappeared," I reminded him, annoyed.

"Besides that."

My brow shot up. "Besides that? Wow, some loving brother you are." I laid my head back on the cold concrete floor, cringing at the spider webs between the rafters overhead. "Why didn't you tell us that before we went back."

"Tell you what?"

"That we could disappear, you moron!"

"Oh yeah, I meant to, but I thought I'd take us back to the right day and we wouldn't have to worry about it."

I smacked myself in the forehead at my brother forgetting such a crucial rule.

"Why would she have disappeared just from seeing her past-self?" Kate asked.

"It was in the notes, but I didn't get too much into them," he mumbled, turning to shuffle through the stacks of notes from our grandpa. "Just said it wasn't a good idea, but I thought it meant your past-self could freak out or something."

"Not that the person would vanish into nothing?" I muttered.

"Look, Holly, I'm really sorry, alright? But we made it back, and you have to admit that until you ran into yourself, the whole thing was pretty incredible."

I sat up all the way and couldn't avoid smiling at my brother. His excitement was contagious. "I guess it is pretty neat. Amazing actually!"

After my near-disappearance act let my brain catch up with what we had just done, I was awestruck. We had gone back in time. Like, actually back in time. I saw myself. I heard Mom and Oliver's voices. "How is this even possible?" I murmured, more to myself than looking for an actual answer. I doubted I'd understand anything my brother had to say on the matter anyway.

Oliver was sifting through stacks of papers on the workbench again. "I have to keep reading through these notes, but I think we made a huge first step."

"Yeah," I agreed, and finally found my feet. Kate held up her hand and rolling my eyes over-dramatically, I reached down to pull her up with me. "We're going to wait to do that again though, right?" I stared at my hands, happy to see them both whole, not at all ready to watch them disappear once more.

"It'd probably be safer if we waited until I have a chance to check through these notes some more," Oliver admitted, and I saw the guilt on his face. He was more upset about me almost disappearing than I thought.

I crossed the basement to reach him and leaned into his arm. His hands stopped shuffling the papers, and he rested his cheek on top of my head.

"I really am sorry," he whispered. "As much as you drive me nuts, life would be pretty boring without you around to bug me. As well as finding ways to get me into trouble," he grinned.

"I forgive you. But can we make a deal now that we know how dangerous this can be?"

"What did you have in mind?"

"No using this alone. Please!" I said sternly. "I don't want you to think you know what you're doing, then have it backfire, and I lose my brother."

"Next time you do this, I want to come along, too!" Kate chimed in brightly.

We turned to look at her, and I bobbed my head, yes, waiting for Oliver to say no. But instead, he agreed, too. "Why not? She already knows about it, and as long as she doesn't tell anyone, I don't see why she can't hang around. Might not be a bad idea to have three people," he nodded.

I held out my hand. "Right then, we'll be the Time Traveling Musketeers," I announced.

Oliver gave me a blank look, but Kate was all for it

and rested her hand on top of mine. "Oh, come on, Oliver," she smiled, batting her eyelashes at him, making him turn three shades of red. "All groups like this have to have a name. That's just how it is."

His lips pursed, but he gave in as we both gave him puppy dog stares. His hand rested on top of Kate's, and I grinned at how her cheeks were the next to turn red.

"Sweet," I said, and we threw our one hand up then let it fall with a laugh.

A door opened upstairs, and all smiles disappeared. I held my breath until I heard Mom. "Oliver! Holly, where *are* you two?"

I glanced at Oliver, and he nodded, shooing us towards the stairs. "She's home early! I'll hide this then I'll be up," he said.

"Down here, Mom!" I called as Kate, and I rushed up the stairs.

"Hanging out with your brother?" Mom asked, setting her purse down on the entryway table with a curious look on her face.

"Yeah, he was showing us something he was tinkering with," I said with a sigh. "You know how he is. He has to tell someone what he's discovered or else he'll explode."

The curious look disappeared, and she grinned. "Yes, yes I do know that. And hello, Kate."

"Hi, Mrs. Peterson," Kate replied politely.

"Did you two enjoy your trip into town?" Mom asked, heading into the kitchen, and carrying several paper bags with her from her shopping trip.

Kate giggled, and I nudged her with my elbow to shush her. Until that moment, I'd honestly forgotten about our walk into town and bumping into Zac. Zac, who had asked for my number and wanted to hang out tomorrow.

Mom's brow went up at Kate's incessant giggling. "So, it was a fun trip, hey? Did something exciting happen, girls? Or should I take a wild guess?"

"No," I insisted as Kate said, "Yes!" at the same time.

Mom burst out laughing. "Alright then, keep it to yourselves, for now." She gently poked the tip of my nose. "But if it has something to do with a boy, just remember, Mom's know everything. And you can share all the details later, young lady."

Yeah, like how we just traveled back in time! I kept the thought to myself, but before she could say anything else, Oliver strolled into the kitchen. Kate ducked her head and turned away as Mom's eyes shifted from my friend to my brother and back again. "Sounds like you three have had a very interesting day." She raised her eyebrows at my brother curiously.

"Oh, I thought it was boring," Oliver muttered, plopping down on a barstool at the breakfast counter. "I had to look after these two. It interrupted my work."

Mom sighed and started unpacking the bags. "I know you love working on your projects, Oliver, but sometimes it's good to get out of the house. Breathe some fresh air. Let the sunlight hit your face every now and again."

He huffed in reply then turned to the fridge, looking for something to eat. I was abruptly reminded that apart from our ice cream, we hadn't eaten anything since breakfast. But my hunger disappeared when Mom shook her head, mumbling about Oliver being like his father. Oliver and I exchanged a look, both pretty sure she hadn't meant to say that so loudly. He looked ready to push Mom for more about Dad, but she was in a good mood, and I didn't want that to change or make Kate feel uncomfortable if it started a disagreement again.

"How was shopping?" I asked, watching her unwrap several items out of brown paper.

She set a beautiful bright blue vase on the counter with swirls of purple and green glass in it. "There's a new shop in town where they do glass blowing," Mom told us, turning the vase so we could see it from all sides. "Fantastic pieces."

Next, she set out a glass figurine of a polar bear, and something in her eyes told me she liked it for more than one reason. Her fingers rested on it, and her eyes suddenly shone with tears before she blinked and cleared her throat loudly. I frowned at Oliver as she turned her back to us, but he shrugged, unsure of what was wrong. Mom liked bears, we both knew that, but this one meant something more to her.

Curiosity had me thinking of the pictures I'd found in the attic and wondering if there was a clue hidden amongst them. Then Mom began telling us about her other finds at the local antique store and Oliver, and I groaned. She was always picking up old odds and ends, but when she pulled out a small, studded box that resembled a treasure chest, all three of us were intrigued and gathered around closer.

"It just called to me," she told us, sounding wistful. Mom never sounded wistful.

When she opened the lid, we stared inside the box at an ornate looking metal key. It was fairly large and looked very heavy. Oliver's eyes widened as he stared at me. My brow furrowed in confusion at why he was so excited. I saw his gaze dart down to the basement and then back up towards the attic. He did it a few more times, his face growing pinched as his frustration mounted. Then finally, it clicked.

No. No way could this be the missing key to the metal box I'd found in our attic! How could Mom find it at the local antique store?

"Pretty neat, huh?" Mom said.

"What are you going to do with it?" I asked, more earnest than I meant to sound. Both Mom and Kate blinked at me.

Mom smiled. "Out of all the pieces I've brought home from that place, this is the only one that you've ever been interested in. An old key," she mused. "I have the strangest kids."

Oliver and I both stuck out our tongues at her, and she laughed, sliding the box to me. "Wait, you're giving it to me?" I asked, surprised. "Wasn't this expensive?"

"No, it wasn't actually. The owner of the store forgot it was even there. I found it tucked away on a dusty old shelf, buried under a few books and a weird looking machine that was broken. I've never seen anything like it before."

I bounced on the balls of my feet. We had to get to that store. If this was the key that we thought it was, then who knew what else we might find that had belonged to Grandpa. But if it *was* Grandpa's key, why had his stuff been taken there? Mom kept all our old things in the attic. I realized it must mean Grandma had taken it to the antique store, or Grandpa had, at some point in his life.

"Thanks, Mom," I told her and picked up the box

carefully.

The key rested on a velvet bed, but the corner looked like it had been pulled up at some point. Later. I'd have to wait until later. Reluctantly, I closed the box and set it aside as Mom asked Kate if she wanted to stay for an early dinner.

"Thanks, Mrs. Peterson, that would be great. I'll just call my mom to check if it's ok," she pulled out her cell and walked to the front of the house.

"Tacos sound good for you two?" Mom asked Oliver and me, digging around in the freezer.

"Tacos sound great," I agreed with a wide smile, my hunger suddenly returning with a vengeance.

My grin widened when I caught Oliver glancing Kate's way. I felt sure that I wasn't the only one who was pleased that she was staying for dinner.

Chapter 2

When dinner was finally over, and we'd helped with the dishes, I grabbed the box that Mom had given me and headed with Kate towards the stairs that led up to my room. Oliver motioned that he'd be up in a bit and said something about tidying his mess in the basement. Mom nodded in approval.

I shot him a worried glance, but he shook his head, and I breathed a sigh of relief. He was sticking to his promise as agreed, and not planning to use the machine without us.

After closing the door to my room, Kate and I sat down on the purple rug in the middle of the floor and stared intently at the decorative box. I had flipped the lid open, and the ornate looking key was in full view.

"Care to tell me what's so special about this and why it's got you and Oliver freaking out?" Kate frowned.

"This key, I think it belongs to the metal box Oliver had to pry open," I said. "Our grandpa's box. But we can't try it out because the lock is ruined now."

"The one for the time machine? Why do you think that? And if it is, why would it be at the antique store?"

"I don't know; it's just a feeling I have. And Oliver thinks so too."

Kate frowned at me once more, clearly thinking that my brother and I both had overactive imaginations.

"Look," I said, pointing to the messed-up corner of the felt. "I think there's something under it."

She squinted at it. "Could be, or it's just old, and you two have gone a little, you know." She twirled her finger by her ear as she whistled. I gave her a playful shove.

"Just saying," she grinned.

"You did go back in time with us, remember? So if we're crazy, so are you."

"Good point."

We stared at it intently, waiting for Oliver to hurry and get his butt upstairs. I wanted to take the key out and pull up the velvet but didn't want him to be upset with me. So we waited. And waited. And we continued to wait.

"Have you heard from Zac yet?" Kate asked, picking at a loose thread on my rug.

I hadn't looked at my phone all afternoon and pulled it out of my pocket to check. There were three new messages, all of them from Zac. I grinned as I opened them and scrolled through. "He says he's really happy he bumped into me at the ice cream store," I relayed to Kate. "And he wants to know if I'd like to hang out at the park with him tomorrow." I beamed at the messages, while at the same time, butterflies began to do a crazy dance in my stomach.

I grinned at Kate. "What should I say?"

"You're going to say yes, right?" Kate asked, scooting closer so she could look over my shoulder.

"I think so…but what about…what if, you know, Jade shows up?"

"Jade doesn't go to parks. That's not cool enough for her. And besides, who cares?"

"Yeah, guess you're right." My fingers hovered over the keypad, but I was unsure of what to text back.

I stared at the screen for a moment, my fingers still not moving.

It seemed Zac was interested in me, but why did he let Jade hang around him so much? What if this was all a setup to make fun of me, and after a few days, a week of Zac hanging out with me, he showed up one day with Jade, and they all pointed their fingers and laughed at me for thinking I could be with him. That I could be anything but the nerdy girl in school?

"You're doing it again, making that face," Kate pointed out. "Stop thinking worst case scenario."

"I can't help it," I pouted and sighed. "You don't think this will end badly?"

"For Jade, maybe, but not for you. He didn't let her get away with pushing you around today. I think Zac's finally tired of putting up with her and that horrible annoying laugh." Kate and I mimicked it together until we were rolling around on the floor cackling like banshees when Oliver finally walked in. He stared at us with one arched brow.

"Do I want to know?" he asked.

"No, not important." I made a quick decision and typed a brief reply to Zac asking what time he'd like to meet at the park. I'd probably have to have Kate or Oliver with me. But there'd be a ton of people around on a Sunday, and hopefully, Mom would give me a little freedom.

"You didn't pull it out of the box yet?" Oliver asked, sitting cross-legged on the floor and staring at the gold key.

"No, I was being a nice sister and waiting for you." I set my phone aside and reached for the key that lay on the red velvet beneath. "You think this would've opened that box before you destroyed the lock?"

The key was cold and heavy in my hand, and the metal had rusted a little around the edges.

"Only one way to find out. We'll have to get it downstairs and test it on the box. The locking mechanism is probably wrecked, but we can at least see if the key fits inside it."

I handed the key to my brother and picked up the box. Using my fingernail, I picked at the velvet until it pulled away from the backing. Carefully, I tugged at it and was able to remove it. "Uh, Oliver? There's a piece of paper in here," I said excitedly. "Something's written on it."

Gently, I slipped it free of the box. The page was worn and crumpled, but the writing was clear on it as I gingerly unfolded it, worried it would tear.

"That's Grandpa's writing," Oliver said in disbelief. "I'm sure of it! What does it say?"

Oliver, this key belongs to a very important invention. If you should ever find it, I must implore you to use it with the utmost care.

When you find this, I know you'll be able to understand what it is and how to use it. I've seen you at work, my grandson, and you have the same mind as me.

But remember, you must always be careful not to be seen and that anything you change in the past can have damaging effects on the future for everyone.

One day, when the time is right, this will come into your possession and the greatest mystery of your life will be yours to solve. Yours and your sister's, Holly.

"Oh my gosh, I can't believe this really did belong to Grandpa!" My hands were shaking as I squinted at the words trying to make them out so I could read it aloud. After a moment I was able to decipher the text…

"Oliver, this key belongs to a very important invention. If you should ever find it, I must implore you to use it with the utmost care."

I paused in surprise and watched my brother's face brighten. "He wrote this to you, Oliver! I don't think it was meant to be in that antique shop."

"Go on," he urged, inching closer as he gripped the key tightly in his hand.

"Wait," I said frowning, "how did he know your name? You weren't even born yet!"

Oliver's smile fell, and he sat back. "You're right…now, this is weird."

The hair on the back of my neck stood on end, and goosebumps broke out over my arms. "Do you think Grandpa came to the future? By using that machine?"

Oliver shrugged. "I don't know; maybe he did…keep reading."

I nodded and readjusted my position on the floor, while at the same time taking in Kate's look of concentration. It was clear that she no longer thought Oliver and I were crazy or that we had overactive imaginations.

I looked down at the paper and continued…

"When you find this, I know you'll be able to understand what it is and how to use it. I've seen you at work, my grandson, and you have the same mind as me. But remember, you must always be careful not to be seen and that anything you change in the past can have damaging effects on the future for everyone. One day, when the time is right, this will come into your possession, and the greatest mystery of your life will be yours to solve. Yours and your sister's, Holly."

I lowered the letter, my mind racing with what we'd

discovered. Oliver reached for it, and I handed it to him. "This is insane," he murmured, reading over the words again. "That's all he said?"

"That's it." He knew our names. The only way he could've known was if he came to our time at some point. "Greatest mystery of our life," I repeated. "What does that mean?"

Oliver shook his head and set the key and letter down. "I'm not sure yet, unless...do you think?"

"Think what?"

"The mystery he's talking about is Dad?"

I gulped and rested my back against the edge of my bed. "Grandpa knew?"

"He knew our names; why would he not know that Dad disappeared? What else would be the greatest mystery of our lives?"

"He wants us to find Dad. How are we supposed to do that?"

Oliver held up the key. "We could use the machine. We could go back to the day he disappeared, or before. We could see where he went and maybe then we can understand why he never came back."

Kate reached out and squeezed my hand. "You keep saying you want to find your dad." It was the first time she'd spoken since I began reading the letter. She was as shocked as my brother and me.

"I do," I nodded.

But this was a lot to take in and the day had suddenly caught up with me. Overwhelmed, I fell silent and let Oliver figure out on his own how we would go about finding Dad. I listened to him ramble about what would be the best time to go back to. I struggled to concentrate on what he was saying; all I could think about was the man's face in the family picture. We could finally meet him, see who he was, and get to the truth of why he left us.

All these years, Mom swore to us that he'd just

walked away. But my gut now told me there was more to the story. Something had happened to Dad, something bad.

"It's getting dark," Kate said suddenly and hopped up. "I have to get home before Mom gets mad at me. Call me tomorrow!" She waved at us both and rushed out of my room. I heard her call goodbye to Mom before the front door opened and closed.

"Holly? Are you alright? You look like you're going to be sick." Oliver's brow creased with concern.

I shook my head and tried to smile. "I'm fine; this is just...it's a lot to take in, you know."

"I agree, but it's good, don't you think? Finally, we're getting a chance to figure out who Dad was and why he left."

"And if he left us by choice," I muttered. "I still can't believe Grandpa knew our names. Do you think we met him and never realized it? At a park or maybe even at school?"

Oliver moved so he could rest his back against the bed beside me. "It's possible."

He fiddled with the key then held it out for me to take. I ran my fingers over the rough surface and smiled, feeling an even stronger connection to our grandpa than I ever had before.

"I want to find him," I whispered firmly. "But what happens after we do?"

"What do you mean?"

"I don't know; I just have a bad feeling about all of this. That whatever happened to Dad could happen to us, too."

"I won't let anything happen to you," he promised, a serious expression on his face. "We're in this together, remember?"

He gave me a rare one-armed hug then pushed to his feet. He said he'd see me in the morning and I watched him leave my room. See me in the morning?

Thinking of tomorrow reminded me that in the morning I'd have to talk to Mom about hanging out with Zac. I set the key and letter back inside the leather box, tucking the box away safely in my desk. Then I grabbed my phone and fell onto my bed.

I guessed everything in my life was going to go crazy at once. The time machine, finding the pictures in the attic, and realizing that my crush actually might like me back.

I spent the next hour reading and re-reading Zac's texts and hoping that my reply sounded ok. I'd sent it so quickly. I scrolled through his Instagram photos, laughing about the funny pics he'd added and thinking how cute his dog was. He obviously loved his dog; he was in so many of the images.

When I turned off my lamp and pulled the blankets up to my chin, I pushed all thoughts of the time machine from my mind. That was a worry for another day. Tomorrow, I had a date.

Chapter 3

"A date?" Mom repeated, standing by the griddle as she made pancakes.

"Not really a date," I corrected, spinning from side to side as I sat on the barstool. "Just hanging out really, in the park, where there are lots of other people."

She eyed me over her shoulder. "Still sounds like a date."

"But we're not going to be alone, alone," I pointed out. "Please, Mom?"

I waited impatiently for her to decide whether I could hang out with Zac that day in the park or not. Worst case scenario, she would ask me to bring Oliver along. Best case, if she didn't let me go by myself, she would trust Kate to hang out with Zac and me instead. I mentally tried to convince her that I would be fine with Zac alone and as she removed the pancakes from the griddle, turning it off, she sighed and set the plate on the island.

"You are to stay at the park," she started. I bounced up and down on my stool, too excited to contain myself. She broke out into a smile and patted my hand. "And I don't want you gone more than two hours. Deal?"

"Definitely a deal!" I shook the hand she held out to me.

"My daughter, on her first date," she sighed as she turned back to the griddle to make the rest of the pancakes. "Why couldn't you have waited a few more years? Like four at least?"

"It's not a date," I insisted again, while inside my head all I could think was... *I'm finally going on a date with Zac Fredericks. I am, not Jade. Me. Weird, slightly nerdy, Holly Peterson is going on a date with Zac Fredericks.*

I wanted to jump and down, run around the kitchen and shout that something good was finally happening to me. But I was pretty sure Mom wouldn't allow me to be alone with a boy I was crushing on.

"He seemed very interested in Grandpa's work though," I added, hoping to convince her even more that we were just going to talk about science stuff.

"I'm sure he does," Mom said, unconvinced.

"He's got the highest grade in our science class," I continued. "He's a really good student."

"Hmm," she frowned, and I saw her lips curl into a crooked smile. "You sound as if you're buttering me up for something, Holly."

"Nope, just trying to make you feel better."

She nodded her head slowly, but her smile said I was not doing a very good job of that. "Just remember our deal. Only the park and you have to be back home in two hours."

"I remember."

"And I want to meet him."

I choked on my mouthful of pancake, chugging my orange juice to wash it down. Mom's brow shot up as she flipped the pancakes over. "Uh, today?" I managed to gasp.

"No, but soon. Unless of course, you don't want me to meet him."

"Sure I do," I said, even though inside I was rolling my eyes. "Why wouldn't I?"

Mom was grinning when she turned to face me. "Worried I'll embarrass you?"

"No," I said too quickly, and she laughed loudly.

"When I was your age, I was worried about boys meeting my parents, too."

I picked at my pancakes and wondered where Oliver was so that Mom could give him a hard time about something. And let me get back to being happy about seeing Zac. "You won't embarrass me, will you?" I asked quietly.

Mom turned off the griddle and sat alongside me.

"Only if you want me to." She grinned brightly, and we both laughed as she nudged my arm with hers. "You're just growing up so fast all of a sudden. It's hard for me to think that you have only one year left before high school."

"What about high school?" Oliver asked through a yawn as he joined us in the kitchen.

"Just realizing your sister is going to be there next year," Mom said, ruffling my hair. "Both of you have grown up so fast; I can hardly keep up."

"We're not that old yet," I argued.

"To me you are. And you're both so smart, and creative. I can't wait to see how awesome you turn out to be." She sniffed hard and wiped at her eyes.

Oliver and I stared at each other, confused. "Uh, Mom? You ok?" Oliver asked.

"Yeah, yeah I'm fine, I just...never mind." She stood, not having eaten anything, and made for the stairs. "I'm going to get cleaned up then I'm going to catch up with some of the ladies for our monthly book club meeting. Holly, please explain our agreement to your brother... about your date, I mean. And Oliver, I expect you to keep her to it."

She smiled almost sadly at us one more time then turned to leave, whispering so quietly I almost didn't catch it, "I wish your father could see you two."

The pancakes I'd eaten sat heavily in my stomach, and I pushed my plate away, unable to eat anymore.

"Did you hear that?" I asked Oliver quietly.

"No, what did she say?"

I repeated Mom's words, and his face fell. "I knew she only put on a tough face to try and keep us from seeing how much she misses him," he frowned.

"You think she believes something else happened to him?"

He bobbed his head, running his fingers through his messy hair in thought. "Yeah. Did you see the way she looked at that polar bear yesterday?"

"Oh, that reminds me, keep a lookout."

"On what? Holly, keep a lookout on what?"

But I was already moving for the stairs. I'd heard the sound of water turning on and knew I had at least ten minutes before Mom would be finished in the shower. With Oliver right behind me, I hurried to the upstairs hall and pulled down the ladder leading into the attic.

"What are you doing?" he hissed. "Mom's home!"

"I need those pictures," I insisted. "Just give me a few minutes. I know exactly where they are."

He muttered behind me, but I climbed the ladder, tuning him out, and tip-toeing towards the pictures. Mom's bedroom and adjoining bathroom were right below where the box was, and the floorboards creaked and groaned with each step I took.

I held my breath, waiting to hear the water shut off and Mom rush out to see what we were doing in the attic above. I uncovered the same old box, pried it open, and dug around until I found the envelope of pictures. Not having time to sort through them now, I tucked the envelope under my arm and hurried back down the ladder.

We were pushing it up into the ceiling and racing to get back to the kitchen when the water turned off. Oliver told me to look like I was eating, and a few minutes later, Mom appeared at the entrance to the kitchen, dressed in her robe, her hair wet, eyeing us both curiously.

"Did you two hear something?"

Oliver swiveled around on his stool sleepily. "Besides Holly's loud chewing?"

I smacked his arm lightly. "You chew louder than I do."

"Pretty sure you're chewing is almost as bad as your snoring."

We bantered back and forth for a moment before Mom rolled her eyes and hurried back upstairs to her room. We sagged in relief, and I pulled the envelope of pictures out from under my butt where I'd hidden them.

"What are you looking for?" Oliver asked.

"I can't look through them here, but I'm sure I saw a polar bear the same as the one Mom bought."

"In the pictures?"

"Yeah, and I think it has something to do with Dad." I glanced at the stove clock. I was supposed to meet Zac in the park at eleven. I had an hour and a half to get ready and figure out what I was going to wear. Oh no, what was I going to wear?

"Holly? You ok?"

I gulped; then I nodded frantically. "Yeah, I'm...I'm good."

"Nervous about your first date?"

I glared at him as I hopped off my stool, taking the pictures with me. "It's not a date. And I'll leave these in your room. I'll put them on your desk under some other stuff, so they're out of sight. You can look through them when Mom's gone."

I wanted to help, but this was my first chance to see if Zac actually liked me or was playing a prank on me. But first of all, I needed to figure out what to wear.

I placed the envelope on Oliver's work table in his room, covering it with one of his notebooks, and hurried back into my own room to figure out my next problem. Clothes! First of all, though, I needed a shower, and then I had to fix my hair. That morning it was deciding to be frizzier than ever. Telling myself there was no reason to panic over a boy, I trudged into the bathroom and spent the entire twenty minutes in a full-blown panic.

I was a bit of a mess as I wiped condensation from the mirror and tapped my fingers on the sink. Today had to go well, not perfect, but well at least.

So later, I could let Jade know all about it.

***

Scuffing my boot on the concrete beneath the bench, I tried not to look at my nerdy Harry Potter watch with the Gryffindor lion on the face. I didn't wear it at school because of what Jade said to me one time, but out here I felt it was safe and it gave me some comfort. Mom bought it for me when I entered middle school. She'd read the books to Oliver and I as we were growing up, and I fell in love with the idea of that world.

Now I guessed I was getting to live in a crazy world all of my own, but instead of wands, there was a time machine controlled by my brother.

Unable to stop myself, I checked my watch again. Quarter past eleven. Zac was late. I looked around the park, watching kids play on the swing-set not too far away, people walking their dogs and drinking hot chocolate from a nearby street vendor. But no Zac.

"I knew it," I whispered to myself as the first tears burned in my eyes.

I leaned back, stuffing my hands into the pockets of my jacket, and waiting for the world to come crashing down around me. It was a setup. Zac was working with Jade after all, and tomorrow morning, they would point their fingers and laugh at the silly girl who thought —

"Holly! Hey!"

My head whipped around so fast, I gave myself whiplash, but there was Zac, running towards the bench. My bench. His hair was damp, and when he skidded to a stop beside me, he bent over double, panting for breath.

"Zac? You alright?" I asked, using the opportunity to wipe at my eyes.

"Yeah, sorry. I forgot to plug my phone in last night, and my alarm didn't go off," he gasped, lifting his head to offer an apologetic grin. "Then I panicked, and instead of texting you, which I couldn't cause my phone was dead, I just took off after my shower."

He certainly looked like he'd dressed in a hurry, and my panic subsided as my nerves kicked in. I shrugged as if I wasn't bothered that he was late. "It's alright. It's not a problem."

Lies, so many lies. Mentally, I was jumping up and down for joy as he walked around the bench and plopped down beside me. "Do you always sleep in so late?"

"Ha, no, but my sister got a new game on the Switch, and we stayed up all night trying to beat it." He tucked his hands in his pockets, mirroring me, and we sat shoulder to shoulder.

"Did you?"

"Did I what?" He frowned then shook his head with a laugh. "Oh yeah, at three in the morning. Our dad came down and finally told us to stop hooting like crazy owls and go to bed."

"Hooting, huh?"

He smirked and started to hoot like an owl. I couldn't help it, I laughed loudly, and he kept doing it, those blue eyes shining brightly until he was laughing too.

He rubbed his hands together and nodded towards the vendor. "Want some? I didn't grab a jacket, and it's kinda chillier today than I thought it'd be."

"Sure."

He stood before me and smiled. His smile was contagious, and my heart backflipped in my chest. With a shy smile in return, I stood and walked alongside him as we headed for the hot chocolate vendor. Zac bought me a cup and handed it over.

"Don't burn your tongue," he added a moment later, grimacing after he'd taken a sip too fast.

I already had the lid off and was blowing on mine. "Aren't you the smartest guy in our science class?" I asked with a grin.

"Apparently only during the week." He laughed, indicating that he'd burnt his tongue.

We smiled as we drank our hot chocolate,

meandering along the trail. The chilly air was crisp as I breathed it in, smelling the first hints that spring was attempting to arrive and push winter away. There was a stream that flowed through the park, and we walked alongside it, the water sparkling in the midday sun. And with each step, my nerves lessened.

Being with Zac outside of school was very different. There was no pressure here in the park, no worrying about who might see us, or caring what I looked like. He even seemed more relaxed than normal, and I wondered how much pressure he put on himself to keep up with his friends, the other cool kids at school. Talking to him now about random things that popped into my head, he seemed like a totally different boy.

"Did you find out anything more about your grandpa? The time dude?" he asked after we found a low wall to sit on in the middle of the park. The fountain was across from us, but it was too cold to be running yet.

"I found some more, yeah, but not exactly what I was expecting."

"Oh yeah? Like what?" he asked eagerly.

I bit my bottom lip knowing I couldn't tell him about the device, but I could at least go over the theories we'd found, written down in Grandpa's notes. "Let's just say he was on the verge of trying to invent a time machine. We found all his old notes and sketches. Pretty crazy stuff."

Zac stared at me blankly before his face broke out into a huge, nerdy grin. "Seriously?"

"Yeah, seriously. It's crazy. I think Grandpa was really onto something."

"I wish he were still alive; I would love to pick his brain about his work." Zac smiled.

"You and my brother both," I mused, then stared intently at the ground. "We found out something else as well. My grandpa had a partner, or at least we think he did."

"Yeah? Do you know who he was? Maybe that person could help you with the notes," he suggested. "Then you guys could build your own time machine. How crazy would that be!"

I shook my head, remembering what else we'd discovered in those notes. The partner had been trying to take the machine away from Grandpa. "All we know is one initial: T. That was it."

Too bad I couldn't tell him about the note and the key. There was so much I'd love to share with him if I could. But that just wasn't possible. Oliver would freak out if he knew I told anyone else about our discovery. Even though I felt I could trust Zac, it wasn't the right thing to do.

Regardless though, the thought of our grandpa seeing us at some point in time because of that machine, sent a chill down my spine. Not a bad one, just one that told me there was a chance he could be in this time zone watching me right now, even though he was dead. My head gave a sudden throb, and I decided to stop trying to figure out all this time stuff and leave it to Oliver.

"T," Zac was whispering, rattling off a bunch of T names. "Guess you'll have to find more clues."

"We found out lots of stuff about my grandpa, and…we also found something out…about my dad."

His face softened as he looked at me. "Your dad?"

115

I took a shaky breath and smiled. "My dad left us when Oliver and I were really young. We don't know anything about him. Mom won't talk about him. But I found all these pictures of us together, hidden in a box in the attic. It's weird." I pulled out the one I still had tucked in my pocket, not willing to let it go. Zac carefully took it. He smiled at the image, then up at me.

"Man, your brother looks just like him."

"I said the same thing," I agreed. "I just wish I knew what happened to him, you know?"

"I always thought your dad had died," Zac said as he handed the picture back. "I knew he wasn't around and you never talked about him."

"I guess he could be dead, but I'm hoping he isn't; though I'm not sure what's worse. Having your dad walk out on you when you're a baby and still being alive out there somewhere, just not wanting you. Or, him being dead." I puffed out my cheeks, staring across the park as if my dad would suddenly materialize and give me the answers. "Sorry, I didn't mean to kill our happy conversation with my sappy story."

"What's sappy about it? You're trying to find your dad. That's inspiring."

I couldn't stop smiling. Zac was still the cutest boy in our grade, and the coolest as far as I was concerned, but sitting with him now, I realized there was a lot more to him. He was sweet and understanding, and at that moment, I think we both understood what good friends we could be.

I wondered if it could ever become more than that. If I told Mom I had a boyfriend, she'd faint.

I glanced at my watch and slouched in annoyance. "I have to get home."

"Already?" he asked, disappointed. "Sorry I was late today. Think we can do this again sometime? Maybe next time for a bit longer?"

I nodded eagerly. "But my brother might be forced to

come along. It's just that my mom doesn't like me hanging out on my own without him."

"Oh, that's ok. I like Oliver. He seems cool. Maybe I could even help you guys with your grandpa's notes if you want."

"I'll ask." I wanted just to say yes, but this wasn't only my thing. Oliver was involved, too.

Zac walked with me until we reached the edge of the park where we would have to head in different directions. We stood there, both shifting nervously on our feet, each waiting for the other to say goodbye.

"I'll see you at school tomorrow?" he asked.

"Yeah, see you tomorrow."

He let out one more hoot, and I giggled as he walked away, tucking his hands in his jeans pockets. I watched him go for a moment, before turning around and heading home. It had all gone way better than I'd hoped and I couldn't wait to get home so I could call Kate and tell her all about it. With each step towards my house, I recalled every moment of the past two hours, and when I reached my front door, the smile was still wide on my face.

When I stomped inside the house, Oliver looked up from the kitchen table.

"Good, you're on time," he said, then looked back down.

"What are you doing?" I asked as I joined him. Several pictures were spread out over the table. "You do realize Mom could be home any minute and you have these photos out for her to see! She'll know we've been in the attic."

"Correction, you've been in the attic. And these aren't those photos."

I looked over them again and sat down. "Oh, wow…different photos. Where did you find them?"

"In a box downstairs labeled photos."

I rolled my eyes and sifted through a stack close to

117

my arm. "What are you looking for?"

"Photos of Grandpa and maybe him with this mysterious partner of his."

I wanted to grab the photos I'd left in Oliver's room, to have another look through those as well, but Oliver was sliding an image towards me.

"This is one of the attic ones."

I took it and held it up. "A polar bear." No wonder Mom was so emotional over that figurine she found.

Standing in the picture was Mom and Dad, holding a stuffed polar bear which appeared to be a toy they'd won from some game booth behind them. They looked young, maybe high school age. Dad had his arm around Mom's shoulders and rested his cheek on her head. She hugged the polar bear tightly to her chest.

"It was probably the first present he ever gave her," Oliver told me. "Hey, do you recognize this man?" He picked up a photo from the table and held it up so we both could see.

There was Grandpa in his lab coat, looking like he was in a classroom of sorts. He used to teach before he retired, but it was the man standing beside him who Oliver was pointing at. The man had white hair pulled back in a ponytail and a weird smile on his face. I blinked a few times then gasped, smacking Oliver on the arm.

"Ow, what!" he exclaimed, rubbing his arm, annoyed.

"You don't remember him?"

"No. You do?"

"Yeah, he was that weird substitute teacher we had for science class when Mrs. Green had her baby last year! He would've taught you, too. Remember? He had this strange accent and always wore his hair in that ponytail."

Oliver's eyes narrowed then widened in recognition. "Wow! That *is* him. What was his name?"

I wracked my brain, trying to remember, but nothing popped into my head. Frustrated, I paced around the room, running through all the names of my teachers from last year. He was only there for a month and I never really liked science class, so I didn't pay attention...

"Mr. Thaddeus Banes," Oliver whispered, staring at me with an incredulous expression. "T."

"You think he's the T guy?" I asked.

"It's possible," he said as the front door opened.

I quickly passed the photo of Mom and Dad back to Oliver, and he stuffed it in his pocket just as Mom entered the kitchen. She frowned at the pile of photos spread across the table.

"What are you two up to?"

"Just looking at some old pictures," Oliver said. "Of Grandpa."

Mom's face softened as she stared down at the images of her dad. "He would've loved you both. I wish he'd been able to hold on just a few more years.

"Hey, Mom," Oliver said and held out the picture we'd just been looking at. "Who's this?"

She looked at the photo, setting her purse down on a chair, and grinned. "A very old friend of your grandpa's. They worked together before Dad retired from research and went into teaching. His friend was amazed he gave up on his work so easily." Her smile faded, and she sighed. "They had a falling out I think. Dad stopped talking about him one day, and I never heard anything more about him."

"What was his name?" I asked, trying not to sound overly excited.

"Thaddeus Banes," Mom replied, and my gut dropped. "He was a strange man, but extremely smart, just like your grandpa. They did some amazing work together. I'm surprised you didn't find out anything about him when you were researching your grandad?"

I shook my head. "Nothing."

"Would it be weird if he was our substitute teacher last year?" Oliver asked.

Mom was taken aback at his question. "Well, yeah…yeah, I would say so. You have to be mistaken."

"Why?" I asked, wondering why she was giving us such an odd look.

"Because Thaddeus Banes died a few months after your grandad," Mom replied. "He's dead, kids. Your substitute teacher had to be someone else." She returned the picture to the table and asked us to clean up the pile before disappearing again.

Oliver and I exchanged glances. We were both sure that the man in the photo was the same man who had taught our science class. Maybe Mom was mistaken? Or maybe…maybe something weirder was going on. But whatever it was, it would have to wait until we could do some research away from Mom who had just reappeared in the kitchen, a curious expression on her face.

"Holly, I forgot to ask you…how was your date?"

I looked at her with surprise before moving towards the fridge in the hope that Oliver hadn't eaten all the leftovers. I could feel my face turning pink at her question.

"It wasn't really a date, Mom. We were just hanging out. We got some hot chocolate and went for a walk and stuff. It was fun."

Mom nodded and grinned. She didn't push the matter, but by the way that she raised her eyebrows, I could tell she knew I was crushing over Zac. I sat back down and concentrated on the food on my plate, hoping she wouldn't ask me any more questions.

I also avoided Oliver's stare and was glad that he hadn't decided to interrogate me as well.

I scoffed down my slice of left-over pie, quickly rinsed my plate and stacked it in the dishwasher. Excusing myself from the kitchen, I headed up to my room so I could call Kate and fill her in on my day. She was the one person who I was keen to share all the details with.

She answered on the first ring and immediately asked how it all went.

"He's so different when he's not at school," I said after running through every moment with Zac, answering every question Kate threw at me. "I think he might start hanging out with us more."

"You mean you," Kate said through her excited laughter. "This is awesome, Holly! See, what did I tell you? He likes you! I knew it! You don't have to worry about Jade."

Thinking of Jade's smug expression and the confident way she behaved around Zac, I couldn't help but worry about her. "What if tomorrow Zac acts like we didn't hang out? What if he goes back to acting like I don't exist! Kate, do you think he'd do that?"

"No, of course, he won't" she replied, but not sounding very convincing. "At least, I hope he doesn't."

"Me too." I laid on my bed, head hanging off the edge as I stared across at the photos of my friends and me on my picture board. "What about you and Oliver?" I asked with a grin, no longer wanting to focus on the Zac and Jade scenario.

Kate huffed and mumbled something I couldn't make out. "I have no idea what you're talking about!"

"Yeah ok, whatever," I teased.

"I don't like your brother."

"You know you're a terrible liar."

She burst out laughing. "Just don't say anything to Oliver, alright? That'd be weird, and I don't want to make it weird."

"Promise I won't tell him you're crushing on him bigtime."

Mom called upstairs, telling me it was time for dinner and I sat up so I could see the clock. I hadn't realized I'd been talking to Kate for over two hours.

"Hey, I gotta go, dinner time," I told her.

"I'll see you tomorrow!" She replied and hung up.

Just as I was about to put my phone down, a text tone sounded, and I looked at the screen to find a message from Zac. I scanned it quickly as the excitement bubbled inside me.

I had fun today. Can't wait to hang out again!

Smiling widely, I quickly typed a reply.

I had fun too. Maybe we can hang out next weekend?

After I sent the message, I froze. Was that a ridiculous thing to do? Had I asked him too quickly? We'd hung out one time, and here I was already asking to hang out again. He was going to think I was the pushiest girl in school. My cell chirped in my hand, and I squinted open one eye to see his reply.

Are you doing anything next Saturday?

I squealed loudly in response, as I read the rest of his text.

There's a movie coming out at the theater in town. It's a superhero movie.

I eagerly typed my reply, warning him that I'd probably have to bring my brother along.

He said that he didn't care since he was going to have his little sister with him. And I could invite Kate, too if I wanted.

That would be a yes! I typed and hit the send symbol.

He sent back a smiley face, and I headed down to dinner, the grin stretching across my entire face. When I sat down at the table, I struggled to hide my excitement.

Right then, I felt happier than I'd felt in a very long time.

Chapter 4

On Monday morning, I was up before my alarm, in the shower, and eating breakfast before Mom or Oliver were even out of bed. When Mom eventually shuffled into the kitchen, she placed her hand on my forehead with a sleepy frown.

"Uh, Mom? What are you doing?" I asked.

She shrugged and made her way to the coffee pot. "Just checking to see if you're sick."

"Why? I feel fine."

"Yes, but you're out of bed without me asking you to get up. Must have been some date yesterday," Mom mumbled with a wink. "Can't wait to see him again?"

I shook my head and didn't bother replying, but smiled as I stared down at my bowl of cereal. I was anxious to get to school and see how today would go. What would Zac do? Would he hang out with his friends or would he stop and talk to me? What about at lunchtime? I couldn't bear to see him with Jade hanging all over him again. Suddenly, I wasn't so hungry and carried my half-finished breakfast to the sink.

"Holly? You were beaming two seconds ago, what's wrong?" Mom asked before I could disappear back upstairs to finish getting ready.

"Nothing, I'm fine."

"You're not fine at all. Is it about Zac?"

I tugged at my black sweater and gave a subtle nod.

"Oh sweetie, no matter what happens, remember you're very young, and he's one boy."

"It's not him I'm worried about," I replied quietly. "It's a girl in my class."

Mom's face hardened. "Jade? Is she still giving you trouble?"

"No...I mean kind of, but it's fine. I'll be fine."

Mom bent down, so we were eye level, and gripped onto my arms. "Listen to me...no matter what that girl says to you, remember you are a very bright young girl, you're beautiful, and people like her only give people like you a hard time because they're jealous. Ok? Ignore her, show her it doesn't bother you, and she'll leave you alone."

"I know, Mom."

"And if she doesn't, then tell me and I'll march down to her house and have a word with her mother."

"Please don't do that!" I begged in horror. "Mom, really, I'll be fine."

She frowned as she smoothed my hair down and kissed the top of my head. "I'll resist the urge to be crazy over-protective Mama bear, for now. Go on, finish getting ready, so you're not late. But if she keeps giving you trouble, make sure you let me know."

I started to walk away, then stopped and rushed back to hug her tightly, before darting upstairs. I knew she hadn't had it easy in this town after Dad disappeared. And it hadn't been easy for her before that. She'd been the daughter of the crazy scientist, and everyone in this small town liked to talk. Jade's mom and my mom had a history together. They'd started as friends, but then my dad came along and fell for Mom instead of her friend. That ruined their friendship.

And now, I wondered if history was going to repeat itself.

As I finished brushing my teeth, Oliver stepped out of his bedroom, his backpack slung over his shoulder, and I followed him downstairs. He grabbed a granola bar and tried to sneak out of the house, but Mom caught his backpack and pulled him into a hug. He pursed his lips then hugged her back.

"Mom? Can I go now?"

"Yes, yes, go," she urged and watched us walk out the front door. "Love you guys!"

"Love you, too, Mom!" I called back, waving. I knew she would watch us until we disappeared from her sight.

Oliver was never talkative in the morning, and I enjoyed the quiet as I walked alongside him, both of us deep in thought. When we reached the middle school, he had to continue to the high school, one block over. He gave me his usual brotherly smile, and a small wave then kept on going, still munching on his granola bar.

I hurried up the steps of the building, through the mass of students slowly making their way there, and found Kate at her locker. "Hey."

She greeted me with a bright grin. "Have you seen Zac yet?"

"No, but I need to ask you what you're up to this coming weekend?"

"Hmm, don't think I'm doing anything. Why?"

"Zac wants to go to a movie, but I know Mom's going to make me bring Oliver. Zac's taking his little sister as well. Do you want to come? Zac told me to ask you."

"Really?" She tugged at a loose strand of blond hair, and I knew her answer before she opened her mouth. "I'll have to double check with my mom, but yeah, I'd love to go."

"You want to see Oliver," I teased.

She nudged me with her elbow. "I don't know what you're talking about." But the smile remained on her face.

I opened my locker and hung my backpack inside, ready to empty it when I chanced a glance down the hall. Zac had just walked in, and as he was quite tall, I was able to see him over the heads of the students milling about. My palms grew clammy, and I tried to swallow the lump in my throat.

I lifted my arm to wave but stopped when Jade's loud laughter echoed down the hall. Kate gave Jade a disgusted look as she pushed her way through the crowd to reach Zac, her followers trailing behind her. I held my breath, waiting for her to attach herself to his side and for him to laugh and joke with her as he always did.

But when Jade reached him, Zac barely seemed to notice her. His eyes scanned the crowd, and I raised my hand. He spotted me, and his warm smile had my stomach filling with butterflies. He left his friends behind, headed right past Jade who was chatting animatedly beside him and maneuvered his way through the group of students. Jade glared at him as he walked away and I swore the entire hall fell silent as he finally came to a stop.

Right in front of me.

"Hey, Holly," he said and leaned casually against the locker beside mine.

"Morning," I replied and stared into his shining blue eyes. "I think your friends are confused," I whispered, leaning in a bit.

He shrugged. "Who cares what they think!"

This wasn't happening. It all had to be a dream, and I was going to wake up to find Zac still hanging out with Jade and her friends. But after I pinched myself, Zac was still standing beside me, asking how the rest of my Sunday had been. For a second, I couldn't get the words to come out. Then Kate gave me a helpful nudge, and I was able to ignore everyone else around us.

"Actually, I think my brother and I found out something kind of interesting."

"Oh yeah? About your grandpa or your dad?"

"Grandpa. Oliver found a picture of him with another scientist." Kate moved closer so she could hear better. "You guys remember that weird substitute last year? The one with the ponytail?"

"Mr. Banes?" Zac asked. "He was strange, smelt like mothballs and had that funny accent. He liked to hum classical music, all the time, too."

Kate bobbed her head. "Yeah, he would always do it in tests. Told us it would boost our brain power. But that habit of his was so annoying. What about him?"

"Well, we found a picture of him with our grandpa."

Kate closed her locker, holding her books in her arm, and stared at me. "You're sure?"

"Yeah, pretty sure."

"And he didn't know who you were when he was teaching us, by your last name or anything?" Zac asked. "That's…strange."

Oliver and I thought so, too. But it gets weirder," I started, then stopped myself short. Kate knew all about the time machine, but Zac had no idea. What would he think if I told him that according to my mom, Mr. Banes died more than twelve years ago?

Deciding to skip that part, I focused on a different explanation instead. "We think Mr. Banes is the T guy, Grandpa's partner, and we're trying to figure out if he's still around." I widened my eyes at Kate, hoping she'd understand what I was getting at, but she was watching something else down the hall.

"Well, he was working here last year," Zac said, sounding hopeful. "Maybe ask a few of the teachers. They might know him."

"Maybe." I looked to Kate then followed her gaze down the hallway.

My pulse pounded in my ears, and I wanted to disappear as quickly as possible. Jade was glaring daggers at me, her thumbs were hooked into her belt, and she was taking in my every move.

She'd been mean to me before, but now I knew I was in trouble. I gulped, my hands shaking so much I nearly dropped my books.

Then Zac filled my vision.

"Holly, ignore her," he said quietly, but firmly.

"Uh? Oh, I'm fine, really."

He reached out and squeezed my hand. "I never liked her, just so you know. She always just hung around and…I don't know."

"I get it," I assured him even though I really didn't, not completely. "Jade is easier to put up with than trying to tell her to go away. Trust me, I know."

He frowned, and I could see that he wasn't sure what I meant by that comment. "I'll walk with you to your first class?" he offered.

Kate said she'd see us later and Zac and I headed down the corridor, although I could still feel Jade's eyes burning into my back. Trying to put her out of my mind, I chatted with Zac about our plans for Saturday as well as the substitute teacher, Mr. Banes. Zac wanted to help me track him down if he could. I was surprised at how involved he wanted to be. He seemed to be genuinely interested in helping me figure out one of the mysteries of my family. And I knew his interest was genuine. I could feel it.

When we reached my classroom, he paused for a moment and smiled. "See you in history class," he said, before walking away and throwing a hoot over his shoulder.

A few kids he passed stared at him like he was weird, but he didn't seem to care. I stepped into first period as if I was in the middle of a dream. I was sure that my crush liked me back. Maybe it would be a good Monday after all.

***

History class was more entertaining than usual. We were asked to form groups for a future project involving a report on an aspect of Ancient Egypt, and we were allowed to choose our group. Kate and I shifted our desks closer together, and Zac quickly joined us, followed by Ben, and TJ, two of Zac's friends. I was surprised at first and a little worried, but once we settled in, we found them to be just as much fun as Zac.

Jade glowered at me the entire time until the bell rang, but I did what Zac suggested. I ignored her. He wanted to hang out with me, and it wasn't up to her to say if that was alright or not.

Our teacher explained that we'd have plenty of class time to complete our project. She said we'd be given time with our group in the library and also the computer lab so we could complete the necessary research. That was exciting enough, but after history class it was lunchtime, and Zac and his two friends walked with Kate and me to the cafeteria. I sat with Kate at our usual table while the boys headed off to grab some food.

"Wow," Kate said, watching the three of them walk away.

The rest of Zac's usual group sat across the way, but they didn't seem put off at all by his decision to sit with us. They met up at the sandwich line, laughing and jostling each other.

"Why can't girls be like that?" I asked, pulling out the sandwich I'd brought from home and my bottle of water. "They all seem to just get along with pretty much everybody."

"A lot of girls just like causing trouble." Kate sighed, eyeing Jade who had just walked in the door.

"Yeah, I think you're right!" I nibbled at my lunch, replaying the day so far in my head.

Jade headed straight for the table where Zac usually sat, and I nudged Kate so she'd turn and look. Zac, TJ, and Ben left the lunch line, walked right past Jade, and joined us. The look on Jade's face was priceless. I've never seen cheeks turn such a bright shade of red. It was hard not to laugh at her astonished expression.

When it abruptly turned to anger, I ignored her and joined in the conversation going on around me. Everyone was talking about our project, and TJ was offering some great ideas.

He looked at each of us for approval, and his excited grin was contagious.

I never thought that planning for a history project could be so much fun.

And when he suggested that we should meet up together at someone's house so we could prepare for the final presentation, we all nodded in agreement.

Zac sat right beside me and now and then, bumped his shoulder on mine. He offered me some of his fries, and we shared them, as well as a few smiles every few seconds. I felt so happy and relaxed around him. It was just like a dream come true.

With a few minutes left before the bell, I stood to throw my trash away and use the bathroom. It was empty when I entered, but when I exited a stall and turned the water on to wash my hands, the door opened, and Jade walked in. Her friends were right behind her. They crossed their arms and glared at me, not saying a word.

I did my best to keep my face blank, but my heart raced, and I was starting to panic.

"What are you doing?" Jade snapped.

"Washing my hands, what does it look like?" I replied, keeping my tone light. "Do you need something? All the stalls are open."

"I'm not here to use the bathroom."

"Ok, then what do you want?" I finished washing my hands and went to grab a paper towel, but she stepped in front of me, blocking my way. "Can you please move?"

"You didn't answer my question. I asked you what are you doing?"

I tilted my head to the side and stared at her. She was wearing makeup, and it was obvious she'd spent time that morning piling her hair into a topknot on her head. "Why do you always try to look so old? We're twelve, Jade, supposed to be having fun, running around outside. Not acting like we're sixteen and in high school."

Her friends gasped, and her jaw dropped. I was a little shocked myself, wondering where my confidence had come from.

"Just let me dry my hands and get out of here." I stared at her.

"No."

I ground my teeth and waited, not sure what to do.

"Stay away from Zac. He likes me, not you."

I stared back at her defiantly. Who did she think she was anyway?

"Whatever you say, Jade!" I locked my eyes on hers, but all the while, I was trembling inside. She had her group of friends with her, and they all stood watching and waiting to see what she would do next.

Jade sighed and tossed her head back. "I'm only going to warn you once, Holly. You're not good enough for Zac. You're just some worthless girl without a dad and a crazy older brother."

I looked at her, a million phrases swirling inside my head. I wanted to stand up to her. I wanted to tell her just to leave me alone. But instead, I didn't utter a single sound.

"You'll never be one of the cool group," she continued, her spiteful tone ringing in my ears. "You'll never be popular. And Zac? Why would he be interested in someone like you, anyway."

"Yeah, Holly!" her friend, Maxine spoke up, her smug stance mimicking Jade's.

I glanced at Maxine in disgust; she followed everything that Jade said and did. I wanted to say to her...*Don't you have a mind of your own?* But still, the words would not leave my lips.

"Think about it, Holly!" Jade's voice had taken on an evil tone. "He probably just wants a good mark for his history project. Why else would he want to work with you? Now stay away from him. *Or you'll get what's coming to you!*"

She emphasized her last sentence threateningly as she turned on her heel and left the bathroom, her group of followers right behind her. I could hear their laughter through the door as it closed behind them.

I stumbled back into the wall and slid down it, hugging my knees to my chest. Tears burned in my eyes, but she wasn't going to make me cry. She wasn't! I was stronger than that.

But what did she mean by...*you'll get what's coming to you?* I didn't doubt that she was capable of doing something horrible. And what she said about Zac...was that true? It couldn't be. No matter how many times I repeated it over and over in my head though, I could not help but worry.

Why was Zac suddenly interested in me? Even though we'd had so much fun yesterday and working on the history project was fun as well, he had never wanted to hang out with me before. I tried to convince myself that he'd enjoyed himself as much as me.

I got to my feet and was wiping my face when Kate burst through the bathroom door, carrying my books. What would I do without her for a friend?

"Hey, are you ok?" she asked, frowning. "We have to get to class."

"Yeah, yeah I'm fine," I lied.

"You don't look fine. What's wrong?" She glanced over her shoulder. "I saw Jade come in here."

"Hmm, no, must've missed her." I took my books with a muffled thanks and followed her out of the bathroom.

Zac was hanging around close by, and he waved when he spotted me. But I couldn't talk to him right now, not without having a full-on breakdown. I gave a half-hearted wave back, turned, and made my way to class. Kate was talking to me, but I was too lost in my thoughts to listen.

Stupid Jade. Or stupid me.

I couldn't quite decide yet, but I guessed I would find out soon enough.

Chapter 5

The rest of Monday passed by in a blur and was filled with me trying not to catch Jade's eye and looking for ways to avoid bumping into Zac. Kate pestered me with questions, but I managed to make up excuses and said I wasn't feeling very well.

"There's something more," she said as the day came to an end and we headed home.

"I'm ok. It's just...my stomach's upset."

She grabbed my arm and pulled me to a stop. "Jade said something to you in the bathroom, didn't she, Holly. I can tell something is going on. What happened?"

Hugging my books to my chest, I quietly skimmed the details of my encounter with Jade and her gang. Kate's eyes narrowed, and she turned around, marching back towards the school. Kids were still loading onto buses and messing around, yelling and laughing.

"Where are you going?" I yelped worriedly, trying to catch up.

"I'm not letting her mess with my best friend," she snapped.

"Kate, it's not worth it!"

"Yes it is," she argued. "She can't keep upsetting you like this. It has to stop."

I managed to grab her and drag her back down the sidewalk. "If you try to confront her like this, you'll get into trouble. You know how she is with the teachers. They all think she's wonderful." I didn't release my hold on Kate's arm until she agreed to let it drop.

"Did she tell you to stay away from Zac?"

I ducked my head, and she groaned.

"Don't worry. I'm not going to do what Jade tells me to." I tried to assure her.

"Yeah, sure. You avoided Zac all afternoon. You had classes with him, and I saw you ignore him."

I didn't want to get into an argument with my best friend, but she was only making me feel worse, although I knew it wasn't on purpose. I just didn't want to talk about Jade anymore. It was nearly the end of March, and then it would be spring break. I'd have a week without Jade around, and hopefully, I could hang out with Zac. After today, I was fairly sure he did like me. Jade must have seen it too. That was the only reason she would have come after me the way that she did.

But I didn't want to risk blurting it all out to Zac. He'd probably think I was a drama queen. Plus, it was kind of embarrassing to suggest that Jade might be jealous because he liked me. It was all so mixed up; I didn't know what he'd think.

"You know, you could always wait until our next project in history," Kate suggested thoughtfully. I could almost see her mind ticking over.

"What do you mean?"

"We all know what Jade's like…she'll come up with something great to impress everybody. And then you can try to embarrass her for once. It'd be perfect," Kate giggled at the thought. "Oh, I'd love to see her squirm."

I nodded in agreement, then stopped suddenly, nearly tripping over my feet. "Oh my gosh! You're a genius!"

"What?" she laughed.

"I've got to get home. I'll call you later!" I replied excitedly and took off at a run, leaving poor Kate standing bewildered on the pavement.

I needed to talk to Oliver, and I could not get home quickly enough. I'd never been so excited to speak to my brother before.

Rushing inside, I dumped my backpack by the door. "Holly?" Mom called from her office.

"Yeah, I'm home!"

"Don't leave your stuff by the door, please!"

I grunted, wondering how she even knew I had done that when she was in her office working. Rushing back for my bag, I carried it with me to the basement, expecting to see Oliver sitting at his workbench. But he wasn't down there. I ran back up the basement stairs and then up another flight of stairs to his room, but that was empty, too.

"Mom? Where's Oliver?" I called loudly, as I raced back down the stairs, panic creeping through me. What if he'd accidentally sent himself back in time somewhere?

Mom came out of her office, glossing over several papers in her hand. "He'll be home around dinnertime. He stayed after school to tutor some students."

"Today?"

She eyed me suspiciously. "Yes, today. What's the problem, Holly? Is there something going on that I should know about?"

"What? Oh nothing," I shook my head. "Just wanted to talk to him about something I learned at school today in science class."

"Oh yeah? Sounds thrilling." Her raised brow said she didn't believe me, but she let it go when I said I was going upstairs to do my homework.

Dumping my bag and books on the bed, I sat down beside them and stared at the ceiling.

Kate's words had given me a great idea, not for when our next presentation came around, but for the one that had already happened. I grinned and imagined going back in time and watching Jade getting up to present to the class but finding her slideshow messed up, or her artifacts missing. She wouldn't be so cool if she had nothing to show after all that boasting. I could take her down a notch or two. Where was the harm? It'd be easy to do. I could sneak in and sabotage it somehow…yeah, I could make it work.

I smiled and rolled over to grab my notebooks and get started on my homework, all the while, formulating a plan in my head to get back at Jade.

***

I didn't get a chance to talk to Oliver until after dinner. He disappeared down to the basement like always, and since it was my turn, I helped Mom to clean up the dishes, then I hurried down after him. He was hunched over his workbench, sifting through more of Grandpa's handwritten notes. He looked deep in thought, and when I reached over to shake his shoulder, he jumped with a startled yelp.

"Sorry," I cringed apologetically, as papers went flying.

He scowled at me, and I helped him pick them up. "I had no idea you were there. You could've said something you know."

"What did you think? I was the bogeyman?" I smiled. "You watch too many of those ghost TV shows."

"It's so quiet and isolated down here," he argued, trying to justify his reaction. "You'd freak out if someone sneaked up on you, too."

With the papers gathered, he plopped back down on his stool, and I paced close by.

"What's up?"

"I uh…I have an idea to run by you, for the next time we take a trip."

"Yeah?" He said slowly, now giving me his full attention. "What were you thinking? And why do you look like you think I'm going to say no?"

I continued to pace, wringing my hands as I spoke. "Well, you know how Jade's been giving me a hard time at school, right?"

139

"Yeah…"

"Don't look at me like that! I don't want to do anything too crazy," I promised. "Just something to put her in her place is all. Gently."

He turned his cap to the back of his head and stared at me curiously.

"What exactly did you want to do?"

"I want to go back to just a week ago and mess up her history presentation."

Oliver puffed out his cheeks and shook his head.

"What? Why not?" I stared back at him, my stomach dropping with disappointment.

"First of all, that's being petty, and secondly, how do you plan on messing up her presentation without getting caught?" he challenged. "That's in the middle of the school day with a ton of people around!"

I sank onto the other stool and sighed. "I guess you have a point."

"Holly, you saw what happened when you saw yourself. What if that happens again?"

"But what if it doesn't?"

He threw his head back, muttering under his breath, "You're pushing your luck."

I picked at the wooden edge of the table, figuring I would have to go with Kate's original plan and mess up Jade's next presentation somehow. I wondered what it would be about and if I could mess her up enough to get payback.

"So what did she do that's got you so keen on revenge?" he asked, interrupting my thoughts.

I shook my head and started for the basement stairs. "No, it's fine. You're right about risking too much. It's not a big deal."

"Yeah, it is if you want to risk all this just to mess her up. She must've done something pretty bad!

I remained tight-lipped but stayed in my spot. Oliver raised his eyebrows encouragingly, waiting for me to explain.

"She and her friends ganged up on me about hanging out with Zac."

"Ganged up on you?"

I hadn't even told Kate the entire story, but if Oliver heard about her bullying, he might be more inclined to help me out. I took a deep breath and spilled every detail of what Jade said in the bathroom, including the way she and her friends acted towards me. Oliver rarely got mad, but when he saw how upset I was, he glared at the far wall and then pulled me into a hug. I hugged him back.

"You're going to tell Mom, right?"

"What? No way," I said quickly, wiping at my eyes to dry them. "No. Jade's mom and our mom know each other, remember? I'm not going to bring up their old rivalry."

"Mom should know, or you should at least tell someone at school."

"No, it won't make any difference. All the teachers think Jade's the perfect student," I argued. "It's really ok. I'll be fine."

Oliver shook his head and walked back to the table. "If we do this, if we even try it, you have to understand how dangerous it would be. We have to plan it perfectly, like better than perfect, so we don't get caught."

"Wait, you're saying you'll do it?" I asked quietly, not wanting to get my hopes up just yet.

"No one messes with my little sister. So yeah, yeah we're going to do this. Somehow."

I squealed with excited laughter and hugged him again. "Oh, my gosh, Oliver! Thank you! You're the best big brother ever!"

"You bet I am."

"So, how are we going to do it?" I asked, bouncing on my feet as I watched him reach for the machine. "Are we doing it right now?"

"What? No, we're going to have to plan this out carefully, and that's going to take a few days." He grabbed his notepad, and after checking some of Grandpa's notes, he started jotting things down that I didn't understand. "The safest way is for us to already be at school when we travel."

"Because we'll land in the same spot in the past," I said. "Right, ok, I get it. So how are we going to do that without anyone seeing us?"

I bit my lower lip, wondering if this was a good idea or not. I pictured the thought of us getting caught, sneaking around the school at night. I could see it now, some night patrol security guard catching Oliver, me, and probably Kate, wandering around the school with a box that had a crazy glowing machine inside it.

"I'm not sure," Oliver replied. "Is there anything going on at your school this week?"

I was about to say no, but then hopped up and down when I remembered. "The spring band concert, it's on Thursday night. We can get in with the other students and then sneak away while the concert is on!"

He nodded along with my idea. "And your history

class? How are you going to sneak into the classroom to do what you need to do?"

I held up my hand, ready for a brilliant idea to pour out of my mouth, but there was nothing. I had no idea what to do, or how to get it done without getting all of us caught. "I'll have to get back to you on that one," I mumbled.

"Think it over long and hard. If we're going to do this, we have to be sure we're not going to mess it up. Got it?"

"Got it."

He went back to jotting down his notes, and I headed for the stairs. There was homework I needed to finish, and I'd promised Kate I'd call her. I started up the steps, stopped, then rushed back to hug Oliver again before racing up the stairs.

My heart was pounding with excited adrenalin over what we had planned. And I could not wait to put it into action.

Chapter 6

"Stop glaring at her like that," I whispered the following morning.

"Can't help it. I'm wondering how I can find a way to get back at her."

Kate shoved a few more books into her locker then closed it. "You going to talk to Zac today at least? He seemed really confused yesterday when you ignored him."

I felt bad about yesterday, but for some reason, I didn't want to open up to Zac about the way Jade was behaving. He said he didn't want to hang out with her, but I had no idea if they'd actually been friends before or if he was just putting up with her? And there was that deep, dark part of my mind that said it was all a bad joke and the whole idea of Zac liking me was just a nasty trick that Jade had planned all along.

"Hey, there he is," Kate said, and before I could say anything, she gave me a little shove forward.

I tripped over my feet and fell right into Zac. He caught me with a soft laugh and steadied me on my feet, smiling at me. "Hey, you ok?" he asked.

"I uh, yeah, I'm good," I rambled, then cleared my throat when a lump formed.

"So um… are you still talking to me? Or did I do something wrong?" He shuffled his feet, and I realized he was nervous, really nervous. "You looked like you were kind of avoiding me."

I stared up at him, surprised at how direct he was being. "It wasn't you," I told him quickly and hung my head. "I kind of argued with someone, and…and it made me upset…that's all," I spied the person in question and froze.

His eyes narrowed, and he glanced over his shoulder

when he saw my reaction. "Jade?"

"Don't worry about it, it's ok," I mumbled.

"Look, Holly, she thinks she's the best, but really, she's just a bully," he insisted turning back to me. "Without her friends to back her up, she wouldn't be half as confident. And besides, I'm sure she's jealous of you. That's just the way she is."

"But she's your friend, isn't she? I don't think she likes me hanging out with you," I said, my cheeks growing hot at the thought of her staring at us.

Zac shook his head. "Like I said before…she always wants to hang out with my friends and I but I don't like her, Holly, and I don't want her bugging you. I'll talk to her if you want, try to make her understand."

"No, no that might make it worse. I'll be fine, don't worry."

"You sure you're ok?" he asked, concerned. It warmed me to hear it.

"Yeah, I'm sure."

"Okay," he smiled.

His blue eyes beamed at me and I felt the familiar tremor of butterflies fluttering crazily in my stomach. We walked side by side down the hall, passing Jade as we went. She tried to get Zac's attention, but he ignored her, and a hush fell over the area. On the outside, I kept on talking to Zac, acting as if nothing was out of the ordinary. Inwardly, I was laughing to see Jade out of sorts and her cheeks reddening as the people around her giggled and whispered before she stormed off. I decided to stay out of her way for the next few days; at least until I had my chance to mess up her spotless reputation even further.

I shouldn't have been so excited to do something that would essentially ruin another person's grade, but I told myself it was karma coming back to get Jade for all the stuff she'd put other kids through, myself included. She was not a nice person, and she deserved what she got.

One way or another, I'd get my chance to get her back and then she would leave me alone.

***

I was able to spend all of history class sitting with Zac since we now had our project to work on. It was the most fun history lesson I'd ever had. We laughed while we worked and as well, we talked more about our plans to see a movie that weekend. I was very excited and couldn't stop smiling. Even Jade glaring at me the entire time did nothing to dampen my good mood.

At lunchtime, Kate and I sat by ourselves. Zac was at basketball training with his teammates in the gym, but it gave me a chance to tell Kate all about my plan to sabotage Jade's history project. I hadn't mentioned it on the phone the night before because I wanted to tell her in person. It was the first chance I'd had, and I was desperate to share the details.

"The one Jade hasn't done yet?" Kate asked, unsure of what project I was referring to.

"No," I corrected on a whisper. "The one that Jade has already done.

"Wait, how are you...oh my gosh!" Kate yelped, and I shushed her as kids around us stared curiously. "Sorry, but are you sure that's a good idea?"

"Why not? That project was such a big deal for her. Could you imagine the look on her face if it gets messed up?" I couldn't eat my food because I was too intent on explaining all the details. I shoved my tray aside. "But the problem is, I don't know when I could sneak into the classroom to do it."

Kate's lips pursed in her thinking face as she picked apart her sandwich. "You know, Mrs. Clarke's planning period is right before our class."

I smiled slowly along with her. I'd completely forgotten. "We'd have to get her out of the room."

"She's not in her room, not normally. I always see her coming from the teacher's staffroom before our class, but if she did happen to be in the classroom, we could always cause a distraction and get her out of there. What are you planning to do?"

"Hide the artifacts for one," I said, tapping my fingers on the table. "And maybe give Jade's presentation a bit of an upgrade."

Everyone had to log into the student computer in the classroom to access their presentations. All I had to do was log in under Jade's account and switch out her presentation with a new one. "But I need her student ID."

Our logins were simple. The first letter of the first name, followed by the first four letters of the last name, and our password was our six-digit student ID number. If I had that, I could get into the computer, use a USB drive to upload a new presentation and then close it out. She'd never notice if I made sure the saved date didn't show. No one paid attention to that.

"I can get her ID," Kate suggested eagerly. "We'll find a way to take a peek at one of the teacher's books."

"We have to get it by Thursday. That's when the band concert is on, and it might be our only chance. That way we can be at school when everyone is occupied in the gym, and we won't get caught."

Kate saluted me, face serious. "Yes, Ma'am. Don't worry, we're going to get it, and then Jade is going to have a fun time explaining why her presentation is so bad."

We toasted with our water bottles, and when I caught Jade glaring daggers at me, I smiled and waved. Soon enough, she'd be the one everyone would make fun of and she would finally leave me alone for good. I could hardly wait for Thursday to arrive.

***

147

By the next afternoon, I was worried we weren't going to pull this plan off. I had yet to get Jade's ID number, and as my afternoon class was different from Kate's, I had no idea if she'd been successful. It was seventh period, and the bell was about to ring to send us home for the day. I needed to know I had her ID so I could get going on the new presentation that would replace Jade's old one. I remembered what her title slide had looked like, but everything after that was going to be very, very different.

The bell rang, and I hurried out of the classroom, rushing to my locker to wait for my friend. I heard running steps and Kate's voice loudly asking people to move as she sprinted down the hall and slid into me with a laugh.

"Did you get it?" I asked.

She nodded, grinning from ear to ear. "Got it! We are in!"

"Oh my gosh, you're amazing!" I beamed at her. "You want to help me get the presentation going? It'll be fun putting it together!"

"Um…yes! Definitely!" she laughed.

We gathered our things and walked out of the school. Just as we reached the pavement that led to the street outside the school grounds, we saw Zac skateboarding our way.

"Hey!" he grinned, hopping off his skateboard and standing alongside us. "How're things?"

"Today ended up being pretty good," I smiled back. "And I think the rest of the week is going to be even better."

His blue eyes sparkled in the afternoon sunlight. "And Saturday? You're still ok to see that movie?"

"Definitely. Kate's keen too," I told him, glancing at Kate. "And Oliver's going to come as well, so it should be fun."

"Ha, really?" he smiled back. "That's perfect then."

He ran a hand shyly through his spiky dark hair. "So, I guess I'll see you guys, tomorrow?"

"Okay, see you tomorrow," I smiled as he hopped back on his skateboard and headed off down the street.

My stomach was churning with excitement, and I couldn't help laughing at Kate when she nudged me in the arm with her elbow. "You two are getting along well," she grinned.

I laughed some more, and we chatted happily all the way to my front gate. I wanted Saturday to come faster, but it'd be here soon enough, and I knew I had other things to focus on in the meantime.

Kate texted her mom to let her know she was at my house and we headed straight up to my room. Mom called a greeting from her office, but I told her we had some history project stuff to work on and we managed to get upstairs before she could bombard us with questions about our day.

Once inside my room, I texted Oliver to let him know that everything was set to go ahead with our plan.

"So, what do you want to put on the slides for Jade's presentation?" Kate asked, clapping her hands and looking almost evil as I booted up my laptop.

"I don't want to do anything too bad," I said quickly. "You know, not something that will get her into trouble, but I definitely want to make sure she doesn't have a perfect grade by the end of it. Maybe we'll throw in some more interesting pictures instead of the ones she showed us?"

We started searching around on the internet for photos of the past presidents and then more recent photos of famous singers and actors. We made up random facts about why they were famous and how much they'd contributed to the world recognition of our country. We laughed as we did it, but tried to keep it under control as we searched for more images. I wasn't a mean person, and I knew I was close to crossing a line that I shouldn't. At one stage, I almost changed my mind about going ahead, but then I remembered Jade's behavior and that thought quickly disappeared. When we had the appropriate number of slides, we sat back and admired our handiwork.

"Well, she's not going to get an A for this!" Kate announced proudly. "This presentation is going to be so funny."

"And all we have to do is hide her artifacts, so she has nothing else to show."

We watched as the last slide fell into place on the screen, a wonderful photo of Jade mid-jump during a cheerleader competition, her face screwed up in a ridiculous expression.

At the sight of that image, I sat back in my chair and frowned. "You think this is going too far?" I asked Kate worriedly.

"What? No, Holly. She's threatening you, and she's made it clear that she won't let up. All because Zac likes you. She has to learn a lesson or she'll never back off." Kate pulled out her phone to check the time. "It's almost dinner time. I have to run."

"Thanks for your help, Kate. So, are you ready for tomorrow night?"

"Yep, my mom said its fine for me to go and watch the concert. So I'll see you tomorrow at school and then before you know it, it'll be showtime."

I headed down the stairs with her and waved from the front door until I couldn't see her anymore.

"You two get much work done?" Mom called from the kitchen, standing by the stove as she cooked up what smelt like a stir-fry for dinner.

"Oh yeah, I think our project is going to be awesome."

"That's great to hear, Holly. I'm sure it was fun working on it together. Now, could you set the table, please? And then go and find your brother. Tell him that dinner will be on the table in two minutes."

I did as she asked and ran downstairs to find Oliver. "Hey, dinner's ready."

"Perfect timing!" he replied, "I'm pretty much finished with sorting out all the details of changing time zones. Did you guys get the presentation taken care of?"

"All finished." I watched him write down a few more notes before he hid everything away. "You think this is going to work?"

"Only one way to find out!"

He was right about that. But part of me suddenly worried we were messing with something way over our heads.

I followed Oliver up the stairs and tried not to think about the mess we might be getting ourselves into.

Chapter 7

At half past six on Thursday evening, Oliver and I met up with Kate at her house, and the three of us started the walk to school. Oliver had sneaked the machine out of the house earlier and hid it in the bushes in the front garden so he could pick it up when we left the house. Mom didn't suspect a thing which was the most important issue.

The school gym was busy when we arrived, and the three of us found seats at the back at the end of a row so we could easily slip out the door. We'd passed by my locker on the way and hid Oliver's backpack with the machine inside it to grab when we needed it later on.

"There's a janitor closet a few doors down from Mrs. Clarke's room that we could use," I whispered to them, as we sat quietly waiting for the concert to begin.

"It might be locked," Kate said.

"We could always use the bathroom I guess."

"There isn't one close to the classroom," Oliver said quickly. "If we use the ones near here, we could be caught by someone from the concert. And I don't think they'd appreciate finding a boy in the girls' bathroom."

I cringed, imagining some poor mother being in there when the three of us materialized out of thin air. "Good point."

"We'll aim for the janitor's closet and just hope it's opened," Oliver said. "If not, we'll have to find somewhere else."

I rubbed my hands on my thighs, concerned that our plan wasn't going to work. Kate and Oliver talked quietly together, but I was too busy watching the crowd around us and worrying about what would happen. We'd come this far though, and I had a feeling Kate and Oliver wouldn't let me back out now. My brother was too excited to use the machine again and Kate, well, Kate was ready for some much-needed revenge against Jade. She was willing to do whatever it took.

The lights dimmed in the gym but remained bright on the school band as the music teacher moved to the front. Everyone applauded for him and the students before he launched into his spiel about what the band was going to be performing. Oliver and I had no musical talent whatsoever, so we'd managed to avoid having to be a part of any band concert.

As soon as the first song was started, the three of us quietly left our seats and moved to the doors, escaping into the corridor. No one even noticed us; they were all too engrossed in the concert and the performances of the kids on the stage. Thankfully, the hallway was empty, and we ran quietly back to my locker. I opened it up and handed the heavy backpack over to Oliver.

Then we made off for the janitor's closet. The closed-door loomed in front of us.

I held my breath as Oliver tried the handle and then sighed in relief to find it unlocked. He ushered us inside and shut the door.

"Right, let's make sure our date and time is right," he said as he set the machine on the floor and checked the page of notes he had. "You've got the USB drive?"

I pulled it out of my pocket. "Right here."

"Good, now remember the plan. I'll go with you inside the classroom and Kate will keep watch outside the door. We'll get in, do what we have to do, and get out. We just have to keep an eye on the time." Without another moment's hesitation, he flipped the switch, and the machine began to glow blue. "Ready?"

Kate and I nodded. Oliver picked up the machine, and we each rested a hand on his shoulders. The brooms and mops in the room vibrated and began to float in the air as everything else began to shake. The blue light expanded and we giggled as it surrounded us and we were lifted off our feet. A loud pop sounded, and then we fell to the floor in the closet. A bell rang loudly overhead followed by an announcement. We climbed to our feet and grinned.

"We did it," I whispered.

Oliver checked his digital watch. "Alright, once the halls are clear and everyone is in class, we'll move out."

Two minutes later, another bell rang, and after waiting a final two minutes to be sure the halls would be empty, we stepped outside. There were a few straggling students, but no teachers. Mrs. Clarke's room was just three doors down, and the door was currently propped open.

With my heart pounding and my nerves ready to explode, I led the way down the hall to the doorway…and just as quickly backed out.

"She's in there," I whispered. "What do we do?"

"Distraction time," Kate said, and before I could stop her, she walked into the classroom, motioning for us to hide by the alcove where the drinking fountains were mounted against the wall. I heard Kate's voice and then Mrs. Clarke's as she answered, but couldn't make out what they were saying to each other.

"What's taking so long?" Oliver asked. "We're running out of time."

I motioned for him to be patient, hoping Kate knew what she was doing.

"I don't see why they need me," Mrs. Clarke replied as I heard her heels clicking on the floor. "And I suggest you get back to class now, Kate."

"Okay, Mrs. Clarke," Kate replied.

I dared to peek out from my hiding spot and noticed our teacher's annoyed expression before I quickly ducked back out of view. Clearly, she was not impressed about being disturbed.

I waited another few seconds then peeked out again to see Kate standing by the door of the classroom. She waved for us to come out of hiding and we rushed to get inside the room.

"I'll stand watch," she whispered, keeping the door open enough that she could see.

I ran straight to the student computer against the wall. Using the ID number Kate had given me, I quickly logged into Jade's account, all the while, my heart pounding anxiously in my chest. "Ok, we're in."

"Upload it. Quickly." Oliver whispered urgently behind me.

I inserted the USB drive, and once I found Jade's original presentation on the computer, I deleted it and uploaded the new one, ensuring to name it in the same way. My hands were shaky, but I couldn't hide a smirk as I exited the folder, pulled out my USB drive, and logged back out. I worried that Mrs. Clarke would be suspicious of the computer being logged out, so I shut it down completely. Hopefully, she'd think it had updated or something and turned itself off.

"Ok, one more thing," I whispered and searched around the room. "We need those artifacts."

"Hurry up, Holly," Oliver was already tinkering with the machine again and keen for us to get out of there as quickly as possible.

"Oh no! She's coming back!" Kate hissed and sprinted over to help me.

The artifacts had to be by the desk somewhere, but I couldn't seem to find them. If Mrs. Clarke was coming, we couldn't get back to the janitor's closet. We'd have to leave from inside the classroom.

"There!" Kate exclaimed, pointing to a box on the floor.

We could hear Mrs. Clarke's steps as I snagged the box and Oliver flipped the switch. "Let's go!" he urged frantically.

Kate rushed back to the door just as the glowing began.
"Kate!"

She clicked the lock in place on the door just as Mrs.
Clarke appeared on the other side and tried to turn the knob.
We could hear the knob rattling as our teacher tugged and
twisted in her effort to get the door open. "Is there someone
in there?" she demanded sharply just as the blue light
expanded, surrounding us.

The lights flickered on and off as I hugged the box of
artifacts to my chest and clung to Oliver's shoulder with my
other hand. Kate lunged for us and latched herself onto
Oliver's arm just as the light became blinding and
everything in the classroom vibrated, the desks sliding
across the floor. Mrs. Clarke banged firmly on the classroom
door, demanding for it to be unlocked.

I bounced on the balls of my feet, pleading for the
machine to work faster. Finally, the familiar pop sounded,
and we stumbled into each other as we landed back in the
present, standing in the darkness of Mrs. Clarke's classroom.
I still had the box of artifacts in my arm and began to laugh
as I realized what we'd just pulled off.

"How do we know if it worked?" I asked as Oliver
powered down the machine, turning it off and pushing it
into his book bag.

But as soon as I asked, a flood of memories appeared
in my head. They were new memories, scenes that had been
created because we had gone back and changed the past. I
erupted into loud laughter as I remembered what happened
in the hours that passed after Mrs. Clarke was able to get the
door unlocked and re-enter the classroom. From that
moment on, the day continued very differently to the first
time we had experienced it.

At first, Kate frowned, confused about what I was
laughing about, but then the same vision appeared in her
head, and she began laughing too.

Oliver grinned right along with us. "I'm going to assume it worked?"

I thought back to that morning and nodded. "Oh yeah, it definitely worked."

And as each vivid memory swirled through my mind, I recalled every single detail.

***

Monday, Two Weeks Ago…

I groaned, watching as Jade stood to start her presentation in history class. It was going to be another long ten minutes of her boasting about her famous ancestor and blah, blah, blah.

"Jade? I can't seem to find the artifacts your mother dropped off this morning," Mrs. Clarke said, searching around her desk. "I swore I had them in here. You didn't happen to move them, did you?"

My brow rose, and I looked on as Jade's cheeks reddened.

"No, but I saw her bring them in," Jade insisted. "They should be there."

"I understand, but I'm afraid the box is not here." Mrs. Clarke mumbled something under her breath and then complained about some students who had been messing around in her room earlier. She then said she'd had to get the principal involved. I frowned, wondering what she was talking about, but it was Jade who glared in anger.

"Are you saying someone stole my grandpa's artifacts?" she snapped, and a hush fell over the classroom.

"Jade, please watch your tone when speaking to me," Mrs. Clarke scolded as Jade turned a darker shade of red. "Now, don't worry, I'm sure they'll turn up. How about you carry on with your presentation without the artifacts for now?"

"But those were the best part!" Jade whined,

devastated not to have the things she'd spent weeks boasting about.

"You still have your presentation, and that's what is most important."

"Yes, Mrs. C," Jade muttered, still sounding annoyed, and I covered my mouth to hide a laugh as Mrs. Clarke eyed her sharply.

"Jade, my name is Mrs. Clarke. Please call me by my full name."

Jade hung her head, grinding her teeth as every pair of eyes in the room was on her. She opened her presentation and began the slideshow. "I did my presentation on an ancestor who served as a soldier in the Civil War." She tapped the mouse, and the next slide appeared.

The entire class erupted in laughter as music blared through the speakers, a Justin Bieber song. I laughed along with everyone else as Mrs. Clarke quickly turned down the volume and asked Jade if she thought this was funny.

"I didn't have that song in my slideshow," she argued.

"Just go on with your presentation...is that a picture of George Washington...riding a donkey?"

Jade turned to stare at the whiteboard, eyes wide. "What? No, I didn't do that."

She clicked through the next slide, and another song started to play. More Justin Bieber. This time there was a map of Middle-Earth instead of the United States as the slide was labeled. She clicked through them faster and faster, each slide filled with a variety of objects and animals until we came to a smiling brown puppy wagging his tail and everyone burst into laughter.

When the last slide appeared on the screen, the class was practically rolling on the floor laughing as she tried to turn it off.

"Jade, stay behind after class. We need to discuss your serious lack of concern for a project that will count as one-third of your grade," Mrs. Clarke stated. "I am very, very disappointed in you."

"That wasn't my presentation!" Jade argued.

Mrs. Clarke shook her head and asked Jade to sit back down in her seat. She called for the rest of the class to calm down, but the sound of giggling rippled through the room as Jade slumped down in her chair. I shouldn't have felt so happy to see her being made fun of, but I couldn't help it. Finally, Jade had got what was coming to her.

I had no idea who messed up her presentation, but I silently thanked them for making my day so much better. Mrs. Clarke called my name to give my presentation next, and I heard another voice apart from Kate's, wishing me good luck.

I turned to see the voice had come from Zac. Zac was grinning at me and giving me a thumbs up. Uh, this day just kept getting better.

***

Present Day...

As we left Mrs. Clarke's room, Kate and I filled Oliver in with what had happened that day in history class. We took it in turns to share each new memory. All the while, we giggled and laughed so much that we struggled to control ourselves and Oliver had to keep reminding us to keep our voices down.

On our way, we quickly stashed the box of artifacts in the janitor's closet and then hid the machine back in my locker. I still couldn't believe we'd pulled off our plan without getting caught or messing anything up. A huge thrill stirred inside me, and a wide grin fixed itself to my face.

When we approached the gym, we could hear the music from the concert spilling out into the hallway. Then, when we opened the door and stepped inside, I spotted someone I hadn't expected to see there at all. Zac. At the sound of the door opening, he turned around and waved eagerly.

"What's Zac doing here?" Kate asked me, but I was just as lost as she was.

I caught Oliver's frown but not wanting to make a scene, I led the way to the three spare seats next to Zac.

"You ok?" Zac asked. "You guys have been gone for a while."

"We have?"

He checked his watch and nodded. "Yeah, you said you just had to go to the bathroom. You sure took a while!"

"Oh...um yeah," I stammered, wondering what on earth he was talking about and where he had suddenly come from.

"Holly?" he frowned at me. "Are you ok?"

I nodded at him quietly as I strained my mind, and was suddenly bombarded by more new memories from the past two weeks. I suddenly realized that after Jade messed up her presentation and made such a fool of herself, a lot of people began to avoid her, and even her close friends stopped hanging out with her quite so much.

Then I remembered that Zac and I had ended up talking all that Monday, and ever since, we'd hung out every day at lunch. As far as tonight was concerned, I'd actually asked him to meet us here so we could spend more time together.

As well, Mom had met him already, and she really liked him.

Bigger still, Zac casually held my hand in his while the music played on making me realize that he and I were now going out together. Kate nudged my arm to find out what was going on. But I waved her off, hoping she'd give up with the questioning and let me tell her later.

I sat silently in my chair and listened to the end of the concert. At first, I was shocked to discover the impact of our decision to go back in time and change a past event. Since doing that, we had changed the flow of events ever since. But when I looked back down at Zac's hand in mine, I smiled and decided I liked this new world that we had come back to.

Then another new memory came to mind. After Jade's messed up history presentation, the confrontation I'd had with her in the bathroom never ended up taking place. And ever since that day, she had not bothered me at all.

We really had done it!

But as happy as I was about how this trip back in time had turned out, I couldn't help the worry that was forming in my head. We had changed the events of that morning in history class two weeks ago, but in doing so, the events that followed had also changed, including my friendship with Zac.

What bothered me the most was that we might also have changed things that we weren't even aware of yet.

Chapter 8

Friday at school was a whole new world, one I very much wanted to get used to. Jade left me alone all day long, and I remembered that we spent our lunches now with Zac's friends sitting at our table. They were a fun group, and it was certainly one of my top ten favorite days of the entire seventh grade.

After dinner that night, Mom checked on whether we still planned to see a movie the following day with Kate, Zac, and his little sister. But when she wasn't looking, Oliver nudged me and whispered to meet him upstairs in his room. I wondered if something was going on with the time machine, and as soon as I could escape Mom's nonstop chatter, I raced up the stairs.

"What's up?" I asked Oliver when I reached his room.

"I've been doing some more researching on Grandpa's friend."

"The supposedly dead Thaddeus Banes? Did you find anything helpful?"

"Well, I found some more stuff about their work, along with some pictures," he explained, motioning to the screen on his laptop. "Every time something was published by them, there was a picture taken of the two of them together. But watch this."

I leaned closer and looked on as Oliver sifted through various pictures on the screen. In each image, Grandpa and Thaddeus stood with an arm around each other's shoulders, grinning widely at the camera. But as the years passed, their hair grew whiter, and they seemed to become less and less friendly towards each other. Until, in the last photos taken of them together, they were standing a few feet apart. Grandpa still attempted a smile, but Mr. Banes didn't even seem to be trying.

"He doesn't look too happy," I mused.

"No, and after a certain year, the papers Grandpa published only had his name on them."

"What year was that?"

He pointed to the letter we'd found with the machine's notes. "1990, the same year Grandpa dated his research we found with the machine."

"Mr. Bane's got to be the T, guy, right? There's no one else."

"I want to say yes, especially when looking at the research Mr. Banes did on his own after 1990. That was after Grandpa supposedly retired and started teaching."

He pulled up another tab on his computer, and I quietly read over the list of works published by Thaddeus Banes. "Time Travel," I read the title of the first one on the list and then scanned the ones following it. "All of these are to do with time travel, experiments, machines, the probability of time traveling. I don't understand. Why didn't he and Grandpa keep working together?"

"Because of this." Oliver tapped a few more keys, and a news article appeared on the screen.

The article was from 2001 and described a heated argument that broke out on a college campus involving our grandpa and an unnamed man who ran off before anyone could stop him. Students in the article reported that the man barged into Grandpa's classroom and started ranting and raving about research Grandpa had hidden from him. Apparently, he accused Grandpa of having a machine that he used only for his gain. Some pushing and shoving started up between them, and several students had to pull them apart.

"This was the same year Grandpa died," I whispered. "You don't think…" I trailed off, worried about where my train of thought was headed.

"I don't know, but it makes sense."

"And then what? Mr. Banes disappeared until he showed up one day as our substitute teacher?"

"Yeah, that's what I don't understand. Nothing makes sense."

I laughed. "Oliver, we've been traveling to the past. That doesn't make sense."

"True." He tapped his fingers on his desk, leaning back in his desk chair. "I just want to know what happened."

I wanted to know what happened too.... how did Mr. Banes manage to show up after he was supposedly dead?. There were too many questions. "You don't think Mr. Banes has a version of Grandpa's machine or something, do you?"

"Maybe. Perhaps Mr. Banes just went somewhere else. That would explain why everyone thought he had died."

"What if he had something to do with Dad's disappearance?" I asked quietly.

Oliver's face paled. He opened his mouth to say something, but then we heard Mom's voice as she made her way up the stairs. He quickly closed his laptop, and we turned to see her standing in the doorway.

"What are you two in such deep discussion about?" she asked curiously.

"Nothing too exciting," I answered. "Just the movie tomorrow. We were watching the trailer again."

"Right, well, how about a movie night with your mom tonight?" She grinned. "Come on, when was the last time we had a fun movie night together?"

I grinned, and Oliver rolled his eyes. He never liked Mom's choice of movies. But I dragged him out of his chair, and we bounded downstairs forced to tuck away our questions about Grandpa and Dad for another night.

***

The following day, Oliver and I headed into town to the movie theater with Kate. Just as we arrived, I glanced up to see Zac making his way down the sidewalk towards us, holding the hand of his little sister. She was seven, and according to Zac, she was a very avid fan of Spiderman. "Hey guys," I greeted them when they reached us. "You must be Sammy," I smiled down at the cute dark haired little girl who looked so much like her brother.

Sammy bobbed her head shyly. "Hello." She wore a long-sleeved pink top and a pleated skirt with long white socks.

"Sammy's been talking about this movie all week," Zac smiled back at me.

He let his sister tug him towards the theater so we could buy our tickets and head in to see the movie. Once we found our seats, I shuffled Oliver in ahead of me and then pushed Kate after him, grinning as I nudged her forwards. I then sat down with Kate on one side and Zac on the other. Sammy sat next to her brother and immediately began to munch on her popcorn.

She was so funny to watch a movie with, gasping in all the right places, leaning forward in her seat when the story got really exciting. And when it was over, we all sat through the credits for that token end scene that always came at the end.

Afterward, we followed along behind Kate and Oliver who were getting on very well and headed towards a nearby diner to grab some lunch. I texted Mom to update her on our day, and she sent me back a stream of smiley faces.

Sammy skipped along ahead of us while Zac and I chatted to each other. I felt so comfortable with him, and it encouraged me to confide in him more. "Oliver and I have been going through some old family pictures and things that we found."

"Oh yeah," Zac's eyebrows shot up with interest. "You said before that you found a heap of photos hidden away in the attic."

I wondered how much I had told him. My memory since the day of our history presentations had become mixed up and a little hazy, so I wasn't too sure. "We just want to find out what happened to our dad."

"You said you guys were looking into a bunch of stuff, right? I'm sure you'll find answers somewhere along the way."

"I hope so."

"Zac! Can I get a milkshake?" Sammy called out abruptly, directing our attention towards her. "Please! Please!"

"You had candy at the movie," he reminded her in a big brotherly fashion.

She grinned widely at him and batted her eyelashes, even going so far as to give him puppy dog eyes and pouting lips before he gave in with an exaggerated groan.

She jumped up and down, and we headed into the diner together, taking up the back corner booth. We all ordered milkshakes, burgers, and cheese fries, and chatted about the movie.

Sammy was certainly hyped up on sugar, and we let her babble on happily about her favorite superhero.

After a while, the conversation turned to other superhero movies, and Zac and Oliver started a debate about the reality of some of them even existing. Sammy listened intently to them talking, but Kate and I contented ourselves with sharing knowing smiles and giggles. Boys were special, plain and simple.

"I still vote Batman as the best," I chimed in at some point.

Zac groaned and Oliver right along with him. "How have you dealt with this all your life?" Zac teased playfully, and I dropped a fry in his milkshake. He fished it out and ate it, grinning the whole time.

"I tried to get her to like someone else, but she insists on Batman," Oliver whined as if my choice in superheroes was the worst ever.

We paid for our food and headed out of the diner almost two hours later, laughing and chatting easily. As we strolled along, I shivered from a sudden chilly breeze. Zac slipped off his hoodie and offered it to me.

"You sure?" I asked, eyeing his thin long-sleeved t-shirt "What if you get cold?"

"I'll be fine. I don't get cold too easily."

I tugged it on and sighed at the warmth of it. I was so wrapped up in my thoughts that I walked right into the back of Oliver who had suddenly stopped in the middle of the sidewalk.

"What's wrong? Oliver?" I asked when I saw him staring intently across the street.

"The antique store," he pointed. "The one Mom went to."

"Where she found the key?" I asked, and he nodded. I remembered what else she'd told us that day and knew that Oliver would want to go and check it out. "The old broken machine she mentioned…do you want to have a look at it?"

He nodded thoughtfully as he stared across the street at the store.

"You don't think it has something to do with Grandpa, do you?" I asked him.

"Grandpa…or Mr. Banes."

"The weird substitute teacher?" Zac asked. "Why would you guys be looking for something of his?"

I waited for Oliver to make up some excuse, but what he said instead made me realize I wasn't the only one who was now comfortable around Zac. I couldn't believe Oliver was willing to share the information with him.

"Mr. Banes used to work with our grandpa," Oliver explained. "And our mom bought something in this shop that belonged to our grandad. She mentioned seeing something else that might have belonged to him as well. Or maybe it belonged to Mr. Banes."

"Sweet, this is like a secret mission," Zac said, rubbing his hands together. "Let's go have a look."

I smiled at Kate, who was just as keen to check out the store as the rest of us. We headed down to the crosswalk, my blood pumping. I was certainly ready to go digging through some dusty old shelves to see what we could find. As we pushed open the door, a bell tinkled overhead.

"Welcome," a man's voice called out from the darkened interior of the room. Shuffling footsteps followed, and a white-haired old man wearing a black suit and bluish-lensed glasses eyed us curiously.

At first, I worried he was going to throw us out for being kids, but he planted his hands on his hips and studied us closely. His expression made me feel as though he knew exactly why we were there.

"Hi," I said, the word coming out more like a squeak

169

than a word.

"Hello, my dear," the old man replied politely. "Anything in particular that you're searching for today?"

I squinted, trying to see his face better, but the lighting was quite dim.

"Just browsing," Zac said when I couldn't get the words out.

"Alright then. Just holler if you need anything and please be careful wandering through the shop.
There are many old and curious items in here," the man told us, closing one eye so he could study us with the other. "Many, many curious things."

"Thanks," Oliver replied, and our group moved deeper into the store, leaving the old man to watch us. "That was odd."

"Just a bit," I murmured, glancing back to try to see the man once more. "Did he seem familiar to you at all? Like we've met him somewhere before?"

Oliver shrugged. "Maybe, but he's probably been in this town forever."

"Yeah, yeah, I guess you're right." Something nagged at me though, and I wanted to go back and ask the man for his name. But Oliver was already heading towards the rear of the store where Mom said she'd found the key. And I hurried to catch up.

Sammy contented herself with a display of old dolls, finding one that was only three dollars. Zac held it and after checking it over, ruffled her hair and said he'd be happy to buy it for her.

"You're really sweet to her," I said quietly, as Sammy moved on ahead to show Kate her doll.

"Sammy's a great kid. I mean, she plays video games. What's not to love about that?"

I laughed. "You're a great big brother."

"Thanks for not thinking it's nerdy, or stupid for her to hang out with us."

"Why would I? She's fun."

He shrugged, and something told me it had to do with Jade. But I couldn't remember any conversation I'd had with him about Jade and Sammy, not even in my new memories. And then I heard Oliver hissing my name through the shop, so Zac and I wound our way through the last few aisles of shelves until we finally found him standing by the rear wall. It was covered in a fine layer of dust and Oliver and Kate were hunched over something towards the end.

"What did you find?" I asked eagerly.

"The broken machine Mom mentioned. Look familiar?"

He stepped to the side, pointing to something on the shelves. It was covered in dust, dulling the knobs and levers on it, as well as the numbers and other words along the cylinder. It was missing part of the box it had been kept in and had certainly seen better days. I ran my fingers over it, wiping the dust off as I turned to Oliver.

"It's like a twin," I whispered, amazed to have found this in the antique store.

"No, not a twin, an earlier model. Look at it. It's like he just hadn't streamlined it yet."

"Or," I corrected quietly, "this is not Grandpa's machine."

Oliver carefully pulled it from the shelf and blew more of the dust off. "We have to take this home with us," he said. "We have to. I want to see how similar it is to Grandpa's."

"Wait, you have something like this already?" Zac leaned over, eyes wide with curiosity. "What is it, anyway?"

"Not sure yet. We think it might be something our grandpa put together. Or maybe Mr. Banes. I'd like to take it home and check it out properly." Oliver turned the machine around.

"What are you doing?" I watched as Oliver turned it

almost upside down.

"Checking for a price," he mumbled. "I can't find a tag on it."

"Why don't we take it up to the front and find out what it costs. We might not have enough money with us anyway."

We'd just used most of our allowances for the movie and the diner. I wasn't sure how much I had leftover, and Oliver was always spending his money on random tools and things for his inventions.

He nodded and before I could say anything else about us not being able to afford it, he hurried past us up to the register. The white-haired old man was behind the counter, polishing some antique pieces of silverware.

"Well now, what have you dug up on my shelves?" he asked, intrigued.

"Something that doesn't have a price on it," Oliver told him, carefully sliding the machine onto the counter.

I watched as the old man's wrinkled and weathered hands turned it around to study it better. His eyes were hidden behind his glasses, but he seemed familiar as if I'd seen his face before. I tried to squint my own eyes and see him in a different light. Why did he look like someone I'd met? We had never gone into that store before so there was no reason for me to know who he was.

"This is quite an interesting piece," the old man told Oliver, studying it closely through his glasses at the end of his nose. "I've had this in the shop for many, many years. I've always wondered what it was."

"I think I know," Oliver said, practically shaking with excitement. "But it needs some work."

"Well, if it needs some work, then I think we can make a deal."

"A deal?" I asked, suddenly worried. What if this man was Thaddeus Banes? Older, a lot older? And hiding behind that disguise? I tried to motion to Oliver, but he was too engrossed in the idea of getting the machine to realize what I was trying to tell him.

"Yes, a deal. That machine is going to need a lot of work, young man. Are you up for it?"

"I sure am!"

I stomped on Oliver's foot, but all he did was grunt and move further away from me. He wanted the machine, and I could see that we weren't leaving the shop without it.

"Tell you what, you take this for free, but you make me a promise. Once you get it working again, you bring it back so I can see it powered up and ready to go," the old man said with a wink as he leaned on the counter. "What do you say?"

"Do you know what it is?" I asked, red flags shooting up in my head that we should not be talking to this guy.

"I have my suspicions." He slid the machine back across the counter to a slack-jawed Oliver who was nodding slowly as he picked it back up in his arms. "Now then, you kids run along. I think you have lots of work to do today, yeah?"

"Oh yeah," Oliver said, beaming at the old man. "Thanks!"

With Oliver carting the machine away in his arms, we left the shop. I was the last to leave, staring back at the old man behind the counter. He gave me a half-hearted wave, and I couldn't shake the feeling that this man knew who we were, one way or another.

"Holly, you coming?" Zac called, and I rushed out the door after him, the bell above the door frame jingling as I left.

Chapter 9

After our visit to the antique shop, Zac told us he was going to take Sammy home and asked if he could then hang out with Kate and me at my house. Oliver said he'd be busy in the basement, so it was fine with him and I texted Mom who also said it was ok. She really liked Zac and sent more smileys back.

We waved Zac and Sammy off then turned and headed towards our street. Oliver hefted the machine up into his arms, and we had to hurry to keep up with him.

"Do you even know what you're going to do with that thing?" I asked

"Not yet, but once I take it apart, I can see what makes this one up, see if it's Grandpa's or if it's someone else's."

"And you're not worried at all about accidentally setting it off?"

"Oh Holly," Kate sighed, "stop worrying so much. Oliver's smart, I'm sure he knows what he's doing."

I watched her stare admiringly at the back of Oliver's head

I elbowed her side, and then her cheeks reddened. "What?"

"You and Oliver," I laughed and rolled my eyes at her.

"You should talk," she grinned back. "What about you and Zac! I can't believe you guys are now going out together."

"We're just good friends!" I laughed, quickening my step so I could catch up with Oliver.

When we reached the house, Oliver headed straight down to the basement and Kate, and I waited for Zac to arrive. I completely forgot I was still wearing his hoodie and I curled up on the couch, wrapping the sleeves around me.

"That was cute, him giving you his hoodie." Kate plopped down beside me with a grin.

"What about you and Oliver," I teased. "You guys seemed to be having some fun today, too."

"Yeah, it was fun." She tucked her legs under her as we stared out the window at the two-lane road. "You don't think it's weird, that I like your brother?"

"Oh, not really," I told her. "I think it's good for him. We've managed to get him out of the house two weekends in a row now." Oliver had also been much more talkative, and I was sure that it was all because of Kate.

When I spotted Zac climbing the steps to our front door a short while later, I hopped up from my seat to let him inside. Just as I pulled the front door open, a loud crack sounded from deep inside the house.

The three of us jumped at the sound, and I whipped around to look behind me.

"What was that?" Zac asked worriedly.

"I think it came from the basement," I said. Then in a moment of recognition, my heart sank. "Oliver!"

Bright blue flashes of light issued out of the open basement door. I rushed towards it, Kate and Zac right behind me. All the items in the living room were vibrating and shaking violently.

Zac staggered to a stop, his mouth dropping open at what was happening around us. The house trembled, and a mixture of blinding blue light and smoke flashed from the basement doorway.

"Oliver!" I yelled and sprinted downstairs, shielding my eyes from the light. "Oliver!"

"I'm here!" I heard him reply, but couldn't see him.

"What's going on?"

"I don't know! It's from the other machine...ours!"

I stumbled around and finally ran into him, Kate and Zac right behind me. I held onto his arm and squinting, saw the machine sitting on the workbench. It was whirring louder than before, and a crackling sound shot out from it in random bursts. Zac found my hand, and I saw Kate hold onto his shoulder, all of us trying not to lose the other as the light grew brighter and brighter.

The same floating sensation came over me, and I felt my feet leave the floor. I yelled in panic, trying to reach for the machine to shut it down. I flipped the switch, but nothing happened.

"Hold on!" Oliver shouted, and then we were spinning around and around until I thought I was going to throw up.

With the same loud pop that we'd heard each time before, we crashed to the floor in the basement again. I groaned in pain and holding my stomach, waited for the sickening sensation inside me to stop.

"What just happened?" Zac whispered, confused.

"Good question," I muttered and looked at Oliver, blinking. The machine sat next to us on the floor, and he scurried to it, staring at the dials. "Oliver?"

But he said nothing. His face paled. "Oh no."

"Oh no? What do you mean, oh no?" I asked sharply. "Where did you send us?"

"Send us?" Zac repeated. "Guys, can someone please tell me what just happened?"

I opened my mouth to do just that when I heard Mom call out from somewhere inside the house. Another voice replied, but it wasn't one of us. Steps moved overhead, and we stared up at the ceiling, watching as we heard the steps move from the kitchen towards the basement stairs.

The door opened and a man's voice, a voice I'd never heard before, or at least couldn't remember, said loudly, "I think it's in the basement!"

Each of us was too frozen with shock to move, and all we could do was sit there on the floor, as step by step, the man made his way down towards us.

But when he reached the bottom step, he paused, as if trying to process the sight in front of him. Then his mouth suddenly dropped open, and he stared at the four kids on the floor in disbelief.

I knew exactly who he was. Those blue eyes…those features and that thick brown hair.

I swallowed hard and whispered without thinking, "Dad?"

I didn't feel the world turn upside down until he replied, "Holly? Oliver? What are you two doing here?"

Book 3
Shocked

Prologue

The basement door opened and a man's voice, a voice I'd never heard before, or at least couldn't remember, said loudly, "I think it's in the basement!"

Each of us was too frozen with shock to move, and all we could do was sit there on the floor, as step by step, the man made his way down towards us.

But when he reached the bottom step, he paused, as if trying to process the sight in front of him. Then his mouth suddenly dropped open, and he stared at the four kids on the floor in disbelief.

I knew exactly who he was. Those blue eyes…those features and that thick brown hair.

Swallowing hard, I whispered, "Dad?"

I didn't feel the world turn upside down until he replied, "Holly? Oliver? What are you two doing here?"

Chapter 1

The basement was dead silent for at least thirty seconds as the man who I knew was my father, changed his expression from worried to confused to finally excited.

I was certain we were dreaming somehow and that this couldn't be real, but eventually, I managed to speak, and the only words I could get out were not very helpful at all.

"What did you say?" I asked, staring and thinking that I couldn't have heard him correctly.

"How are you here?" he asked quickly, throwing a look over his shoulder, obviously worried that Mom was going to come charging down the steps and see us. "*When did you come from?*"

Why wasn't he more freaked out at seeing his grown kids? How did he even know what we looked like at this age? He hadn't been around…had he?

"We've come from the year 2017," Oliver replied, as Dad reached out a hand to pull him to his feet.

They hesitated only for a moment and then threw their arms around each other in a tight hug. Oliver clung to Dad and tears burned in my eyes to see them together. Dad's gaze fell to me. Oliver stepped aside so I could hug him too. Suddenly, it didn't matter how this was possible. All I wanted to do was hug my dad. I ran into his arms, and the second they closed around me, I knew this was real.

He kissed the top of my head and lifted me off my feet, clutching an even tighter hold before he finally released his grip. He kept an arm around me and rested a hand on Oliver's shoulder, as though he was afraid we would disappear. "I don't understand," he replied, "…and who are your friends?"

I'd completely forgotten about Kate and Zac and

abruptly turned to introduce them. "Guys, this is our Dad...Robert." I couldn't believe I was saying that name, my Dad's name, and that he was actually standing beside me. "Dad, this is Zac and this Kate."

"Nice to meet you," Dad said in greeting, a warm smile wide on his face.

Kate smiled back, but Zac was staring blankly ahead. "I'm sorry, what's going on?" he finally murmured.

"Poor Zac hasn't done this before," I said with a grimace.

"Wait, how do you know who we are?" Oliver asked quickly. "I don't get it. You disappeared years ago. I was only small, and Holly wasn't even born yet. You haven't been around since...have you? What's going on?"

Dad sighed heavily and opened his mouth to explain. But there were more footsteps overhead, and he placed a finger on his lips.

"Robert? Did you find it?" Mom's voice echoed down

to the basement. I froze in my spot, not daring to move.

"Not yet! I'll be up in a minute!" he called back.

I heard a baby's loud laughter and realized with amazement that it must be baby Oliver up there. I shook my head in awe at the thought of Oliver as a real live baby on the floor above us.

When Mom's steps told us she had walked in the other direction, Dad sagged and ushered us further into the basement. "It isn't safe for you to be here."

"Why not?" I demanded more earnestly than I meant. "We wanted to meet you."

"You will meet me. Well, …you've just met me…but you'll meet me again. It's all very complicated. You have to understand though…you're not the only ones with a time machine."

Oliver and I exchanged a glance. "Thaddeus," Oliver whispered.

Dad straightened, his brow furrowing in worry. "Yes, how did you know?"

"We found all of Grandpa William's stuff in the attic," I explained. "And then we found another time machine at the antique store in town…with a key and a note from Grandpa. He wrote about someone called T, and we figured it had to be Mr. Thaddeus Banes."

My head suddenly pounded as I tried to make sense of everything going on around us. "What's going on, Dad? What happened to you? Why did you disappear and where did you go?"

My mind was spinning. I had so many questions that I wanted answers to. But Dad simply shook his head. "I can't tell you," he muttered hurriedly. "You have to figure it out on your own, but you have to be careful, do you understand? Time travel is a very complicated process, and if you mess with it in the wrong way, things can change and sometimes they can go terribly wrong."

"Is that what happened to you?" Oliver asked.

Dad didn't answer right away, and that was enough of an explanation for me. "I wish I could spend more time with you kids right now, but you have to get back to your own time span. And you need to get going now!"

His tone had become a little frantic, and I could see that he was on edge. For some reason, he wanted us to return to our own time zone as quickly as possible.

"Who are you talking to down there?" Mom suddenly called from the top of the stairs.

"Just talking to myself, Mags!" Dad replied, and despite the strange situation we'd found ourselves in, it warmed me to hear Dad call our mom that. Mags. Everyone else called her Maggie or Margaret, but not Dad. She let it slip one time that he always called her Mags.

"Talking to yourself, Dad?" I smiled. "I guess craziness runs in the family."

He grinned back before quickly hurrying to the bottom of the stairs and peering up. The four of us scrunched further back into the shadows. I reached for Zac's hand to squeeze it encouragingly, but his expression was still one of total shock.

"Why don't you start the movie? I'll be up in a minute!" Dad called out to Mom.

"Okay," Mom replied as she walked away again.

On his way back towards us, Dad stopped and stared at the machine on the floor. Fear crept onto his face as he bent down to pick it up.

"Get yourselves back to your time zone," he instructed as he handed Oliver the machine. "And whatever you do, stay away from Thaddeus. That man is dangerous, and he'll do anything to get what he thinks is his."

"Is there any way we can see you again? In our time zone?" I wanted him to say yes, but he shook his head.

"I don't know, kids, I really don't." He rested a hand on both our shoulders then dragged us into another embrace. "I love you both very much. I want you to know

183

that. No matter what happens, I love you both more than anything else on this earth."

Instantly, I felt it…. the love of a dad I'd never had the chance to know. I also knew he would never have left us if he'd had a choice.

Quickly kissing the top of my head, then Oliver's, he stepped back. "Now go, before you're here too long and you mess something up."

I wondered what exactly we could mess up, all we had done was talk to him. But I had no time to ask that question. Oliver was already pushing buttons and levers on the machine, and I huddled close to him as Dad moved to the stairs. I held tightly to Oliver with one hand and Zac with the other. Kate wrapped her hand around Oliver's arm. The familiar blue light grew and surrounded us. I heard Mom call in a panic from upstairs, but Dad ignored her voice and stood there the entire time, watching as we vanished from sight.

When we landed back in the present, we crashed to the floor. My head spun with thoughts of what had just happened, and I was unable to move from my spot.

"We met our dad," Oliver whispered in awe. "We actually met him."

"And he knew who we were!" I stared back at my brother, the realization of what we had just done, finally sinking in.

I wished we could have stayed longer and asked more questions, but deep down, I knew that remaining in the past wasn't a good idea.

Oliver pulled himself to his feet and carefully set the machine back on his workbench beside the one we'd picked up at the antique store.

"Can someone please tell me what just happened?" Zac frowned as he stared at each of us in turn. "What…what happened? The light and that man…I thought you said your dad was gone?"

I swallowed hard and smiled. "I guess there are a few things we should explain to you."

On the outside, I was calm, but inside I was freaking out. Zac was going to think we were crazy people who had just transported him to another world or something else just as weird. He was going to run out the front door and tell everyone at school I was the weirdest person he'd ever met. He'd never talk to me again. All my hard work getting Jade to be unlikable and making myself stand out, would be for nothing. I'd be right back where I started.

I was frantically trying to think of the right way to explain when Oliver began talking. "We found our grandpa's old-time machine in the attic. I got it working, and we've used it a couple of times. This last time, it went off by accident and somehow transported us back about thirteen years and a few months...back to when our dad was still here. Then, we came back to the present."

My jaw dropped, and Kate's face displayed a look of utter surprise and worry as she glanced at Zac. I held my breath, waiting for him to get up and leave in disgust, but instead, he found his feet and joined Oliver at the workbench.

"Time Travel! This is incredible! Everything your grandpa studied, this is what it was all for? This is what he was working on?"

"Yes."

Zac pointed to the other machine. "And you think this thing we got at the antique store is another time machine?"

"Something like that. I was trying to take it apart to see how it was made so I could compare the two. But our grandpa's machine from the attic suddenly turned itself on somehow. And then, well, you know the rest."

Zac scratched his jaw in astonishment. "It took us back in time!"

I glanced at Kate. She frowned, just as confused as I

was. Everything happening here was a mystery that neither of us understood. I waited for Zac to say this was all too much, that he was leaving us to our crazy inventions and going home. But instead, he went from looking horribly confused to grinning at Oliver and asking question after question about the machine and how it worked. Kate and I hung back. The two boys ignored us, but for the moment, that was fine by me. I needed to get out of the basement and clear my head.

"Let's go upstairs," I said to Kate.

"Good idea," she smiled. "We'll leave the nerds on their own for a while."

I nodded in agreement at her comment as we headed up to the kitchen. Glancing at the clock, I wondered when Mom would be back. The thought of her catching Oliver and Zac in the basement, followed by all her questions about what they were up to, ones I did not know how I would answer, began to worry me more than anything. I got out two glasses and filled them with water from the fridge door, then handed one to Kate.

"So, that little trip was unexpected," she mused with a grin.

"That's one word for it." I sipped my water thoughtfully. "We saw my dad; we actually met him in the flesh…I can't believe it. I keep thinking this is all a dream."

"It's not, Holly. Trust me, it happened. You met your father." She drummed her fingers on the counter. "It's crazy though, how did he even know who you guys were? How was that possible? He found a bunch of kids in his basement. Why would he even suspect that two of them were his kids and that you'd come from the future?"

"After what we did with Jade and everything we've seen so far, I'm wondering if there's anything that's not possible." I glanced absently around the kitchen and suddenly realized that the walls were a different color. "How long has my kitchen been blue?"

"Huh?"

We stared around the space that before had been painted a light shade of yellow, but was now blue. My mom wasn't a big fan of blue, but now the kitchen was painted blue. "Oliver!" I bellowed. "Oliver, get up here!"

"It's just paint," Kate was saying. At the same time, however, all I could think about was Dad's warning about messing with time travel and that staying in the past too long could cause things to change or go wrong.

"What?" Oliver asked as he and Zac ran into the kitchen.

I spread my arms wide, motioning to the walls. "Well?"

"Holly, what are you going on about...oh no!!"

"Exactly! What have we done, Oliver? What did we change?"

"What's wrong?" Zac looked around him. "I don't get it."

"The kitchen walls have changed color since we were here last." Oliver scratched his head as he spun around in a slow circle. "Huh, that's really weird."

"Is it bad weird or good weird?" I reached out to gingerly feel the wall, not sure why I was scared to touch it. But seeing the blue paint made my gut twinge with worry that we were messing with things we shouldn't be.

"I'm not sure, but it's just paint, right?" Oliver said, although even he couldn't hide his concern.

"Yeah, I guess so." I sighed, my stomach clenching in a tight knot as I tried to convince myself that it was just a color and wasn't important.

The four of us stood in silence in the kitchen for a long few minutes before my head whipped around at the sound of a car. Mom was home. I heard the car door slam. Zac and Oliver grabbed a seat and sat at the kitchen bench. Kate and I started laughing for no reason at all except to make it look like we'd been sitting there the whole time. It

187

didn't take long for Mom to appear at the door.

"So, kids, how was the movie?" she asked brightly.

"Pretty good," I announced, "but Batman is still better."

"Of course," Mom grinned. Zac and Oliver rolled their eyes. "I take it the boys don't agree?"

"Nope, not even close." Zac checked his phone and stood. "I have to get going. Thanks for having me over, Holly. I'll see you at school?"

"Yeah, definitely!" I smiled happily at his words. Then, realizing everyone had turned to stare at my enthusiastic response, my cheeks began to burn.

Zac said goodbye before hurrying to the front door. I wanted him to stay so we could talk more about what he'd seen plus I was enjoying having him around. But Kate was the next to realize how late in the afternoon it was and decided that she needed to get going too.

After they'd both left, Mom turned to us with a smile, "So, today was fun?"

"Yeah, the movie was good. And we swung by the antique store afterward," Oliver said, then immediately cringed. I nudged his foot with my own, unable to believe that he'd mentioned our visit to the antique store. He widened his eyes at me.

"Oh yeah?" Mom looked at him with interest. "Find anything cool?"

"Oh, just some beat up old machine that Oliver's going to waste his time tinkering with," I replied quickly. Then, deciding I had to ask or I would die of curiosity, I added, "Hey Mom…"

"Hmm?"

"When did you paint the kitchen blue?"

It was Oliver's turn to stomp on my foot, and I winced as I waited for Mom to answer.

"I painted it blue years ago; you know that."

"Oh, that's right," I lied. "But I thought you always preferred yellow?"

She set the stack of mail that she'd been flipping through down on the benchtop. "Are you feeling okay? You know blue is my favorite color, it has been since after I had your brother. Are you saying I need to update my paintwork?" She nibbled her lip as she looked around the kitchen. "I guess it's been a few years. I should probably give it a freshening up."

"Yeah, maybe." I nodded, glancing hesitantly towards Oliver.

He immediately motioned towards the basement, indicating for me to follow. "I'm going to get back to what I was doing."

"Ok hon," Mom smiled at him.

"I'll come too," I added and headed after him.

Mom nodded without looking up, and we darted downstairs, away from the new blue kitchen and a Mom who now liked blue instead of yellow.

But all I could think was…what have we done?

Chapter 2

I watched Oliver pace around the basement, mumbling under his breath. "So?" I said, fear building inside me.

"So what?" he asked without stopping his pacing.

"What are we going to do to fix this?"

"We can't just fix it, Holly. Our dad saw us. Our actual dad saw us and met us. He talked to us!"

"Yeah, but why did that change things here? Mom now has a new favorite color, and she said she painted the kitchen blue years ago. How can that be?"

"I have no idea!" Oliver sighed as he continued to pace.

"Plus, he already knew who we were," I reminded Oliver, still in awe of hearing our Dad say our names.

Right then, I wished more than anything we could have taken our father from that time zone to our own so that we could have him with us. But when I gave the idea some more thought, I blanched. Sinking onto a nearby stool, I realized what that would have meant.

If we'd been careless and grabbed hold of Dad as we returned to our own time, we would have completely changed the past. Oliver was already born then, so he would still be here. But I hadn't been born yet. So, I would probably have faded away to nothing, and now I wouldn't exist.

"Holly? Are you okay?" Oliver frowned. "You look like you're going to throw up." He shoved a trashcan towards me in case I needed it.

I rolled my eyes at him. "I'm not going to throw up in the trash!"

I crossed my arms over my chest and nudged the bucket back towards him. I wasn't sure how I felt.

Everything was too confusing right now. In the time zone we'd just been to, Dad was living happily with Mom, and they had baby Oliver, but I hadn't been born yet. So how did he know he was going to disappear from our lives? And how did he know who we both were? I wanted to close my eyes and pretend it was all a dream, but at the same time, I couldn't have been happier that we'd seen him, face to face.

"Do you think anything else has changed?" I asked Oliver quietly. "Apart from the color of the kitchen walls, I mean?"

Oliver leaned against the workbench beside me. "I don't know, but we won't find out by hiding in the basement. Tomorrow, we'll do some more poking around and see if we notice anything. But until then, we shouldn't freak out about it. And no more using the machine for a little while. I'm not even sure what set it off this afternoon. That was weird!"

If Oliver didn't know, then I certainly had no answers for him. He was the tech genius, and I was just the tag-along sister. Realizing none of my questions were going to be answered, I decided to head upstairs. I wanted to chat with Kate and Zac to make sure they were both okay after our sudden trip to the past. At least Kate had time traveled before. But for Zac, it was his first time, and I was sure he had questions. I also wanted to be certain he wouldn't tell anyone about what had happened.

Mom was busy in her office, humming loudly to herself when I passed by her door and headed up to my room. Closing the door firmly behind me, I picked up my laptop and logged onto the instant messenger a lot of us at school used when talking to each other. Technically, we did have a history project that we were supposed to be working on, so if Mom asked why I was hiding away in my room, I could use that as an excuse.

I logged in and was not surprised to see Kate there already. I had no chance to click on her name before a message appeared on my screen…

Hey, that was insane today! Are you and Oliver okay? We left kinda fast.

We're okay. I typed back. *I just wanted to check on **you**!*

This last trip into the past had left me feeling pretty nauseous. That hadn't happened after the previous trips we'd trialed. I hadn't wanted to tell Oliver, but this time, my head felt almost scrambled, and my stomach was still rolling around like it was on a roller coaster ride.

I mentioned to Kate that we wouldn't be using the machine for a while; not until Oliver could figure out what had gone wrong. We didn't want anything unexpected to happen again. She sent back a pouty face, but when I told her she could still come over and bug Oliver, she sent a smiley.

I laughed as I scrolled through my list of friends. Zac was new to the list, and I smiled to see him online, too. My phone started ringing, and I picked it up, answering it without looking at who the caller was. "Hello?"

"Hey, Holly," Zac said just as I sent my message to him.

"Hi! I just messaged you!" A fluttery sensation filled my stomach as I pictured his smiling face in my head.

"Ha Ha, it just came through! I can't believe you messaged me, just as I rang your phone. But...how are you? I thought I'd give you a call because today was pretty uh...crazy, huh?"

"Crazy is one word for it!" I replied. "Are you sure you're ok with what you saw?"

"Part of me still can't believe it's real," he exclaimed. "We actually went back in time! Man...that's crazy! I can't think of any other word for it! I mean...who else can say they've gone back in time? It's like finding myself in the middle of a sci-fi novel, or something."

"Yeah, that's how we felt the first time we tried it," I agreed. "But um...I do have to ask...you know you can't tell anyone about this, right? I mean...no one at all!"

"That's okay, Holly. You don't have to worry about that. I won't be telling anyone, I promise!"

I let out the breath I'd been holding.

"Today was the most fun I've had in a long time," he added. "I wanted you to know that too. And I'm not just talking about traveling back in time and meeting your dad. That was super cool. But I really enjoyed the rest of the day as well...it was fun hanging out with you!"

I smiled, tugging on a strand of my hair, while at the same time, butterflies did a crazy dance in my stomach. "I had fun, too, Zac. Do you want to hang out again sometime?" I asked shyly.

"Sure!"

"Sammy can always tag along. She's so cute. And it was so much fun today...the date thing, not just the time travel...not that today was a date, though. I mean, we were all just hanging out and everything," I was rambling and wanted to kick myself for letting my mouth run away from me.

He laughed through the line, and I breathed a sigh of relief when he replied. "I kinda liked today being a date for us. And Sammy had a great time with you guys.

193

She kept asking me about you when I got back home."

He was so easy to talk to, and the butterflies in my stomach settled a little as we chatted about normal things...the movie and then the idea of hanging out on the following weekend. At some point, the conversation turned to our history project and what we needed to do to get it finished. It felt natural talking to Zac; I couldn't believe I'd allowed someone like Jade to stand in my way for so long.

Technically, I'd managed to get her back for the way she used to treat me. But when I thought of what I did to her by messing up her history presentation, I couldn't help feeling guilty. What if by changing that day in class, other things had changed as well? She still appeared to be on the bad side of our history teacher, even though she'd always been her favorite student before. And although Zac said he had never really liked her that much, what if I'd changed things that should have happened between them? Not that I wanted Zac to end up with Jade, but I couldn't stop thinking about the blue kitchen downstairs and how one tiny event could start a chain reaction and change other things that followed.

That afternoon when we visited Dad, we'd only been in the past for a couple of minutes. Regardless, we'd somehow gone back and made things different...permanently. I was about to admit all of this to Zac when he interrupted me and prevented me from blurting out the truth. "Hey, my parents are calling me for dinner."

I looked at the time, and then I heard Mom calling to me as well. "I didn't realize we were talking for quite so long," I replied. "Sorry."

"Why are you apologizing? I don't mind. Talking to you is fun," he said, and I smiled even more. "I'll text you tomorrow. And you don't have to worry about me. I won't say a word to anyone about you know what."

"Thanks, Zac…it's really important that we keep it secret. And maybe if we use the time machine again, you could come with us?"

"Definitely! I'm always up for an adventure with you guys. Bye Holly."

My heart gave another flutter as I said goodbye and hung up. Zac was so cool, and my crush was now bigger than ever. I told Kate on messenger that I was going to eat dinner, and that we could keep chatting later on. Even through her reply, I could feel her rolling her eyes at having to wait. Maybe later we'd talk about her crush, too. I knew she was more interested in Oliver than she was letting on. Smiling at the thought of my best friend crushing over my brother, I logged out, shut down my laptop and rushed downstairs.

With each step, I wondered if I'd notice any other unusual changes. And if so, what they could be.

Chapter 3

Much to my relief, we managed to get through to Sunday without any other obvious differences showing up. After all the excitement the day before, I looked forward to chilling out in front of the television. Sunday was a day when we would often all laze around watching movies. But as soon as Oliver woke up, he disappeared into the basement. And apart from resurfacing to make himself a sandwich for lunch, he had not shown his face all day. Mid-afternoon came and went, and Mom began to stare worriedly at the basement door.

"Your brother's up to something," she murmured. "Will you please go and check on him?"

"Why me?" I asked, completely engrossed in the movie on the TV screen.

She paused the movie. "Please go and make sure he hasn't electrocuted himself or something. Then I'll let you decide where we're going out to eat tonight?"

"We're going out tonight?"

"I thought we could use a treat. Now go, scoot," Mom said with a laugh and shooed me off the couch. "And tell him his favorite episode is on next!"

I rushed downstairs, excited for a night out with Mom. I wished it could be the four of us, but we'd have to wait to see Dad again. I'd hardly slept the night before, thinking about how different our lives would be if he hadn't disappeared.

"Oliver! Mom wants to know when you're going to finish up. We haven't seen you all day," I called as I reached the bottom of the stairs.

"Hmm," he managed to respond, and I heard tools clinking as I moved closer.

"What are you doing?" I stared in surprise to see he'd managed to almost completely dismantle the machine we had bought at the antique store. The pieces lay scattered all over his workbench. Most of them looked weird to me, but I recognized a few as matching parts on Grandpa's working machine. Wires jutted out of a metal panel, and other things looked like coils from Star Trek instead of our world. "Mom says your favorite episode is on next."

"Episode of what?" he replied without looking up.

"Episode of Star Trek. Come on! Leave this stuff alone for a little bit. Mom says she's taking us out tonight as well."

Oliver set his screwdriver down and pinched the bridge of his nose. "Really?"

"Yeah, so let's not make her change her mind. All this stuff will still be here when we get back."

"I just…I can't stop thinking about what Dad said. He's counting on us, you know, to figure this out. So is Grandpa. And I don't want to let them down."

I hadn't even stopped to wonder what seeing Dad meant for Oliver. So much weight fell on him now, to understand what happened to Dad, and our grandpa, too. After hearing he got in a fight with Thaddeus, I started to worry that Grandpa might not have died of a heart attack as Mom was told. I didn't want to think someone would go so far as to cause his death, but all the clues were starting to point that way. It bothered me even more after seeing Thaddeus last year even though Mom thought he had died.

"You won't fail them," I assured Oliver. I grabbed his shoulders and locked eyes with him. "You're the smarted kid around. Dad knows it, and so did Grandpa. Why else would he have left us that note and the key?"

He shrugged, not looking convinced by my words of encouragement.

"I bet Grandpa went to the future, our futures, and he saw you become some famous scientist, just like he was," I went on. "I bet you take this machine that Grandpa built and

197

you show the world all these incredible discoveries that can change the planet and—"

"Ok, ok, you've flattered me enough," he interrupted just when I was getting ready to throw some more compliments his way. "Let's go watch Star Trek with Mom. Help me cover all this up first, will you?"

I helped him put Grandpa's machine back in its box, and we hid it in a darkened corner of the basement behind a pile of old suitcases and bags, so it was out of sight.

The rest of the parts he collected into another box and hid that elsewhere to make sure that if someone found them, they wouldn't be found at the same time. I watched him cover both boxes with a sheet and then stack more boxes around them.

"Wow, you're paranoid, you know that?" I teased.

"What's wrong with that? I don't want Mom accidentally stumbling on this stuff and disappearing. Do you?"

I froze. "I hadn't thought of that," I whispered, horrified. "Think that's what happened to Dad?"

"No, maybe...I don't know." He motioned towards the stairs. "Come on; we'll get back to this mess later. Where are we going for dinner?"

"Wherever I decide," I smirked as we climbed the stairs.

"You know where I would choose."

"Yeah, but it's my choice tonight," I reminded him.

He grumbled behind me, and I grinned wider, knowing already I was going to pick the place he would have chosen. We were more alike than I cared to admit in so many different ways.

Though one thing I was sure of, he was the smart one of the family. I just hoped he could figure out all this time machine stuff so we could use it safely in the future.

And when I thought again about Dad's warning, a tremor of fear caused goosebumps on my skin. Had we already caused changes that could not be undone? And if so, what were they?

While I hoped that it was only Mom's favorite color that had changed, somehow I suspected there might be something more; something that we were not yet aware of.

Chapter 4

Dinner that night ended up being burgers, thick shakes, and cheesy fries at our local diner. Mom told me we could have gone anywhere, but the diner was always our favorite. I liked our small town and everything in it. And that included our local burger restaurant.

When we pulled back into our driveway afterward and made our way to the front door, I still had my milkshake in my hand. Double chocolate malted milkshakes were my all-time favorite, and I always saved them until last. Gulping down some more of the icy liquid, I winced when my forehead throbbed.

"Brain freeze!" I squealed, as Mom got her keys out to unlock the kitchen door.

Oliver and I waited impatiently to get inside and continue with the last episode of Star Trek. But Mom blocked the doorway, frozen in her spot; her face suddenly blank as she switched on the light and stared into the interior of our house.

"Mom? It's a brain freeze, not a body freeze," Oliver teased, but still, she didn't move. "Mom?"

"Get back in the car and lock the doors, right now," she whispered firmly, pulling the door closed again.

"What, why?" Oliver asked.

"Do as I said. Don't argue!" Mom's tone made Oliver give me a shove towards the Tahoe, and we climbed in, locking the doors.

"What's going on?" I frowned.

Oliver shook his head, straining to see as Mom stood in the driveway and pulled out her phone. We tried to listen as she spoke, her voice shaky and unsure. "I think…I think someone has broken into our house."

A chill came over me, and I grabbed the handle of the door hard enough to turn my knuckles white. Who would break into our home? Mom was talking faster now, running a hand through her hair as she nodded, looking ready to cry. I wanted to go out there and hug her, but when I started to unlock the doors, she heard it and waved her hand for us to stay where we were. She stayed on the phone, and about five minutes later, the local sheriff arrived with the deputy behind him, lights flashing, drawing the attention of the whole street.

As Mom talked to Sheriff Biggins, the deputy was already opening the kitchen door, flashlight in one hand and his other on his holstered gun. I couldn't believe this was happening on top of everything else we'd experienced these past few days.

Sheriff Biggins talked to Mom, patting her on the shoulder.

He nodded his head towards us, and she knocked on the window of the driver's side.

Oliver unlocked the door and popped it open just as Sheriff Biggins followed the deputy into the house.

"It's okay, kids," she said, her voice shaky. "They're just checking to make sure…make sure the house is empty."

"Why would someone break into our house?" Oliver asked, confused.

"I don't know. Sometimes bad people just do bad things."

We all fell into an uneasy silence, waiting for Sheriff Biggins to emerge. It seemed to take forever before lights began appearing inside the house and the two men exited.

"There is no one inside, and this door is the only one unlocked," Biggins informed Mom. "I'll have a car with a surveillance team remain outside your house tonight, Mrs. Peterson. But tomorrow, I'd recommend getting a burglar alarm installed. I think it would be a good idea."

"Thanks, Sheriff," Mom said sincerely. "I'll certainly do that."

"The place is a mess, I'm not going to lie," he added. "Just take it slow tonight and make a list of everything that's missing…though, to be honest, I'm not sure what they took."

"What do you mean?" Oliver asked over Mom's shoulder.

"Well, son, the TV is still there, so are the laptops and computers…I'm not sure what they were looking for, but I can almost guarantee they left without it." He gave Mom a one-armed hug as she stared dumbfounded back at him. "If there's anything else you need, Maggie, give me a call, day or night. I know it's been hard all these years, and this, no one should have to deal with this."

We climbed out of the car and left Mom outside talking quietly with Biggins and the deputy. The second we stepped into the kitchen, the rest of the world fell away.

A mess wasn't the right word for it. Someone had come inside and torn our house apart.

Every kitchen cabinet and drawer was open with its contents spilled over the floor. Dishes were broken, and I carefully edged around the shattered glass fragments, moving deeper into the house.

My mouth fell open to see the couch where we'd spent so many nights lazing around watching movies with Mom, damaged, stained and torn. There were tables and cabinets overturned as well as various trinkets and household items scattered everywhere.

I saw everything, but nothing seemed to process. I looked from one spot to the next. The person who entered our house hadn't left any spot unchecked. Even the family photos that had lined the walls had been torn down and ripped from their frames.

A hand fumbled for mine, and I glanced over to see Oliver in the same confused and angry state of shock that I was in. Our home had been brutally invaded and damaged. I hadn't realized I was shaking until I felt Oliver's firm grip trying to steady my hand.

Neither one of us seemed to know what to say so we remained silent as we stared around us. I knew we should check upstairs, and in the basement, but at the sound of a gasp from behind us, we turned to see Mom standing in the kitchen, her hand over her mouth, and angry tears in her eyes. Without a sound, we went to her, and the three of us huddled together in the midst of the destruction left behind by one person's hatred.

"We're going to get through this," Mom assured us, holding us at her sides. She kissed the top of my head then Oliver's. "We're going to make it through this crisis just like we've done everything else."

I nodded, hugging her tighter.

"We will, Mom," Oliver promised. "We have each other. We'll be okay."

"You two are staying home from school tomorrow...maybe Tuesday, too. Let's get the glass cleaned up at least, and tomorrow, tomorrow we'll work on everything else. Why don't you check your rooms, first? Hopefully, they haven't been touched."

Reluctant to take the first step, I felt fearful of what I'd find. I shuddered at the thought of some strange person going through my closet and my dresser, touching everything I owned. But with Oliver holding my hand, I managed to find the strength to keep moving.

Before we even reached our rooms, we were faced with a sight that chilled me to the core. "Mom!" I yelled, my panic setting in worse than ever. "Mom!"

I heard the pounding of her steps as she raced up the stairs. "Holly? What's wrong — oh no!" she gasped, and her hand flew to cover her mouth as she skidded to a stop beside me.

The attic ladder had been pulled down, and a trail of debris hung over it, littering the hallway.

Boxes were ripped apart, and photos were scattered everywhere amongst the wreckage. They were pictures that Oliver and I had already seen of course, though Mom didn't know that. They had been in Oliver's room, but now they covered the hall. And Mom obviously thought they'd come from the attic. Not that it mattered anymore. Slowly, Oliver bent down and reached for a few of Dad holding us. He stared down at them.

"Is this…our dad?" he whispered.

He was a better actor than I was and I bit my tongue to stop myself from saying anything. Mom nodded slowly as she took the photos from him, then bent down to gather more. We helped her scoop them up as she sank to the floor, resting her back against the wall. Oliver and I sat on either side of her, unsure of what to do. Tears slipped from her eyes, and she smiled sadly as she ran her fingers over Dad's face.

"He was so happy," she told us. Her voice was shaky with emotion. "We loved each other, loved our lives and when you two came into the world, I'd never seen a happier father. He would hold you both so close as if afraid he would lose you…" She trailed off and sifted through the photos until she found one of Dad holding Oliver. "He told me he was going to teach you all he knew; show you all his technology know-how, build robots with you and do so many other things."

Oliver smiled as she handed him the picture. "I never knew Dad was into tech stuff."

"Yeah, it's where you get your brains. From him and your grandpa. Those two would disappear for hours together in your grandpa's lab. Two peas in a pod." The next picture was of Dad holding me as a baby. She cried even harder as she let me take that one from her. "When you came along, Holly, he called you a mini-me. He would've given up anything for you two."

She began to sob, clutching the pictures in her hands. "Mom?" I asked worriedly and put my arm around her. She rested her head on my shoulder, and Oliver held her too. I'd never seen her cry that way before and my heart hurt from seeing her pain, the pain she'd suffered all these years.

"I'm sorry," she gasped between sobs. "I'm sorry. I don't ever talk about him…and I'm sorry you think I hate him, but I don't…your father…I miss him so much."

"We don't think you hate him, Mom," Oliver told her firmly. "We just thought the whole thing was too hard to talk about."

She nodded against my shoulder. "That day, I know he didn't just walk out on us."

I locked eyes with Oliver over Mom's head for a brief second before she wiped her eyes on her sleeve and lifted her head. "You do?"

"Yes. Your father loved us all too much to just disappear. Something happened to him, stopped him from coming back to us. For years, I did everything I could to find him. I know you two think it's because of your grandpa that everyone in this town thinks we're all a bit strange," she said with a bitter laugh. "But it's mostly because of me, because of what I did after he disappeared."

"What did you do?" I asked.

"I searched and pleaded, I begged for the Sheriff not to give up looking for him. But there was nothing to go on." She wiped her eyes again and breathed heavily. "I would've kept it up, but there was talk amongst our friends in the town. They were worried about my sanity and you two. I realized that if I didn't stop, if I didn't find a way to let your dad go, they'd think I was unfit to look after you and I'd lose you both as well."

She reached for our hands, kissing them, and for the first time in my life, I understood my mom. I knew why she was so hard on us to do well, and why anytime we mentioned Dad, she became defensive.

She was keeping us from falling down the same rabbit hole that had almost cost her life, her sanity and nearly had us taken away from her. I knew she was strong for raising us on her own, but now I realized just how incredible she was.

"He'd be so proud of you both," she said, gently pushing away Oliver's hair from his forehead. "So very proud of his prodigy and his bright, curious little girl."

"You think?" Oliver asked, sounding almost like a little kid again.

"Definitely." She let go of our hands so she could pick up the photos that lay in her lap. "Would you like to see these?"

We bobbed our heads eagerly, and she began with the first one, starting with their wedding day. She placed it down in front of us, and I stared at the image longingly. They looked so in love and so happy.

She went on to tell us all about the dad we'd never had a chance to meet; apart from the precious few minutes that we'd had with him the day before. Every picture brought a new memory that had Mom smiling brightly, and soon the three of us were laughing as she told us about Dad's terrible singing. Though, according to Mom, it was the only thing that helped get Oliver to sleep on so many nights. She told us about the way Oliver would ride around on Dad's shoulders, both of them howling like wolves at the moon. And when I came along, she said his singing became even worse as he carried me around the house in his arms, making up new lyrics about mermaids and princesses.

It didn't matter anymore that the house was in shambles, nor that it would take time to get everything tidied again. They were just belongings, household stuff. Whereas sitting there alongside Mom and my brother, listening to Mom's memories, that was real. We stayed in there in the hallway late into the night before we finally reached the last picture of Mom and Dad hugging each other tightly, her holding up a stuffed polar bear.

"He always found me a polar bear," she murmured. "Every year for our anniversary and my birthday and Christmas. I'd get a new miniature statue or a stuffed animal. My closet is filled with them."

"Maybe it's time you put them out somewhere," I suggested. "Show them off."

"You know what, I think you're right!" She patted my leg and then stood, stretching her arms over her head. "Alright, I vote we camp out in my room tonight, pop on a movie. What do you two say? We can tackle this in the morning after a huge stack of pancakes."

I was more than happy with her idea, staying close to them both would be the only way I'd get to sleep.

I went into my room to grab my pillow and some pajamas, but as soon as I stepped one foot in the doorway, a shiver ran down my spine at the thought of an invader going through my things. Thankfully though, my bed hadn't been touched.

When I went to my desk to see if my laptop still worked since it had been carelessly tossed onto the floor, I glanced out the window, and the hairs on the back of my neck abruptly stood on end. I wasn't sure what caused me to peer out into the darkness. I spotted the squad car that was parked out on the street as promised but there was something else that had caught my eye. The more I stared, the more convinced I became that there was a dark figure hidden behind a large oak tree on the other side of the road. I blinked, rubbing my eyes, and pressing my nose to the glass. All I could see, however, was the gentle rustle of the long unmown grass in the evening breeze.

Deciding I had imagined the figure and was simply being paranoid, I then hurried to my mom's room to get settled in for the night. But no matter how hard I tried, I could not shake the feeling that whoever had invaded our home was still out there, watching us.

Watching me.

Chapter 5

I tossed and turned all night long, unable to sleep. But I wasn't the only one. Mom woke several times during the night; I heard her padding through the house, double-checking the locks and windows. Oliver couldn't seem to get comfortable, and when the sun finally cast an early morning glow through the curtain, I gave up trying to sleep any longer and just lay there, staring at the ceiling.

When we eventually decided to get out of bed and face the aftermath, we headed downstairs and began with the kitchen. With brooms and dustpans in hand, we swept up the glass, tossing it in the trash bin. Mom followed with the vacuum cleaner to be sure she picked up all the tiny shards. Once we'd cleaned the floor and the counters, she began making breakfast, and within minutes, the smell of pancakes filled the kitchen. I helped flip them on the griddle until each of us had a nice tall stack.

We tucked in at the breakfast counter to eat, but I struggled to get them down, and before long, they were churning in the pit of my stomach. I picked at what was left on my plate, glancing at my family. They looked as tired as I felt, but Mom seemed determined to get the house tidied as soon as possible. She drained her cup of coffee and set the mug down with an affirmative nod.

"Right, I'm going to call the alarm system company that Sheriff Biggins recommended and a locksmith to change the locks on the doors as well. Hopefully, it won't take too long to get everything sorted out. Then we can get on with the rest of the house." She picked up the phone and dialed a number. Five minutes later, she was yelling at someone on the other end, and Oliver and I couldn't help but laugh.

"I'm not waiting two weeks to have someone come out to my house," she snapped in her best mom voice. "My home was broken into last night, and I have two kids. You think making me wait for the insurance company to contact you is going to help? And why does that even matter?" She paced around the kitchen, nodding her head, but whatever the person was saying only set her off again. "Look, I don't care what your policies are, but please get someone out here today, or you'll be getting a visit from the sheriff!"

Two minutes later, she was smirking and thanking the person before hanging up.

"They'll be here this afternoon," she grinned as she searched for the number of a locksmith. That call seemed to be much easier. Barely five minutes later, she set the phone back in its place on the benchtop and planted her hands on her hips, observing the scene around her.

"Remind me never to get on your bad side," Oliver mumbled.

Mom winked and tied her hair back in a blue bandana. "I don't think you two could ever be on my bad side. But I wasn't kidding when I said everyone in this town thought I was losing my mind. Your mom's got a crazy side you will hopefully never see."

With her leading, and putting on some very loud, bouncy music to flood the house, we set to work. As we went, we kept a list of anything that was destroyed beyond repair so Mom could tell the insurance company and we could buy replacements.

"On the bright side," Mom said, after wiping sweat from her brow and retying the bandanna in her hair, "I never liked those dishes, but now we can get new ones."

That was how we looked at each room we cleaned. It was springtime anyway, so it was the perfect time to clean out the house. I thought the day would have dragged by, but by two o'clock, the main floor was cleaned and organized once again.

My cell phone buzzed on the kitchen table, and I hurried to see who it was.

"It's Kate," I told Mom. "Can I take a break?"

"Yeah, I think we're done for today unless you two want to tackle your rooms."

I hugged her one more time before I bolted upstairs, deciding I could chat while I cleaned. I was eager to get my room back to some semblance of normal and was still considering scrubbing it from top to bottom. I loathed the fact that someone had been in there touching everything I owned.

By the time I reached the top of the stairs, Kate had hung up. I called her back. She picked up on the first ring and started rambling before I even managed to say hello. "Where were you today? Rumors are going around, and Jack said that his dad was at your place last night. He said your house was broken into! Are you guys okay? Was the person still there—"

"It's okay!" I interrupted her. "We're fine, all of us are fine. But it was all so scary!"

"Oh my gosh, Holly! What happened?"

"While we were out last night, someone broke into our house," I explained as I bent down to pick up the schoolbooks that had been dumped out of my backpack. Every pocket had been emptied, and the contents were thrown all over the room.

"We had to watch the sheriff come in and search the house. It was really scary!" My voice shook with the memory. No matter how much I told myself we were safe, I was still scared and anxious. I wasn't sure that our house would ever feel safe again.

"I can't believe it! Do you want me to come over? Do you need anything?" The concern in my friend's voice rang in my ear.

"No, it's okay. Thanks for offering, Kate. But I think I'll be back at school the day after tomorrow. We're going to need another day to get our bedrooms and the rest of the house sorted."

"They went through your bedrooms?"

"Yeah, my clothes were everywhere. It's weird and creepy! But Mom called the alarm system people this morning. They should be coming out soon to get us all hooked up, and a locksmith is coming too. Mom's not leaving anything to chance."

"I can't imagine how crazy that is. You're sure you don't need anything?" She was such a good friend, and I wondered if she was already on her front porch, ready to rush over if I said I did need her.

"No, I don't think so. Except maybe your notes from today and tomorrow. I hate missing school."

She sighed loudly. "Really? Holly, your house was broken into. I think you're allowed to miss a few days of school."

"But I'll get behind and—"

"Seriously?" she scolded. "You don't need to worry about school right now!"

"Yeah, I guess you're right. It's just so weird though because nothing was taken."

"Like nothing at all?"

"No, all our electronics are still here, and everything of value is still lying around. Even Mom's jewelry is still in her room. Whoever broke in damaged a lot of things, but they didn't take anything."

"What about the...you know what?" she whispered.

I frowned, not sure what she was talking about; then it registered as I pictured the metal case that held the time machine. The one really important thing that we'd completely forgotten about. "Oh no!"

Sprinting from my room, I skidded to a stop at the top of the stairs when I heard Mom talking to someone out on the porch. While she was distracted, I rushed down the steps to the basement, almost tripping on my feet, only to find Oliver had beaten me.

"Is it still there?" I blurted, startling him. I stared around wildly, and although the basement was a mess, half the boxes hadn't been disturbed. Oliver stood beside the pile, not moving. "Oliver, did you hear me?"

"Yeah, yeah the machines are safe...it's as though he was interrupted or something. Why tear the whole house apart, but stop here?"

I saw where he was pointing and realized the intruder had been two stacks of boxes away from the machines before he stopped his search. Last night when I was in my room, I knew I'd seen someone out on the street. Had it been the guy who broke in? I staggered backward until my calves hit the steps. As I sat down, I heard Kate calling my name, but I wasn't able to respond. Oliver, his brow furrowed with worry, crouched before me and took the phone from my hand. He said something to Kate then set the phone down.

"I saw him," I managed to whisper.

"Who?"

"Last night when I looked out my bedroom window...I saw someone standing in the shadows across the road, but I thought I'd imagined it. What if I didn't? What if we interrupted whoever it was when we came home?"

He scratched absently at the back of his neck. "It's possible I guess, but the only unlocked door was the kitchen one. We were right by it the whole time. We would have seen him trying to escape." I heard the doubt in his words as he continued. "You didn't see anything, Holly. He's not going to come back. And besides, there is an alarm system being installed today."

"That might not work if this person can magic their way through walls," I mumbled.

Oliver straightened suddenly and threw a glance over his shoulder at the undisturbed boxes. "Yeah...but that's impossible, right?"

"So is time travel."

My phone buzzed beside me with a text, and I saw Zac's name. I needed a distraction and numbly told Oliver I was heading back to my room. He barely nodded at me as I trudged up the stairs and closed my bedroom door. Sitting in the middle of the floor, I texted Zac back. He was just as worried as Kate. It was nice to know my friends cared about me.

I spent the rest of the afternoon texting back and forth with Zac and Kate while I organized and cleaned out my closet, my desk, and every inch I could reach. It kept my mind busy. But as the sun set and darkness closed in, I wondered about the shadow-figure I had seen the night before.

My mind swirled with images of him moving in closer and closer; waiting to make his move and come back for whatever he hadn't found the first time.

Chapter 6

The following afternoon, by the end of what would have been the school day, I felt that my room was finally clean and tidy. I'd hung my clothes back in the closet and put everything else back in its place. I was waiting for Kate to text me, but I wasn't expecting the doorbell to ring.

"Holly! You have a visitor!" Mom yelled up the stairs.

I checked my phone. Kate would have texted me first. I shoved a stack of books onto the shelf where they belonged and hurried downstairs. To my surprise, I saw Zac smiling shyly on the front porch, a bunch of colorful flowers in his hand. Mom stood by the open door, grinning at me.

"Hey, Holly," Zac said when I reached him. "I uh, I thought I'd stop by and see how you were doing and all." He fiddled with the flowers in his grip.

"Thanks, Zac," I replied. "That's so nice of you."

He glanced at the flowers as if he'd forgotten he was even holding them. "Oh, and um…these flowers are for you. I thought they might make you smile after what you've been through and all. I wasn't sure what else to do."

I heard a hard sniff and glanced over to see Mom watching us both, holding her hand to her mouth. I widened my eyes at her and waited for her to walk away, but she didn't seem to catch the hint.

"Mom? Mind if I go for a walk with Zac in the park?"

"Sure, sure, go have fun, but be back by dinner, okay?"

I grabbed my jacket off the hook by the door and in my rush to escape my mom, I still had the flowers in my hand as we headed towards the park. One look back told me Mom was still watching and when we turned the corner and were out of sight, I sighed in relief.

"What?" Zac said, but he was already laughing.

"She's so embarrassing sometimes."

"Ah, I think all parents are like that." He kicked a rock down the sidewalk, his hands in his pockets. "You sure you're ok? Kate said you were pretty shaken up. I can't even imagine coming home to something like that."

I ran my fingers over one of the flowers then brought them to my nose, smelling them for a few seconds. They tickled my nose, and I grinned, but my smile didn't last long.

"Nothing was taken," I told him as we walked. "Nothing at all. But Oliver and I think he was interrupted. Or her...whoever it was. They were close, though, really close to finding the machines."

I didn't want to think about what could have happened if those were found. Zac moved closer until our arms touched and I welcomed having him with me. "Thanks for coming over, Zac. It means a lot, you stopping by and all."

"Well...we *have* traveled through time together, so I think it's the least I can do," he smiled.

We entered the park and found a bench near the pond and several weeping willows. The light breeze rustled their branches, and I was happy sitting there watching them with Zac at my side. I asked him about school the past couple of days, and he said history was boring without me. But our group had managed to get a heap of work done for the history project.

"Lunch was kinda quiet all around," he said. "Everyone's a bit freaked out about your house being busted into like that."

"What do you mean? It happens all the time on the news."

"Yeah, maybe in other places, but Jack said his dad was really surprised. There hasn't been a break-in reported for at least five years," Zac informed me. "Our town's pretty sleepy I guess, and our crime rate has never been high."

I hadn't thought of it in that way. "It is really strange," I mumbled. "And I'm sure I saw someone later that night, hiding behind a tree across the road. But it might've been a shadow. Or I could have just imagined it."

"Did you tell anyone?"

"Just Oliver. But he thought the same thing I did, that it was just me seeing shadows." I sat quietly for a moment before speaking again. "I wish it had never happened. There's enough drama going on in my life to worry about someone breaking into our house."

"I hope I'm not part of the drama," he grinned. But at the same time, he seemed worried that I might say yes.

"No, of course you're not!" I gave him a friendly shove. "I'm so glad we're hanging out together."

"Me too," he smiled. His expression then became more serious. "You're so much nicer than the other girls at school, Holly. I think you're really cool."

I grinned back, my heart soaring at the sound of his words.

At the same time though, I could not help thinking of Jade and what I had done to her history project. If Zac knew about that, I wasn't sure he'd still feel the same way about me.

When he started talking about school again and offered to give me his notes, I managed to push my guilt aside; but only momentarily. Because all of a sudden, I was confronted with the one person I had not expected to see.

Jade and her group of friends walked towards us. Jade wasn't dressed as nicely as she usually was and there was no hint of anything except anger on her face. She blocked the sidewalk, her friends spreading out to make a wall.

"What do you want?" Zac asked, annoyed. "Can you move?"

"No, I don't think I will," Jade snapped, staring at me as she said it.

"What's your problem?" Zac frowned at her. "Stop being a bully and just move."

"I like the park, and I'm allowed to be here, too," she snarled.

"Go for it," Zac shot back. "We were just leaving." He reached for my hand and held it, but I couldn't bring myself to say anything in defense.

Jade's eyes narrowed as she tapped her toe and crossed her arms. "What's the matter, Holly? Can't think of anything to say after what you did?"

My eyes widened in panic. But there was no way she could know about us going back in time to mess up her project. No way. It wasn't possible! I hadn't said anything, and I knew Kate wouldn't. So how did she know?

"What are you talking about?" Zac demanded, stepping partially in front of me.

"She's the reason I'm currently flunking history!"

"What?" I gasped. Surely, her family tree project wasn't causing her to fail the class. And besides, she had always been the teacher's favorite before. I thought she had managed top marks in everything else she'd submitted. My palms grew sweaty, and I shook my head. "No, that's not true. And I didn't do anything to you."

She smirked. "You're a terrible liar."

"If she says she didn't do anything then I believe her," Zac said, his tone becoming angry.

"Oh yeah? Then why did I overhear Mrs. Clarke saying that right before our history lesson, Kate sent her off to help someone who didn't even need her help? Then, when she came back, she found some kids locked inside her classroom messing with something," Jade yelled, drawing the attention of a few other people in the park. "And on top of that, my box of artifacts went missing!"

"I don't know what you're talking about," I tried to say, but she was shaking her head again.

"They were found hidden in a janitor's closet."

"Yeah and…?" Zac scoffed, trying to push me even farther behind him. "Anyone could have put them there, even you."

"Why would I do that?"

"I don't know…to try and get even more attention than you already do! Now, if you'll excuse us, we have somewhere we need to be." Zac, still holding my hand firmly in his, guided us around Jade and her friends.

Jade yelled after me, but Zac told me to tune her out, and soon enough we were back on my street. That was when I pulled him to a stop.

"What's wrong?" he asked, giving me an odd look.

"Don't worry about Jade. She's just trying to lay the blame on someone. It's got nothing to do with you."

"Actually…it has," I said slowly, hanging my head.

There was only one time I'd felt this bad, and it was when I accidentally broke one of my mom's favorite dishes. It had been given to her by our grandma, and I knew that she treasured it. I was so scared to tell her that for weeks, I pretended it just vanished into thin air when really, I'd hidden the pieces away in my closet. When I finally told her, the words came out in a rush, and I felt so ashamed for lying to her.

That same horrible feeling hit me now, and I wanted to crawl away and hide somewhere. The longer Zac stared at me, the more his expression filled with concern and the worse I felt.

"I…I did do something…to mess up Jade's project," I said it quietly, half of me hoping that he didn't hear.

He stepped back and shook his head. "What? No, you wouldn't that."

I struggled to continue, but I knew I had to confess.

"It's just that she was so horrible to me, she's been mean for so long, and something just snapped," I rambled. "And then we found the time machine, and I had this crazy idea to get back at her. And so, we messed up her project, and then things changed, and after that, things with you were different—"

"With me?" he asked, his frown deepening.

At the same second the words left his lips, I clapped my hand over my mouth, realizing I'd said too much. He shoved his hands into his pockets and narrowed his eyes, confused. "What do you mean with me? And the machine? You used it to get back at Jade?"

I would have wrung my hands together, but I was still holding the flowers. "During the night of the band concert, we used the machine to go back to the day of the history presentations. I didn't think it would change other things as well. I just wanted to mess up her project a bit."

He blinked rapidly, and I knew he was thinking back over that night when Kate, Oliver and I disappeared from the gym, saying we had to use the bathroom.

He seemed more confused than ever, and I needed to explain. "When we originally went to the concert, you weren't even there. Kate, Oliver and I sneaked into the classroom and uploaded a different file for Jade's project, one that Kate and I put together at home. Then we hid the artifacts," I confessed. "But it was just meant to be a prank! I just wanted to embarrass her. Then when we came back to the present…you were there. And then…you and I were kind of going out and, well…" I trailed off and watched as he connected the dots for himself.

He stared at me silently as he tried to process my words.

I bobbed my head, not sure what else to do. "Zac, I'm sorry…I should've told you, but I was worried you'd think I was crazy."

He nodded absently, staring at the ground.

222

"Are you…are you mad at me?"

"Mad? No, but…I'm confused I guess. You and I weren't seeing each other very much until you went back and changed Jade's project. Is that right? And then after that, we were like…together?"

"Yeah, I guess."

"And you have no idea what else you might've changed?"

I shook my head. "But everything's been fine, hasn't it? I mean, we're still friends, and it was just Jade's project that was messed up."

"Except you did to her exactly what she's always done to you."

I shrugged, trying to smash down the guilt that persistently got worse the longer he stared at me, his face filled with disappointment. "I'm not sure I see what's so wrong with that." I stammered.

"Really? Wow, Holly, that's just…wow."

"What? She was mean to me for years, and when I finally decide to get her back, I become the bad guy?"

"Yes!" he declared loudly. "Don't you see? When you do what the bully does, you become the bully! You take on the mean girl persona, and that…that is not who I thought you were."

"That's not fair," I argued, tears burning in my eyes. "You have no idea what she did to me!"

"I know she was horrible to you, and I get that it was bad, but you can't sink to her level." He stepped back again, and my chest tightened. "You were willing to risk getting into a heap of trouble and being just like Jade so that you could get a little revenge. Maybe you guys finding that machine wasn't such a good thing after all."

My jaw dropped, and the flowers fell from my hands. "How can you say that? I got to meet my dad because of it!"

"Yeah, and you've also messed with people's lives! You've changed the way your mom sees things. You've changed things for Jade. Maybe you've even made things happen between us. Who knows what else you've changed!" He turned around and started to walk away.

"Zac! Wait a second!"

"No, I'm going home…see you at school tomorrow or…whenever. And ask Kate for her notes. I'm sure she'll fill you in on anything you need to know," he yelled over his shoulder, not stopping.

I stood on the sidewalk staring at his retreating back until he was gone from my sight. Tears blurred my vision, and angrily, I wiped them away. My life had been so much simpler before, but now it was turning into a huge mess! And it was all my fault.

Hugging my arms around me as a chill breeze picked up, I stepped over the fallen daises, not feeling I deserved them or even wanted them anymore, and I headed home.

"How was your walk, hon?" Mom asked when I walked in the front door.

"Fine," I managed to say without sounding upset. "I'm going to finish tidying my room, and Kate's going to call me soon, to give me some notes I missed."

"Ok. I think we're doing takeout tonight. I'll let you know when it gets here."

"Sounds good!" I ran upstairs and closed my door. Kicking off my shoes, I fell face first onto my bed, clutching my pillow tightly to my chest as tears spilled from my eyes. I'd always told myself I would never be the girl who would cry over a boy. And here I was crying because Zac was disappointed in what I'd done.

What I had wanted was to make Jade feel bad; the way she'd made me feel on so many occasions. But I never imagined I'd turn into the same type of girl she was because of it.

A soft knock came at my door before Oliver opened it a crack. "Holly? Are you crying?"

"No," I said, my voice muffled from my pillow. "Go

224

away."

My door creaked open, and I lifted my head enough to see him step inside.

"I said go away," I muttered the words and turned my back on him. "I don't want to talk."

"I thought you were just out with Zac. What happened?" My bed shifted as he sat on the edge of it. "Holly, come on. You know you'll feel better if you talk about it."

I sniffed hard, wiping my face on my freshly cleaned pillow and not caring. "He found out…about what we did to Jade."

"How?"

I gave him a quick rundown on what had happened at the park and how I couldn't stand to keep the secret from Zac anymore, not when he knew about the machine. By the time I finished explaining, I was crying all over again, and Oliver looked torn between annoyance at Zac and his own guilt.

"Why do you look like that?" I asked, wiping my face on my sleeve. "You didn't come up with the idea, remember? I did. I'm the one who suggested we mess with her project."

"I know, but I agreed." He hugged me, and I leaned against him. "I get where Zac's coming from, but you're not the only one to blame for what happened. Sometimes, when people get pushed too far, they have to push back. Maybe we went a little overboard, but you can't let this hang over your head forever."

"Feels like it's going to," I mumbled.

He chuckled. "You're in seventh grade, Holly. Trust me; there's plenty of years ahead of both of us for messing up. Let this one go." He poked me in the ribs, trying to get me to smile.

"And Zac?"

"He's just one guy. But I'm sure he'll come around

eventually. Don't worry about it."

He gave me one more tight squeeze before he stood and left me alone. He was right, but it only made me feel marginally better about what we'd done. I took off my tear-stained jacket, as well as my pillowcase, and busied myself with putting the last of my books back on their shelves. I tried to convince myself that Oliver was right and we had more important things to worry about.

But even so, the guilt inside me sat heavily in my stomach, and I could not rid my mind of Zac's disappointed expression.

I didn't want his opinion of me to mean so much. But it did.

And I wondered if he'd ever want to talk to me again.

Chapter 7

The next day at school was a disaster. Zac barely even nodded in my direction. I glanced his way a few times, but it was obvious he was ignoring me. Adding to my distress was Jade, who glared angrily towards me, but I managed to avoid further confrontation by staying as far away from her as possible.

It seemed my worst fears had been realized and I was right back where I'd started a few weeks earlier. Zac was barely acknowledging me, and Jade was throwing repeated mean looks my way. I couldn't believe that things could change so rapidly. Especially because everything had been going so well.

Along with these issues, I was filled with an eerie sensation that I was being watched. The feeling increased as time went by and I developed a new sense of paranoia that continued to grow in the back of my mind. I worried that whoever had broken into our house was going to come back. He had clearly been interrupted before finding what he was looking for. And if that was the case, there was a good chance he would return.

Meanwhile, Mom took a couple more days off work to get the rest of the house in order and to deal with the insurance agency. And finally, towards the end of the week, the house was restored to a semblance of order.

When she eventually returned to work, she was faced with a compulsory evening conference that was to be held somewhere in the city. It meant she'd be leaving us at home alone. As she grabbed her purse and prepared to walk out the door, I saw the hesitation on her face.

"We'll be fine, Mom," Oliver told her. "Really. We have the alarm system and everything."

"I know, I just…I can't help feeling that I should be staying here with you."

"It's ok. You've already said that we need to get back to normal," I pointed out. "And you have our permission to call us every half hour if it'll make you feel better."

She chewed on her bottom lip, her frown deepening, but finally, she relented and held out her arms to hug us. "Alright, but if either of you starts to feel uncomfortable, you call me right away. Promise?"

"We promise, Mom!" I said, pushing her out the door.

Though she'd put on a strong face the past few days, we could both tell she was barely holding it together. The insurance money was going to take a little while to come through, and until the house was back to the way it was, I didn't think Mom would return to her usual self. Though to be fair, the kitchen was still blue, and I suspected more than ever that somehow we were responsible for that man breaking into our home. I hadn't said it out loud, and neither had Oliver, but we both knew the truth. Whoever came to the house had been looking for one thing…Grandpa's time machine.

I mumbled something to Oliver about going to finish my homework and headed for the stairs. But he grabbed my arm.

"What?"

"I'm going back," he said simply and then turned for the basement.

"Wait, what? Oliver!" But he had already disappeared through the basement doorway.

I followed after him and found him already at the workbench, fiddling with the time machine. "Hold on a second. We decided we wouldn't use this for a while! What do you think you're going to do?"

"I'm going back to that night of the break-in," he informed me without turning around. "And I'm going to see who did it. You coming or not?"

I thought of how disappointed Zac looked after I confessed my crime against Jade, but this was different, right? If I went with Oliver, it wasn't as though we were going back to mess with anyone.

Or at least I didn't think we were.

I knew that messing with Jade had been reckless on my part. And that had led to a fallout with the boy I'd been crushing on for years. I wasn't sure that we should be using the machine again without giving it more thought.

Oliver's plan could get us into serious trouble. "Can we talk about this for a minute? Please?"

"Why? I know you already have your suspicions of who broke into our house. And so do I. I'm not going to sit around and wait for him to come back. I can't."

I wasn't sure how to stop my brother. I had a bad feeling about what he was suggesting. I didn't think it was a good idea. But at the same time, I wasn't about to let him go alone. "I'm calling Kate."

"Why?"

"Because we promised each other that if one of us goes back, all three of us do, remember? I'm calling to let her know." I was already searching for her name on my phone when he opened his mouth to argue. But he took one look at the determination on my face and changed his mind. Rolling his eyes, he turned back to the machine while I silently begged for my friend to pick up.

"Holly?"

"Kate, is there any chance you can come over to my house? Like…right now?"

"I think so. Why? What's up?"

"Oliver has some crazy idea to go back to the night our place was broken into," I answered quietly as I climbed the stairs so Oliver wouldn't overhear. "I'm hoping you can help me talk him out of it."

"Does he know who broke in?"

I almost said Thaddeus Banes, but I wasn't completely sure. And I hadn't seen anything, but a shadow that night so there was no point accusing a supposedly dead man of this crime unless it really had been him.

"No...maybe...I don't know. But I don't think this is a good idea. Mom's gone out, but still...what if something goes wrong? Like very wrong? This person could hurt Oliver."

"Alright, I'll be there as fast as I can," she promised and then hung up.

I paced the front entry impatiently waiting for Kate's knock, and when it finally came, I dragged her inside, shutting and locking the door behind her.

I hurried back to make sure the alarm was set, just in case, and then nodded to the basement door. "He's downstairs."

Together, we raced down the steps to see Oliver had set the machine on the floor in the basement and was adjusting the knobs. He barely offered a glance when Kate and I approached him. "Ready to go?" he asked.

"First, there's something Kate needs to tell you," I said, and mimed for her to talk to him.

She took a deep breath, and I waited for her to give him some crazy speech that would convince him not to go back, but instead, all she said was, "Let's do this!"

"What?" I yelped. "Kate! You're supposed to talk him out of it!"

"Holly, he's right. And you know it! You guys started something the day you found this machine, and now when things get a little crazy you're going to miss a chance to see who's behind all of this?"

"It could've just been a burglar! We could be walking into a very dangerous situation!" I tried to argue, but I could tell from Oliver's set face that he wasn't about to back down. And neither was Kate.

Sighing with frustration, I pleaded, "Guys, seriously, this is beyond ruining someone's project at school. This is dangerous, really dangerous. What if we get hurt? What if something happens to the machine and we can't get back?"

"Then let's make sure nothing happens to the machine," Oliver suggested as he stood.

I ran my hands through my hair, searching for options. I could let them go without me, but if something happened to them, if they were injured or hurt in some way, or even worse, if they never came back, I couldn't live with myself.

Knowing I was going to regret my decision, I stepped forward, and Kate acknowledged me with a pleased nod.

"Mom will be back in a few hours," I reminded my brother as he picked up the machine. "We have to be back here, or she'll think we were kidnapped. Got it? No wasting time. We get there; we see a face, we leave. Deal?"

"Deal." Oliver nodded in agreement.

He inhaled a deep breath and then told us both to hold on. Kate and I grabbed his arms as he flipped the switch on Grandpa's machine. I was growing used to the strange sensations that happened when we were yanked from the present and sent abruptly into the past. But the second that my feet hit the floor in the previous time zone, I knew something was wrong.

We were in the basement, and the light was off as it should have been since we had gone out for dinner. But the house was eerily quiet. Not a single sound could be heard anywhere.

"Are you sure this is last Sunday night?" I whispered as Oliver checked his digital watch.

"Yeah, and it's twenty minutes before we got home from the diner. The intruder should be in the house." Holding onto the machine, Oliver moved slowly towards the basement stairs, craning his head in an attempt to hear if anyone was on the floor above us. There were no footsteps, no sounds of rummaging, nothing.

"I don't like this," I urged. "Oliver, let's just go back."

"Not yet," he whispered. "Just wait a second."

The sudden click was so loud in the silence of the basement that it was near deafening. "Yes, just hold on for one second," a man said from the shadows of the basement. My stomach dropped to the floor as I gulped. "Now then, let's see what you have in your arms, son. Flip on the light."

"No," Oliver said fiercely. But the man shifted against the shadows, and a sliver of moonlight caught the shiny object in his hand.

"Don't make me hurt you. Turn on the light. Now!"

"Oliver, just do it," I whispered, hoping he understood what I meant by that.

The machine was our only chance to get out of this. We had to leave immediately. I glanced over my shoulder to my brother, trying to make him understand that we needed to leave, but he couldn't see my face in the darkness. I winced when the light clicked on. It was Kate who had flicked the switch, and she stood trembling in fear as she stared at the man across the room.

A man who we all recognized straight away.

"Thaddeus Banes," Oliver whispered. "You're supposed to be dead!"

The old man appeared more haphazardly put together than he had in his pictures with Grandpa. His hair was mostly gone except for a few gray strands on the sides. His eyes twitched angrily, and the hand holding the revolver was shaky. I stepped back, trying to get away from him and the lingering smell of mothballs and cigarettes. My nose crinkled and I tried to move even further back when he reached out and snagged my arm. He was faster than I expected for an old man and I winced as his fingers dug into my flesh.

Oliver and Kate yelled in panic, both ready to charge forward. But Thaddeus aimed the gun at them, and they slid to a stop.

"Now then, we're all going to have a nice little chat, aren't we?"

"About what?" Oliver snapped. "Just let her go, and we'll talk about whatever you want."

"Not while you're holding that machine. Set it down gently on this stack of boxes, and step away."

I saw Oliver's grip tighten on the machine in his hands, but the second Thaddeus aimed the revolver at me, Oliver put the machine down and backed away.

"There," said Oliver. Now let her go."

233

I heard the old man's teeth grinding before he shrugged and shoved me back towards Oliver and Kate. Oliver caught me in a hug before he pushed Kate and me protectively behind him. Thaddeus wasn't paying any attention to us, just the machine at his side. His eyes were wide, and I thought for a second, tears were glistening on his cheeks at the sight of it.

"You found it…after all these years, William's grandson found it and got it working. Marvelous, just marvelous," Thaddeus whispered in awe. "I knew. I knew that one day I would find it, find what he'd kept from me all these years. What they both tried to stop me from finding."

I frowned when he said both, but this wasn't the time to consider his words.

"For good reason probably," Oliver muttered.

Thaddeus lifted his head and leered at us. "You're just like him, aren't you? Thinking you know best, thinking that this science can only be used for one purpose and one purpose only." He licked his lips, and his hands shook even more. "He never understood, no one ever understood! All I wanted was to show the world what we'd discovered. But William…he locked it away, claimed it was too dangerous."

He laughed madly, and I gulped, realizing we were stuck in the past with a crazy man holding a gun. "And here are his grandkids," he smirked, "using it to mess around with things they don't understand."

"We're trying to find our dad," Oliver corrected him sharply.

Thaddeus laughed even harder. "Your dad? Oh, well then, by all means, enjoy your search."

"What's that supposed to mean?" I whispered. "You…what did you do to him?"

"It wasn't my fault," Thaddeus said with a casual shrug. "Your dad poked his nose where it didn't belong…so I sent him away."

"Where?" Oliver asked. "Where did you send him!"

"Ah, ah, temper, temper," Thaddeus warned and lifted the revolver again. "I'm the one asking questions here tonight, not you. Besides, you're not even supposed to be here. But I had a feeling…a feeling that somehow my plan would work out the way I'd intended and I'd catch you in the act."

I didn't want to hear any more. Thaddeus knew about Dad, but I doubted he would tell us anything to help us understand what had happened. We'd have to keep looking and find Dad on our own like Grandpa's note had told us to. Thaddeus was unstable, and right now we just needed to grab the machine from him and get back to our own time zone. But the gun was a problem. Somehow, we needed to get the gun away from him so we could get to the machine. My head was spinning frantically as I watched Thaddeus mumble to himself as he leaned over the device, running his fingers along it, mesmerized by what he saw.

Looking around, I suddenly knew what I had to do. The shelving unit behind Thaddeus was filled with old books and a heap of boxes. If I could topple it over, so it landed on him, it might give us the chance we needed. With no way to tell Oliver what I was planning, I took a few tentative steps towards the wall of the basement and held my breath. Thaddeus was too distracted and didn't notice me moving.

Oliver slid a sideways glance towards me, subtly shaking his head, but I indicated the shelf with a nod, trying to make him understand. He shook his head, more fiercely this time, but I was already moving.

"Fascinating," Thaddeus whispered loudly. "I would never have considered using the coils like this. And the power source…one wrong adjustment and it could blow the entire thing up. He actually managed to get it stable…all this time, I knew he'd figured it out. I knew it!"

I inched my way past Thaddeus and around the shelves. Finally, standing behind the shelving unit, I readied myself for what I was about to do. With my heart pounding and my palms sweaty, I placed my hands on one of the lower shelves and pushed.

Nothing happened. It didn't budge.

But I wasn't giving up. Thaddeus was still bent over the machine. I climbed up onto the bottom shelf then made my way higher and higher. Using all my body weight, I pushed with every ounce of strength I had. The shelf groaned and creaked, and by the time Thaddeus turned, it was already crashing down on top of him. He yelled, but the sound was muffled, the shelving unit pushing him to the floor and the gun skittering away from him.

I landed on top of the pile with a yelp of pain. Kate grabbed my hand to yank me to my feet as Oliver reached for our precious time machine. I saw that it was covered in some fallen debris and I prayed that it wasn't damaged. Thaddeus' hand flew out and grasped a firm hold of my ankle. At the same time, he struggled to escape the weight of the shelf on top of him. With a yell, Kate grabbed a thick hardcover book that lay at her feet and smacked him on the head with it, until he released his grip.

"Let's go!" Oliver shoved us towards the stairs, then followed us to the top, slamming the basement door behind him. We could still hear Thaddeus yelling, so we pushed a large armchair in front of the door to hold him off a little longer.

"Come on, let's go!" I bounced on my feet, wanting to get out of there before Thaddeus came charging up the stairs to attack us again. "Oliver!"

"Ok! Ok!"

He flipped the switch on the machine, and we held on tight as the blue light surrounded us. With a loud pop, we disappeared from the living room…but the second we landed, I knew something was wrong.

"What happened?" I asked frantically, as I stared around the house and focused on the unfamiliar blue sofa.

"This is all new stuff. We have all new furniture...Oliver!"

"We went too far forward!" He fiddled with the knobs, and I heard him curse, something Oliver never did. "It looks like the coil was damaged! I'll have to fix it before we can use the machine again."

"How far forward did we go?" I asked, waiting for one of us, or for Mom to suddenly appear.

"Twenty years!! No! I don't know if I can fix this!"

"Twenty years??" Kate gulped.

My heart was pounding. We had to do something. "Your workbench. Let's start there. Maybe all the things you need are still in the basement!"

I saw the doubt on his face, but now was not the time for doubting. We had to fix the machine and get back to our real time zone.

I didn't want to think about what would happen if we became stuck twenty years in the future!

Chapter 8

Creeping from room to room, we firstly did a careful but very quick check of the house, and to our huge relief, we found no one at home; that was a plus at least. But in the process, we saw that Oliver's room was void of any tools or his usual boxes of gadgets. We then rushed down to the basement, tearing open box after box, praying we'd find something useful.

"Found it!" Oliver yelled.

Kate and I ran to the back corner of the basement. "Those are the parts from the old machine we found in the antique store," I said over his shoulder.

"Yeah," he said, digging through the contents that had obviously remained packed away.

I stood by, praying he would find whatever he needed to fix the broken coil on Grandpa's machine. He'd set the device on the workbench, and it was still glowing blue. But the light was intermittent, and now and then, it shot out a stream of sparks.

After a few endless seconds of digging around inside the box, he pulled his arm free. "Got it!" he cried, holding up a copper coil that looked similar to the one that had been damaged. But it wasn't the same. Even I could tell the wiring was different.

"You sure that'll work?" I asked as he ran to his workbench.

"It has to. Otherwise, we're stuck here!"

I paced back and forth. Kate did the same but went in the opposite direction, wringing her hands with worry. I wanted to tell my best friend that everything would be fine and that we'd get back home, back to our proper time zone, the one where we were supposed to be. But I had no idea if that would be the case. And the longer it took Oliver to fix the machine, the worse my panic grew. Until finally, it threatened to swallow me whole.

Finally, we heard Oliver's excited voice. "Done! Who's ready to go home?" he announced proudly.

"Oh my gosh!" Kate replied, her face filled with utter relief. "Let's go!"

Oliver tucked the machine into his arms and made for the stairs.

"What are you doing?" I asked. "What if Mom comes home?"

"The easiest way to tell if we're in the right time zone is to land in the living room with all our original furniture. Trust me; we'll be fine."

I didn't argue and trailed him and Kate up the stairs. He set the machine on the floor and fiddled with the knobs and dials that would get us back to our time. When he told us it was ready to go, he stood, holding the machine in his arms as we took up our designated places beside him. He flipped the switch, and I prepared for the trip home.

Then, in the sudden blink of an eye, I knew something wasn't right…for some reason, my gut told me we should run, but run from what? The hairs on my arms stood on end, and every instinct in me said we had messed up big time.

At first, it was a gentle rumble, like thunder in the distance. It vibrated beneath my feet and shook the walls. Then the subtle shaking turned to tremors, shooting so hard through the wooden floorboards they started to pull up out of the floor. Earthquake. It had to be an earthquake! There'd been no intense shaking the previous times we did this so what had changed? Panic set in and I wanted to tell him I'd changed my mind. But it was too late. The shaking turned violent, sending me to my knees, with Kate, my best friend beside me.

My brother, on the other hand, whooped with excitement. I guessed he thought that the new part had caused a power boost. Typical Oliver to think this was something to be jumping for joy about, instead of freaking out. He was the genius. He should be the one realizing that something was wrong, terribly wrong.

We pulled ourselves up using the furniture and clung on tightly so we could stay on our feet. Kate's face was pale, and she opened her mouth in fear. I was sure my expression was no different.

Trinkets and books from around the room lifted into the air, hovering all on their own as if gravity no longer affected them. The shaking that had paused for a moment picked up again violently; I waited for the house to collapse on top of us, burying us alive. Bad idea, this was a very bad idea! Whatever part Oliver used had messed up the machine somehow, it must have. Cracks appeared in the walls, and I clung to Kate's hand.

Oliver backed his way towards us. He grabbed my other hand, gulping. "I think we made a mistake," I swore I heard him yell, but the crackling sound that filled the room stole his words away. I took a breath to reply, and a gust of air snatched my voice away from me.

Then, for a split second, time stood still. A heavy silence enveloped the room. I wasn't sure what was more frightening, the silence, or the shaking of the objects as they hovered before our eyes. It was the same and yet so different. What had we done wrong?

Abruptly, it seemed that time sped up as everything blurred into a faded haze. I squeezed Kate and Oliver's hands tighter, but they were pulled away from me. My gut twisted as I was lifted off my feet, my scream dying in my throat. I felt as though we'd been whipped into a tornado as everything spun in a frantic motion around us.

A few seconds later, I landed on my butt and heard grunts from Kate and Oliver, too. I opened my eyes, blinking as I tried to take in my surroundings.

Very different surroundings.

I had a sinking feeling our experiment had worked.

But instead of being overjoyed and excited, I was terrified.

Completely terrified.

The house was our house, but it was dark and dank. Cobwebs hung from the ceiling, and a few inches of dust covered the tables and furniture around us. The air was heavy, and all the windows looked like they were boarded up.

"Oliver?" I whispered, my voice cracking. "Oliver, what happened?"

He ran his hands along the coffee table, frowning at the dust as it fell from his fingertips. "I don't...I don't know," he whispered and checked his watch.
"It's the right day and time, but this...this isn't our home. It can't be."

Slowly, I walked around the living room. The furniture was familiar, but it was old and dilapidated, covered in dirt and stains, and the cushioning on the sofa was ripped in various places. The wind whistled through the boards covering the windows, and when I reached for a light switch, I found there was no power. It was our home, but no one had been here in years. Where was Mom? What had we done?

"Oliver, I don't like this. We need to get out of here."

"And go where? We came from twenty years in the future; we can't just go back there again."

"So we're stuck here? We don't even know where here is?" I spun around, hoping that if I shut my eyes tightly enough, everything would magically return to normal.

But that didn't happen. Instead, everything remained the same. Dark and dank and dirty.

I spun around again and spied Kate, clasping her hands nervously as her whole body trembled. For a horrible second, I'd forgotten my friend was with us. What about her family? Her house?

"Kate, we should check your place, too. See what's going on," I suggested frantically.

She nodded but didn't say a word. Oliver nodded too and hoisted the machine up into his arms. "Let me grab a bag and then we can head out. Hopefully, we'll find some answers in town."

I hoped so. I wanted to know where our mother was. The fact that she wasn't in the house terrified me almost more than I wanted to admit. Inside, I was screaming that we'd messed up big time. What had we changed? We still had our machine. Thaddeus didn't have it, and it didn't make sense that by going into the future we'd changed something that would affect the past like this.

Oliver disappeared upstairs; I guessed to look through his old room and find a backpack. When he came back down, his face was white, and his hands were shaking.

"Oliver? What's wrong? What's up there?" I asked, not sure I wanted to hear the answer.

He shoved the machine in an old bag I didn't recognize.

Slinging the bag onto his shoulder, he replied, "Nothing, let's just get out of here."

"No, not until you tell me what you saw." I stepped in front of him, blocking his escape and grabbing his arms. "It's not…it's not Mom, is it?"

"What? No," he grunted and grabbed the straps of the bag tightly in his hands. "But I wasn't kidding when I said there's nothing up there. Our rooms…they're completely empty. I'm not sure we ever lived here with Mom. Ever."

I couldn't move after he spoke. It wasn't possible, couldn't be. We'd lived here all our lives.

"We'll find her, Holly," He whispered and squeezed my hand. "Let's just get out of this place first; it's creeping me out."

Numbly, I nodded and followed him out the front door, Kate walking beside me. We held hands as we went and I felt her shaking just as much as I was. We had no idea what we'd find at her house. But the farther we walked along the street, the more I knew that something was horribly wrong. All the houses appeared dilapidated and rundown as if the area had been deserted at one point or another. The yards were overgrown, and there was no one else in sight; no one on the streets anywhere. It was overcast and cold. I wished I would have looked for a jacket to wrap around myself or something to keep the chill out of my bones, but there was no point going back now.

"Oh no," Kate whispered, and I looked up to see her house.

Or what was left of it.

"Where…where are my parents? Guys…what happened here?" she asked, clutching at my arm.

There were broken panes in every window, and the walls were discolored and dirty looking, the paint cracked and stained. Oliver walked to the front door, but Kate was too scared to follow. He rang the doorbell a few times, but I guessed it wasn't working when he pounded his fist on the door instead. On the second hit, it shuddered and fell right in off its hinges. It landed with a thud and Kate gasped beside me.

"Mom! Dad!" she screamed, bolting into the house before I could catch her. "Mom!"

"Kate! Hold on!" Oliver rushed in behind her. "Wait for me!"

I reached the front door as the house groaned from their combined weight. Although from the outside, it looked solid enough, the interior seemed ready to collapse. "Oliver! Get her out of there!" I yelled, watching the house vibrate. "Oliver!"

I saw dust and dirt fall from the ceiling. I held my breath, listening as Oliver tried to tell Kate they had to leave. She was crying, still calling out for her parents, but they weren't there. No one was there, and it was all our fault. I wasn't sure what exactly we had done, but I knew it was because of that machine.

"There's no sign of them," Kate whispered as she sank to her knees on the grass outside, tears streaking down her dirty cheeks. "Where are they if they're not here?"

"We'll figure it out," I told her as I knelt beside her. "I swear we will. We'll get to the bottom of this. Kate…Kate," I stammered. "I'm so sorry. This shouldn't have happened! It's all my fault; I know it is."

"All our fault," Oliver corrected bitterly. "And it was my idea to go back again."

"To catch whoever broke into your house," Kate muttered, wiping her face with her hands. "But we made a pact, remember? To always go back together and we all made that choice."

I stared at her, worried that this was too much for her, for all of us.

But she was stronger than that. "You guys are my friends," she insisted, climbing to her feet and planting her hands on her hips. "And friends stick together. Period. We'll go into town and see what we can figure out, right?" With a firm nod of her head, she added, "At least we won't have school for a while!"

I attempted a grin, but try as I might to remain positive, my voice shook with fear. "Yeah, no school..."

At the same time, however, I wondered what we would find instead.

Chapter 9

I hoped we'd leave our street behind and walk right into our tiny, bustling town, but unfortunately, that was not the case. The houses gave way to the park, and beyond that, there should have been a lively street lined with shops and people.

But the town was dead silent.

"No…no! How is this possible?" I yelled in frustration. "What did we do to cause this?"

"I don't know," Oliver whispered, too shocked to say much else. "The only thing we changed was…oh no."

"Oh no, what?" I snapped. "What did you just think of?"

"Thaddeus, he saw Grandpa's machine," he whispered. "He saw how it worked."

"Do you think he made one just like it?" Kate gasped.

"He must have," Oliver sighed. "He had probably been trying for years, and could never get it completely right. When he saw Grandpa's, that was all he needed."

"But how could he suddenly cause the town to be in ruins?" Kate argued.

"He must have gone back in time to years ago," Oliver shook his head in disgust. "And somehow, he caused everything to change."

Oliver's words took a few seconds to register in my head as I tried to process the impact of what we'd done, of what Thaddeus must have done after we left him in our basement.

"Why would he destroy the town though?" Kate asked the question that I was unable to. "Why would he do that?"

"We don't know when this happened. It could have been before we were born, back when Grandpa still lived here," Oliver said. "Come on, let's keep going. Maybe we'll find a phone we can use."

"And call who?" I asked.

Kate had already pulled out her cell phone, but it wasn't working. I didn't bother trying mine, knowing I'd probably get the same result. We technically weren't supposed to be here so whatever phones we had on us were obsolete now.

As we walked down the center of the main street, doors creaked on hinges, and every window was either broken or boarded up. The ice cream store we went to just a few weekends before was dark and empty. Shadows lurked inside, and I moved closer to Oliver as we passed.

I noticed how Oliver's shoulders stiffened and he picked up the pace as more creaking sounded from the surrounding shops. "There's a payphone on the corner up ahead. Anyone got a quarter?"

"Who exactly are you going to call?" I asked as I patted down my pockets and came up with nothing. Kate managed to find a quarter in her pocket and handed it over.

He took the coin and picked up his pace. "Sheriff Biggins. He should know something, right?"

"You think the police department is still up and running?"

"Only one way to find out." He slipped the coin into the phone and held it to his ear. "It's working. That's a plus I guess."

He dialed the number, but within seconds, I knew he hadn't got through. He hung his head, pressing the earpiece harder against his ear as if wishing whatever he heard would change. "Nothing." He slammed the phone back into the receiver making Kate and I jump. "The number has been disconnected."

A bell chimed lightly nearby, and we whipped around, bracing, ready to take off at the first sign of danger. But all we saw was an old man calling to us.

"Is that the guy from the antique store?" I squinted, trying to make out his face. He looked older than I remembered.

"Hurry!" the man was yelling and waving his hand more frantically.

"Let's find out what he wants," Oliver said and gave us a gentle nudge. "What could be worse than what we've already seen?"

We took off back down the main street and slipped into the antique store as the old man held the door open for us. The second we were inside, he closed it and flipped the lock closed.

"Are you three crazy? What are you doing here? You're not supposed to even be in this part of the country anymore!"

"You remember us?" I asked, as he removed his glasses and cleaned them hastily on his shirt.

"Of course, I do. You're the children of Maggie. And you're...Kate. There is no reason for you to be here. You've put yourselves in great danger. Oliver and Holly, I'm certain your mother is in a right state, wondering where you are! And Kate, what will your parents think of you running off like that?"

My jaw dropped, and I didn't have to look at my brother and best friend to know they were most likely mirroring my expression. How did this man know us? How did he know our parents? And he called our mom, Maggie, not Margaret like everyone else did. I watched him rush to the front window and carefully lift a dusty curtain aside and peer out.

"You're lucky I found you as quickly as I did. Why did you leave your homes to come here?"

I shook my head hard. "No, just wait for a second! This is our home. What happened? And who are you? Why are you here if the entire town is a ghost town!" My gaze shifted around his shop and although it was dustier than before, all the junk remained, filling the large space.

He dropped the curtain and backed away from the window, his face paling beneath the few dim lights overhead. "You…you don't know?"

"Know what?" I yelled, Oliver and Kate both turning to me in surprise.

I never yelled. I was usually the quiet one. The girl who put her head down and tried to get through the day. But this? This was too much for any kid to handle. We thought we knew what we were doing, thought we had everything under control, and now…now everything was just gone as if it had never existed.

"You three, you came from the past, didn't you," the old man stated.

"Not sure what you're talking about," Oliver replied, but the man obviously didn't believe him.

"There is no need to hide the truth from me. I know you bought that old machine from my shop, young man."

"That isn't the machine that got us here, we used a different one," I said, and immediately clapped my hand over my mouth, cringing as Oliver rolled his eyes at me. "What? Maybe he can help us. Maybe he knows all about what's going on. Mom found that key here, remember?"

"Indeed she did and for a good reason," the man frowned at us.

We faced him at the same time. "Who are you?" I asked again, quieter this time and in a state of disbelief that this man could know who we were.

He sighed heavily and sat down on a tall, metal stool that he appeared to keep by the window.

"That is a very long story and one I'm not sure you're ready to hear. How about we start with what happened to the town and save my identity for later, hmm?"

I wasn't sure that was good enough, but then my stomach growled loudly. I guess it had been a while since we'd eaten anything, or just stopped moving. The old man smiled softly, and I had the weirdest feeling that somehow, I knew who he was.

"How about some dinner and I'll tell you all about it while you eat?"

He didn't wait for an answer but weaved his way around the various shelves, his heavy steps sounding on a set of wooden stairs somewhere near the back of the store.

"Can we trust him?" I whispered.

"Do we have much choice?" Kate offered. "He might have some answers! I say we at least hear him out, try to find out what happened to our parents." She was wringing her hands again, and I reached out to stop her before she hurt herself.

"We'll find your parents, Kate, I promise."

"Kate's right," Oliver said. "I have a feeling whoever this guy is that he's wrapped up in this mess just like we are."

Oliver headed down the aisle and around the shelves, Kate hurrying behind him to catch up. I smiled when I saw him reach back and hold her hand to guide her.

I waited a few seconds before I followed, glancing around the shop for any more clues as to who this man was. It would take hours to go through every item on the shelves, and we didn't have that kind of time. Making my way towards the back, I followed the sounds of the man's voice as well as my brother's. When a picture caught my eye though, I hesitated, not sure if it was even real.

The picture hung on the wall in a frame; it was quite small, but it was there all the same. I reached out and removed it from the nail that it hung on, wiping my fingers over the glass to stare down at an image that my brain screamed could not be possible.

There, smiling as we stood shoulder to shoulder, was a picture of Oliver and me.

But we were older, much older, and both holding diplomas from some college. Clutching the picture in my hand, I ran up the stairs to confront the old man and figure out what game he was playing at.

Chapter 10

When I reached the second floor of the store, I was surprised to see what was essentially a tiny apartment. The man had his back to us, standing at the counter and stove as he made us something to eat. Kate and Oliver were talking quietly together, the time machine in the bag sitting on the floor at Oliver's feet.

"What's wrong?" Kate asked when she saw me appear in the doorway. "Holly, are you ok?"

Gripping the framed picture in my hand, I moved past her and stood beside the old man as he cut up vegetables to put into a large pot. Without a word, I moved the picture in front of him. His hand stilled. Forgetting about the uncut vegetables, he turned to stare at me.

"Where did you get this?" I demanded, my voice shaking.

"Holly? What is that?" Oliver asked, but I refused to move it away from the old man's sight.

"Who are you? I want a name. Otherwise, the three of us are leaving."

"Leaving would not be wise," the man told me quietly, wiping his hands on a towel before he reached for the framed picture. "May I?"

Reluctantly, I let him take it and watched as he ran his fingers over the faces I knew belonged to Oliver and me. He sighed and moved to sit down at the table, plopping down hard and hanging his head.

"I was so proud of you both that day," he whispered. "Mags was, too. Our kids were all grown up and graduated. It was amazing to see."

"Wait, what?" Oliver asked, his words strained as he peered over to see the framed photo.

I gulped and realized why the old man seemed so familiar when we'd first met him. It took a few seconds before the word finally escaped my lips, and when it did, it was barely audible. "Dad? No, but you…you're old. You can't be…"

"And yet, here I am." He set the picture on the table and took hold of my hand, squeezing it gently. "I wasn't kidding when I said it was a long story. And now that you're here…I'm not even sure where to begin."

"The beginning?" I suggested as tears burned in my eyes. "Dad? Why…why didn't you say it was you when we were here in your store the last time?"

He laughed warmly. Despite him being so old, I knew that it was him.

"Would you have believed me?" he asked. "And besides that, I couldn't risk telling you too much, too soon. I've been watching over you three, the best I could. You, your brother, and your mom."

"But she came into this store. She bought things from you. She didn't know it was you?" Oliver asked, surprised.

"She did joke about me looking familiar, but she didn't say she thought I was her long-lost husband, no." His eyes took on a faraway look of longing. "Oh, how I've missed her, and you two, all these years. Trapped, being able to see you, but not being able to see you, all at the same time. That was what he wanted…to make me suffer for the rest of my days."

"What who wanted?"

The old man, who I now knew was my dad, pushed out of the chair and nodded to another picture on the far wall. "Who do you think? That rotten old man just couldn't leave me alone. Oh no, he had to make life as bad as possible for my family, all because I refused to help him finish what he and William had started."

On the wall hung a photograph. It was of Grandpa and Thaddeus, smiling brightly. Alongside them was our dad when he was young. They all looked so happy in that picture, as though they were best friends.

"You knew about the time machine," Oliver stated. "You helped them work on it?"

"Well, I only worked on it with your grandfather. By the time I came along and married your mother, he'd stopped working with Thaddeus."

I opened my mouth to start asking him more questions, but he held up his hand to stop me.

"I'm going to finish making you something to eat and then we can sit down and talk about everything that's happened since your grandfather's death, and why the town is very different from how you remember it."

Not having any other choice, the three of us took our seats at the table and watched the old man, who was actually our dad, make us dinner for the first time.

***

Soon afterward, the fork clattered into my empty bowl, and I leaned back, anxiously waiting for Dad to start the story. I'd never eaten so quickly before, but all I could think of was how we were finally going to find out what happened to him all those years ago. He finished eating and pushed his bowl aside. A smile lit his face as he looked at us, his kids, and leaned back in his chair.

"Just before your grandpa died," he started, as we leaned closer to catch every word, "he gave me the notes as well as the machine itself to keep safe. I kept them up in the attic where I knew no one would get to them by accident."

"Until we came along, of course," I replied.

His smile widened. "Yes, but you two were meant to find them."

"We were?"

He nodded in answer to my question and opened his mouth to continue, then changed his mind and held up his hand. Getting up from his chair, he began rummaging around in a nearby drawer. He pulled out a large notepad and a pen and returned to the table. "This might help since this story gets a little...complicated."

He marked one end of the page with an X and wrote down a date. "This is when your grandpa decided to stop his work, at least with Thaddeus. He packed everything away and told everyone he was finished with that line of work, as he wanted to dedicate the rest of his days to teaching," Dad explained. "That was until your mother met me. I had a huge interest in science and technology, just like your grandpa. And we became good friends."

"Then you two started doing research together?" Oliver asked, his eyes never leaving our dad's.

"We did," Dad replied. "Your grandpa showed me all of his notes, and we set to work on the machine once again, quietly of course. Your grandpa didn't want anyone else to know. Within a few years, we managed to get it working, and then together, we took our first steps into the future." He marked another X. "Sadly, it was soon after that, your grandpa passed away." Dad marked one more X on the sheet of paper, two years later.

"But on that first trip, what did you see? Where did you go?" I had so many questions that I wanted to be answered.

"You mean when," he said with a wink. "I went far enough into the future to see you kids. And your grandfather and I didn't go just once. He was fascinated to see what you and Oliver would end up doing."

A look of pure pride came over his face as he stared past us at the far wall as if seeing us all grown up again.

"But then things changed. Thaddeus found out what we were up to and he started coming by. We thought nothing of it until he tried to break into the house to steal one of the machines that we'd built."

"One of the machines?" Oliver cut in. "How many did you guys make?"

Dad tilted his head back and forth. "Enough to ensure we had one that worked properly. The one you have with you, of course." We all glanced at the backpack as if to make sure it was still there.

"It was on one of our trips to the future that we realized something." Dad continued. "After Thaddeus attacked your grandpa at the university, we went to the future and found that Grandpa was no longer there. And what was worse...I had disappeared, too."

"How is that possible?" Oliver shook his head, scrunching his face in thought. "What changed?"

"That was precisely what we needed to figure out. By the time we came back, we had found your grandpa's lab had been broken into, and several key parts had been stolen." He marked another spot on the paper. "We couldn't prove it was Thaddeus and for a few months all was quiet...until your grandpa was found dead in his home. The doctor said it was natural causes, but..." He trailed off, and a shiver ran down my spine.

"You think it was Thaddeus?" I whispered, and Dad nodded. "But why?"

"He wanted the time machine to himself, and he wanted to get your grandfather out of the way. I stopped all research after that, shut down the lab, and went about a quiet life with Mags. I assumed everything was fine until one day when I left the house."

"And you never came back," Oliver murmured. "Thaddeus took you away from us?"

He fell silent for a few long moments, and I wondered if he was going to continue or not. He tapped his fingers on the table and his frown deepened before he sucked in a deep breath.

"Thaddeus found me in town one day. He had a machine of his own, but the thing didn't work properly. He switched it on, and I was thrown far into the future. Somehow, I wound up switching places with an older version of myself in the process. The older version came back, and my younger other self was lost somewhere in the void of space and time," he mumbled. "I couldn't very well go home looking like a sixty-year-old man. So, I didn't go back home at all."

My head hurt trying to keep track of what was going on, but then I gave up trying to understand what had happened. I trusted that this man was our dad and he had come back from the future. And our dad, the younger version who should still be living with us now, was trapped somewhere else. I grunted in frustration, mixed with sadness and rested my head on the table. Part of me wished we had never found this machine. But if that had been the case, then we would never have found our dad.

"Is there a way to get you back?" Oliver was asking when I finally lifted my head again. "To swap you back to your normal places?"

"There could be, but that's not your biggest concern right now."

"Why not? We want you back," I argued.

He patted my hand. "And I would like to be back with both of you and your mother, but as you can see, something has changed in this town."

"Our parents," Kate said so quietly, I almost didn't hear her. "What happened to them?"

Dad stood from the table and paced to the counter, leaning heavily against it. "It's strange. I can remember this town the way it was before; the way it was when you first came into the shop. But since then…it's been overshadowed by what Thaddeus did. Ever since his involvement, this has happened."

Fear grew in the back of my mind, but I didn't want to jump to conclusions.

"Before your grandpa died, Thaddeus came out with an invention. It was his own time machine, and he wanted to use it. William, your grandpa, fought against the idea, tried to stop him from moving forward, but then, of course, he died, apparently from a heart attack. So it was left to me to try and put an end to what Thaddeus was doing."

"What was he actually doing?"

Dad turned around to face us, shoulders slumped, and I saw the defeat on his face. "Thaddeus was using the machine to change major events in his life, with no care for what else it might change."

"And he messed up the town? How?"

Dad grimaced. "That, I'm afraid was my fault, and your mom's. She worked with me to try to build another machine so we could counteract Thaddeus' new invention and put a stop to him."

My heart was pounding in my chest, and I felt sick to my stomach at what he was going to say next. "What happened?"

"Thaddeus found out about our plans. That was when he threw me into the future, and my older self was brought back here." His hands gripped the counter harder. "It gets worse I'm afraid."

"Worse how?"

Silence fell over the kitchen as we waited for him to speak.

"Thaddeus bought out the town and then he ruined it. Drove everyone out," he whispered. "I had nothing to stop him with. I was just an old man in an antique store. I watched as every shop was closed down, people were forced to move away. He ensured his revenge was carried out against our family and anyone who thought they could help us."

"And Mom?" I asked, leaning closer. "Where is she? Where are we supposed to be?"

He folded his hands on the table, not meeting our eyes. "Your mom ranted and raved on and on about Thaddeus and the time machine, about how he's the reason Grandpa was dead and that I was gone," he murmured sadly. "She wouldn't give up, and in the end, they took her away, locked her up in a hospital facility for the mentally unstable. And you two...you're now supposed to be in the care of a guardian."

"A facility? For the mentally unstable?" I didn't believe it, didn't want to believe it! Mom couldn't be locked up in one of those places. It was impossible! "We have to see her; we have to get her out! We have to do something."

"I'm afraid you can't just walk in and see her," Dad said sternly. "It doesn't work that way."

"Why not?" Oliver yelled and both Kate and I stared at him amazed. He was furious, his face was red, and his hands were balled into fists on the table. "She's our mom, your wife!" We're going to go see her, and we're going to fix all of this."

"It's not your fault this happened," Dad pointed out, and the three of us cringed.

"What's wrong?" he asked. "What did you do?"

We'd been so wrapped up in what had happened to our dad that we hadn't yet told him of our own ordeal. So, after taking a deep breath, Oliver launched into the story about how our house was broken into and the three of us went back to see who had done it. We told Dad about finding Thaddeus in the basement and how he managed to take a close look at Grandpa's time machine.

"I guess whatever he saw, he used. Then he created his own version of it and changed things," Oliver finished, his voice shaking with anger. "It's because of us that our mom is locked up and the town has died. We can't just leave it like this. We have to do something."

259

I expected a lecture, something, anything from Dad to make us feel bad for what we had done. But instead, he simply got up from the table and moved slowly around the tiny second-story apartment, mumbling under his breath. I couldn't hear what he said, but when he turned back around, he was shaking his head.

"I'm sorry. It won't be possible. If you try anything, you risk making things worse than they already are," he said with finality. "We'll just have to make the best of this."

"Where are my parents?" Kate asked.

"Safe and sound living in another state," Dad assured her. "I'm sure they're extremely worried about you."

"And us? Who's this guardian you said is supposed to be watching out for us?" Oliver asked, getting up from his chair and standing toe to toe with our dad. "Who is it?"

Dad suddenly looked very uncomfortable. "You have to understand, all of this happened when you two were still very, very young."

"Who is it?" I demanded, jumping to my feet. "Just tell us!"

"Thaddeus!" Dad yelled back.

He sighed heavily, his whole body seeming to cave in on itself. "Thaddeus took the two of you in as foster children when your mom was taken away. There was no one else around to care for you."

My jaw dropped, and Oliver moaned in desperation. "How...how could you let him take us?"

"No one believed I was your father," Dad muttered. "I was merely the old man who lived above the antique store. They would never have allowed me to keep you. But Thaddeus, he was a millionaire willing to take in two kids who lost their parents to terrible circumstances. And it was another chance for him to get revenge against me."

"We're not going back to him," I said, stomping my foot for emphasis. "I won't! And I want to see Mom. Where is she? Just take us to her!"

"You won't be allowed inside! Don't you understand? The place is owned and operated by Thaddeus! The second you show your faces he'll be rushing back to claim you two. And he'll know you're not the same Oliver and Kate who lived with him before. He will know that you've come from another time zone and are aware of the truth!" Dad stormed away angrily, but I sensed his anger wasn't meant for us.

He sank into an old armchair, resting his elbows on his knees and holding his face in his hands. His shoulders shook, and I heard a strangled sound erupt from deep inside him. "Dad?"

"I tried," he whispered fiercely, "I tried everything I could to get her out of there. But I'm an old man. I can't bust through windows and climb over walls. I couldn't do anything to help her! Or you two. All I did was get myself tangled up in this mess when I should have left it all alone."

"You and Grandpa, you were discovering something amazing," I insisted. "Something that could change the world for everyone. You didn't do anything wrong. Thaddeus did."

"The second he started poking around, I should have ended it."

"He would have figured out something eventually," Oliver said, stepping forward. "Look, you couldn't do anything before, but you didn't have us with you. We're here now, and we have Grandpa's machine. All we have to do is figure out how to use it properly this time, to set everything right."

Dad lifted his head, tears glimmering in his eyes. "And if everything becomes even worse than it is now?'

I looked to Oliver, and he nodded in agreement at what he knew I was about to say. "I think we're willing to take that chance."

Turning to Kate, I stared at her determined to keep her safe, "Kate, you need to be with your parents. It's too dangerous to come with us."

"Oh no, you're not getting rid of me that easily," she argued. "We got into this mess together; we're sticking together until the end. That was our deal! Remember? Let's go see your mom and kick Thaddeus Banes' butt."

Oliver stuck his hand up in the air, and she turned to him with a grin. They high-fived each other before doing the same to me.

The three of us turned to look at Dad, waiting expectantly for his response. He glanced at each of us in turn, and a sly smile spread slowly across his face.

He pushed to his feet and rested one hand on top of ours and the other underneath, holding all our hands together. "I can't guarantee any good coming from this, but I'm not about to let you go alone. Let's go find your mom and then maybe we can find a way to fix this mess and get our lives back, once and for all!"

We lifted our hands with an excited yelp as he locked eyes with each of us.

"We'll get a few hours' sleep and then get going so we can reach the hospital by morning. And on the way, we can start planning what time zone to go back to so we can stop Thaddeus for good!"

I nodded firmly in agreement and pushed aside my underlying fear of what lay ahead. We had contributed to this mess, and it was up to us to make things right again.

I looked at Kate and Oliver, their eyes shining with excitement and I saw that my brother still had a firm grip on my friend's hand. Even though I was worried about Kate, I was glad to have her with us, and I could see that Oliver felt the same way.

As Kate had said, we would stick together until the end. I just hoped we could recreate the past and get our lives back.

But I knew there was only one way to find out.

Chapter 11

By the time Dad announced that we were ten minutes out from the facility, my legs were bouncing so hard in the back seat of Dad's beat up Chevy truck that Kate finally rested her hands firmly on my knees to try and get me to stop.

"It's going to be fine," she said with an anxious smile.

I nodded, and my legs stopped for a few seconds at least. "Okay, Dad, let's go over the plan again. What are we going to do if we can't just walk in and see Mom?"

"I'm going to distract the front desk nurse. I'll make a commotion and you three are going to sneak past her and into the hallways. Last I heard, your mom was being kept in the east wing," Dad added. A few choice words came out of his mouth, and we muffled our laughter before he added, "Sorry, I don't normally speak that way, but when it comes to Thaddeus, I can't help myself. I would just like to see him put in a jail cell where he belongs."

"Maybe we'll make that happen." Oliver patted the machine on his lap which was still hidden away in the backpack.

We had debated leaving it at the antique store for safekeeping, but it was our only chance of a fast getaway. Once we saw Mom, we needed to go back in time and take her with us. Unfortunately, though, Dad said he had to stay here.

"I've been messed up enough already," he said sadly. "I don't want to drag another version of myself into the present, or past, or anywhere else it doesn't belong."

I closed my eyes for a moment and pictured the four of us living together again, the happy family I knew we could be.

So far, it hadn't been the right time for that to happen. Not yet. I promised myself we'd get there, though. And in my mind, I promised Dad that somehow, we'd get him back, so we could be that family and put all this crazy time travel stuff far behind us.

"As soon as you find your mom, I want you to get out of there, understand?" Dad said as he pulled off the main road onto a winding one leading through a dense forest and up a hill. "I need you to go back to the day you hid everything in the basement, before the break-in. Get the machine out of the basement and take it somewhere safe. Then stay away."

"Are you sure that'll be far enough back?"

"If that's the point when everything changed, it should work. Everything stems from that day."

Oliver and I exchanged a worried glance, but it was all we could do. If that's what Dad thought would work, then we had to trust him. He parked the truck, and the four of us piled out. We drew our hoods over our heads from the jackets Dad had found for us, and he led the way up to the imposing brick building.

The view from the top of the pine tree covered mountain was spectacular and would be beautiful if the place wasn't technically a prison for our mom.

We made our way to the rear where there was a large wrap around porch with a few people sitting at tables, playing cards and talking quietly. Men and women in scrubs were close by, watching the patients. Dad led the way up the few steps and straight inside. A frumpy woman with blond hair sat behind a short desk with two beefy guys not far behind her.

"How can I help you today, sir?" she asked brusquely and I could tell that her smile was fake.

"I'm here to see Thaddeus," Dad stated loudly, and I paused as panic filled my entire being. What was he doing?

For a horrible second, I wondered if we'd been tricked, but then Dad turned back to us, winked, and slammed his hand on the countertop making the woman jump. "Thaddeus Banes! Where is the old codger! I need to have a word with him! The voices said so!"

Dad continued to rant, and the woman backed away from her desk as the two men moved closer. Dad yelled louder, swinging his arms wildly around, creating a spectacle. Oliver grabbed my arm and nodded his head towards the right. There, above the doorway was a sign that said, East Wing. We knew that our mother was down that long corridor somewhere, but as we turned to go, I worried about leaving Dad. What would they do to him? What would happen if Thaddeus appeared? Dad said that he wasn't always on the premises, but that didn't mean he wasn't here now. The men grabbed Dad by the arms, and the woman began speaking into a phone. We had no more time to wait. At any moment, she would look up and realize the three kids who had just been alongside the old man had vanished.

We walked at a brisk pace until we were through the doors, then we ran, peering into every room that we passed. Names were added to some of the doors, and I skimmed each of them, searching for the name, Margaret. At the end of the hall, we hit a T-intersection and spun around in a circle, wondering if we should go right or left. Oliver bounced on his feet, mumbling under his breath before we decided to split up. He went right, and Kate and I took the left hall, my heart beating wildly in my chest as we ran.

"She has to be here," I whispered as I frantically checked every room. "She has to be—"

"Holly!" Oliver called to us from the other end, and we bolted back in his direction. He pointed through a narrow window into a room. A woman sat in a wheelchair, staring blankly through a window covered in bars.

The name by the door said Maggie. "It's Mom," he gasped.

"Is the door locked?" I asked, turning it sharply. To my surprise, it opened. "Let's go."

Oliver hesitated and then followed me in, while Kate stayed outside to keep a lookout. Mom didn't even turn around, she just sighed heavily and held out her hand.

"What pills am I getting today? The funny green ones, or the pretty blue ones?"

"Mom?" I said as I watched a shudder pass over her body. "Mom, it's Holly, your daughter. Oliver's here too, and we're not...we're not from this time." I was worried that talking about time travel might make things worse, but we couldn't stand there wasting the few precious minutes that Dad had managed to give us.

"We came to take you with us and make everything right again," Oliver added. "Mom?"

She failed to respond and fear spiked inside me. But then suddenly she was on her feet, as though somehow we had managed to get through the fog in her head. She hugged us to her, crying. "My kids! My real kids! You found me; I knew you would. I knew somehow you'd figure all this out!"

We hugged her back, tears spilling from my eyes at my guilt over getting her into this horrible mess. "Dad's here, too. Well, old dad," I explained quickly. "He distracted the orderlies. We're getting you out of here, going back to fix everything up."

She cupped our cheeks in her hands, beaming at us. "Smart, just like your dad. Wait...you said he's here?"

"Old dad, from the future," Oliver corrected. "It's a long story, but there's no time. We have to go. Now!"

"Guys! We're in trouble!" Kate yelped a second before an alarm sounded throughout the building.

266

Kate managed to step back into the room just as the door closed and a heavy lock clanked into place. "No!"

All four of us rushed to it, tugging on it, desperate to get out, but the door wouldn't budge.

"The machine! We have to use it. Now!" I told Oliver, and he nodded, placing the bag on the floor of the room. We gathered around as he set the right date and time. Loud yelling could be heard from the corridor, and I urged him on, willing him to hurry.

Faces appeared in the window of the door. A key grated in the lock and before Oliver could even flip the switch, the door was thrown open, and orderlies rushed in, grabbing us and yanking us away from our only chance of escape.

"Get off me!" Mom yelled. "Get away from my kids!"

"Now, is that any way to behave, Maggie?"

My blood ran cold at the sound of that voice, and I knew instantly who stood in the doorway behind us.

Thaddeus Banes leered as he glanced from the machine then up to Oliver, Kate, and finally me.

"Well now, isn't this a surprise! My foster children have come to visit their mother, though something tells me you two are quite different. Is that correct?"

He bent down and picked up the machine. Oliver screamed at him to put it down. But Thaddeus didn't listen. Tucking it safely under his arm, he ordered the guards. "Take them away. We have much to discuss. All of us."

Our screams and fighting did nothing as we were dragged out of Mom's room, through the facility.

Desperately, I tried to shake off the hands that held me, but it was no use. The firm grip on my arms was too strong. And as I stared down the bleak hallway that stretched out ahead of us, I knew we were in terrible trouble.

Would we ever leave these this place again?

Book 4
The Final Journey

Chapter 1

I woke up groggy and confused. When I looked around and stared at my unfamiliar surroundings, I was filled with a crippling panic.

The walls were painted a sickly green, and bars were covering the window. As I swung my legs over the bed and my feet hit the floor, I strained to remember what had happened. Then all of a sudden it came tumbling back and the memories appeared in my head one after another.

We were in some type of messed up present time...and...Dad. We'd found Dad! But he was old Dad! I glanced around the room, and the full impact of what had happened made me gasp as if the wind had been knocked right out of me.

"Mom!"

We'd found Mom locked up in this strange facility and it was all because of Thaddeus! We were trapped here in this place for the mentally unstable because of him. I had no way of knowing how long we'd been here, or even if all the others were still here. But I had to get to Oliver. We had to find both our parents, and we had to find Kate!

I sprinted to the door and banged on it until my hands hurt, but the orderlies standing in the hallway ignored me. There were bars on the window, and I could barely make out their shapes through the colored glass.

"I shouldn't be in here! Let me out!"

"Pipe down," one of them grunted thumping on the other side of the door.

"Open the door! Where are my parents? Where's my brother?" I banged on the door again, my palms going numb as I continued to yell. But the orderlies ignored me.

I pressed my ear to the door and listened for other sounds, perhaps sounds of Oliver and Kate also trying to get out of their rooms. There was nothing except silence. Kicking the door, annoyed, I hoped for some sort of reaction. But all I managed to do was stub my toe. I stared back at the locked door defiantly.

I wasn't going to give up; not now that we'd found Dad. Except he was the wrong dad. And to get the dad we wanted, the one who had disappeared from our lives long ago, one of us would be forced to jump way into the future to find the real one and bring him back. My temples gave a sharp throb at the idea of how messed up everything was now, all because of me finding that stupid machine.

But at the same time, if I hadn't found it, we'd never have found Dad at all, and we'd also never know there was a chance of bringing our original dad back to us.

"Let me out of here!" I hollered one more time.

There was still no response, no one to open the door and allow me to escape. I paced around the tiny room, rattling the bars on the window every time I passed, just in case. I needed to think; I needed to come up with a plan. But even if I did bust out of this room, what then? I had no idea where anyone else was, or the machine, or how to even use it!

"Holly!"

I froze at the whispering voice. "Oliver?"

"Yeah, down here."

"Down where?" I spun around, searching for the voice. I had no idea where it was coming from and for a horrible second, I thought that maybe I was going crazy after all.

"Down here. On the floor near the wall. Hurry up!"

I stared at the large bed that stood against the wall. Oliver's voice was coming from beneath it.

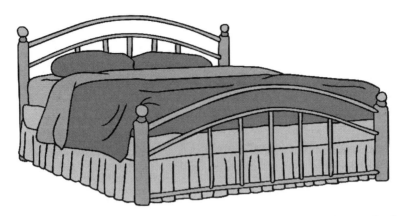

Glancing at the door, I could see no faces through the window, so I sank to the floor, lifted the bedsheets and peered beneath the bed. At first glance, all I found was a dark space and a dusty floor. But when I crawled further underneath, I spotted what looked like a vent cut into a section of the wall. With the bed placed directly above it, I had no idea the vent existed. Then I heard Oliver's voice again and knew I hadn't imagined it.

I shimmied further under the bed. "Oliver?"

"Yes," he called back. "Kate's in another room on the other side of mine. If we're going to get out of this, we need to get that machine."

"Yeah, but we have no idea where the machine is!"

"Do you think Thaddeus is going to let that thing out of his sight? I guarantee it's with him in his office," Oliver's words poured out in a rush. "I know where his office is. I saw it when they dragged us down the corridor. We need to get out of here and get that machine. And we need to get Mom."

"What about Dad?"

"I think he might have to stay here, so we can figure out how to get his other self back."

I worried about losing Dad, even if he was the old version. Any dad in our lives was better than no dad at all. But all we could do was hope that Oliver's idea would work.

272

"I take it you have some genius plan?"

"Maybe," he replied. "If we can get out of these rooms."

"Well, Thaddeus can't keep us in here forever. That's illegal, right? I mean, technically, we're in his care," I cringed at the thought. "Can't we report him for abuse or something?"

"He owns this place so he can probably do whatever he wants and no one would know about it," Oliver muttered. "It's not like we have any other family to complain to."

A cold chill shot down my spine at the notion of Thaddeus having such control over us. I asked Oliver again what his plan was.

"He's going to want to talk to us soon, I guarantee it. He's too curious about everything we've done not to ask us about the machine and what we did to get it working. The second we get to his office, we need to find the machine, knock him out, grab Mom and Kate, and get out of here."

"And go where exactly?"

"Back to the time zone that Dad said we needed to go to. We have to stop Thaddeus from ever finding the machine in the basement," Oliver replied. "Then, we have to find a way to get Dad and destroy the machine. For good."

"You do realize that none of our plans have worked yet?" I said quietly, glaring at the vent as if I could see Oliver instead. "And I mean, none of our plans at all, not a single one. Every time we've messed something up."

"Okay, Holly...be a negative Nancy! And anyway, do you have any better ideas?"

I rolled my eyes. "Just saying...every time we've gone back to do something small, something else changes. What if this time we go back and make things even worse?" I hated to imagine what could be worse than this, but there was always a chance.

"We won't, have a little faith."

I was trying, but after seeing how dark and depressing our world could be, it was hard to think of ever getting back to our happy lives, or imagining finding a way to have Dad there with us again. To have a chance to grow up with him, see him with Mom and be a complete family was something I'd always dreamed of.

I wanted to talk to Oliver some more about it, to try to figure out a few more details. But he mumbled something about hearing keys, and when I tilted my head towards the door, I heard them too. It was the sound of something loud and clanking moving closer.

Quickly, I shuffled back out from under the bed and jumped to my feet, just as voices sounded in the hall, and a key turned in the lock. I watched the door open and found myself staring at a stern-faced woman in a blue uniform, wearing a nurse's cap.

She stomped inside and glowered at me. "Dr. Banes would like to speak with you, now."

"Sure, why not," I mumbled as I stepped nervously forward.

She followed me out of the room, grabbed my upper arm, and dragged me down the hall.

"Wait, is my brother coming?" I asked, staring back over my shoulder, and digging my feet in. "Stop! I want to see my brother! Let me go!"

"Dr. Banes will meet with him in due time," the nurse informed me and pulled harder on my arm. I winced and tried to pry away her cold fingers, but her nails dug in. "Don't make any more trouble for yourself," she warned.

I let my legs go limp and plopped down onto the floor. The nurse tripped and almost fell to the floor herself. Yelling for the orderlies, she glared at me. "Really, what will Dr. Banes think of you?'

"I don't care! I don't want to see him without my brother! Let Oliver out right now!"

"OLIVERRRRRR!!" I screamed his name at the top of my lungs, but the two orderlies appeared and simply picked me up by my arms and carried me down the hallway.

I kicked and flailed, but there was no getting out of their hold. The nurse, who strode purposefully along in front of us, smirked at me over her shoulder then turned and led the way down the long hallway. I tried to bite back my fear, but couldn't control my trembling as the men set me down outside a solid wooden office door. The nurse knocked, and a voice on the other side beckoned her to enter. She swung the door open to reveal Thaddeus seated behind a large, timber desk. His hands were folded on the desktop, and he offered up a pitying smile that I knew was completely fake.

The orderlies shoved me forward, and the nurse pointed to a chair. "Sit down and behave yourself."

I stared defiantly back at her, and her scowl deepened so much, I thought it might become permanent.

"Thank you, that will be all," Thaddeus said to the nurse. "Please wait outside."

She did as he asked and the door closed with a horrible sense of finality. I refused to look at Thaddeus, and instead, allowed my eyes to wander around his office. I was convinced the machine had to be there. Oliver knew what he was talking about, he always did. So where was the machine?

"I must admit, I did not expect to see you or your brother anytime soon, at least not the versions who understood what was happening," Thaddeus began. "Part of me hoped I would never see you, but now that you're here, I do have several questions I'd like you to answer."

I said nothing and kept my gaze averted.

"We don't have to make this more difficult than it is," he went on. "This life is admittedly very different from the one you led before. However, if you allow me to explain, I think you'll find there are certain…advantages to remaining here in this present time."

I sniggered at him in disgust. "You know, for being a genius and all, you're pretty stupid. Why would I want to be here where my mom is locked up in some tiny room, my hometown is gone, and I still don't really have my dad? Why?"

A smile remained on his face as he sighed. "In this life, you'll be able to gain access to whatever college you want. You can travel, you can see the world, you can do and have so many things that were not available to you before. In that other life, you were trapped in an insignificant little town with a mother who barely earned enough money to make ends meet."

My eyes shot to his. I glared at him, and he smirked. "You have so much potential, Holly, just as your brother does. He could study under me; learn everything I know. He could change the world."

"Like you did? You made everything worse! You ruined our lives!"

"If your grandfather had simply done as I'd asked, if he had been ready to take that last step, we would never have found ourselves in this situation!" His face turned bright red, and he shot to his feet. "That machine was meant to be our destiny, and he tried to take it away from me!"

He pointed as he bellowed, and I shifted my gaze to see Oliver's bag sitting in the corner of the room.

Alongside it, sat the time machine. It was right there, so close. I stared at it, willing myself to leap for it. But I had to get past Thaddeus, and a nurse plus two orderlies were standing guard outside the door. What chance did I have?

At the same time though, I knew the second I left that office, I'd never get another opportunity.

I had no idea what time zone the machine was set to, or if it had even changed since we arrived. But I needed to get the machine and get away from Thaddeus so I could fix this mess for good.

I inched forward in my chair, making it easier for me to bolt towards the machine. I was much closer to it than Thaddeus who would have to run around the desk to reach me. I was aware of the orderlies and the nurse outside the door, but I had an idea to solve that problem.

There was one thing making me hesitate though. I was scared to use the machine alone. Oliver always told me I was smart, but he could think on his feet, he knew how to fix that thing if something went wrong. If it malfunctioned, if it broke along the way, I'd be stuck wherever it dumped me, and there was a chance I could end up in a place without Oliver to help me make things right.

I stared at the machine, hesitant and uncertain.

"Now then," Thaddeus suddenly said, causing me to jump in my seat. "I believe that you, your brother and I, have all got off on the wrong foot. I propose we start over."

"Just like that?" I said, hoping I sounded nervous because of what we were talking about, and not because of what I was building up the courage to do.

"Yes. Your grandfather and your father both saw flaws in my plans. But you two, you have so much you can help me to achieve, starting with telling me all about your adventures together. I want every detail, where you went, who you spoke to…"

He kept going, but I stopped listening as a new part of my crazy plan appeared in my head. During our first adventure back in time, I saw myself, and I started to disappear. If I used that machine and dragged Thaddeus with me…all he had to do was see himself and he'd be gone! Finished! I gulped at the idea of technically ending someone's life, but he was the reason Dad left us, and probably the reason that Grandpa died. He was the reason for all of this. Thaddeus wasn't a man. He was a monster. And I was going to stop him.

Knowing if I waited any longer I'd lose my nerve, I gripped the arms of the chair, took a deep breath, and lunged for the machine.

"Stop!" Thaddeus bellowed. I ignored him and flicked the lock on the office door as I passed by.

I sank to the floor and grabbed the machine, flipping the switch and holding on tight as Thaddeus hurried towards me. He grabbed for it, but I grasped it even more firmly and twisted it away to prevent him from reaching the switch. Blue light slipped out, surrounding us. As he yelled at me, the orderlies banged on the door, trying to force it open.

"What have you done?" he shouted, yanking even harder. But I had a death grip on the machine and wasn't about to give it up. "Stop! You don't know what you're doing!" he yelled hysterically.

What he said was true, but I wasn't about to stop now.

Blue light filled the office. The walls, his desk, and the items on top began to spin and shake. His hands almost knocked the dials out of place, but I stumbled back from him, clutching the machine to my chest.

Then I realized too late what was about to happen. Disappearing from that time zone, I landed hard on an office floor...without Thaddeus. He'd let go too soon.

"No!" I muttered, filled with frustration as I pushed to my feet. Now I'd have to find another way to make him face himself. But at least, I had the machine.

When I glanced around, my brain registered the fact that I was still in the facility. I gulped as I realized how bad of an idea this was. I hadn't done anything except go back to the day we'd arrived in town. This meant I had a chance of running into myself.

But that also meant I could find Oliver and Kate!

I dug around the office until I found a bag that could hold the machine. Hands shaking, I managed to get it tucked out of sight, and I quickly slung the bag over my shoulder. Then, quietly and slowly, I opened the office door. There were no orderlies and no nurse.

All I had to do was get out of the building and find a way to get back to town...without running into myself and disappearing for good.

Chapter 2

Following the path that led along the side of the road, I set off at a fast pace in the direction we had come from. Although it had only been a short drive in the car with Dad, it took much, much longer to walk. By the time I saw the familiar streets of our town, still rundown and haunted looking, several hours had passed, and I was exhausted.

I sat on the ground for a few minutes to rest my cramped legs. On the bright side, when Oliver, Kate and I had originally landed in this old and shabby township, I was sure it had been a little later in the day. Because of this, I now had time to get prepared and avoid the chance of bumping into myself.

The machine on my back was heavy, but I wasn't about to remove it, just in case. I might not have seen Thaddeus when I left the facility, but that didn't mean he didn't know where I was, or what I was up to. That man seemed to show up where we least expected him, and this time…this time I was going to be ready.

All I needed to do now was find Oliver. I had to stop him from going to the antique store and making plans to go to the facility with Dad. Instead, I had to convince Oliver to come with me. And at the same time, I had to avoid allowing my other self to see me.

Scrambling to find a place to hide out and watch for them to arrive…watch out for me to arrive…I decided the ice cream shop would be the best choice. I found an unlocked door that led to the darkened interior and hunkered down inside to wait. It wasn't until I was alone in the quiet of the shop that I realized how hard I was breathing, and how hard I was shaking. My nerves were so on edge that I was struggling to maintain control.

I knew I needed a new plan to get Thaddeus back with me so I could make him see himself, but for that, I needed Oliver.

By the time I heard voices breaking through the hovering silence, I was no closer to understanding what I was about to do. I couldn't let myself see myself, but I had to get Oliver away from Kate and…me.

"This is going to get confusing," I whispered aloud as I moved towards the windows, cringing when I bumped a few boards and caused them to fall to the floor with a crash.

Outside, Kate, Oliver, and the other Holly jumped and looked cautiously around before quickening their pace. Suddenly, our walk down Main Street made a lot more sense, as I knew exactly what was going to happen. Soon enough, they were going to reach the pay phone and then the old version of our dad was going to step out of that antique store…

I froze in my spot when the realization dawned on me…I should have gone to the antique store first! What had I been thinking? I almost smacked myself in the forehead with frustration for not realizing my mistake sooner.

With little time to spare, I sneaked quietly out of the ice cream shop and sprinted across the street just as Oliver reached the payphone. Knocking gently on the door of the store, I begged silently for Dad to hurry and open it. I needed to get inside and out of sight before Oliver and the others turned around and saw me. Finally, I heard the lock click free, and a very confused older version of my dad poked his head out.

Without saying a word, I rushed inside and closed the door. "I have to hide in here somewhere, so I don't see myself!"

"Holly?"

"Yes, Dad, it's me," I said and watched his eyes widen as he stood in shocked surprise, staring at me.

"Look, I'll explain soon, but I know you're our dad and I know you were about to go outside and call that group of kids in." I pointed through the window to Oliver, Kate, and my other self. "You still need to get the three of them off the street but is there somewhere I can hide until it's safe to talk? Please? Something bad has happened, and I need your help!"

He sputtered for a moment before he managed to say, "Hide in my back office, down there, quickly."

I nodded and raced through to the back of the store out of sight. A moment later, I heard the front door open and Dad's voice calling out to Oliver, Kate, and the other me. Soon after, they entered the shop, and I peeked out of the office door to see the recent event play out all over again, just like pressing rewind on a movie.

Eventually, their steps disappeared upstairs and I sat down on the floor, staring at the machine in the bag. I waited impatiently for Dad to come back down so I could explain everything and get his help.

***

I wasn't sure how much time passed while I waited. But the entire time, I kept a close eye on the machine, scared it would somehow disappear, and my plan for using it against Thaddeus would fail. I still had no real idea of what I was doing and my stomach ached from worry over Oliver, the one I left back at the facility. And Kate. And Mom and Dad. The thought of them all stuck in those tiny rooms in that horrible place ate away at me, and especially the fact that Mom had been locked up there because she was considered a crazy person.

Everything was so messed up, and it was technically all my fault. I was the one who had gone poking around in the attic and found the machine.

And although we were able to meet our dad, what if we couldn't fix anything? What if all we were doing was reaffirming that he wasn't meant to be with us and now we'd never have a chance to get our family back together again? As I sat there, the doubts piled up around me, and it became harder and harder to believe any good was going to come of this.

The doorknob suddenly turned, and I quickly wiped the tears from my cheeks. When the door opened, Dad stood there, his brow creasing with worry the second he saw me.

"Holly? Are you okay?"

I sniffed hard and tried to smile.

His face softened, and he sighed, holding out his arms. "Come here, kiddo."

I didn't want to break down and cry, but seeing Dad standing there, not the Dad I should've had, but a much older version that got dragged into this mess just like we did, had me crying hard as I went to him. He hugged me close, just as I always imagined him doing when I wished he was around. I began rambling on about something or other when he chuckled in my ear.

"What's so funny?" I mumbled as he dabbed at my cheeks with a handkerchief.

"You are just like your mother, that's what," he smiled. "Always forgetting to see the good possibilities before you rush towards how horrible everything is."

"But everything's so messed up! Look at what we did to our hometown! And Mom, and what happened to you...all of it is so bad!" I hung my head as the weight of our latest mistake hit me again. "I know what happens at the facility. You can't go there!"

He opened his mouth as if to ask me how I knew that, then gave his head a little shake. "Okay, we won't go there Holly, but you have to keep holding onto hope that we'll figure this out. Everything will be alright again."

"How do you know?" I asked. "How? Every time we've used that machine, things have become worse, not better. Either that or we've changed things without even realizing it! What if we do something and we can't go back...if we ruin everything for good? What then?"

"We won't," he promised and held my hands tightly. "You are two of the brightest kids ever. You and your brother have already done things I never thought you'd be capable of."

"I think most of it was by accident," I mumbled.

His smile widened. "Maybe. But you know your grandpa didn't get the machine to work for him either until a freak accident! He was stuck for years on those plans of his until one day he was so mad that he kicked the thing, and then it worked. Just like that."

"So, you're saying we should kick it?" I suggested.

He shrugged. "Metaphorically speaking, you should kick it I think."

I wasn't sure that made sense, but then I heard footsteps coming closer, and Oliver's voice. "Hey, Dad? What did you want to show me?"

284

Oliver stepped into the doorway and blinked a few times before his face screwed up. "Holly? What…wait, why are you down here…" His gaze drifted past me to the machine on the floor. "What's that doing down here? I left it…I left it upstairs."

"Different machine," I told him, "and I'm a different Holly."

"Right, yeah, cause that makes sense," he muttered. I watched him run a hand through his hair as he blew out a heavy breath. His cheeks puffed out, and he looked as though he was either going to throw up or that he desperately needed to sit down and sleep for a while so he could pretend this was all a bad dream. I knew the feeling well.

He stared at me for a moment longer before speaking. "So…exactly what time zone are you from?"

I glanced from him to Dad then down to the machine. "It's complicated. But I'm here now, and I need your help. You and Kate and me, Mom and Dad…all get stuck in that facility for the mentally unstable with Thaddeus," I explained briefly. "We were separated, and when I saw the machine, I took a chance. I meant to bring Thaddeus back with me—"

"What? Why would you do that?" Oliver's voice rang out in alarm.

Dad shushed him and took a quick peek into the shop, making sure Kate or the other me hadn't come to investigate all the ruckus. He gently closed the door.

"Because…I may have come up with a plan." I wrung my hands nervously, unsure if he would go for this or not. "Remember when I first accidentally saw myself?" I held up my hands, recalling the way they'd disappeared before my eyes. I shuddered at the idea of it happening again and pressed myself even deeper into the office, just in case the other Holly came poking around. The door was closed, but I knew myself all too well. I was nosey by nature, and a closed door wouldn't stop me from bursting inside to see what was going on.

"Yeah, but what does that have to do with Thaddeus?" Oliver frowned.

Before I could answer, Dad's eyes lit up, and he grinned. Then he started shaking his head. "No, absolutely not. I will not have you going through with it."

"What do you mean, no?" I asked quickly. "Come on, we get Thaddeus to see his other self, and then he disappears. It's perfect!"

"No, it's too dangerous. I do not want you attempting to drag Thaddeus around with you and that machine! It's too risky, and I will not have you and Oliver risking your lives."

"But Dad, this could fix everything!"

"Or it could make everything worse; it could ruin what few chances you have of getting things back to the way they were," he argued. And a few more worry lines seemed to appear on his face. "Trust me, kids, Thaddeus is a smart, dangerous man. I know you think this is a good plan, Holly, but he always manages to figure everything out before you even finish knowing what you're going to do."

Oliver glanced at me nervously as Dad paced around

his office. "Dad, what happened back then? On the day you disappeared. You never actually told us."

"I poked my nose in Thaddeus' business, trying to get him to stop."

"Dad? Please just tell us what's going on here," I urged.

He had that same worried look Oliver would get when he was overthinking something for school or a new invention of his. But after a slight pause, Dad sighed heavily and then began to speak. "The first time, Thaddeus contacted me and said he wanted to meet and talk things over. I wanted nothing to do with the project, not after your grandpa purposely tucked away all the notes and hid the machine. He'd given me that locked box for a reason and I planned on keeping it secret, keeping it safe as your grandpa requested I do."

"The letter we found from Grandpa," Oliver said slowly, "it said something about solving the greatest mystery of our lives. That was finding you, right?"

"Well, he had gone into the future alone and when he came back that last time...he was different, worried." Dad sank onto a stool, pulled his handkerchief from his pocket and took his glasses from his nose to clean them. "We packed everything up, the machine, all his notes, everything. Then not long after that, he passed away, and I never looked at the notes or the machine again. I couldn't bring myself to mess with something that had brought so much tragedy into his life, and mine. Your mom missed him terribly. She could barely stand to talk about him, so I let his memory rest in peace, along with all of his work."

I exchanged a confused glance with Oliver, but he was too busy watching Dad.

"Then," Dad continued, replacing his glasses, "Thaddeus began contacting me. He called at first, sent a few messages and your mom and I ignored him. We went about our lives, I taught at the school, and we enjoyed our time together with you kids, as a family." His eyes narrowed and his body hunched.

"Dad? What happened next?"

"He showed up at the house when I wasn't at home," Dad whispered angrily. "Upset Maggie so much. She was in a panic, thinking he was there to hurt her or one of you. When she told me, I threatened him, warned him to stay away from us.

"So, what happened?" I asked, already knowing it wouldn't be that easy.

"He said if I wanted him to stay out of our lives, I had to meet him and bring William's notes." He hesitated for a second before he went on. "So I agreed to meet him at the storage lot that's just down the road from here."

"What?" Oliver exclaimed, but Dad held up his hand.

"I showed up, even though I had no intention of giving him anything he could use. I planned to see what he had and destroy it all for good. Get him off this time-machine madness and be done with it. Maybe even figure out if he had anything to do with your grandfather's death and get the police after him." Dad smiled sadly. "But the second the door closed on that storage unit, I knew I'd made a big mistake. I'd underestimated him just as everyone else had and I wound up paying the price."

"So, you remember all that?" I asked, really wishing we could get out of this confusing timeline and back to normal.

"Yes, I remember it all. My young self was thrown through the years until I was an old man. When I landed back in the storage unit, Thaddeus was waiting for me with the news of what had happened…and with the knowledge that I would never see you kids or Maggie, again."

"But Mom, she would've understood," I argued. "You could've gone to her and told her what happened!"

"It wasn't that easy. How could I go back to her? And how could I explain it to you kids? I look like your grandpa, not your dad." He shook his head. "No, it was safer for everyone if I stayed away. Though it killed me to do it."

I felt so sad at the pain in his words as he spoke. "But I had to stay away from you three, and from a distance, I watched Maggie fall apart because I'd disappeared."

I rested a hand on his shoulder. Oliver did the same. He reached up to hold both our hands as he sniffed hard, fighting back the tears.

"We're going to fix this," Oliver said sincerely. "We'll find a way to get our family back together again."

"I can't let you keep bouncing around through time. I will not let your mother lose the two of you permanently. I won't."

"But if we don't do anything then we're stuck in this present," I reminded him gently. "Dad, we can do this. Oliver and I, I know we can. You have to trust us. We're your kids, remember? I'm pretty sure Oliver is just as smart as you are."

"And Holly's as crazy brave," Oliver said, glancing at me. "She came back here from the facility all by herself to stop us from walking into a trap."

Dad still didn't look convinced. But we had no other options.

"Uh, Holly?" a voice sounded from behind Oliver.

The three of us whipped towards the door that we hadn't heard open. I realized that thankfully, it was only Kate standing there and not my other self. She looked horribly confused. She pointed at me then turned and looked towards the stairs. She blinked a few times, then blinked again before stepping inside to join us.

"Whatever…" she said, shaking her head trying to process the fact that I was standing in front of her. "I'm assuming something went wrong?"

I stared at her blankly then laughed as I hugged her. "This is why I love you," I told her as she hugged me back. "Nothing bothers the great Kate."

"I wouldn't say that…but, you're here from…what…the past or the future?"

"The future. And yeah, I'm here because things went wrong, really wrong."

Kate nodded slowly. "Okay, so what do we need to do now? And we'd better hurry before the other Holly comes downstairs and finds you here."

Dad stood up from his stool and placed the machine on his desk. "Your grandad always talked about some failsafe switch, a reset in case something went wrong while the machine was in use," He peered at it closely, turning it over to check underneath. "The question is…where is it?"

He set the machine down again and spun it around, removing the back panel. Oliver looked on, fascinated as he leaned closer and watched Dad pull out a bundle of wires that seemed to run through the entire system. I peeked inside the machine and shook my head. It was very complex looking, and I was relieved that Dad and Oliver were there with me.

"So, what would the failsafe switch do?" Oliver asked as Dad separated the wires carefully and slowly until we were all staring down at a rainbow of color.

"It was meant to take you back to the first time you used the machine. And by doing so, the theory was it would erase all the flow-on effects of your time travel. That was the theory, mind you."

"Back to the very first time?" I asked hopefully, but not ready to believe it could be that easy.

"Well, that's debatable since it depends on which one of you used it first," he mumbled, reaching further inside the machine. "The point was to go back and prevent everything that was caused as a chain reaction. As you can imagine, it's much easier said than done and I know he was still working on it before he packed it all away. But I have no idea if he managed to make it work or if the ideas were all still in his head." Dad bit his lip as his hand searched for something.

Then his eyes widened, and he laughed in triumph. "There it is!"

There was a click, and the lights of the machine switched from blue to red as it hummed to life once more. I took a step back, not sure what was about to happen. I watched Dad work the wires back into the machine and reattach the panel.

"So, what do we do now?" Oliver asked. "Where is it going to take us?"

"Who used the machine first?" he asked.

"I did, but I used it on my own to get Holly's school book back."

"And then you later used it for all three of you, right?" Dad asked. We nodded. "Then with any luck, your grandpa worked out the bugs before he passed away. And it will now take you back to that moment."

"Just like that?" I asked, staring at the machine, and filled with doubts. "It can't be that simple!"

"There is a small chance the switch's use was not fully realized," Dad said, tilting his head back and forth, "but this is your best option for resetting what's been changed and getting things back to normal." He stared at us long and hard before passing the machine to Oliver. "I have faith in you both, I really do!'

"As do I," a deep voice grumbled from the doorway. My heart pounded in fear at the sound of the familiar voice. "Well now, isn't this just a lovely reunion."

"Thaddeus," Dad whispered and shoved us all behind him protectively. "How?"

"I have my ways, don't you worry about that," he said, grinning as he glanced from us down to the machine glowing red in Oliver's arms. "Now then, what's this about a new addition to the machine? I'd love to hear all about it."

Chapter 3

Oliver's hands tightened around the machine. Thaddeus hadn't taken his eyes off it either, but so far he'd made no move to try and take it away. All he wanted was to get his hands on it and keep it away from us, to stop us from destroying this new timeline he'd created.

But we were going to make it right. We had to.

"Fascinating how much William hid from me during all our years of working together," he mused. "And so much you kept from me as well, Robert. I don't understand your reluctance to work with me. Think of all we could accomplish together! You and your kids, we could be famous, everyone would know our names for centuries to come! We could change the very foundations of the science world!"

"No, I told you before, I will not work with you," Dad insisted firmly. "I will not work with you. Not now, not ever and you will not get your hands on my kids. Get out of my shop, Thaddeus!"

Thaddeus huffed in the doorway, blocking it completely. "Why would I do that? You think you can threaten me? You know who I am in this world, right? There is nothing you can do to me, Robert. Nothing."

Oliver's arms gripped even more firmly around the machine. Kate and I sidled closer to him while Dad stepped towards Thaddeus, trying to block his sight. The lights were still glowing bright red, and I didn't want to lose this chance of resetting everything we'd done. It was a long shot at best, but right now a long shot was better than being trapped in this horrible present we'd caused to happen from bouncing around so much, thinking we knew what we were doing. The trips we took now seemed so stupid.

Going back to mess with Jade's project, getting the chance to put her in her place...I would do anything to take it all back. I'd put up with Jade's bullying forever if it meant never having to experience what we were going through now.

Slowly, I reached around and placed my hand on Kate's arm as she grabbed hold of Oliver's. Dad was still arguing hotly with Thaddeus, demanding he let Maggie out of the facility; promising they'd leave town and Thaddeus would never see them again. But the mad doctor's cackling was enough to tell me that was never going to happen.

"You are going to come with me now, all of you. We are going back to the facility, and we will work this out." Thaddeus stared at us with his beady blue eyes.

"You don't understand what's happening here," Dad argued. "The very foundations of time could be unraveling as we know it because of what you've done!"

"Or because of what your children have done," he shot back. "They're the ones who started us all on this new path. If anyone is to blame, it's them."

Dad's eyes narrowed with hate. "Don't you dare lay the blame on them! You did this! You were greedy, always wanting more. And when William tried to stop you, you made sure he could never challenge you again. But you're going to cause irreparable damage if we can't fix this. Why don't you understand what's happening here?"

"I understand quite well," he snapped back. "You are once again attempting to thwart my plans, my greatness!" he bellowed. "I thought sending you to the future and bringing your older version back would have been enough to teach you a lesson, but it seems, you are due for another. An even harsher one."

"You can't do anything worse to me," Dad stated, lifting his chin in challenge.

"Oh, can't I? How about I start with shutting down your store and locking you up deep in my facility. How about I cut off any access you may have had with your wife," Thaddeus muttered. "How about—"

"Dad?"

I froze at the sudden sound of my voice, the voice that was coming from my other self. Ducking as low as I could, I hid behind Dad so that the other Holly wouldn't see me.

Thaddeus' mouth snapped shut with an audible clack as he whipped around frowning. "You!" he gasped, staring in stunned shock at my other self. "Where did you come from?"

"Upstairs," I heard myself smartly reply. "Why are you here? Where's Oliver?"

From my hiding spot behind Dad, I hissed at my brother. "Now! Do it now!"

Oliver fumbled with the machine, and I saw the worry on his face. He was struggling with the idea of leaving the other Holly behind even though I was technically going with him. "Here goes nothing," he whispered, and I heard a click as he flipped the switch on the machine.

Instead of a blue glow flowing out and surrounding us gently, the entire building shook violently as a bright red light exploded outward. I heard myself scream as she...my other self...was thrown back into the shop and the office door slammed shut, trapping Dad and Thaddeus inside with us. I cringed as my gut rolled and nausea rose to my throat. Dad fell backward into Oliver, grabbing hold of his shoulder. Thaddeus fell right behind him, clutching at Dad's arm. Dad tried to shake him off, but Thaddeus dug his fingers in deeper. As the objects in the office swirled around us in a tornado of shape and color, I knew we were in serious trouble.

A popping sound filled my ears, making me partially deaf as my feet left the ground. The five of us were thrown through a tunnel of light, soaring through space and time. I had no idea where we were going, or where we'd land, but all I could hope for was the basement of our house, back to the very first time Oliver used the machine.

My head and my mind spun wildly as I gripped a firmer hold of Oliver's arm. And then, with a thud, everything around me stopped spinning, and my feet hit the solid floor again. I blinked in confusion to find us back in Thaddeus' office at the facility.

It was the last time I used the machine. "No...no this can't be right," I muttered, horrified by where we'd landed. "Oliver! We can't be here!"

Thaddeus beamed as he fixed his jacket. "Well, that worked out very well now, didn't it?"

He'd barely spoken the words when Oliver let out a yelp of alarm, and the red light burst outwards again, catching us all in its grasp.

"No!" Thaddeus tried to break free.

But the light tugged him back towards us as we yelled then disappeared with another loud pop. It seemed that we were all in this together until the machine decided it was finished with us.

We were thrown through time once more, and I clung to Kate's hand as she did the same to mine. I had a brief moment of regret that I had ever brought her into this mess now that we had no idea how it was all going to end. Then, with another loud thud, we landed hard once more, this time in our dilapidated and broken down living room, covered in rips and dirt and stains.

I frowned seeing the house so damaged and in such disarray, but there wasn't much time to linger on that thought. Thaddeus grunted and covered his mouth as Dad tried to steady himself and remain upright. But the machine wasn't finished with us yet.

"What's happening?" I managed to gasp just as it hummed loudly in Oliver's arms and we were sucked up yet again, out of that timeline and tossed around like leaves in the wind.

There was no answer to my question as we touched down again and again...in our living room in the future, then back to the basement, over and over it picked us up and flung us around until I couldn't see straight anymore. I felt as though I'd been squashed by a massive weight.

When we landed in the janitor's closet of the school, we all hit the floor, holding our heads and our stomachs. Music played from outside the room, and I realized it was the night of the concert when we'd gone back to mess with Jade's project.

"It's going back to every occasion the machine was used," Dad mumbled, his voice shaky as he quickly sucked in a breath. "I hadn't realized how many times you'd used it."

"Back to every time?" Oliver gasped. "Why...why would it do that?"

"William...must not have finished working on it," Dad replied and shook his head as he grimaced. "I can't take much more of this, kids. How many times did you use the machine?"

"We should be...should be almost finished," I promised, counting off all the separate occasions on my fingers and figuring where we had left to go. "What happens when we reach the end of the line?"

"I don't...I don't exactly know. Your grandpa never told me if his experiments were a success or not. I have no idea what's going to happen."

"I do," Thaddeus snapped and lunged for the machine. "Give that to me!" He struggled towards it as Oliver attempted to yank it away. We tried to shove Thaddeus off while music blasted from the gym through the hallways of the school.

Oliver kicked at Thaddeus, desperately trying to keep him away, but then the machine hummed and the light shifted from red to blue and back again. Dad's arms bumped the knobs, and I heard them clicking before they began spinning crazily in all directions. The humming grew louder until I heard nothing else.

The bright light filled the interior of the small closet, blinding all of us before an ear-splitting pop resounded in my head. I winced as I was thrown away from everyone else. I couldn't see, I couldn't hear, and all my strength disappeared. I sank down and allowed myself to drift.

***

"Oliver!"

I bolted upright in bed, drenched in a cold sweat as the early morning sun poured through my window. I blinked against its harshness as I reached down to feel the familiar comforter that covered me. I glanced around my bedroom frantically. Everything appeared normal.

"What?" I whispered as I tossed the covers off and carefully opened my door to see the hallway. The house wasn't falling down around me, and it looked just as it had before this whole mess started. Just remembering it all made my head ache and I winced as I hurried to the bathroom to splash some cold water on my face. But then a sudden wave of dizziness hit me hard.

A time machine? Had I really just been thinking that was real? The house was fine, and I was here like I always had been.

"Crazy dream," I whispered and shook my head as the last bits of sleep left me feeling weirdly off kilter. My headache worsened, and I blinked and rubbed at my temples. "Wow, did you have to leave me with such a bad headache?" I muttered as if my dream could be held accountable.

When I stepped out of the bathroom a few minutes later, Oliver was just opening his bedroom door, running a hand through his messy hair and yawning, still in the sweats that he'd slept in. I stopped and stared at him, watching his face shift from what he looked like now, to the way I swore I'd seen him recently. The Oliver in my dream looked different to the version standing in front of me. I continued to stare and his brow furrowed.

"Holly? What's up with you this morning?"

"Huh? I uh…nothing, nothing at all," I said quickly but didn't look away.

"Holly…I have to use the bathroom."

"Yeah, sure," I said and moved away from the doorway. He was about to close the door when I called him back. "Oliver? Do you, uh, do you remember anything weird from the past few days?"

He rubbed the back of his neck as he yawned again. "No, why?"

"Nothing you were working on in your room?"

"Working on?" Now he looked downright confused. "What would I be working on in my room?"

"I don't know, some new invention or another…a machine maybe?"

He blinked as he stared at me blankly then burst out laughing. "Good one, sis, really funny." He closed the bathroom door leaving me standing in the hallway feeling like I was missing something major, but I had no idea what it was. I stood there a few minutes longer, rubbing my forehead and wondering what was wrong.

My dreams had been crazy, so much running around with Kate and Oliver…and Mom, she'd been there too, mixed up somewhere in the middle of it all. Then there was this old guy who kinda resembled Oliver, a much older version of him. And that other old dude. I shrugged it off as I wandered down the hall, peering into Oliver's room as I passed.

"Messy as always," I whispered and rolled my eyes.

He was going through what Mom referred to as his obnoxious rebellious stage. Posters covered his walls, and his guitar sat against the far wall. Music sheets were

298

everywhere, and dinner plates were stacked high on the floor. Mom would have a field day if she came up here to see this mess. I ducked back into my own room to get dressed in jeans and a black hoodie. I pulled my hair back in a braid and grabbed a pair of heavy black boots along with my ragged backpack that was covered in stickers of skulls and crossbones. I bounded down the stairs and dropped my bag by the door before hurrying into the kitchen for breakfast.

"Morning," I said to Mom as she glanced up at me.

I stared at her, caught off guard. The mom in my dreams had been completely different from the mom before me. That one had been put together, not falling apart, well for at least part of the dream. She was nothing like the woman who stood before me at the counter, her brow furrowed with worry lines and gripping a cup of coffee like it was the only thing keeping her alive.

"Your brother up yet?" she asked.

"Yeah, he is." I dumped cereal into a bowl, still trying to piece together my dreams as I poured in some milk. "Hey, Mom? Did Oliver ever invent anything?" I asked around mouthfuls of flakes.

She set a stack of papers down, probably her latest manuscript of some dark story or other that her publisher was hounding her for. Mom was known for her creepy, horror stories that gave her quite a reputation around town, though I wasn't always sure it was a good one. "Invent anything? Besides how to drive his mother crazy and be totally messy all the time? No, course not. Why?"

"Dunno, had a bunch of weird dreams last night."

"And your brother was an inventor? Huh, that'd be interesting, I guess."

"Yeah, yeah it would."

I held onto my cereal bowl as I shut my eyes, trying to remember what else had happened in that dream. But all it did was give me more of a headache. I finished eating and ran back upstairs to brush my teeth, passing Oliver on my way. He was dressed all in black; his jeans, t-shirt, shirt, and boots all blended into one dark color. His hair was gelled, and he had a confident smirk on his face.

For a split second the image of a completely different version of my brother flashed into my mind. I stopped at the top of the stairs, watching him play air guitar before he disappeared into the kitchen. Within moments, he and Mom were bickering about something or other, and I rolled my eyes. He was the usual Oliver. Just like normal. Not sure what I was thinking, but those dreams had thrown me for a loop. I brushed my teeth, checked my hair one more time, then called goodbye to Mom as I raced out the front door so I could wait for Kate like I did every morning before school.

The weather was chilly, and I shoved my hands into the pouch pocket at my front. When I reached the end of the street, I danced around on the sidewalk as I looked back for Kate. A cold wind whipped by and I shivered, mentally begging Kate to hurry up so we could get to school before I froze my feet off. I bounced on the balls of my boots, wishing I'd worn thicker socks. Finally, I saw her blond head of hair as she ran down the pavement and skidded to a stop right by me.

"Hey, sorry," she exclaimed as we took off again, walking into the wind. "I had the weirdest dreams last night, slept through my alarm. And I was in such a hurry; I forgot to grab my jacket."

I glanced down at what she was wearing, thinking how cold she must be when I realized what she'd said. "I had some really weird dreams last night as well!"

"Really? What did you dream about?" she asked me curiously.

I told her as much as I could remember about the strange dreams that still filled my mind. "We were time-travelers or something; it was crazy. But this morning, I woke up and felt like it was real; like it had really happened."

"Right, because time travel is possible," she scoffed with a smirk. "You're just crazy yourself."

"You never know, I guess." I was suddenly feeling very uncomfortable, so I asked her about her dream to get off the topic.

She blushed and looked away. "Oh, come on, it can't be that bad!" I grinned.

"It's not that it was bad," she murmured. "It's just kind of embarrassing...I dreamt about your brother."

"Oliver?" I said laughing. "Oh man, he's really got into your head lately."

"Can't help it, he's so cute looking, and those songs of his are cool." She gave a dramatic sigh, holding a hand to her chest as if she was going to swoon. "I could listen to him sing all day long. And guess what...he gave me a thumb drive with all his songs on it, yesterday."

"Yeah well, I'm pretty sure he likes you," I informed her and watched her cheeks redden further. "But no matter how good his singing is, it's not like Mom's ever going to support him. She thinks he's wasting his time and that he's going to end up ruining his life."

"He's always been a bit wild."

"That's what happens when you grow up without a dad I guess." My steps slowed as we neared our school. I whipped around, squinting back down the sidewalk past the other kids arriving. I could've sworn I'd heard someone calling my name, but there was no one there.

"Holly? Come on; we're going to be late!" Kate yelled from the front steps.

"Right, sorry," I said and ran to catch up to her.

We darted up the steps into the warm school building and moved through the crowd to our lockers. Most of the students stayed clear of Kate and me, and I was just fine with that. Oliver had set a reputation for both him and myself when he was here, and I let everyone think I was just as wild as he was. It made it easier to get through the day. There was less drama when I only had one friend to worry about. I crammed my backpack in my locker as I chatted with Kate about our classes for the day. We were both dreading another day filled with boring classes we had no interest in.

"Don't look now, but it's Miss Thing herself coming down the hall," Kate muttered darkly. I turned and rolled my eyes as Jade and her friends strode towards us. The sight of her pink top turned my stomach; that and the beaming smile that was plastered on her face. She was always smiling as if she'd never had a bad day in her entire life. It was annoying. I leered at her when she made the mistake of glancing our way. She lowered her head and hurried past us to get to her first class.

"Well, guess I'll see you in history class," Kate said before heading towards her own classroom.

"Yep, see you then." I grabbed my binder and closed my locker.

I turned around to dive into the bustling crowd just as the five-minute warning bell rang, and found myself walking right into someone. "Hey, watch it!" I snapped as my binder fell to the floor and burst open, scattering papers everywhere. "Seriously? Why don't you look where you're going?"

"*Sorry*," a voice replied sharply, and I glanced up to stare into the face of Zac.

"Oh, hey," I mumbled quickly, but he was already shoving my binder at me and straightening up. "What's wrong with *you*?" I frowned at him.

"*Nothing*, I'm fine," he snapped, and before I had a chance to say anything else, he stormed away.

I watched him move on down the hall, gripping firmly onto my binder when he paused to talk to Jade. The two of them laughed at something he'd said and then he gave her hand a quick squeeze before continuing to class.

I ground my teeth as I stepped into first period and took my seat to the right of Jade. She stared pointedly at the board as I leaned in closer. "I see you and Zac are getting awfully close."

"We're just friends," she insisted quietly, her hand trembling as she held her pen tighter.

"Sure, whatever you say. But you'd better just be friends!"

She slumped in her seat as I glared at her through the entire period. We left that class, and I did the same thing in our next class, smirking when she squirmed in her chair. By the time history class rolled around and Zac tried to talk to her, she wanted nothing to do with him. Good. He shouldn't want to talk to her; he should want to be with someone like me. I had no idea why he was interested in her, anyway.

But to make matters worse, our teacher made us pair up for some dumb assignment. I sat with Kate while Zac scooted his desk closer to Jade's.

All through class, I watched them talk quietly and laugh

about something or other. My lips twitched with growing aggravation until, by the end of the class, I had successfully destroyed the cap of my pen from chewing on it so hard. We were barely out the door when I purposely turned back and stuck out my foot just as Jade exited the classroom. She tripped, and I faked a gasp of shock as Kate stood laughing alongside me.

"Oh Jade, I'm *very* sorry! I didn't see you there," I said and bent down. "Let me help you."

"Why don't you just get away from her?" Zac said, stepping in front of me and blocking my path. "Just go away and leave her alone. Just leave everyone alone."

I glowered at him as Jade scrambled to her feet, clutching her books to her chest and hiding behind him. "I didn't do anything wrong," I said in an attempt to defend myself. "I was just trying to help her,"

"You know this problem you have against the world? It's getting really old, Holly."

"What problem? I don't have a problem!"

"Oh no? Then why do you act like you hate everyone?" He glared at me openly as the students around us fell quiet. "You never used to be like this, and then one day it's like you snapped. You're mean to everyone for no reason. Why?"

I shifted uncomfortably on my feet. "I don't know what you're talking about."

"Yeah you do, and that's the problem. You've changed. Most of us used to be your friends, remember? And then one day you decided you hated everyone." He scoffed as he guided Jade past Kate and me. "Whatever...just leave us alone, alright? Be miserable all by yourself."

My jaw dropped as he moved towards the cafeteria, talking quietly to Jade. "Seriously?" I said to Kate, raising my eyebrows sky-high.

"I don't know what he's going on about," Kate said as

she stood beside me, twirling her hair around her finger. "But you're not alone; you've got me at least."

I flinched at her words. But at the very same time, part of my dream from the night before came rushing back to hit me full in the face. This wasn't right, none of this felt right.

We entered the cafeteria and took our usual table so we could watch everyone else. But today I found myself staring absently out the window. Kate was talking about her earlier classes and what had happened with some girl or another, but all I did was nod as she chatted away.

I couldn't put my finger on the problem, but everything about today, how I was acting, what I was saying, what I was wearing, was wrong...I suddenly felt very uncomfortable in my own skin. It was like I'd pulled a different version out of the closet and slipped it on without realizing what life I was stepping into.

I felt as though I'd fallen into someone else's life completely and the Holly I was now...was not the real me.

"Man, I have to stop eating ice cream before bed," I mumbled when lunch finally ended, blaming the sugar for giving me crazy dreams and feeling so weird. "I'm going to the bathroom. See you in class," I told Kate as I headed into the girl's restroom.

It was empty, and I set my binder on the ledge by the sink as I stared long and hard at my reflection. I tugged at a strand of hair that had come loose from my braid then poked at my cheeks and picked at my dark purple fingernails. I felt like me, I looked like me, but at the same time, I knew that the Holly staring back was different. I closed my eyes, remembering my dream a little more. Then my eyes abruptly shot open to see another version of me, laughing and joking around with Kate, Oliver, and Zac. Even Zac's kid sister. I knew that had never happened, but it had been so real in my dream. I was friends with Zac and lots of other kids.

And Jade…in my dream she bullied *me*, not the other way around. She tried to make *my* life miserable, told *me* to stay away from Zac. He had protected *me* from her. I saw it vividly, saw him stepping up and telling her to leave me alone, telling her to mind her own business. But that hadn't actually happened, had it?

None of it made sense, and suddenly, I wished I could go back to that dream where I was liked and had lots of friends to hang out with; where Zac, the best looking boy in our grade, actually liked me.

The bathroom door opened and Jade walked in. The second she spotted me, she froze. I felt the words rise to my throat. I wanted to give her a hard time about Zac or anything else I could think of. But I forced myself to swallow them down, grabbed my stuff, and rushed past her without saying a word.

Clutching my binder to my chest, I pushed through the crowd of kids in the hallway, apologizing every time I nudged someone and getting very strange looks in return. Another headache started at my temples, and I swore I was seeing flashes of this very same hallway from a different time…from my dream? I didn't know, but things were becoming very confusing. I wanted that moment again, to be talking to Zac, laughing with him, not having him angry at me for picking on Jade.

There was a time not so long ago when Jade was the one making fun of me. The thought hit me for a second time, but this time it was more intense; her threatening me in the girl's bathroom as her gang of supporters looked on, made me extremely nervous that it was going to happen all over again.

I froze mid-step and nearly fell over. No, that wasn't right. Jade had never been mean to me, not outright at least. She wouldn't dare. I was the one who was mean to her. And yet those images still appeared in my head, our roles reversed and Zac being there for me, not her.

When I finally got my feet moving again, I saw Kate waiting for me outside our science class. As soon as I reached her, she poked me in the shoulder. "You ok?"

"What? Yeah, yeah I'm fine," I mumbled. "Perfect, why?"

"You're all pale, that's why. Did something happen in the bathroom?"

I was going to say no, but when Jade passed us and made her way into the classroom, we both caught her curious stare. Kate glared at her, and she almost sprinted to her seat.

"Did something happen with you and Jade?" Kate asked.

"No, she came into the bathroom while I was there, but nothing happened." I took a deep breath to steady my unstable nerves and motioned to the doorway. "Let's just go into class. I can't be late again."

"That's for sure!" Kate nodded in agreement. "Mr. Banes loves giving out detentions too much," she added as she stepped inside the doorway.

My feet wouldn't move. "Mr. Banes?"

"Our science teacher, yeah," she said slowly. "You know, Holly? The man who teaches our science class?"

I gulped as the name reverberated through my head. My gaze slipped from Kate to the man sitting behind the desk at the front of the room.

His glasses were perched at the end of his nose, and his beard and the wisps of hair at the sides of his head were gray. From where I stood, he looked perfect for the part of a mad scientist, and my mouth dropped open as a new flood of memories hit me hard. But whether they were from my dream or were real, I couldn't decide.

Either way, I knew this Mr. Banes, and it wasn't because he was my science teacher.

Chapter 4

"Holly? What's up? You coming in or what?" Kate asked.

She sounded far away. It was like all the air had been sucked from my lungs as I stared at our teacher, sitting behind his desk while he waited for everyone to file in and take their seats. The hair on the back of my neck stood on end. I did not want to go in, not into this classroom, I just couldn't.

"Holly," Kate said louder, snapping her fingers in my face and making me jump. "What is with you today?"

I wanted to tell her that this man was a bad guy, that we shouldn't let him see us…but that was crazy! Wasn't it?

"Girls, please take your seats," Mr. Banes said. The sound of his voice made me take another step back into the hall. He frowned at us both and pushed up from his desk. "Holly, what seems to be the problem, this time? You forget something in your locker?"

My mouth worked a few times before I gave a quick shake of my head and moved towards my desk near the back of the room. Kate slid into hers beside me. The bell rang, and Mr. Banes closed the door, diving right into his lesson, one I had no interest in paying attention to. The longer I listened to him talk, the more my mind played tricks on me, and I heard him saying other things…threatening my family… But that wasn't possible. He didn't know my family, my parents. Did he? No, he couldn't. No one knew my dad because he ran off when I was a baby.

But just like before, I felt the gnawing sensation that all of this was wrong. Horribly wrong.

For reasons I couldn't explain, I hated this man. I hated him so much, I glared at him all through class and when the bell finally rang I dreaded the idea of having to see him again tomorrow. And the next day and the next, not after what he did to my family…

I winced as my head throbbed painfully, and when I got to my feet, I nearly fell into my desk.

"Holly? You don't look too good," Kate said worriedly. "Maybe you're getting that bug everyone else has. You're very pale."

My knees felt shaky, as did my hands. "I think I'll go to the nurse. I'll um…I'll talk to you later, okay?"

"Okay," she said as she took a few steps to follow me. "Do you want me to come with you?" I shook my head, and she shrugged before telling me she'd text me later.

I kept my head down, but it hurt to walk, and I cringed every time I took a step. I passed the janitor's closet near the front of the school, and another image appeared in my mind. It was of Kate, Oliver, and me landing there after using the time machine to do something…something to do with Jade's project? I groaned. Now I really was sounding crazy.

"Time machines," I mumbled under my breath. "No such things as time machines, Holly. You're losing it; you're totally losing it."

When I reached the nurse's office and told her how unwell I felt, she took my temperature, frowning as she checked the thermometer. "Bit of a temp. I'm going to go ahead and send you home for the day. You walk to school, is that right? I'll call your mom to let her know. Do you need her to come and get you?"

"No, no I'll text her. It's okay, I can make it," I assured her. After a skeptical glance back at me, she gave me a note to hand to the main office and then told me I could go.

I did as she asked and then swung by my locker to grab my bag before trudging home. At least I wouldn't have to see Jade or Zac for the rest of the day. When I reached my house, I opened the door and called out to Mom, but there was no answer. I dropped my bag at the stairs and wandered into the kitchen where I found a note on the fridge.

My publisher called me in for a meeting. We're having a late lunch/dinner. There's leftovers in the fridge.

I'll be home late.
Mom xx

I rolled my eyes, texted her and said I was at home with a slight fever, but not to worry, and disappeared upstairs to wallow in my bedroom. She texted back, making me promise to lie down and take it easy and to let her know if I felt any worse.

Dropping down onto my bed, I tried to clear my mind, to not think about any of the weird stuff that had happened that day. Eventually, I felt myself relax and drifted off to a not so restful sleep…

I was running, and someone was with me. Oliver? And Kate. They were both there, but I couldn't figure out where we were or what was happening. Then suddenly we were in a room, and there was a blue light surrounding us. I glanced around, hearing the same voice from that morning when I arrived at school, calling my name. It sounded familiar. I knew that voice, knew it really well, but whose was it? I wanted to see the person's face, know who was calling out to me. Then there was another voice…maybe more? I couldn't tell. But I didn't stop running. The blue light blinded me, and I winced when my feet left the ground then thumped back to the floor with a thud. The scenery changed, so did Oliver and Kate…and me. I yelled, asking them to tell me what was going on. Then they ripped away from me, and I was left alone as the light changed from blue to red. I was terrified, but of what, I had no idea.

A sound of cruel laughter filled my ears, and I thrashed around, tangling in the bedsheets. Finally opening my eyes, I stared around my room and glanced at the clock on my bedside table. I'd been asleep for less than an hour, but it felt like a lifetime. With my head pounding even worse than before, I turned over, closed my eyes, and tried to forget about the nightmare I'd just had.

***

When I woke, my room was shrouded in darkness. Groggily, I looked around. The dream this time was worse than the last, and I felt even more off-kilter. I rubbed my eyes as they adjusted to the darkness that had fallen while I was asleep. I couldn't believe I'd slept that long. My head still hurt, and I wasn't sure what was real and what wasn't. The house was quiet around me, and a weird image of it being deserted and rundown flashed in front of me. I shook my head, and the image was gone again.

"You're fine," I told myself. "There's nothing wrong with you. You've had some weird dreams, that's all. They're just dreams!" I said it over and over before I finally managed to get to my feet and flip on the light. I stared at my bedside clock and gasped at how late it was.

Midnight! I'd slept right through until midnight! In an effort not to wake anyone, I tip-toed from my bedroom to the bathroom and then to the kitchen to find something to eat.

The longer I stood there, the more I sensed that everything was wrong, all of it. I rubbed my forehead, trying to smooth the sensation away, but it only grew worse. Flashes of Mom in this kitchen, the walls yellow, then blue. Me in the kitchen with Oliver as we made breakfast on the weekends. Seeing Kate and I laughing…and Zac. I held my head, waiting for the strange scenes to stop. There were more bright flashes of blue and then I was falling through a tunnel of light, and when I landed…I saw the hazy figure of a man I recognized immediately.

I wasn't sure how I knew him. I swore I'd never seen him before. But then I realized. "Dad…it was Dad," I whispered. And suddenly it was like I was waking up all over again, except this time, I knew exactly what had happened.

"NOOO!...Oh, NOOO!"

The kitchen spun around me as everything came

rushing back. My memories were a mess. How had this happened? We'd been using the time machine reset to fix everything and now…now I had no idea where the machine even was.

"Oliver." My gaze shot to the stairs. He'd been with me when it all happened. And Kate. And Thaddeus and Dad. What went wrong? We were supposed to be making all of this right. But instead, we'd created new versions of ourselves. It was an even bigger mess than ever.

I had to get to Oliver. Scrambling into action, I bolted up the stairs and banged on his bedroom door. When he didn't answer, I threw the door open and charged in, shaking him awake as hard as I could. I yelled his name until his eyes finally shot open. He yelped in alarm until he finally realized it was me.

"Holly? What are you doing? Is the house on fire?" he grunted through a yawn. "What time is it?"

"It doesn't matter. Do you remember?"

"Remember what? Can you get off my bed? I have a test in the morning." He rolled over and tugged the comforter back over his head. I yanked it off, throwing it onto the floor. "What!" he snapped as he shoved me away. "You trying for the most annoying sister of the year award, or what?"

"Do you remember everything we went through with Kate and the machine…and Dad. Do you remember Dad? You have to remember!" I tugged on his arm, desperate for him to understand what I was talking about, but his eyes narrowed, and he sat up, pushing away from me.

"What are you talking about?"

"Dad…we found him, remember? We met him, and you look just like him, and you act just like him. And he was helping us, said he was so proud of us." I searched his eyes for any sign of recognition, but he only glared at me. "Please, Oliver you have to remember!"

"What's wrong with you, huh? You think it's funny to

313

sit there and act like you know our father? Seriously, Holly, just go back to bed and stop talking about someone you don't even know."

"Oliver! You have to remember!" I yelled, grabbing his shoulders and shaking him hard.

"Go away!"

"What's going on?" Mom snapped from the hallway, flipping on Oliver's bedroom light and blinding us both. Oliver grabbed his pillow to cover his face as I blinked against the harsh light.

"Holly? Do you know what time it is? We all have to be up early in the morning. And you're not well. Get back in bed." She shuffled over in her slippers and planted her hand on my forehead.

"I'm fine, Mom," I argued.

"No, you're burning up. Get back into bed, right now. I'll bring you some medicine."

"I can't!" I pushed her hand away. "Oliver," I tugged on the comforter again. "You have to remember! Just think about it, please! The machine and us going back in time! And Dad, we met Dad!" I repeated, hoping something would trigger his mind to realize that this was all a lie.

Mom froze and her eyes filled with what looked like confusion at my words. "What did you just say?"

I swallowed hard, not sure I should go on. But I had no choice, not if we were going to figure out what had gone wrong. "We found the time machine. And we found Dad. We figured out what happened all those years ago," I rambled on excitedly even as they both glared at me. "This isn't where we're supposed to be! And it's not ho we're supposed to be! You don't remember. But I do! Our science teacher, Thaddeus Banes, he's at my school, and he did this! He messed everything up!"

Mom shook her head, and Oliver began to look worried as though I really was a crazy person and had lost all sanity.

"I found the machine in the attic, and you fixed it." I stared at Oliver.

"What machine? And how did I fix it?"

"You're a nerd, Oliver, you're a computer nerd, and you invent stuff just like Grandpa and Dad," I told him, willing him to remember. "You got the machine working again, and we...we went back in time. We did all this stuff and this, this is all messed up now!"

"Enough!" Mom yelled so loudly I jumped. "Enough of this right now, young lady. You are to go back to your room, and I do not want to hear another word from you until morning. Do you understand?"

"But Mom—"

"Go back to bed. Now! You're grounded, do you hear me? You cannot run around saying that you met your father, the man who left us all when you were a baby!" Her face was red, and she was furious as she guided me out of Oliver's room and back to my own. "I want you in that bed, and I want you to go back to sleep. You are not to say one more word about any of this nonsense, do you understand?"

"It's true though!" I argued. "Please, listen to me for five seconds! We can fix this; we can, we can get Dad back. But you have to remember! You both do!"

Mom threw her arms up with a yell of aggravation, and I clamped my lips shut. "Holly, please stop, alright? You were dreaming, that's all. You did not meet your dad, and you are not going to fix anything!"

Angry tears welled in my eyes as I crossed my arms, my mind racing with how I could convince her that this was all real and that our present situation was not real. "Please, Mom, why would I lie about this? Why?"

"Obviously you want attention because you're clearly not getting enough already!"

I couldn't hold my tears back any longer. They streamed down my cheeks. I had nothing more to say. Mom wasn't going to believe me unless I had proof. The hurt in her eyes had me mentally kicking myself for acting so rashly. I backed into my room and closed the door just as she wiped at her own eyes and marched back to her bedroom, slamming the door hard enough to shake the walls. I sank to the floor behind my door and held my face in my hands.

I was awake, really awake to what was going on here. But I had to find a way to convince Oliver and Kate that the machine was real. If only I could find it, then that would do it. They'd have to believe me then.

I climbed into bed and spent the next hour making a plan for the following day. One way or another, I swore to myself, I would make everything right, make it all the way it was supposed to be.

If we were ever going to get our real lives back, I had to find a way. I just had to!

Chapter 5

When I woke up, I heard Oliver and Mom moving around. But I didn't want to get up and face them. Eventually, there was a light knock at my door.

"Holly? You awake?" Mom asked as she opened the door a crack.

I kept my eyes closed and pretended to be asleep as her steps moved closer to my bed. She sat down alongside me and pressed her hand against my forehead, smoothing back my hair.

For a second, I almost gave in. But there was nothing I could say to her yet that would make up for what I'd said. I'd been wrong to jump all over her and Oliver like that. For them, Dad had been gone for years, and they were hurt and upset by my outburst.

But they had no idea how close Dad really was.

She bent down and kissed my forehead. I kept my eyes closed and waited until her steps retreated and she closed the door.

As soon as she was gone, I sat up and spotted a note on my bedside table. I scanned it quickly.

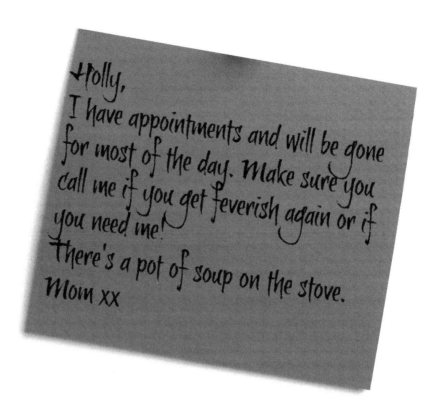

Holly,
I have appointments and will be gone for most of the day. Make sure you call me if you get feverish again or if you need me! There's a pot of soup on the stove.
Mom xx

She would be leaving soon. And with Oliver at school all day, it was the chance I'd hoped for. I threw my covers off all the way so I could hurry and get dressed.

As soon as I heard them both walk out the front door, I stepped into the hallway. I planned to dig through the house and see what I could find. Something had to be left behind from our multiple times bouncing from one year to the next. I was not going to give up until I had done a thorough search.

Because I'd found the original machine in the attic, I decided to start there. Tugging on the rope for the ladder, I pulled it down so I could climb up into the dusty darkness. The attic was filled with more stuff than I remembered and I planted my hands on my hips, wondering where to start.

Figuring I would do what I had done last time, I started on the right side of the attic, and one by one, opened every single box. By the time I'd worked through most of them, I was annoyed and frustrated.

"Nothing! There's nothing up here," I ranted as I shoved another useless box to the side.

Only two more remained, but after I opened them and dug through some old clothes of Oliver's and then a heavy box filled with books, I gave up, glaring at the dust floating in front of my face. Growing more and more frantic, I hurried down the ladder and did something I never thought I would do.

I went into Mom's room and tore it apart. Somewhere, she had to have the pictures of Dad from before he disappeared. I was going to drag them out into the light so she could see them. Maybe they would help jog her memory. But after going through every inch of her closet, and her dresser, her room was in a shambles, and I was no closer to finding anything I needed at all. I moved onto Oliver's room, followed by my own, and then the hall closet, giving each of them the same treatment. But there was nothing packed away anywhere!

I decided there was nothing left to do but go through every inch of the house. I left no closet or cabinet, or drawer unchecked. I was desperate, desperate to find the answers I needed. And I was determined that we were not going to be stuck in this messed up timeline.

***

I worked my way through the basement, finally reaching the last stack of boxes and old suitcases in the far back corner. When the front door opened, I heard footsteps on the floor above but didn't stop my search until Mom's yell exploded.

"Holly! What did you do to the house!"

I cringed as she stomped around on the floor above me.

"Holly! Where are you? Holly, you'd better answer me right this second, or you will be grounded forever!"

I decided it would be better to head upstairs than to give her a chance to find me in the basement surrounded by another mess. Slowly, I made my way up and saw her standing amongst the mayhem that was now our living room, shaking her head, her eyes bulging.

"Hey, Mom," I said lightly, as she turned around to stare at me like I'd gone insane. "I uh, I didn't think you'd be home so early."

"What...what is going on?" she asked quietly. She used her quiet Mom voice, the one I was well aware of. It meant that no matter what I said, there would be no way to explain the situation and it would be impossible not to end up grounded for life. "Is the whole house like this?"

I scratched my cheek and tried to shake my head, "I was looking for something."

She took in a deep breath. "Looking for something?" she repeated.

"Yeah, I think I misplaced it, and it's really important."

"And you decided to destroy the entire house trying to find it?"

I nodded. "Yeah, but don't worry, I'll put everything back. I promise."

Mom hung her head and dropped her purse on the couch. "Holly, please tell me this has nothing to do with what happened last night?"

"Well, no…" I started to say, but she groaned, throwing her head back. "Just wait, Mom, hear me out. Please!"

"No, not another word. I don't want to hear any more about your dream or what you think is real or not real! You have destroyed this entire house! What were you hoping to find?"

"Proof," I said before I could stop myself.

"Proof of what?"

I mumbled my answer. But she couldn't hear it and ordered me to repeat it. "Proof that what happened in my dreams is real, that they're not dreams." She stalked away from me and into the kitchen. I followed along behind her. "I know it sounds crazy, but I'm telling you the truth! There is a time machine. Oliver and I used it to go back. We found Dad!"

"No, you didn't!" She planted her hands on the counter as she stared me down. "None of this is real, and you need to stop talking about it, right now. I'm worried about you, Holly, can't you see that? You're going through an episode of some kind, and if you don't get it under control, I'm taking you to a therapist."

"A therapist, really? You'd rather believe that I'm

321

crazy rather than the fact that I've found Dad?"

"You didn't find him, alright! None of us did!" she yelled back.

"But we did. If you give me a chance to find the proof, I'll show you; I'll get you both to remember!"

"No, we're finished. You are not to talk about this again. Tomorrow, you're going back to school, and then you are coming straight home every day for the rest of the semester. Then, you're grounded for the entire summer and until Christmas for all I care!" She was breathing heavily as she finished, but I wasn't going to stick around. I couldn't. I started moving back toward the front door. "Holly, what are you doing?"

"It's okay, Mom, I'm going to make this right. You just have to trust me."

I grabbed my cell phone off the coffee table, and while she was still yelling for me to come back and clean up the house, I took off out the front door, running as fast as I could as I headed to the park. School would be over in a few minutes, and I texted Kate as soon as I reached a park bench, out of breath with a cramp in my side. I asked her to meet me on her way home. I was just hoping she'd remember what we'd all been through. She mentioned having dreams the other night, too and there was a chance she'd dreamed about the way Oliver was supposed to be, not this weird rocker guy who didn't know how to make a time machine work.

I paced around the bench, unable to sit still while I waited for her. I half expected Mom to come after me, but I texted to tell her I was in the park and would be home soon. She didn't text me back, and I didn't bug her again, figuring she needed time to cool off.

"Holly!" I heard Kate yell and turned around to see her waving her arm over her head as she raced towards me. "I got your text, what's going on? I thought you were still sick?"

"No, I'm fine, but listen, the dream you had the other night, what was it about?"

She tugged on her backpack straps as she eyed me with a frown. "The dream I had about your brother?"

"Yeah, was there anything else going on in that dream? Anything you can remember?"

"No, we were just hanging out. It wasn't that big of a deal. Is this really why you asked me to meet you here?"

"Yes and no." I puffed out my cheeks as I debated my next move. "Look, I need you to hear me out, alright? Can you do that?"

"Sure, I guess," she said sounding uncertain.

I took a deep breath before launching into the story of what had happened since finding the time machine in the attic. I had to give her credit. She sat there on that bench and listened to every word without interrupting me even once. When I reached the part about finding the town empty and our parents gone, she glanced around worriedly as if everyone would disappear while I was talking. But as I came to the end of the tale, I saw the skepticism on her face begin to fade and in its place was confusion as well as something else I couldn't place.

"And that's how we got here," I finished finally. "We were trying to reset everything we'd done. But Thaddeus grabbed at the machine, and it malfunctioned."

"And now we're stuck in some alternate time warp thing?"

"Yes!"

"And how is it that only you remember?" she asked quietly.

"I don't know. Yesterday, something made me remember...I was dreaming, but then I started seeing how we used to be." I plopped down beside her, holding my head. It had started to ache again, and there was a throbbing in my temples. "I'm not really like this...I'm not a mean person," I told her. "Neither of us are."

323

"We're not mean," she argued until I stared at her pointedly and she had to admit that we really were pretty horrible.

"In the present time zone that we're supposed to be in, Jade's the bully, not us. And Zac and I…we're kinda dating." I smiled as I looked around the park picturing his smiling face and the day I'd met him in this very spot.

"We had our first date here actually."

"Sounds nice," she said, but I could tell I was losing her.

"And you and Oliver like each other," I added. "I know you kind of like each other now, but in our *real* time zone, you *really* like each other."

She stared silently back at me. I sighed. "None of this sounds familiar. None of what I told you?"

"I want to say yes," Kate told me, patting me on the shoulder, "but no, nothing."

I held my face in my hands, feeling ready to cry all over again. There had to be a way to get her to remember. "I'm not about to give up. Not now." I pushed off the bench and started towards Main Street.

"Holly? What are you going to do?"

"I don't know yet, but I've got to do something…" I trailed off and sat back down quickly, trying to hide behind Kate when I spotted a familiar face across the park from us. He sat on a bench and appeared innocent enough, feeding the birds, but the hair on the back of my neck stood on end. He shouldn't be there.

"Are you hiding from Mr. Banes?"

"I'm telling you, he's the one behind all of this," I whispered. "Look, I have to go. I'll text you soon, and when I do, please make sure you text back. Okay?"

She started to answer, but I didn't give her a chance before I was on the move again, hurrying through the park and doing my best to keep out of sight of Thaddeus. He didn't seem to notice me, and I made it out of the park without him so much as turning around.

I shoved my hands into my jeans pockets and traipsed down the sidewalk. My cell vibrated a few times, but it was just Mom telling me I needed to be home for dinner. I texted her back saying that I would. But I knew that depended on what happened next.

I turned the corner, heading towards the one last hope I had when I ran right into Zac.

"Oh, sorry," I mumbled, locking eyes with him.

"Holly," he said, but there was nothing nice about his tone. He didn't even stop to chat. Instead, he stepped around me and kept on walking.

"Hey, uh Zac?" I called out, unable to stop myself.

He stopped but didn't turn around.

"Listen, I'm…I'm sorry for how I've been acting," I said quickly, "but I promise I'm going to make things right."

That made him turn and his brow wrinkled. "How are you going to do that?"

"Just…you just have to trust me," I said lamely. "I have to go, but I'll see you again soon, and next time, next time everything will be better. I swear it." I whipped back around and ran the rest of the way to the antique store. Stepping cautiously inside, I heard the bell jingle loudly overhead. "Hello?" I called out.

I heard a gruff voice muttering loudly along with shuffling footsteps. The second the older version of Dad came out of the office, he looked down at me and then pointed to a sign by the door. "Can't you read? No kids allowed."

"What if it's your own kid?" I asked.

For one second, I thought I had him, but then he barked a laugh, and my shoulders sagged. "I have no kids, now beat it."

"Nope, not leaving that easily." I started towards him. "We need to talk, Dad, we have a lot of catching up to do."

Chapter 6

"Listen, kid," Dad said as he followed me around the shop. "You need to get out of here before I call the cops."

"Can't, have to find something first."

"There is nothing in here for you to find," he argued. "And I'm not your dad! I don't have any children!"

He'd said that about ten times already, as well as continuing his threat to call the cops. But so far he was following right behind me as I scoured the shelves for a part of the machine, something to show Kate and Oliver.

"Yes, you do have children. You have me, and you have Oliver," I informed him. "And your wife is Maggie. You lost her because you got mixed up with some guy named Thaddeus Banes. There was a time machine, and events got out of whack. You were thrown into the future and then dragged back as your older self."

Dad laughed behind me. "You sure do have one heck of an imagination, girl, but none of that's true. Time machines don't exist. Go back home and shove your nose in another book. Better yet, I'll give you a book for free if you promise to leave my shop! Not a bad deal, right?"

"Not leaving," I said, and he mumbled in annoyance. Ignoring him, I continued to browse the shelves. "There has to be something here!"

I expected him to go off and make that call to the police, or to leave me alone if he thought I was crazy. But he did neither, and every time I glanced over my shoulder, he was there, watching me closely. I went up and down every small aisle, climbed on top of a step stool to check the high shelves, and finally glanced towards the one place I hadn't thought to look…the storage room at the back of the store. Before he could stop me, I darted behind the curtain, ignoring his yelling at me to get out of there before something fell on my head, and he was sued for damages.

But the second I stepped into that back room, I knew I'd found the object I was looking for. I felt it like a pulse in the air. The room was a mess, but I let my feet guide me, moving around the rubbish on the floor and the stacks of boxes before I reached the item I wanted to see so badly. It was tucked away on the floor in the back corner, a very familiar silver box.

Dad was still threatening to drag me out and to get the Sheriff onto me, but I continued to ignore him while I searched for a screwdriver to get the box opened.

"I mean it, kid! Ten seconds and I'm calling the police," he yelled as I pried open the lock and lifted the lid. Dad started his countdown as I sat on the floor in relief to see what was there, covered in dust, but exactly as I remembered it from the first time I saw it. "Three, two...what is that?" he demanded as I walked back through the shop and set the machine on the front counter.

"That is what I was looking for. Know what it is?" I asked, holding my breath in hopeful anticipation.

He walked over to it slowly, running his hand along the top of it as he gulped a few times, his eyes widening. He gave himself a little shake as he glanced from the machine then back to me.

I saw his eyes brighten with recognition the instant that it all rushed back. He moved as fast as his old body could manage around the counter to hug me. "Holly! You...you're my daughter!"

I nodded my head against his chest and hugged him back just as hard. Tears of relief spilled from my eyes. "Dad! I don't know what happened, but something went wrong. I almost didn't remember! And I didn't think you were going to remember either!"

"But you did, and now I do...I think." He frowned as he stepped back to the machine. "We were in a closet, right?

And Thaddeus, he tried to take the machine away from Oliver. Your brother," he said suddenly, "where is he? And your friend?"

"They're at home, but they don't remember," I said, full of frustration. "I told Kate everything that's happened, but she thinks it was all just a dream. And Oliver, he won't even sit still long enough for me to try to explain."

Dad tapped his fingers on the counter, lost in thought. "The reset, it was working, but I don't think we can use it again. Too risky."

"Then what do we do? I don't want to stay in this totally messed up time warp! It's not right!"

"Give me a few minutes to think. And you need to get Oliver and Kate here as fast as you can."

"What are you planning?"

He grinned and my hopes lifted. "A way to make everything right again, using your original plan."

"What plan?" I asked, struggling to remember that detail.

"You said the only way to fix everything was to get rid of Thaddeus for good. And to do that, we have to go back to the very beginning and make him see his other self."

"Are you sure you want to do that?"

"Well, I think it's our only hope. And right now, he's probably just like the rest of us, with no memory of what happened after we used the reset switch." Dad nodded firmly, giving the idea some more thought. "Yes, I think his memory loss will work in our favor. Go and get your brother and Kate, and hurry back. The longer we stay here, the less chance we have that Thaddeus won't remember."

I quickly hugged my dad one more time. He kissed the top of my head, then I was gone, out the door of the antique store and racing towards the park.

On the way, I texted Kate and then Oliver, begging them both to meet me, telling them it was urgent. Kate replied and said she would be there, but Oliver didn't respond straight away. I texted him three more times before he finally said he was on his way. Kate arrived first, rushing towards me. But I didn't want to tell her any details until Oliver arrived. I tapped my foot impatiently until eventually, I spotted him. I waved him over and told them both to follow me.

"Holly, Mom's really upset with you by the way," he said as they jogged to keep up with me. "And anyway, where are we going?"

"Trust me!" I threw back over my shoulder.

"Trying to, but you're acting like a psycho," he muttered from behind me. I didn't slow down or stop at all until we were outside the antique store.

"Here? Why are we here?" Oliver frowned.

I stepped inside, and they followed me, whispering to each other behind my back.

"Dad?" I called out, scanning the store for any sight of him.

"Dad? Seriously?" Oliver snapped. "Holly, what is going on with you? Our father isn't here!"

"But he is," Dad said as he shuffled towards us. "Oliver, it's time you and Kate remember. You need to know the truth."

"The truth? What truth?" Oliver glared at me like I was a traitor and crossed his arms over his chest as he stared at the old man in front of him. "You're too old to be our dad, so whatever trick you're playing on my sister, it ends right now. Let's go," he said and grabbed my arm.

I tugged myself free. "Stop, Oliver! You and Kate, you just need a reminder, and it'll all come back," I told him.

"What are you talking about?" he asked hotly. I nodded to the machine in Dad's hands. "What is that?" Oliver shook his head, clearly frustrated.

"The machine we've been using to get from each time zone to another," I explained. Dad set the machine down on the counter and flipped the switch, to get the gears whirring and the blue lights flashing. "Pretty cool, huh?"

Oliver and Kate both stepped closer, their eyes focused on the blue lights as if in a trance. Their faces scrunched in confusion, and a few seconds later, they were both holding their heads as they tried to process what was going on. Dad shut the machine off.

"Dad?" Oliver gasped suddenly. "Holly?"

"What...what happened?" Kate shrieked, grabbing her stomach. "Oh man, it's all coming back. And I don't feel very well."

I hugged Kate, squealing with joy to have my friend back. I tackled Oliver in a hug next, and he patted me on the back, still not quite sure what was going on.

"Hey, Oliver... are you with us?" I asked him.

"Yeah, sorry," he said, turning to me sheepishly. "I guess I should've listened to you."

"Usually a good idea," I smiled.

"So, what's the plan now?" he asked. "What are we going to do to fix this mess?"

"Thaddeus Banes," Dad said as he glared at the door to his shop. "We need to find him."

"What, why?" Oliver looked from Dad to me and back at Dad again. Then his mouth dropped open in recognition. He shook his head and grinned. "I thought you said getting Thaddeus to see his other self was a bad idea."

Dad nodded. "I did, but we're down to no other option."

"I'm in," Oliver replied with no hesitation whatsoever.

Kate nodded eagerly. "Me too. Let's get this finished."

"Right then," Dad said. "Girls...Thaddeus is your science teacher...do you think you can come up with a way to get him to the storage lot, the one that's down the road from here? Once you're there, the three of you need to use the machine to take him back to the very beginning.

Back to when this mess all began."

Dad looked at us as he twisted the knobs on the machine. "You must go back to the day, years ago, when I agreed to meet him at the storage unit. That was the day he took me away from my family. It's the only hope we have of returning to our original selves."

"Why not just bring him here?" I frowned.

"You land in the same place you leave from, remember?" Oliver reminded me. "The easiest way to make this work is to be in the storage lot when we land."

"Oh, of course, good point," I nodded.

"You'll have to get him to unit number 56. Both Thaddeus and my younger self will be there."

Kate and I exchanged a worried glance as Dad and Oliver tinkered with the machine, wiping the rest of the dust from it, and triple checking that the date was set right.

"What if he remembers before we can get him there?" I asked.

Dad smiled softly. "I have faith that you will know what to do. Have a little faith in yourselves. You can do this." He clapped his hands together. "Now, any suggestions for tracking him down?"

"He's still in the park," Kate said, and I blinked in surprise. "I saw him still sitting on the park bench."

"Do you think you can somehow get him to the storage unit?" Dad asked.

Kate bobbed her head. "Yes, I do," she announced suddenly. "That storage place is right by the park. I have a perfect idea, and it's better if I go on my own." She grinned confidently at me. "I'll text you soon. See you guys there." Before I could say another word, she bolted to the door.

"Be careful," Dad warned her. "He might already remember."

Kate nodded and took off, the door banging closed behind her. I just prayed that whatever her plan was, it would work.

Oliver picked up the machine, holding it gingerly against his chest as if terrified it was going to be taken away from him again. I knew the feeling well and followed him and Dad nervously to the back door of the store.

The storage facility wasn't too far from the shop, and we made it there in decent time. Kate texted to let us know that she and Thaddeus were on their way. How she'd convinced Thaddeus Banes to go with her was beyond me, but as the minutes ticked by, I finally heard her voice.

"It was headed this way, and it looked badly hurt," she sobbed. I could tell she was fake crying.

"Are you sure it was a kitten?" Thaddeus replied, sounding out of breath. I smirked remembering all the cat pictures in the classroom. This version of Thaddeus was a cat lover. Score one for Kate.

"Yes, it was tiny, but I saw it hobble in this direction. It was badly injured. I'm sure it's leg is broken! And I know how much you love cats. I thought you could help."

Dad squeezed my shoulder then Oliver's before he darted out of sight, just as Kate and Thaddeus turned the corner, entering the lot. Thankfully, there were no staff or security people around to stop us.

"I think I can see it, over there against the wall," Kate pointed urgently as Thaddeus stepped inside the gate, not seeing me.

But he spotted Oliver, clutching the machine to his chest. It was glowing subtly, and Thaddeus came to a sudden stop as Kate rushed in behind him, blocking off his backward escape.

Thaddeus took a few more steps, lifting his hand to point at the machine. "Who are you? And what...what is that thing?"

"An end to this game you started," Oliver told him.

"Game? What game?" Thaddeus reached up and rubbed his forehead. "I'm here to help an injured kitten, not play some game!"

He shook his head as confusion spread across his face. He staggered a few steps, and for a moment I thought he was going to collapse. But all of a sudden, he cackled loudly. When he straightened, I knew our luck had run out. He had his memory back. "Why don't you just hand that machine over, son, before you hurt yourself?"

Oliver shifted the machine in his arms and grinned. "Never." His eyes shot to me, and he nodded.

This is it! I said to myself and burst into action.

Chapter 7

"Oliver! Now!" I yelled as I slammed the gate shut, locking it closed with a heavy padlock that was hanging open on a chain.

Thaddeus cursed as he spun around, but he was surrounded by Oliver, Kate, and me. He wasn't getting away from us, not this time. We closed ranks, and the machine glowed brightly in Oliver's hands. Thaddeus tried to shove past us, but I tripped him up, and he hit the ground hard, grunting in pain. Kate and I each grabbed hold of his shoulder with one hand and reached for Oliver with the other. We couldn't let Thaddeus escape. The blue light surrounded us all. Then the ground shook beneath our feet. Thaddeus fought to get up, but he was an old man, and we were three very determined kids.

"You don't understand!" he tried to argue.

But we were done listening. One second, we were in a completely warped version of the present time, and then, after a loud pop echoed around us, we crashed to the pavement, still in the storage lot, but in a very different year. The three of us jumped back as Thaddeus swung his fists wide attempting to hit us. His steps were uneasy, and he staggered to his feet, not able to move well enough to be a threat.

"Are we in the right time?" I asked.

Oliver checked his digital watch. "Oh yeah, we're right on time...for once!"

Thaddeus' eyes widened as he realized what we'd done. He struggled to his feet. "No, no! Get me out of here, right now!"

"What's the matter? You don't want to say hello to yourself?"

He stared at me in full panic before he launched himself at Oliver, trying to get to the machine. It dropped to the ground and Thaddeus dove for it. Oliver shoved him off as Kate rushed over and picked it up, carrying it deeper into the storage facility.

"Get to 56! Go!" Oliver yelled just as Thaddeus managed to throw Oliver off. "Run!"

Kate and I took off at a dead sprint, searching for the right number garage. We made a sharp left turn, and I counted off the numbers in my head. "Come on, come on," Kate whispered under her breath. "There! It's down there!"

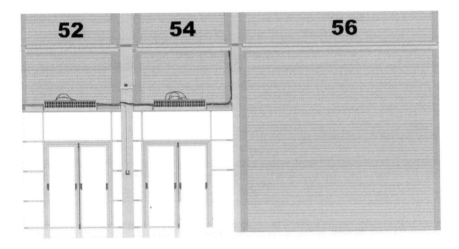

I glanced over my shoulder to see Thaddeus still chasing us, just as planned. I knew he'd go after the machine the second he realized where we were, especially if he believed there was a chance he could get out of here without running into his other self. He wasn't about to let it out of his sight, not when it was his only way of getting back to the present.

But this time, it was going to be the right present.

I hoped.

The other Thaddeus Banes was, in fact, in number 56 at this very moment with another man I very much wanted to see. We stopped at the garage in time to hear their voices yelling. I banged on the door just as Thaddeus was feet away, screaming at the top of his lungs for us to give him back the machine. I yelled louder, calling out both men by name when finally, the door gave a grumble, and someone inside slid it upwards, revealing a makeshift lab. There, standing side by side was another Thaddeus and a young version of my dad. He frowned at me in confusion, then at Kate holding the machine.

"Holly?" he asked, completely bewildered. "I told you guys not to mess with that thing!"

"What is this, what's going on?" the other Thaddeus demanded.

"No," the same voice echoed behind us. I whirled around to see the Thaddeus we'd brought with us frozen in shock and horror as his eyes locked onto his younger self. "What have you done! No!"

The Thaddeus in the storage unit tried to turn, but Dad was faster. He grabbed hold of the man and shoved him forward, causing him to trip and fall into the other version of himself. I watched the pair fall to the ground in a tangled heap. The two Thaddeus' grappled with each other, but it was too late. Their hands were already disappearing.

In a flash of light and a blur of color, I watched them fade away bit by bit until they vanished completely and there was nothing left of Thaddeus Banes.

He was gone from all timelines.

Gone from our lives.

For good.

When I turned, I saw Dad hugging Oliver and reaching to pull me into his arms as well.

"We did it! We actually did it!"

Part of me waited to hear Thaddeus laughing as he came out from some other storage unit, tricking us yet again, but as the seconds ticked by and nothing happened, I knew it was finally over.

"I don't know what's going on or how you did it," Dad said, "but I am so glad to see the last of that man. And I am so proud of both of you."

I was about to tell him exactly what had happened, every detail of the crazy adventure we'd just been on when Kate let out a panicked yell, and we all whipped around to stare at the time machine suddenly coming to life. It sparked and sputtered, shaking so hard it leaped off the pavement. Dad dragged the three of us away from it, placing himself in front of us protectively.

"We have to get back!" I argued, trying to go forward as the blue light pulsed out of the machine. It seemed to be breathing as if it had a life of its own. "Oliver! What do we do?"

A heavy wind gusted around us and suddenly it felt as though someone had hold of my ankles, sliding me back towards the malfunctioning box. Kate and Oliver screamed as all three of us were pulled away from Dad. He reached for my hands, but my grip slipped, and I was unable to grab hold of him. The second that Oliver, Kate and I were back to back with the machine at our feet, the blue light surrounded us. It was so bright that I was blinded by it. I yelled for Dad, but then we were shooting through space and time all over again. I strained to see, terrified of where we'd wind up this time. We'd messed everything up again; even though we had finally managed to rid ourselves of Thaddeus Banes. We twisted and turned longer than we had any other time and I heard Kate and Oliver yelp in alarm. But when I reached out, I found myself alone in the bright spiral of blue light.

I was sure I could see flashes of Oliver in the light, and Kate, then Zac and Mom and Dad, everyone who had been included in this wild adventure of ours appeared. The images flew by too fast for me to follow and understand exactly what I was seeing. I reached out, again and again, my fingers breaking through the light, scattering it like stardust until it surrounded me. I could do nothing as it

338

glittered before my face. Dizzy and light headed, I feared this fall through time would go on forever.

Then, rather than a sharp pop which was the usual sound we heard when we'd arrived at our destination, the sound of an explosion rang loudly in my ears.

Chapter 8

At first, I didn't dare to open my eyes, petrified at what I might find. But rather than the hard surface of a floor, there was something soft beneath me.

I opened one eye, then another, and blinked as I stared around my bedroom.

I hesitated as I threw back the covers and glared into the morning sunlight pouring through my window. I studied every small detail, searching for any sign that this was the wrong time zone, or another messed up version of the present. But the color of the walls was right; my furniture was in the right place, along with my school things. I searched for the machine. I could not see it anywhere.

"Am I back?" I said aloud and carefully climbed out of bed.

This time, I remembered every detail of what had just happened. Thaddeus was gone, but we'd left Dad behind. How could that be?

I stared around my room, trying to process the memories.

Something buzzed, and I jumped, hand to my chest, ready to brace for being thrown through time again. But it was only the sound of my cell phone on my desk.

I picked it up to see a message from Kate. I read it once, then I read it again, shaking my head to clear my vision so I could read the message a third time.

"Project? What project?"

I texted her back, panicking that I'd been thrown into a completely different time zone. Though, compared to the other issues we'd faced, a late project was far from terrible.

I held my cell anxiously as I waited for her reply and the second my cell buzzed in my hand, I skimmed the message and frowned. The family tree project? Was the presentation today? I closed out the message and checked the date on my phone, sinking back down on my bed. Monday morning, the day we were supposed to give our presentations to the class. The week that all the crazy time traveling began.

Closing my eyes, I thought back over the weekend that had just passed and saw it in two different ways. The first version was the time I'd found the boxes in the attic and discovered the time machine. But the second version had my eyes shooting open and holding my breath, not willing to believe it could be true.

My memory of the second version was of me working on my family tree project which now rested on my desk. Slowly, as if scared it would disappear in front of me, I crept over and stared down at the poster. The entire thing was filled out. Mom's side…and Dad's. Dropping my phone, I snatched up the chart, eyes blurring as I saw Dad's name proudly displayed beside Mom's.

"Hey, Holly? You up yet?" Oliver called as he knocked on my door.

"Yeah, yeah I'm up!" I exclaimed and rushed to open my door, still holding my project. He stared at me wide-eyed as I almost ran right into him.

"Uh, you alright?"

I nodded slowly, squinting at him, unsure. "What do you remember?"

"From what exactly?" he replied just as weirdly. He glanced down the hall towards the top of the stairs before leaning in closer. "Holly?"

"Yeah?"

He frowned at me. "The machine…do you remember it?"

I let out a massive sigh of relief. "I was worried *you* wouldn't remember!" He gave me a quick hug, the relief filling his features as well.

I frowned at him. "We were with Dad and then the machine…it sucked us back to when? Back to the day we used it for the first time. Is that even possible?" I threw the questions at him one after another.

"I guess so. I mean everything else has been possible, so why not that, right?" He ran a hand through his messed-up hair and blew out a heavy breath. "Everything we went through…it hasn't happened yet. But…I remember bits of this past weekend, the version where everything was normal…it's all a bit hazy but I don't remember any mention of a time machine."

"That's because I didn't have to search in the attic for information for my project, so I never ended up finding the machine."

"What do you mean?" he asked, confused.

I held up the family tree chart and pointed to the spot where Dad's name was filled in. "All the details about Dad and his family, they're on here... so that means—"

"You kids up yet? You're going to be late for school!"

Our eyes lit up at the same time. And in unison, the two of us both whispered the same word... "Dad!"

We took off together down the hall. Our father, the real version of our dad who wasn't an old man, stood at the bottom of the steps, holding a steaming cup of coffee in his hand as he eyed the both of us curiously. We rushed downstairs, and he barely managed to set his coffee down before we both threw our arms around him. He laughed warmly as he wrapped us in a tight hug.

"Well now, why can't you guys be this happy every morning before school?" he asked as he stood back smiling at each of us. "What's going on with you two, anyway? You act like you haven't seen me in years."

"We haven't," I blurted out before I could stop myself.

Dad's eyes narrowed. "What do you mean? Holly, Oliver, what's going on?"

We exchanged a glance, but I nibbled on my lip and said nothing. I guessed Dad might not remember what we did to Thaddeus. It was probably a good thing, and I didn't care too much as long as our dad was here to stay, and we could finally be one big happy family.

But then he looked down the hall towards the kitchen where we heard Mom humming loudly to the radio. He moved closer to us and winked. "Have I ever told you both how proud I am of you?" he whispered.

"You remember!" I whispered excitedly, and he

343

hugged us both again.

"I can't believe you did it!" he said and kissed the top of my head. Then he kissed Oliver's as well. "I was gone for so many years and then finally...finally, I was thrown back to the very beginning, and I got to see the two of you grow up the way a father should. I've been here since the start, and I was able to be here for both of you." He choked on the last words and wiped quickly at his eyes. "You are two amazing kids; you know that?"

We both hugged him again, each of us struggling to believe he was really there.

Oliver pulled away for a moment, glancing thoughtfully towards the stairs. "The machine, what happened to it?"

"After all the problems it caused, I took it and I...I destroyed it."

My jaw dropped, and Oliver's eyes almost bulged out of his head. "You did what? Why?"

"So, no one could use it again, that's why," Dad stated simply. "You both risked so much to get this family back together. I wasn't about to let anything tear us apart, not again." He took a deep breath as he studied us, laying a hand on both our shoulders. "I remember everything that happened to me. I remember being taken away from you both and being trapped in the future. I remember everything you had to go through to get us back. I couldn't imagine any of us ever going through that again."

"The machine's actually gone?" Oliver muttered.

"It's a good thing," I said, agreeing with Dad. "I would say I wished we'd never messed with it, but then we wouldn't have you back, Dad. And now we do, so that's all that matters."

I stared at his handsome face, the young version of our dad, and my heart swelled with love.

He beamed down at us as Mom called out from the kitchen, "You three going to stand there all day or come in here and eat breakfast? Oliver and Holly, you're going to be late for school!"

"And you have a presentation to give today," Dad reminded me.

"Yeah, I do," I nodded, remembering how that had gone the first time around.

Oliver and I followed Dad, as I tried to come to terms with the fact that we had our dad back and he was in our lives for good. He gave Mom a sweet kiss on her cheek, and she leaned into him, grinning widely, oblivious to the nightmarish experience we had all been through.

"You feeling good about your presentation today?" Mom asked.

"It'll be fine," I said and ate my breakfast quickly so I could hurry and get dressed. I had faced so much. Surely I could manage a simple presentation in class. But my head continued to whirl with visions of what we'd been through and the realization that we had actually all made it back.

Taking a moment between deciding on an outfit and fixing my hair, I stopped to glance over my project notes. I could see there was a lot more information than I'd had before. Dad, it seemed, had been able to fill in a lot of blanks for me about Grandpa's career, his scientific discoveries and Dad's career in science as well. Of course, there was no mention of any time machines. But I still couldn't believe Dad was downstairs, laughing with Mom as if he'd never been absent from our lives.

Part of me was sad we'd missed out on the last twelve years with him, but when I paused before leaving my room again, I finally noticed the framed pictures that were scattered around, showing us all as a family from the day I was born.

I realized then that if I closed my eyes and thought hard enough, I could remember Dad being there. He taught me how to ride my bike; he helped Oliver with his first major science project. We'd eaten dinner together every night and played games on the weekends. There was even a memory of Oliver and I tackling Dad into a huge pile of autumn leaves in the backyard.

Yeah, I remembered all of it, and it boosted my spirits so much that I skipped out the door. No matter what happened in class, I was determined that nothing would spoil the realization that we had our dad back and we were all safe.

Oliver and I waved to Mom and Dad who stood on the front porch together, leaning into one another as they watched us walk down the street.

"Man, we did it!" Oliver said. "Can you believe it!"

"I know!" I grinned. "The whole thing is crazy! I wonder if Kate remembers anything. She didn't act like it when I texted her earlier."

"Guess we'll find out soon enough."

My steps slowed, and Oliver frowned back at me.

"What's going on? Everything's back to normal, better than normal now."

"Yeah, well, that means Jade is still at school, ready to give me a hard time. And the last time I talked to Zac we were in that strange messed up time warp…and he didn't exactly like me. No one did. And," I added as he grabbed my arm and pulled me along, "everyone thought I was weird and a bully, It wasn't the nicest situation."

"To be fair, you were ranting and raving about a time-machine to me and probably to Kate, too. You were acting pretty strangely. But that wasn't you, Holly, it doesn't matter."

"Yeah, but still, I had no friends. No one like me apart from Kate…and you didn't want to know about me either. It was just hard, alright?"

He gave me a one-armed hug. "It's going to be fine, I promise. And you're going to knock them all dead with that presentation of yours. I can feel it."

"And Jade?"

"You have to stop letting her ruin your day," he argued. "Seriously, she's one girl, and she's nothing compared to my little sister."

"You're just saying that to be nice," I mumbled.

Oliver pulled me to a stop again, and when I met his gaze, I saw a look of pride on his face as he grinned. "Do you realize what you did for all of us? You took on Thaddeus Banes, alone. You went back in time without us, and you risked your life. You took off from that facility with the time machine, on your own, to try and fix everything. You never gave up when none of us could remember what had happened. Imagine if we were still stuck in that nightmare of a future! But we're back here now because of you, Holly! You're an insanely brave and incredible girl, and don't ever forget it!"

I sniffed hard to hear such admiration from my older brother and brushed a tear from my eye. "I guess you're right about Jade. At least she can't say *she* ever fought against a real-life mad scientist and went on a mad chase through time, right?"

"That's the spirit. Pretty sure you're now winning coolest kid of the year award."

I grinned back. Oliver and I were still talking when I heard Kate call out our names and run up to greet us both. She was bouncing on the balls of her feet as she clutched her books to her chest, smiling brightly at Oliver, and only Oliver.

I watched his cheeks turn bright red as he rubbed the back of his neck and glanced shyly at the ground.

"So, you guys remember, right?" she whispered suddenly, and we both sagged in relief.

"Oh my gosh, I was so worried I wouldn't be able to talk to you about anything," I said as I gave her a quick hug.

"When I woke up this morning, I wasn't sure, but then it all came back." She turned to Oliver and stepped a little closer. "Hey…uh, Oliver?"

"Yeah?" he asked, his expression torn between smiling and frowning.

"This weekend, do you uh, want to go catch a movie or something?"

He swallowed loud enough for me to hear and I hid a smile behind my hand. "Like…like a date?"

"Maybe…if you want to."

My eyes shifted from one to the other as the silence stretched on. I was about to stomp on Oliver's foot when he moved closer and kissed Kate on the cheek. When he moved back again, her face was firetruck red, and he was having a hard time forming words.

"Yeah...yeah...that'd be fun," he managed to mumble. "Um...see you guys after school." He hurried off, his backpack hanging loosely in his hand.

When he started whistling, I burst out laughing and nudged Kate playfully with my elbow. "Wow, you're going on a date with my brother!"

"Is that weird?" she asked, suddenly looking panicked. "You can tell me if it's too weird."

"Nope, not weird at all. I'm very happy for you both."

She put her arm through mine, and we giggled over the fact that she had just come right out and asked my brother out on a date. But Oliver's reaction was the funniest part of all.

At our lockers, we dropped off our bags and grabbed the books we needed for our first few classes. Everything was going well until I heard Jade's voice echoing loudly down the hall. I groaned, resting my head on the locker door.

"Oh, come on, you already know how it turns out," Kate nudged me.

"I do, but that doesn't make me feel any better." I slammed my locker door shut and stepped out into the hall traffic without really looking, and stumbled right into someone else. "Oh my gosh, sorry!" I muttered as my books fell to the floor along with the other person's. I crouched down to help pick them up when I realized who was in front of me. "Zac!" I swallowed hard, waiting for him to glare at me again, or snap. But instead, the look he gave me caused butterflies to do a wild dance in my stomach.

"Yeah," he said laughing. "That's my name!" His smile was friendly as he scooped up my books and we stood up together. "Holly? You ok?"

"Yeah, course," I said quickly. "Thanks, I uh, sorry for running into you."

"No big deal. You ready for history class today?"

"Sure, why not," I rambled. "You?"

He shrugged one shoulder, and his eyes brightened. "Bet your project is more interesting than mine. I'll see you in class later, okay?"

I nodded and raised a hand to wave as he hurried off to catch up with his friends further down the hall. More butterflies filled my stomach as I realized that Oliver was right…the crazy time warp where everyone hated me, including Zac, no longer existed.

By the time history class rolled around, I was anxious to see Zac again. But the second Jade stepped into the classroom, I groaned and slouched down as far as possible in my seat. She purposely stopped at Zac's desk, blocking my view of him as she chatted excitedly about her project until the bell rang and class started. I hoped her name wouldn't be pulled first, but when it was, Kate and I exchanged annoyed glances as we were forced to listen to her presentation all over again.

Except for this time, when we went up to look at the artifacts she'd brought, there was no snarky remark about me not having a dad. She glared at me, but that was because Zac was still there looking when my group came along, and he happened to point a few things out to me that he thought were cool. Her lips thinned, and I could tell she was itching to dive in between us. I ignored her, not wanting to make a scene.

When Zac went to sit down, she leaned towards me and whispered, "You can't have him!"

I lifted my gaze to hers but remembered everything Oliver told me. She wasn't worth my time, so I merely smiled and returned to my seat, leaving her glaring at the back of my head.

And all through my presentation and the rest of class, I didn't care, not anymore. I'd been through too much craziness to let one girl give me a hard time over a boy. I'd nearly lost my entire family and had to fight to get them back. Jade was just a bully, and she wasn't going to bother me anymore.

When lunch came around, Kate and I went to our usual table, gossiping about Jade's presentation. "You know, it was boring if you really think about it," Kate was saying as she opened her bottled water.

I nodded absently but was too busy watching Zac and his friends to respond.

Perhaps it was Kate's confidence that morning with Oliver that motivated me to do what I did next. But without giving it much thought, I pushed back from the table, grinned at Kate as she gasped at what I was about to do, and headed across the cafeteria to where Zac sat with his friends.

When I reached the table, one of them spotted me and tapped Zac on the shoulder.

"Oh, hey, Holly," Zac said with a smile.

"Hey," I said and nodded to the empty chair beside him. "Mind if I sit down?"

Zac's friends fell quiet as he reached over and pulled the chair out for me. "Nah, I'd love it."

Tucking my hair behind my ears, I sat down and leaned on the table as we began chatting just as easily as we had that day in the park, a day he didn't remember. But I did. And this moment was so much better.

We were laughing with his friends over which was our favorite superhero when a shadow suddenly loomed over the table.

"What are you doing?" Jade snapped.

Zac stiffened and opened his mouth. But I spoke first. Locking my gaze on Jade's, I said, "Sitting here talking. What are you doing?'

"You can't sit here," she argued, then smirked, "Tell her Zac."

"It's fine if Holly sits here," he said in return.

Her smile faltered. "This is our table!" She crossed her arms. "We always sit together at lunch. Always…and I won't let her take my spot!"

The cafeteria grew quieter around us at Jade's raised voice, but I kept my eyes on her. "You know what, Jade, you're just a bully," I said, and her jaw clenched. "You've always been a bully. I don't know why and I honestly don't care anymore. I'm going to hang out with whoever I want, and you can go about your day, doing whatever you like doing. But so that you know, bullies usually wind up alone. It's never too late to turn yourself around."

Her jaw dropped, and I caught the smirk on Zac's face, his eyebrows raised in surprise. Jade's friends shifted uncomfortably and tugged on her arm. She jerked away from them, pointed her finger at my face, then stormed off without another word, her crowd of followers hurrying to catch up.

"Sorry," I said to Zac after she'd gone. "I know she's your friend."

"No, not really," he shook his head. "She likes hanging out with us. But, I'm glad you said what you did. I should've said it a long time ago."

I took a deep breath and blew it out, feeling a huge weight lift off my shoulders. "What are you doing this weekend?" I asked before I could stop myself. I waited, my stomach clenching with worry that he'd turn me down.

But instead, he shrugged and smiled. "Hanging out with you!"

Butterflies fluttered inside me as I answered. "Cool, I think it's going to be a great weekend."

His grin widened. "You know, there's a Spiderman movie coming out!"

I rolled my eyes and gave his shoulder a playful shove. "Everyone knows Batman's better.

In that instant, I knew we were going to be alright; all of us. Time was going to keep moving forward like it was supposed to, and for the first time in a long time, I had no worries about what tomorrow would bring.

***

I hope you've enjoyed the Time Traveler series.
If you have time to leave a review, I would love to hear what you
think!
Thanks so much!
Katrina x

BEAUTIFUL & POSITIVE BOOKS FOR GIRLS

KIDS LOVE THESE BOOKS!

OTHER POPULAR SERIES
FREE ON KINDLE UNLIMITED

EBOOKS & PAPERBACKS

THANK YOU

We really appreciate and love
our readers! You are amazing!
If you loved this book, we would really
appreciate it if you could leave a review
on Amazon.

You can subscribe to our website
www.bestsellingbooksforkids.com
so we can notify you as soon as
we release a new book.

Please 👍 Katrina's Facebook page
https://www.facebook.com/katrinaauthor
and follow Katrina on Instagram
@katrinakahler

Printed in Great Britain
by Amazon

72167223R00203